THE
LAST QUEEN
OF
ENGLAND

A Jefferson Tayte Genealogical Mystery

Other books in this series

THE
LAST QUEEN
OF
ENGLAND

A Jefferson Tayte Genealogical Mystery

by

STEVE ROBINSON

THOMAS & MERCER

Published by Thomas & Mercer, Seattle

www.apub.com

Amazon, the Amazon logo, and Thomas & Mercer are trademarks of Amazon.com, Inc., or its affiliates.

ISBN-13: 9781477818541
ISBN-10: 1477818545

Cover design by The Book Designers

Library of Congress Control Number: 2013920535

Printed in the United States of America

For Karen

House of Stuart & Orange 1603-1714

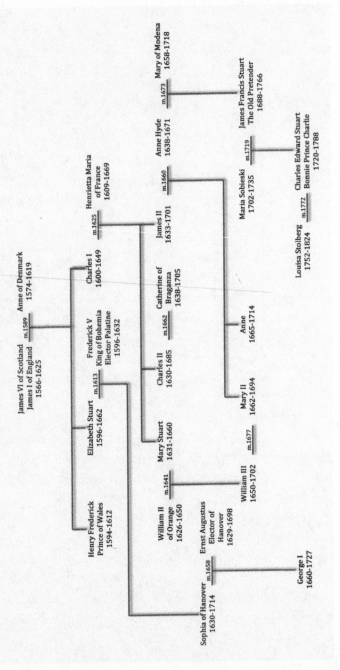

Prologue

Three months ago.

Julian Davenport owned a penthouse apartment in Bermondsey, overlooking Tower Bridge. He drove any one of three expensive cars and had a second home in Aspen where he spent most of his winters. His London-based real estate business was lucrative, his trophy wife was a surgically enhanced conversation stopper, and their two spoiled-brat teenage daughters doted on him, if only for their generous weekly allowance. Davenport must have thought he had it all, but his dark-haired visitor in the smart grey suit knew he was about to deny him everything.

'Let's get this over with,' Davenport said, avoiding eye contact as he invited the man in. 'My wife's due home.'

Davenport was a short, skinny man with a quick manner and a curt tone. He wore leather slippers and a plush white dressing gown that he was still tying as he turned away from the door and shuffled across a spacious lounge of white leather furnishings and exposed floorboards.

'Don't touch anything you can't afford,' he added. 'Which means don't touch a damn thing!'

The visitor wore thin leather driving gloves, which he removed and slipped into his pocket as he followed Davenport into the room. He didn't once take his eyes off the back of the man's head—a tangle of long, mousy threads that looked wet, like he'd just taken a shower.

Davenport slumped into an armchair. 'Have a seat.'

'I'd prefer to stand. Do you have the item?'

Davenport made eye contact at last. He nodded and reached down beside him. 'Here,' he said as he brought a slim oak case into view. He placed it on the coffee table and slid it towards his visitor.

'It's all original,' Davenport added. 'Nothing's missing.'

On seeing the case for the first time, the visitor rushed to it and picked it up, studying the unremarkable object as though it were something of exquisite beauty.

'Take it easy,' Davenport said. 'It's three hundred years old.'

The visitor knew exactly how old it was. He flung the lid back and caught his breath as his eyes fell on the contents: a parallel ruler, a sector, a pair of callipers, and several other mathematical instruments set into a green velvet inlay. He traced his fingertips over the cool brass work, and the hint of a smile twitched at the corner of his mouth.

'Is it there?' Davenport asked.

The visitor returned the case to the table and removed one of the items: a rectangular protractor. He studied it closely, then put it back and moved on to the callipers.

'Can you hurry it up?' Davenport said. 'I already told you, my wife's due home.'

The visitor ignored him. He would not be rushed. He removed the parallel ruler and turned it slowly in his hands. Then he paused, eyes narrowing as he brought it closer.

'Can you see it?' Davenport asked. 'I had no idea what I was sitting on until I got your call.' He scoffed. 'Some heirloom, eh? Dad never told me anything about all this.'

'That was careless of him.'

'You're telling me.'

Davenport was on the edge of his seat, rubbing his palms together. 'So that's it, right? It's what you're looking for?'

The visitor nodded. The digits were engraved on the brass, small but visible to his keen eyes: four binary numbers, one decimal. They were a reminder to him that his life had purpose, and now that it was time to fulfil that purpose, he felt something primeval stir within him. He tensed to suppress the feeling and placed the item carefully back into the case.

'So when will you have the rest?' Davenport asked.

'Soon,' the visitor replied, closing the case as he flourished a handgun from beneath his jacket and shot Davenport twice in the chest.

Chapter One

Jefferson Tayte was in London, sitting on the pavement somewhere near Covent Garden, waiting for an ambulance to arrive. It was the middle of a wet Sunday afternoon in September, and the frightened faces that had previously scattered now formed into a concerned crowd around him, despite the rain that made the blood on his tan linen suit spread like dye. It was not his blood, but he would have traded places with the man in his arms in a heartbeat.

Tayte had very few friends—maybe only one true friend if he were honest with himself—and judging from the seemingly impossible amount of blood Marcus Brown was losing, Tayte was mournfully aware that unless help arrived soon, his friend was not going to make it. Jean was there, too, no more than a blur in his periphery. Marcus had only just introduced them. Two hours ago they were sitting in a restaurant enjoying a very British Sunday lunch, chatting and laughing over roast rib of beef and fine wine as Tayte got to know Jean and he and Marcus continued to play catch-up on all the years that had passed since they last saw each other. All Tayte could think about now was the blood and his friend, and why anyone would want to shoot him.

What were you working on, Marcus? Who did this?

Right now, Tayte had no idea, but he did know that some of the answers had to be back there in the restaurant: threads of conversation still hanging in the air, yet fading rapidly now after the confusion that had followed. He knew he had to piece them back together again if he was going to make any sense of what had just happened.

———⌣———

Rules Restaurant was lively when Tayte and Marcus had arrived, each carrying a battered leather briefcase that seemed to compete in terms of whose looked the most tatty and travel-worn. Tayte had flown in from Washington, DC, twenty-four hours earlier to attend the International Genealogy Convention at London's O2 Arena, although his main reason for coming to London was to see Marcus. He wanted to congratulate his friend on his recent retirement from The National Archives, where Marcus had worked most of his life, and Tayte wanted to thank him in person for all the support he'd given him over the years. It only occurred to him recently that he'd never really done that. Marcus was the only person who had been there for him after his adoptive parents died, when his friend was a visiting professor of family history in America, and Tayte, who was suddenly left alone and without any real sense of identity, had never been in greater need of direction.

Rules was apparently Marcus Brown's only consideration when any kind of celebration was called for. It wasn't cheap, but you get what you pay for, Marcus had said, and he'd insisted on 'getting the check' as he put it, playfully mimicking Tayte's American phrases as he often did. He'd also pointed out that the place had been going since 1798 and that it was the oldest restaurant in London, so they had to be doing something right.

The restaurant decor was old-world cream and red, with red and gold carpet and mahogany chairs and tables hiding beneath starched linen. Sections of the ceiling were made up of domed glass panels, and the walls were a mosaic of framed caricatures and old photographs of famous patrons. The staff, in their white aprons, black blouson jackets, and bow ties, conjured images of Paris, although Tayte had never been there. He might have believed his friend's motives for bringing him to Rules were it not for the woman waiting for them at the cocktail bar. Marcus was quick with the introductions.

'This is my good friend, Professor Jean Summer.'

She wore a black dress and patent heels, and Tayte thought she looked a little on the bony side, although he had to concede that next to him most people did.

Marcus leant in and kissed her hand. 'Jean was at a loose end this weekend so I invited her along. You don't mind, do you?'

Tayte just smiled.

'Jean's a historian, specialising in all things royal and London, aren't you, dear?' Marcus said. 'Very handy to know. I'm sure you'll have plenty to chat about.'

'Maybe not all things quite yet,' Jean said. 'But I like to think I'm getting there. Wherever *there* is.' She gave a small laugh and held out her hand.

Tayte shook it. 'JT,' he said, holding on to his smile until it felt awkward.

He put her in her late thirties. She had brown shoulder-length hair, and he thought her lipstick looked uncomfortably bright on her face. His initial impression was that she was trying too hard, and there was something about her that told him she'd left her glasses at home today: her eyes looked pinched and unsettled, like her contact lenses were irritating her. As blind dates went, this was about as obvious a setup as there was.

The penny really dropped when they were seated at their corner table looking into the restaurant. Casual conversation dominated the entrées, after which they each raised a glass to someone or something. Marcus toasted Tayte for turning forty a few months earlier, and Tayte toasted Marcus on his retirement. Jean, who was already a full glass of wine ahead, followed with a toast to herself to celebrate her decree absolute, making her divorce final, which explained everything. Not that Tayte minded. She was proving good company, and if she was in on Marcus's little dating game then he figured she was the one who had been shortchanged.

They were partway through the main course when Tayte asked Marcus what he'd been working on since he'd retired. It was a throwaway question to which he expected the usual ten-minute monologue about whichever family history Marcus was currently researching. Instead, Marcus scratched his goatee and began to fidget and play with his food like he was chewing over his reply. When it came, it was too brief to be taken seriously.

'Nothing,' he said. Then he pushed his glasses up on his nose and carried on eating.

Tayte just laughed at him. 'Nothing? I don't believe that for a minute.'

Marcus Brown and family history were synonymous. He'd published many books on the subject, and Tayte knew he wasn't about to stop doing the one thing he loved just because The National Archives had stopped paying him a regular salary.

'Come on, Marcus,' Tayte said. 'You're always working on something.'

Marcus coughed into his hand and fidgeted again. He looked like he was trying to hold back a smile—trying not to crack. It took him a while to settle, and when he did, he leant in low over the table.

'Not now,' he said under his breath. 'And certainly not here.'

Jean's smile was laced with intrigue. 'What are you up to, Marcus Brown?'

Marcus shook his head, but Jean wasn't giving in that easily.

'Anything to do with Queen Anne?' She turned to Tayte. 'It's been the hot topic with him all month.'

Marcus's smile surfaced at last. 'Look, I'm literally sworn to secrecy,' he added. 'Please, can we leave it at that?'

'How about the Bonny Prince?' Jean said, grinning.

Tayte admired her persistence, but it seemed that Marcus did not. He waved a hand over the table, urging Jean to lower her voice. His eyes were suddenly wide, his smile gone.

'Okay,' he whispered. 'I am working on something, of course I am, but I really can't talk about it now. I'm meeting some people first thing in the morning, and let's just say that they're the kind of people who like to keep their secrets close to their chest.'

'And you can't tell us who it is?' Tayte said.

Marcus stared at him and sighed. 'No,' he insisted. 'Look, maybe after the show. I'll put you both in the picture then. We'll go back to my place for a nightcap. Emmy hasn't seen you yet, Jefferson. I'm sure she'd like that. We can talk about it there.'

Tayte was a great lover of musicals, and he'd seen just about everything going at least twice. They were going to see *Les Misérables* at the Queen's Theatre on Shaftesbury Avenue after the meal—another of Marcus's treats—although Tayte was beginning to wonder if that too hadn't been arranged on account of Jean. He sat back in his chair and eyed Marcus with a measure of puzzlement, knowing that he wouldn't enjoy it as much this time around for wondering whose family history demanded such caution and why Marcus was being so secretive about it. He let it go for now and topped up the wine glasses, lingering over Marcus's, thinking the wine might loosen his tongue.

'So what's your topic for tomorrow?' he asked, changing the subject.

Marcus had been a key speaker at the genealogy convention for many years, and this year Tayte knew he had something controversial planned.

'Technology,' Marcus said, relaxing again. 'Specifically the World Wide Web and how it's changing the way we genealogists do our job—and not necessarily for the better.'

Jean seemed surprised by his negativity. 'Surely the Internet's making things easier, isn't it?'

Tayte agreed.

'In many ways, yes,' Marcus said. 'Access to archives has never been easier, but there are serious downsides. There's a price to pay.'

'How so?' Tayte asked.

'Well, take e-mail for example. People don't write to each other anymore, do they? Once my generation's gone, the written letter will be consigned to social history. Tell me, Jefferson. When did you last write a letter?'

Tayte had to think about it. When the occasion came to him, he smiled, wide and cheesy. 'It was to you,' he said. 'I wrote you on your sixtieth birthday.'

'That was five years ago.'

'I still wrote you.'

Marcus looked sympathetic. 'It was an e-mail.'

'Was it?'

Marcus nodded. 'You see my point? Letters are key to genealogical research, and they're becoming obsolete. Photographs are going the same way.' He looked genuinely saddened by the thought. 'How many connections have you made going through boxes of old letters and faded sepia photographs? How many assignments would have fallen flat without them?'

'Too many,' Tayte agreed.

'I can't see genealogists of the future fervently poring over their clients' old e-mails, can you? Where's the fun in that? Where's the excitement and the scent of time that so often accompanies the discovery?'

He had Tayte there, too. Tayte's methods were straight out of the 'Marcus Brown School of Family History.' Tripping back into the past through an old letter and a few photographs represented everything he loved about his work. It wouldn't be the same without the sensory triggers he currently took for granted.

'So what's the answer?' Jean said.

'I'm not sure there is one. As I said, technology is changing things and not necessarily for the better.'

Such sobering thoughts and the unanswered question of what Marcus was working on preoccupied Tayte for the rest of the meal. By the time the coffee arrived, the conversation had fallen to small talk, which made Tayte as uncomfortable as ever. Marcus led most of the topics, and they were all so transparently designed to get Tayte and Jean talking that it became laughable.

'Marcus tells me you're working on your first book,' Jean said, sipping her coffee.

Tayte could have kicked his friend right there under the table. He laughed to himself instead and slowly pushed his thick crop of dark hair back off his brow, pausing to hide his face in his hand.

'Is there anything he hasn't told you about me?'

'I'm sure there must be something,' Jean said. The wine had added something playful to her smile. 'What's it called?'

Tayte held on to his answer too long.

'Come on, Jefferson,' Marcus cut in. 'Don't be shy.'

Tayte shook his head, thinking that his friend could be so embarrassing at times, and just for once he wished he'd call him JT.

'It's called *Across the Pond*,' he said. 'It focuses on the ancestral ties between America and the UK. I figured that as so many non-native Americans can trace their roots back to the UK, there should be a market for it.'

Jean nodded. 'Maybe I can get you to sign a copy for me someday.'

Tayte felt his cheeks flush and laughed at the idea.

When Marcus settled the bill ten minutes later, Tayte thought he looked far too pleased with himself, supposing that the blind date was no doubt money well spent to his mind. The black-suited attendant waiting for them by the door helped Jean into her coat, and through the grey windows Tayte could see that it had started to rain. He rarely wore a coat, but on this occasion he chided himself for forgetting how damp London could be. He didn't realise Marcus had fallen behind until he turned around to ask how long they had before the show. His first thought was that he'd intentionally dropped back to give him and Jean a moment to themselves—another of his matchmaking ploys—but when his eyes found his friend again, he wasn't so sure.

A slim, fair-haired man wearing blue jeans and an untucked black shirt was sitting at the bar with a leggy brunette who looked like she hadn't long left school. The man had to be close to Marcus's age, Tayte thought, although he gave the impression he was trying to look closer to the girl's. He had one hand on her St Tropez–tanned thigh and the other was on Marcus's arm. The man was talking through his smile as though he'd just bumped into an old friend, but Marcus did not return the smile. Tayte watched his friend jerk his arm free, and he was about to go and see if he needed any help when Jean distracted him.

'How long are you in London?'

Tayte turned to her. 'Marcus didn't tell you?'

'I suppose he thought it would be nice if I found something out for myself.'

Tayte glanced back at Marcus. The other man was still smiling. It all seemed amiable enough apart from the body language, and there was something about that smile that made Tayte uneasy. Marcus looked tense and Tayte wished he could hear what they were saying. He wanted to step closer, but he was suddenly aware that he was ignoring Jean, so he tried to stay with the conversation.

'Sorry,' he said. 'I fly home tomorrow night, after the convention. Did Marcus invite you to that, too?'

Jean nodded. 'I said I'd get back to him.'

'I know what you mean. Genealogy conventions aren't everyone's idea of a fun day out.'

'That's not quite what I meant.'

It took Tayte a while to realise what she did mean. 'Oh,' he said. He laughed to himself. 'See how this date goes first, right?'

'Something like that.'

Tayte was about to ask her if she'd made a decision, but when he turned and looked into the restaurant again, he saw that Marcus was heading towards them. Tayte thought he looked troubled, but as if to contradict his take on the situation, the fair-haired man at the bar was still smiling.

'Anything wrong?' Tayte asked.

Marcus shook his head. 'No, just an old acquaintance I'd rather not have bumped into today.' He took his coat from the attendant and slipped it on over his sports jacket. 'Come on, let's get a cab and go see that show.'

———

Tayte snapped his collar up as soon as his loafers hit the wet pavement outside. Maiden Lane was a narrow street, lined with four-storey buildings that had a few shops and other eateries at ground level. He left Jean and Marcus sheltering beneath the restaurant canopy and went to secure the black cab he'd seen along the street to their left, towards Covent Garden. Despite the rain the area was busy with sightseers and shoppers, many of whom were linked in pairs between their umbrellas, eating up the pavement. Somewhere ahead he could hear a street performer laughing into a PA system as he told his audience not to try this at home.

He pushed out onto the road between the cars that were parked bumper to bumper along the kerb. The taxi he had his eye on—the only taxi he could see—was further down than it first looked. He waved as he drew closer, and he had to smile to himself when someone else got in and the taxi pulled away. He looked back towards the restaurant as another black cab turned into the street.

Touchdown, he thought.

Being the big Washington Redskins fan he was, Tayte started to run for that touchdown now, the cool sensation on his back letting him know that he would soon be soaked to the skin if he didn't make it. The taxi's light was on, which was a good sign. He supposed it was making a drop-off, and he wished it would slow down so he could be there waiting for it when it did. He picked up his pace a little but soon had to slow down again. He was panting by halfway.

'Still gotta lose a few pounds, JT,' he told himself, having lost count of the number of times he'd said that.

The taxi stopped in the street directly outside Rules Restaurant, and when Tayte saw Marcus and Jean make a beeline for it, he smiled to himself again and thought how typical that was. If he'd wanted to impress Jean, he'd just failed miserably. He stopped running and tried to control his breathing as he walked, returning Marcus's wave as the driver got out of the taxi.

That was when Tayte knew something was wrong.

A taxi driver getting out of his vehicle for a customer without baggage was unusual enough, but this man, dressed in a long black coat, was wearing a full-face plastic mask—the kind sold in novelty shops. The dark-haired figure walked casually around the front of the cab towards the restaurant, and Tayte could see now that he had no passenger, so he wasn't dropping off. He also knew that black cabs didn't usually operate on a private hire basis, so the driver wasn't there to pick up a prearranged fare. And why the mask?

The first gunshot didn't seem real.

Tayte froze and just stood in the road as he watched the action unfold, as though he'd just stepped into a movie set. All of a sudden he could smell the rain in the air, mingling with the kitchen fumes from the vents along the street. People around him began to run as others crouched and kept still. A woman screamed somewhere nearby, and a young boy began to cry. Tayte saw them through a gap between the cars, the mother holding the boy to her with one arm while the other held out an umbrella like a shield, useless as that would be.

Then slowly, still unable to believe what was happening, Tayte turned back to the man in the mask. His gun was levelled at Marcus. There can't have been more than six feet between the two of them. His friend was clutching his shoulder where the first bullet must have struck. He watched Marcus shake his head at the gunman, slowly and purposefully. Pleading. All Tayte could think about was that his friend needed him and he was too far away to help. His awareness was so heightened that he thought he saw the second bullet leave the muzzle, and the sound it made brought everything into painful reality.

No! Tayte yelled, but no sound came out. He began to run again, eyes fixed on Marcus as he watched his friend stagger and fall. He saw Jean then. Marcus was down and she was beside him, looking up at the man in the mask as Tayte watched him turn the gun on her. He didn't think about it. He jumped at the nearest car and slid across the wet bonnet, falling hard onto the pavement on the other side. The gunman seemed to be taking his time over Jean. At least that's how it looked to Tayte. He saw him stoop to pick up Marcus's briefcase, the gun trained on Jean's head the whole time. As Tayte picked himself up, he grabbed a shopping bag from someone beside him and hurled it.

'Hey!'

The bag landed short and spilled its contents, scattering several CD cases. Then Tayte was running again and he had no idea if he'd make it. He had all the man's attention now, and as he drew closer, he could see that the mask the man was wearing was a comedy caricature of Prince Charles. It was surreal. He took in the big ears for a split second, and then all he could think about was the gun that had now turned on him. He didn't stop. He didn't know why, but he just kept running, thinking that although they had only just met, at least he'd bought Jean some time to get away.

The shot came instantly.

Tayte knew it had missed him when he heard a car windscreen shatter. The sound of the glass breaking startled him more than the shot itself. Ahead, Jean was on her feet, recoiling from the shove she must have given the gunman as he squeezed the trigger. Now the man was running back to the taxi, and Tayte silently thanked Jean for choosing fight over flight, if she'd really had a choice.

As Tayte arrived beside her and the taxi sped off in a screech of tyre rubber, they exchanged brief glances and turned their attention to Marcus. Tayte removed his jacket and dropped to his knees. He sat and held his friend in his arms with his jacket pressed to his chest. There was so much blood washing out over the pavement with the rain that Tayte was surprised his friend was still alive. His eyes were wide open, his glasses spattered with blood on the pavement beside him.

'Marcus? Can you hear me?'

Tayte got something back. It could have been 'JT,' but he wasn't sure.

'Marcus! Stay with me, you hear?'

A crowd began to gather around them. People were pouring out of the restaurant.

'An ambulance is on its way,' Tayte told him, speaking slowly as he looked around for one of the restaurant staff, hoping it was true. Someone nodded back at him. 'Just stay with me, Marcus. Stay with me.'

Marcus drew a sharp breath and coughed. 'My briefcase,' he said, struggling to get the words out through the inky blood that was bubbling from his lips.

Tayte shook his head. 'It's gone.'

'You must find it.'

'Don't worry about it now.'

Marcus closed his eyes and somewhere in the real world Tayte heard a siren. It seemed to stir his friend again. He felt his fingers bite into his arm.

'Treason!' Marcus said, his eyes locked in a faraway stare. 'Hurry!'

'Treason?' Tayte repeated. 'What do you mean?' He needed more to go on. He needed his friend. 'Marcus?'

Tayte shook him but he knew he hadn't felt it. The pressure on Tayte's arm had left him as suddenly as it arrived, and in that moment he knew his friend was gone.

Chapter Two

Detective Inspector Jack Fable worked for the Metropolitan Police Service at New Scotland Yard. His real name was William Russell Fable, but he'd been called Jack for so long now because of his middle name that it eventually stuck. 'A terrier with a bone,' someone had once said, and he still was. He had no idea who William Fable was any more. He thought his parents would have liked that other guy better, but it was too late for that now.

Fable was fifty-six years old, had passed up early retirement a year ago, and would do so again if he made it to sixty. He figured either the job or the cigarettes would eventually kill him, but he'd be damned if he was going to depart this world through the slow decay of boredom. He'd been a DI for as long as he could remember. Maybe twenty years—he wasn't counting. He had no ambition beyond his current grade because he liked to get things done, and it was plain to him that the higher up the ladder you climbed, the more bureaucratic bullshit you had to deal with.

He was an iron-faced man with neat medium brown hair that was thin on top and combed to one side with a fixing product—it wasn't quite a combover. Not yet. He shaved twice a day and didn't feel that people in authority should dress down for the job. He liked suits, always black and with the tie to match. If he was old school, then he was a dying breed, and more was the pity to his mind.

Fable hated being at his office almost as much as he hated being home at his one-bed flat in Blackfriars, but both were necessary evils. His office, like his flat, was little more than a shell, with plain cream walls and a blue-grey carpet that struggled to find any kind of cohesion with the rest of the environment. There were no ornaments, no photographs, just a teak-effect desk with the standard issue metal wastepaper basket, a few chairs, and a coat stand.

He was sitting at his desk looking down on two familiar scene-of-crime photographs from a double homicide in Bermondsey, which after three months was beginning to go cold. He held them between nicotine-stained fingers and stared at them like he was waiting for something to change—something that might give him a new angle beyond the limited forensic evidence they had.

One photograph showed a man in a white bloodstained dressing gown, slouched back on a leather armchair. The blood was concentrated in the middle of his chest where two bullets had ended his life. The other image was of the dead man's wife, lying in a pool of designer shopping bags in the entrance hallway. She'd been shot once in the head—9mm, point blank—and it was some small grace that she probably hadn't felt a thing. He put her death down to bad timing, plain and simple. If she'd tried on one more pair of Christian Louboutins, they probably would have saved her life.

Fable laughed sourly to himself. 'The evil that men do,' he said with a rasping, barrow-boy accent, the product of a tough East London childhood and too many cigarettes.

He studied the woman's image for a long time. She made him think about his own marriage, which was something he'd tried once a long time ago, but he'd always known it wouldn't work for him. He gave the phrase 'married to the job' a whole new definition. He shook his head, thinking it a mercy that the kids weren't home as he turned back to the photograph of the man who had once been Julian Davenport. He'd been the target—no doubt about it.

The scenes of crime officers had lifted plenty of prints from the apartment, but they hadn't found a single one that led anywhere. It seemed like a cold-blooded assassination, and as things stood there was still little to go on. With no prior offences, Davenport was as clean as his apartment, and as far as Fable knew, the man had no enemies. There was no sign of a struggle, which was telling, and no known motive. The only thing that kept Fable going on this case was that he supposed the killer had to be known to his victim. They often were. He just had to find the connection.

'Jack? You got a minute?'

It was the chief and he was gone again before Fable had a chance to look up. Fable always kept his door open when he was at his desk; he didn't like to be shut in. He sighed and reluctantly slipped the photographs back into his desk drawer. He'd never known a murder case he didn't take personally. He just couldn't stomach the idea that some low-life out there thought they were smarter than he was— thought they could do whatever they damn well pleased and get away with it. He'd made it his business to prove such people wrong, and sooner or later he usually did. He supposed that was why the Bermondsey case was getting to him.

The chief, or Graham Tanner, as he was called in the regular world, was someone with whom Fable had had too many run-ins over the two years since he'd made the rank. So many that they largely left each other alone these days because neither wanted the grief any more. That suited Fable just fine. He supposed Tanner saw him as some kind of threat, but that was his issue. He wasn't going to lose any sleep over it. In the greater scheme of things, people like DCI Graham Tanner came and went like seasonal flu.

Fable's desk phone rang and he picked it up. The voice at the other end told him there had been a shooting near Covent Garden. He was to go to Maiden Lane and take over the investigation.

Chapter Three

The witness interviews took place in the upstairs function rooms at Rules Restaurant. The place had been closed, and Maiden Lane was shut off while the SOCO team went about their work. Talking to DI Fable and going over everything that had happened had been as useful to Tayte as he hoped it had been to the police. The golden hour—that all-important first hour of investigation after a crime has been committed—worked both ways. It had forced him to focus. Now, as he left the restaurant for the second time that afternoon, he had a number of questions neatly ordered in his mind, all of which boiled down to who wanted Marcus Brown dead and why? Finding the answers wasn't going to be easy, he knew that, but he wasn't going home until he had.

The crime scene was still busy outside as he walked the street under escort. It had stopped raining, although the air was still damp and cool. He passed several spotlights on stands and people in blue paper-like oversuits. He wasn't really taking much in, unable to look anywhere near the spot where his friend had been gunned down two hours earlier. He saw Jean waiting for him beyond the galvanised barrier on the busy corner of Maiden Lane and Bedford Street and thought she couldn't have been there long. They had been told that someone would take them home, or to the hotel in Tayte's case, after the interviews were finished. Tayte thanked the uniformed constable who let him through the barrier and he gave Jean a pensive smile.

'The car won't be long,' Jean said over the din of city traffic that was in constant flow to and from a nearby junction with the Strand.

Tayte nodded. 'Great,' he said. 'I'd like to get out of these clothes.'

The blood on his shirt and trousers had dried to a dark crust. He'd lost track of his jacket and didn't care to have it back. He checked the time on his 1980s retro digital watch, and the glowing red LED digits told him it was almost five o'clock.

'You okay?' he asked.

There had been little time to talk about what had happened before now, and when they did have the chance early on, the inclination hadn't been there.

'I keep hearing his voice,' Jean said.

'Marcus?'

'The gunman.'

'He spoke to you?'

Jean nodded. 'He pointed that gun in my face and told me I'd brought it all on myself. That I shouldn't have got involved. I don't know what he thought I knew, but I was sure he was going to kill me, too.'

That worried Tayte. Whoever had killed Marcus clearly thought the two of them were working together.

'Did you tell the police?'

'Of course.'

'Did they offer you any kind of protection?'

Jean shook her head. 'They gave me a card with a number to call if I was concerned about anything.'

That worried Tayte even more. 'Same here,' he said. 'In case I recall anything else that might be important.'

A black Range Rover caught Tayte's eye as it drew level with them and slowly mounted the kerb. It had blacked out windows and brand new plates, and Tayte instinctively stood in front of Jean as the nearside rear door opened. A man he'd seen recently got out and stepped towards them.

'Michel Levant,' the man announced.

He grabbed Tayte's hand before he had time to react and pumped it lightly but exuberantly. Tayte did little to return the gesture. It was the man Marcus had been talking to at the cocktail bar before they left the restaurant. Over the man's shoulder Tayte caught the smooth sheen of a tanned thigh in the back seat of the car just before the door closed and the driver pulled away.

'And you must be Jean Summer,' Levant said with a soft French accent, his voice thin and melodious. 'Marcus has mentioned you.' He held out his hand and Jean ignored it. Then laughing it off he turned back to Tayte. 'But he has never mentioned you. American?'

Tayte nodded. That much must have been clear from the restaurant. He didn't elaborate. He was a firm believer in trusting your instincts, and everything about this man told him he was bad news.

Levant's smile faded. 'I wanted to offer my condolences,' he said. 'Marcus Brown was a great man. The best in his field. He will be greatly missed.'

Tayte wasn't in the mood for this. 'Look, who are you and what do you want?'

'I am Michel Levant,' the man said again, as if his name alone explained everything. He produced a silver calling card with all the flair of a close-up magician. 'International probate genealogist,' he added, punctuating the words.

Tayte read it. 'So you're an heir hunter? Same question. What do you want?'

'I want to offer you my services,' Levant said, sounding wounded. 'I believe that Marcus was on to something important and that he was killed for what he knew. He was, I am sure, as much a friend to me as he was to you.'

Tayte doubted that.

Jean stepped in. 'What makes you think we're interested in pursuing Marcus's work?'

Levant laughed to himself again—a small laugh through pursed lips that made his expression somewhat effeminate.

He was beginning to annoy Tayte. 'And what makes you think we'd need your help if we were?'

Levant eyed him seriously. 'It is simple. Intrigue and friendship will demand that you pursue his work—human nature will not let you rest without answers. And you need my help because I am the best at what I do.'

Tayte met Levant's eyes. 'Not where I come from you're not.'

Levant might have hit two out of three right, but Tayte had mixed feelings when it came to dedicated probate investigators: people like Levant who made their money connecting heirs with their fortunes, sometimes taking as much as forty percent for themselves. The business was entirely unregulated. It had become a magnet for the unscrupulous, and while Tayte knew many good people in the field, he had the feeling that this particular heir hunter was only talking to them now because he could smell a finder's fee.

The police car they had been waiting for arrived, temporarily slowing the southbound traffic.

'Look, excuse us,' Tayte said. He took Jean's hand and pushed past Levant. 'We're not interested.'

'But wait, I don't know your name.'

'That suits me just fine,' Tayte called back as he and Jean got into the car.

Chapter Four

Tayte had arranged to meet Jean for a drink later that evening. They needed to talk about what had happened, and Tayte needed to work out what he was going to do about it. Somewhere neutral was the idea, but Tayte received a call from Jean not long after the police had dropped him back at his hotel, inviting him to her place for dinner, which he accepted. He thought Marcus would have liked that.

It was just after seven in the evening when he arrived at her door, and it was almost dark outside. He'd brought along a bottle of wine that he'd picked up near the hotel and a bag of Hershey's chocolate miniatures from the supply he'd brought with him from home. Giving wine and chocolates to Jean made it all feel like a proper date, although that wasn't his intention. They had Chinese takeaway delivered, and Tayte, scrubbed up in a fresh tan linen suit, sat in an old leather chair by the window with his briefcase beside him. He had no idea why he'd brought it along; it was just out of habit. Neither he nor Jean had much of an appetite, so they decided to drink the wine first and save the meal for later.

Jean's flat was on the eleventh floor of a recently developed high-rise in the Docklands area, facing east along the River Thames. It was cosy, Tayte thought, as he waited for Jean to return from the kitchen with the drinks. The kitchen doorway led off the sitting room, and another went back out into a narrow hallway where he'd passed three further doors that he figured led to bedrooms and a bathroom.

He sighed for the hundredth time in as many minutes and gazed around at all the books that were lined on shelves against the walls. Larger tomes were piled like occasional tables beside the seating, which was covered with colourful throws. He was thinking about Marcus's wife, Emmy. He'd called her when he got back to the hotel, but predictably she wasn't home. The police had answered on his second call, and he imagined her house had been overrun all afternoon. He supposed she would be at the hospital or maybe with family by now, and he hoped someone was taking care of her. As close as he and Marcus had been, he couldn't begin to imagine how Emmy was feeling right now. He'd go and see her before he flew home, although he had no idea now when that would be.

A tinkle of glass announced Jean's return with the wine. She pulled out a low table between the chairs, set the wine down, and then sat in the other chair and curled up her legs, facing Tayte. She'd changed into jeans and a pastel blue jumper, and she was wearing her glasses now—the makeup gone. Tayte thought the natural look suited her better.

'Thanks,' he said as Jean handed him a glass. The wine was red. He took a sip. 'Not bad.'

'I don't know much about wine, I'm afraid,' Jean said. She smiled. 'It's red, white, or rosé. That's my limit.'

Just as long as it contained alcohol, Tayte didn't really care what colour it was or what it tasted like. 'I noticed a couple of motorcycle helmets on my way through. You ride?'

'It's the only way to get around town.'

Tayte had difficulty imagining Jean on a scooter. She didn't seem the type, but what did he know? 'And the other helmet? Your ex-husband's?'

Jean smiled at him as if she'd just been caught with her hand in the till. 'My son's,' she said. The baggage was out.

'Does he live with you?' The question just came out. Tayte had no idea why he was acting so interested.

'Off and on,' Jean said. 'He prefers to stay with his dad.'

Tayte nodded and gulped his wine. Small talk was definitely not his thing. He decided to change the subject, eager to go over the conversation at the restaurant earlier. He needed to know if Jean had any more insight into what Marcus had been working on, and more than anything, he hoped it would take him closer to finding out why it appeared to have led to his murder.

'Do you think you were close with any of those questions you asked Marcus at the restaurant?'

'I don't know,' Jean said, 'I've been thinking about it all afternoon. He was keen to shut me up, wasn't he?'

'Yes, he was, and I've been thinking about it all afternoon, too. Especially about what Marcus said just before he—' Tayte couldn't continue without pausing first. 'Before he died.'

'Treason?'

Tayte nodded. 'You mentioned a Bonny Prince. Bonny Prince Charlie, the Jacobite?'

'That's right.'

'And the two words fit together, don't they? Jacobite and treason?'

'Very much so,' Jean said. 'But not in the twenty-first century. The Jacobite risings happened more than 250 years ago.'

Tayte wished he had Marcus's briefcase. Although he hoped DI Fable and his team would turn something up at the house, he knew how particular Marcus was with his paperwork. Whatever he was working on was likely to have been with him at Rules, and his killer clearly knew how important it was.

'And what about Queen Anne?' Tayte said. 'You told me she'd been the hot topic with Marcus all month. How might she fit in?'

Jean shook her head while she thought about it. 'I really don't know,' she said. 'Anne succeeded William III, her brother-in-law, in 1702 and reigned until 1714, when the Hanovers came to the throne. Since the Act of Union between England and Scotland was passed during Anne's reign, she became the first monarch of Great Britain and the last queen of England. There were more Jacobite risings soon after she died, one in 1715 and another in 1745. Marcus wasn't so much interested in the Bonny Prince as in Jacobitism in general. It's all basic history stuff.'

Tayte considered what he knew about the Jacobite movement, most of which he'd gleaned from movies about Bonnie Prince Charlie and books by authors such as Robert Louis Stevenson. He quickly concluded that he didn't know much at all and decided to let the professional bring him up to date.

'How about a little history 101?' he said. 'What was their beef?'

Jean sipped her wine and settled back with the glass. 'It began in 1688 with the Glorious Revolution, when Anne's father, James II, fled England for France and thus abdicated the throne. The situation was later aggravated by the 1701 Act of Settlement, which was passed during William III's reign, just before he died and Anne came to the throne. She and her sister Mary, who was William III's wife—although daughters of James II, who was a devout Catholic—were equally devout converts to the Church of England. The Act stipulated that only those of the Church of England faith were eligible for succession to the throne.'

'And that placed the Hanovers next in line?'

'That's right. It ensured that in the event of Anne dying without issue—which she did—succession would fall to the Electress Sophia of Hanover, rather than to James II's Catholic son, who was also called James and was later known as the Old Pretender. Anyway, the Electress died a few weeks before Anne, so the title fell to Sophia's son George, who in 1714 was crowned King George I. The Act of Settlement still stands today.'

Tayte scoffed. 'I thought all your British kings and queens came to power by right of succession through the divinity of God, not man.'

'And there's your beef, as you put it. The Jacobites essentially stood for what was arguably right—maintaining the line of kings through the direct Stuart bloodline and James II. When Anne died, she became the last of the Stuart monarchs, and the uprisings against the Hanovers gained momentum in an attempt to restore the bloodline.'

'Because the Hanovers only came to power by virtue of their faith?'

'More or less. You see, the Electress Sophia of Hanover was—now let me get this right. She was Queen Anne's first cousin once removed, descended from the Stuart line through James I's daughter, Elizabeth. George I was Anne's second cousin and something like fiftieth in the line of succession.'

'Fiftieth?'

Jean nodded with enthusiasm. 'It's an unprecedented figure.'

'And all because of the Act of Settlement?' Tayte said, letting Jean know that he was paying attention.

'Precisely. You could argue that it changed all the rules, interfering with the intended line of kings to suit man's purpose. Although the bloodline has survived, if to a lesser extent. The Windsor ancestry—or I should say the Saxe-Coburg-Gotha ancestry, as it was before it was changed to something that sounded more British—still runs all the way back to Alfred the Great.'

'But theirs is not the true, direct bloodline?'

'Not if you take religion out of the equation. If the Act of Settlement hadn't been passed, we'd have an entirely different monarchy. They were very political times.'

'Sounds like a master stroke.'

'I suppose it was. I try to remain impartial, but you can see the Jacobites' point, can't you?'

'And the Jacobite movement died out some 250 years ago?' Tayte said. He was trying to understand why Marcus had used his dying words to urge him to hurry.

'Not exactly. Many Jacobite societies exist today, and there's still plenty of support for the Stuart bloodline, largely in Scotland and to the north of England, and perhaps surprisingly in America.'

Tayte grinned. 'Actually, that doesn't surprise me at all.'

He'd traced many American families back through Scottish immigrants in the 1700s, many of whom were transported for their Jacobite leanings. He drained his wine back and went for the bottle.

'Do you mind if I help myself?'

'Fill your boots,' Jean said. She checked her own glass. 'I must be talking too much. I've hardly touched mine.'

Tayte sat back again and got comfortable. 'And what are the odds of a twenty-first century uprising these days?' It seemed laughable, but he had to ask. 'I'm just wondering how treason fits into the picture.'

'I think the odds are very slim,' Jean said. 'Since the current heir to the Stuart bloodline—one Franz Herzog von Bayern of Bavaria—has shown no interest in pursuing a claim, I doubt that any related action against the Crown is on anyone's agenda today—treasonable or otherwise.'

Tayte was impressed. 'Marcus was right about you,' he said. 'You really know your stuff.'

Jean smiled. 'It's mostly classroom material. I still keep in touch with a few students from when I taught at university who could really blow your socks off if you got them on to the right subject. Are you hungry yet? All this talking's brought my appetite back.'

'Sure,' Tayte said. 'Let's eat.'

Somewhere in Greater London a shirtless man knelt before a raging fire. The light cast his shadow back across a derelict room, illuminating exposed brickwork, high broken windows, and a tangle of iron pipework. He reached towards the flames with a narrow length of pipe and stirred the white coals again for good measure until the heat on his bare arm was almost unbearable.

You never leave loose ends, he thought. *You tie them up before you move on. No time for complacency. No time to sit around. Not now.*

As he retreated from the flames, he considered the business he had to finish tonight. He turned his attention to the battered briefcase beside him and eyed the initials MB on the clasp. He grabbed it and opened it upside down, spilling the contents in front of the fire, covering the dusty floor with certificates of births, marriages, and deaths: connections to people whose lives he would sooner remain forgotten.

Kneeling among the records, he fed them slowly and purposefully to the flames, topping off the pyre with the briefcase itself. He watched it all burn, and when he was satisfied, he put his shirt and coat back on and headed for the door. He had already removed from the briefcase the one thing he dared to keep: a black address book. He took it out from his coat pocket as he walked, smiling to himself now as he flicked through the pages, thinking, *S is for Summer.*

⌣

'We get it in cardboard cartons back home,' Tayte said, digging his fork into a plastic tray of Singapore noodles and letting the tangled food slide onto his plate beside the char siu. They were eating at the breakfast bar in the kitchen. The oriental aromas made his mouth water.

'I know,' Jean said. 'I've seen it on telly.'

'Right.'

'I think I'd prefer cartons.'

'Why's that?'

'Well, I'm sure the food wouldn't sweat so much, and I don't know, it always looks so romantic when you see a couple in a film curled up with chopsticks and the carton between them.'

Tayte loved Chinese food, but he didn't think there was anything romantic about it. 'It still sweats,' he said, crunching into a prawn cracker.

They ate thoughtfully for a few minutes, and then Jean said, 'So where do we go from here?'

Tayte picked up on the 'we' part straightaway. He was going to do whatever it took to help the police find his friend's killer, but he figured he'd be doing it alone.

'I intend to follow in Marcus's footsteps if I can,' he said. 'You know, go through the same research. It could bring his killer after me. Could be dangerous.'

'I know,' Jean said. 'But I can help.'

Tayte didn't doubt it.

'I think I'm already involved,' Jean added. 'Whether I want to be or not.'

She had Tayte there. He drew a long breath and held it briefly while he thought it through. 'Okay,' he said. 'I had an idea to go to The National Archives first thing in the morning. Marcus might have spoken to someone about what he was working on. Maybe one of his old colleagues knows something. We might even be able to pick up his research from the record logs.'

'Great,' Jean said. 'I can give you a lift.'

'On your scooter?'

'Who said it was a scooter?'

When the meal was finished, they went back into the sitting room and sat together on the sofa.

'You know you can stay here tonight if it's easier,' Jean said. Her cheeks flushed. 'I just meant we could get a head start on things tomorrow, that's all.'

'I didn't really come prepared,' Tayte said. He could see there was no hidden reason for her asking. No romantic agenda.

'My son always leaves a few things here,' Jean said. 'I've got a new toothbrush you can have and—' She paused and tested the sofa with her palm. 'I'm sure it's comfy.'

It was clear to Tayte that Jean didn't want to be alone tonight, and he was flattered, even if it was just for the company, but he couldn't stay.

'I expect I can find you a clean t-shirt,' Jean continued. 'Elliot's into the baggy look. There must be something you can squeeze into. Sorry, I didn't mean it to come out like that.'

Tayte smiled. 'That's okay. No offence taken.'

There was an edge of desperation to her tone that he found hard to refuse, but he knew it wouldn't work. He liked his own space. It was what he was used to.

'I'd appreciate the company,' Jean added, confirming his thoughts.

Tayte fidgeted. 'Look, Jean. I'm sorry, but I just can't.'

'Okay, that's fine,' she said, forcing a smile that was easy to see through.

'So how old's your son?' Tayte asked.

'Twenty.' Jean laughed. 'Going on twelve most of the time.'

Tayte laughed with her as though he knew exactly what she meant, but while a part of him thought it would be good to know what it was like to watch your child grow through adolescence, he really had no idea and doubted he ever would. It didn't really bother him. It was just curiosity.

'So you must have been married a while,' he said.

'Twenty-one years. We were keen to start a family straightaway. We had big plans, but I didn't want to go through it again. Some mothers take to it better than others, I suppose. I don't think Daniel—that's Elliot's father—was ever happy about that. I found out that he'd been seeing other women for several years, and he must have finally found someone he wanted to settle down with or I suppose it would have gone on longer.'

'What a rat,' Tayte said.

Jean agreed.

'So that's where Elliot is tonight?'

'No, he was supposed to be here. I think he's staying with friends. He often does.'

'You *think*?' Tayte said.

Jean sighed. 'If I'm honest with myself, we don't get on that well. Communication's not a strong point. He's always been closer to his father and it's been worse since the breakup.' She stood up. 'Do you fancy a hot drink before you go?'

'Sure. Any chocolate?'

Jean looked surprised, as though she hadn't figured Tayte for a hot chocolate drinker, despite his contradicting waistline. 'I have no idea,' she said. 'Let me go and see.'

She was gone several minutes. When she returned, Tayte came away from the window where he'd been watching the lights on the Thames and sat down again. Jean handed him a thick-rimmed mug that was just right for his supersized hand.

'Mind, it's hot,' she said. 'It's a little past its use-by date, too, but I think you'll live.'

Tayte thanked her.

'So now it's your turn' Jean said. 'You're obviously not married. Ever tried it?'

Tayte laughed. 'No,' he said, categorically, like anyone could tell that he wasn't the marrying type. But that wasn't really it. The laughter was more of a defence mechanism, a reflex action equivalent to putting on a brave face because marriage seemed as unlikely and as scary a thing to him as having the nerve to ask someone out on a date in the first place.

'Why not?' Jean asked.

She was direct. Tayte admired that about her, even if it was beginning to make him feel awkward. He had an image of the 'why not' fixed in his head: Sandra Greenaway, senior prom, 1987. Since that night he'd gone through all the responses he could imagine, and he couldn't think of a single one that hurt him more than when she'd taken two steps back and laughed at him along with her friends.

'I guess my work keeps me too busy,' he said.

It was a white lie and a lame one at that, but he knew his fear of rejection ran far deeper than Sandra Greenaway, and he didn't want to get into it just now.

'Marcus told me your parents died when you were young,' Jean said. 'That must have been tough.'

Tayte had to smile. 'You don't mince your words, do you?'

She slapped her own wrist. 'It's the by-product of a career in further education. I don't mind if you'd rather not talk about it.'

'No, that's okay,' Tayte said. He was happy just to talk about something else. 'I was seventeen. They were on the return flight to DC from a vacation in the Florida Keys. I would have gone, but I was studying for college exams. That was the excuse anyway. Truth was, I didn't want to go. I didn't much like flying then, and I've hated it ever since. They put the crash down to some malfunction or other.'

'I'm sorry,' Jean said.

'It was a while ago now. I'll fly when I have to, but I always try and talk myself out of it first.'

'So coming over this weekend must have been a big deal for you?'

'I'd put it off too long,' Tayte said, wishing now, in light of what had happened to Marcus, that he hadn't. 'I'm getting a little more used to it though, and I'm glad I didn't talk myself out of it this time.'

'No,' Jean agreed.

Tayte sipped his chocolate. 'Anyway, going back to my parents. I only found out that my mom and dad were really my adoptive parents after the accident. I've been looking for my roots ever since.'

'And are you any closer to finding them?'

Tayte thought about that and slowly shook his head, thinking that he was probably the only professional genealogist on the planet who didn't know a damn thing about his own ancestry. How ironic could life get? He started to think about all the dead ends he'd arrived at over the years, reminding himself of how little he still knew. He thought about the many DNA samples he'd sent to one registry and another in the hope of finding a match with one of his biological relatives, but nothing had come of it. The memories made him oblivious to the fact that the conversation had stopped.

'Well,' Jean said. She got up, collected the cups, and headed for the kitchen.

Tayte didn't mind the questions, and he hoped he hadn't offended her; she'd been open enough with him all night. He just didn't like to talk about it—didn't like the answers that kept coming back to remind him of his failings.

'I suppose it is getting late,' he said, glancing at his watch without really noticing the time. He collected his briefcase and followed Jean into the kitchen. 'I'll say goodnight then. Let's meet at Kew tomorrow. Nine a.m. sharp.'

'I'll give you my mobile number. In case there's a problem. You never know.'

'Good idea,' Tayte said. He reached into his briefcase and pulled out the first thing his hand fell on. It was one of Marcus Brown's early publications, and seeing his friend's portrait on the back cover made him catch his breath. After a lengthy pause, he handed the book to Jean and forced a smile. 'Here, you can write it in this. I'll see you tomorrow.'

The lift opposite Jean's apartment looked inviting as Tayte said goodbye and closed the door, but he fought the urge and took the stairs instead, reminding himself that he needed the exercise. He padded down them, listening to the echo of his footfall, thinking about Jean and how much he knew it would have meant to her if he'd stayed. He felt mean, and it began to play on his conscience. He knew it would have sooner or later, but he hadn't expected it to happen quite this soon. He was about halfway down when he heard the door at the bottom of the stairwell open and close again. Soon after that he passed a man in a dark coat who was on his way up, two steps at a time.

'Evening,' Tayte said, not really looking at the man.

He received no reply and hadn't expected one, thinking that London was no different from any other big city when it came to passing strangers. He made it all the way into the lobby, past an abandoned night desk, and out into the quiet street before he stopped and turned back. The truth was that he didn't want to be alone either after what had happened, and seeing Marcus's image again on the book as he'd handed it to Jean just made him feel worse.

He took the lift this time, riding it back to the eleventh floor, smiling for the camera above his head. He had his words fully formed into a neat sentence by the time he heard the *ping* and the lift door opened. What he saw when it did made him forget them in an instant. The man he'd passed on the stairs was standing with his back to him at the door opposite the lift—Jean's door. In that same slow second he thought it was a little late for callers, that Jean would have said if she was expecting anyone else, and that the coat the man was wearing looked worryingly familiar. It made him think about the man in the mask from Maiden Lane earlier, and any question he had as to who this man was disappeared when the figure turned around and started shooting at him.

Tayte lurched sideways as the gunman turned and the bullets arrived, making little sound until they hit something. One ripped through his sleeve, maybe his arm. He wasn't sure. All he felt was a tug at his jacket as it tore through the material and shattered the mirror behind him. He dropped his briefcase. Then as the lift doors began to close he felt something sting, and he knew he'd been hit.

He didn't have time to dwell on it.

Another shot was fired, muted like the others, only this time it was accompanied by the sound of splintering wood, as if the gunman had just shot through the lock on Jean's door and kicked it in. He heard it slam open and bang against the wall, and his finger was already on the lift door-release button. He kept close to one side as he repeatedly tapped it, and when it was fully open again, he peeked out. The man was gone, and the door to Jean's apartment was tellingly wide open.

It seemed to take Tayte forever to think what to do. He knew he couldn't just run in there or the man would shoot them both. Then he saw the fire extinguisher: a big red one. He grabbed it and ran inside, driven by the thought that this man had killed his friend, and he'd be damned if he was going to stand back and let Jean Summer share the same fate.

His resolve buckled when he saw the man again. He was in the hallway. The light was out, but the sitting room door was open, and against the glow from the city lights beyond the window, Tayte saw a coal black silhouette standing in the doorframe. As the man turned around, Tayte ran at him with the extinguisher. He thrust it at him. The gun went off and Tayte hit him with it again, knocking him down.

'Jean!'

She was there, hiding in the dark. Even so, Tayte knew from the size of the apartment that it wouldn't have taken long for the gunman to find her. She came at him like a wild animal, leaping over the gunman and knocking Tayte back. He looked for the gun but couldn't make it out in the half-light. Then the dark figure on the floor began to stir.

'Come on!' Jean urged.

Tayte backed away.

Jean was already at the door. 'Here, take these.'

Two crash helmets were thrust into his stomach and he felt like he'd suddenly awoken from a sleepwalking episode, wondering where he was. He saw that Jean already had a leather jacket on. She had a pair of boots in her hand, and he heard a metallic jangle like she'd just picked up a set of keys. Then they were heading for the lift.

Inside, Jean began to pump the button for the basement parking level. 'Come on, damn you. Come on!'

The door began to close. A shot was fired, wild and untrained. It peeled the plaster from the wall outside, and they moved away from the opening. The gunman was out in the hallway now heading straight for them. Tayte watched him run at the doors, eyes on the gun the whole time as he thrust the silencer forward, presumably in the hope of jamming it between the doors and forcing the safety mechanism to open them again. It was a close call but he didn't make it. Tayte ducked back as the gun clanked against the doors. Then they were descending.

Tayte reacquainted himself with his briefcase and gave a nervous laugh. 'I changed my mind.'

Jean was putting her boots on. When she'd finished, she took the smaller of the two helmets from Tayte and put that on, too. 'I'm glad you did.' She nodded at the other helmet. 'See if it fits.'

Tayte didn't really care. Attracting police attention for not wearing a helmet seemed like a good idea right now. The helmet was an open face type. It was tight, but he got it on.

'He would have seen the helmets,' he said. 'He'll know where we're headed.'

'Then get ready.'

They watched the countdown together. Four, three, two. They reached the lobby.

'Next level,' Jean said.

They ran as soon as they could fit through the gap in the doors, and they were instantly lit up by the harsh overhead strip lights. The motorcycle area was off to the right, and they kept running. All Tayte could see were scooters, and he hoped Jean hadn't been teasing him about the kind of bike she had. None of them looked big enough to carry him, let alone both of them. They passed a blue 4x4 and the view opened up. He could see a few sports bikes now and something big with a yellow tank. It had panniers and high mudguards, and Tayte thought it looked like it belonged in a Dakar rally. He watched Jean bend down and take a key to the U-shaped lock that was dangling from the front brake disc. He eyed the BMW roundel and the letters R1200GS on the tank.

'You've gotta be kidding me.'

Jean climbed onto the thing like she was mounting a horse, and somewhat disconcertingly Tayte noticed that her feet could barely reach the floor. Behind them a door opened and slapped hard against a concrete wall.

'Are you just going to stand there?'

Tayte swung himself on, grabbed the pillion handrail with one hand, and cradled his briefcase to his chest with the other. The engine fired up and Jean rocked the bike forward, tipping it off the centre stand, dropping it several centimetres. Then they were moving again, racing for the exit.

Tayte looked back. He hadn't had a good look at this man yet. Somewhere close by he heard glass pop and shatter, and he decided not to try. He shrank into himself, clutching his briefcase tighter. The gunman was right behind them, running fast, showing no sign of letting up. Another shot fizzed by, taking out one of the overhead lights.

'Brace yourself!' Jean called.

Tayte looked up again and saw why. They were heading towards a barrier and the bike wasn't slowing down.

'It's automatic on the way out!' Jean called.

Automatic or not, Tayte had never seen a barrier of any kind respond as quickly to an approaching vehicle as he knew this one would have to if they were to clear it in time. Jean ducked as they approached and the barrier began to lift. The bike slowed a little then, but sitting on the back, Tayte was higher than he knew he needed to be. He closed his eyes and ducked after Jean, leaning forward as best he could with his briefcase between them as they arrived and the barrier broke across the top of his helmet. An alarm began to sound. Then the engine revs picked up again and they turned out into the night.

Chapter Five

An hour later, Tayte and Jean were climbing into the back of a silver Audi saloon. As soon as they felt it was safe to stop, Tayte had called Fable's number from the card he'd given him, and by then Fable already knew about the incident at Jean's apartment building: several people had reported the disturbance. Fable had told them to stay put at the twenty-four-hour service station Tayte was calling from; a car was on its way. He'd also said that he was keen to talk to Tayte about another matter concerning something that had been found at Marcus Brown's home earlier that day.

As they settled into the journey, Tayte thought the setup didn't feel quite right. He wasn't particularly worried, given that Fable had said the car was coming for them. It was just that he felt sure the two suits sitting up front were not regular police officers, detective grade or otherwise, and the car didn't exactly seem like police issue either, not that he really knew what the inside of an unmarked police car should look like. He couldn't put his finger on it, but he thought the whole thing had more of a military feel.

He asked the obvious question. 'Where are we headed?'

'It shouldn't take long, sir.'

That's all the reply he got, and after exchanging bemused glances with Jean, he decided to sit back and keep quiet. Ten minutes later they began to track the Thames to their left, following its dark course for several minutes until they arrived at a roundabout at the top of Lambeth Bridge. They went straight over and turned right. Jean gave Tayte a nudge, indicating the floodlit facade of the grey building complex they were heading for.

'MI5,' she mouthed.

Tayte had no trouble reading her lips, but he did have trouble trying to understand why they were being taken to the home of the British Security Service. He relaxed a little when the car arrived at Thames House and he saw DI Fable waiting for them. As they walked under escort, Tayte further explained what had happened at Jean's apartment, putting his finger through the hole in his jacket sleeve as if to prove it. His arm was okay: barely a scratch that he'd cleaned up in the service station men's room.

'The building's night watchman wasn't so lucky,' Fable said. 'His body was found behind the desk where he'd fallen. Two bullets in his chest.' He turned to Jean. 'There's a forensics team at your flat now. You'll need somewhere else to stay tonight.'

'What about my bike?' Jean said. 'Do I get a lift back to the service station when we're done here?'

'I get the feeling you won't be needing it for a while,' Fable said. 'Let me have the key and I'll get it picked up for you.'

Jean handed it to him and described the bike. She still had the brake disc lock in her jacket pocket. The ignition key was all he needed.

'Registration?'

'H15 TRY.'

Fable smiled. 'I'll see that it's taken home for you.'

'No, not there,' Jean said. To Tayte, she added, 'Where are you staying?'

'The Hyatt Regency in Marylebone.'

'Have it taken to the hotel,' Jean said. 'I'll stay there until this is over.'

They were escorted to a meeting room. There was a long oval table in the centre with twenty or so chairs around it and dark windows to Tayte's right as he entered. There were three other people in the room: two men in dark suits and a woman in black and white dogtooth. All wore serious expressions.

'Good to meet you, Mr Tayte,' one of the men said. He was a slight man with a nasal tone to his voice. 'Ms Summer,' he added, greeting Jean. The man didn't give his name and neither did anyone else.

Tayte put his briefcase on the table, and they were invited to sit down. Fable placed two manila folders in front of him.

'I was going to call you about this first thing in the morning,' Fable said. 'You told me yesterday you were a genealogist like your friend Marcus Brown.'

Tayte nodded.

Fable slid the folders closer. 'We found these at Mr Brown's home and wondered if you'd take a look.'

Tayte opened the folders. The first contained a three-month-old newspaper cutting of a double murder in Bermondsey: Julian Davenport and his wife. Fable quickly filled Tayte in on the high-level details of the case. Beneath the clipping was a sheet of A3 paper folded twice. It showed Davenport's ancestry dating to the 1600s with plenty of gaps, particularly further back, as Tayte would have expected.

The second folder contained another ancestry chart much like the first: a left-to-right expanding pyramid of names also going back to the 1600s. The subject on this chart was a man called Douglas Jones, and according to his entry, he had died twenty years earlier.

Tayte sat back in his chair. 'They're ancestry charts.'

The woman in the dogtooth suit came back at him before he could elaborate. Her tone was sharp and to the point. 'We know that much, Mr Tayte.'

Tayte gave her an apologetic smile. He laid the charts out side by side and studied them more closely. His only idea at this point was to see if any of the names matched, but there were so many, and the handwriting was small and written by Marcus Brown, which added another level of difficulty. He didn't quite need his degree in palaeography to read his friend's writing, and he knew he could sit there and work through it, but he didn't think that was what the people around him had in mind.

He turned one of the charts over, thinking it wouldn't mean anything even if they did share a common name. It would prove that the people on the charts were related, but so what? Then as he leant in and smoothed the paper out, he noticed a small three-digit number by the crease where the folds converged on the chart for Julian Davenport. He checked the other chart and noted that it had no such marking.

'Unless Marcus singled a name out,' Tayte said under his breath. 'Then it would mean something.' He felt the room close in around him. 'Can I get a pencil? It might be an ahnentafel number.'

Someone handed Tayte a pencil and he wrote down the number, 594, in large print so everyone could see it.

'Ahnentafel?' Jean said, asking the question that must have been on everyone's lips.

Tayte looked up. 'It's a German word that literally translates to 'ancestor table.' The system's been around for centuries. It was invented by an Austrian historian named Eytzinger and later popularised by the genealogists de Sosa and Stradonitz. Basically, it's a construct that allows us to show someone's ancestry in text form, either as a numbered list or even as a binary table.'

Tayte put his finger on the chart entry for Julian Davenport. 'Using the system, everyone on this chart has a unique reference number in relation to the subject.' He turned to Fable. 'Your murder victim, in this case.'

'How does it work?' the woman in the dogtooth suit asked.

Tayte smiled. 'The beauty really lies in its simplicity. The subject is always number one. The father is double that and the mother is double plus one.' Tayte started writing numbers against the names.

'So Davenport's father is number two on the chart. His mother is number three.' He wrote the numbers in. 'His paternal grandmother will be number five—that's twice the father, plus one. And his paternal great-grandmother will be twice that plus one again, which makes her number eleven. It's easy once you get the hang of it.'

The man with the nasal voice was over his shoulder. 'So this three-digit number. Who does it point to?'

'Well, the numbers haven't been written in on the chart, and it would take a while to do that,' Tayte said. 'But fortunately the system provides us with an easy way to get there. I mentioned a binary table a moment ago.'

Heads nodded.

'If we convert this three-digit number to binary, we can use that number to point directly to someone on the chart.' Tayte looked around. 'Anyone know the binary conversion for 594?'

The only man in the room who hadn't spoken yet—a big man with a military style buzz-cut—picked up the phone at the end of the table and hit a couple of buttons.

'I need a numeric conversion,' he said in a baritone voice. 'Decimal to binary, 594.' He nodded, then looked at Tayte. 'Get your pencil ready.'

Tayte wrote the numbers down as the man called them out.

'One-zero-zero-one-zero-one-zero-zero-one-zero. Okay, got it. Thanks.'

Tayte showed everyone what the number looked like written in binary: 1001010010. 'The first time I saw this,' he said, 'I thought it was a magic trick. As I've said, the leading digit is always number one and represents the subject, in this case Julian Davenport. Then a zero translates to 'F' for father, and a one is 'M' for mother. Another way to look at it is like this.' He scratched the first digit and wrote FFMFMFFMF.

He went back to the chart. 'So our number 594 is Julian Davenport's father's father's mother's father's mother's father's father's mother's father.' He traced a finger across the generations as he spoke, arriving at an entry beside which he wrote the number 594. 'That's nine generations from the subject. A direct line of descent to a Reverend Charles Naismith, born 1668 and died 1708. When Marcus wrote that number down on this chart, it's like he drew a big red circle around Naismith's name.'

Jean scoffed. 'It would have been easier if he had.'

'I guess he didn't want to draw too much attention to it,' Tayte said. 'It must be important though, and I wouldn't mind betting our man Naismith also appears on the other chart.'

He checked. The name was there and easy to find now that he had the dates. Naismith had twin sons according to the charts. Julian Davenport was descended from one and Douglas Jones from the other.

'If you want to know what Marcus Brown was working on,' Tayte continued, 'then the Reverend Naismith is your way in.' He sat back in his chair. 'Now is anyone going to tell me why MI5 are so interested in his murder?'

The woman in the dogtooth suit answered. 'We understand that Marcus Brown was concerned about something we now believe could be a threat to our country's national security. I'm sorry the matter wasn't treated with more urgency when he first made contact with us, and I can assure you that will be addressed. But, since he was murdered before we had the opportunity to speak to him, we have to suppose that the threat is real until proven otherwise.'

'And you want me to help identify that threat for you?'

It was clear to Tayte that these were the people Marcus was going to meet—the people who liked to keep their secrets close to their chest, as Marcus had put it.

'You seem very competent at what you do, Mr Tayte,' the woman said. 'And you told Inspector Fable yesterday that you and Mr Brown were close friends. Can you think of anyone better qualified?'

Tayte couldn't.

'We need to know where all this leads,' the woman added, tapping the charts. 'In short, we need to know what Marcus Brown knew.'

Tayte drew a deep breath. *A threat to national security? What the hell were you into, Marcus?* His friend's dying words replayed through his mind. *Treason…Hurry…* This was all so much bigger than he'd imagined. He looked at Jean for confirmation that she still wanted in. She nodded back at him.

'Okay,' Tayte said. He gathered up the charts. 'First thing in the morning we need to visit The National Archives.'

Chapter Six

For their protection, and no doubt because the British Security Service wanted to keep them close, Tayte and Jean spent the remainder of the night at Thames House, sleeping in basic but comfortable accommodations. Early the following morning they took the Great West Road out of Central London, and thirty minutes later the same silver Audi that had picked them up the night before arrived at The National Archives in Kew. It was another government agency building, this one home to almost three hundred million documents spanning a thousand years of history.

Tayte recognised the modern stone building as soon as they came in sight of it. He'd only been there once before, when he'd travelled to England on a cruise ship because he wouldn't get on an aeroplane. That was years ago, but the building's architecture was hard to misplace. It reminded him of something between an air traffic control tower and a compressed multistorey car park. The windows on the first two floors were tall and angled towards the ground, while those on the higher levels were no more than narrow slits that ran around the building, layering the stonework so as to allow in as little damaging UV light as was necessary.

They parked in the visitors' car park, and Tayte and Jean got out of the back as the two efficient-looking Security Service officers who had been assigned to them for the duration got out of the front. The taller man was called Hampshire; the other was Hues. Neither spoke much, not even to each other. Fable wasn't joining them. He had a murder investigation to conduct and a new lead to follow from the genealogy charts: Douglas Jones. They all wanted to know who he was and where he fitted into the picture.

As they paced beside a large rectangular pond towards the building's main entrance—a tall cube-shaped glass appendage with a pyramidal roof—Tayte kept turning the data over in his head to keep it fresh. He had the charts in his briefcase, but he wanted to commit the information to memory. *Charles Naismith. Born 1668. Died 1708.* The reverend was their way in, he'd told them, and he hoped he was right.

In the foyer, Tayte checked his briefcase with security, and they were met by the chief executive of the Archives, who introduced herself as Victoria Marsh. Someone had called ahead and she was expecting them. Tayte put her in her early fifties. She had ash blonde hair and wore a light green trouser suit. When she smiled at him, he thought her face carried the weight of a loss shared.

'We were all so shocked to hear about what happened to dear Marcus,' she said, leading them past a line of visitors who were already queuing for their readers' tickets. 'I was asked by Detective Fable to show you the records Marcus had requested in the last three months. Is that correct?'

'Yes, ma'am,' Tayte said. 'And thanks for your co-operation. I know it's short notice.'

They cleared the security checks and Marsh turned and locked eyes with Tayte. 'Just catch whoever did this, will you?'

They took a lift to the first floor where they passed the Open Reading Room and continued to the Document Reading Room. It was a large space, like any modern open-plan office, with grey carpet, overhead fluorescent lights, and swivel chairs arranged around honeycomb-shaped desk pods. Every pod had a numbered cube at its centre, and all were vacant because the regular visitors had been held back for now. They were taken to a pod adjacent to the windows, and a member of security staff who had been waiting for them resumed his duties as they approached.

There was a strict no-talking policy in the Document Reading Room, which was never going to be a problem for officers Hampshire and Hues, who stood rather than sat at the opposite side of the pod. The only sound Tayte could hear was the background hum of the air conditioning. Victoria Marsh indicated the records that had already been laid out for them.

'I'll leave these with you,' she said, exercising her executive prerogative to contravene the rules. 'If you need anything else, just ask a member of staff to contact me.'

Tayte smiled and mouthed a silent 'Thank you' as Marsh left. He was so used to keeping quiet in such rooms that he thought nothing of the fact that on this occasion they were the only people there to disturb. He looked at Jean and then at the records. Every document at The National Archives was referred to as a record, whether it was a single sheet, an entire book, a newspaper, or a photograph. If it had a catalogue number, it was a record.

There were only two records for them to see, and Tayte thought there might have been more given all the work Marcus had put in on the charts found at his home, but he knew much of his friend's research would have been focused on birth, marriage, and death certificates, which were held at the General Register Office. His research would undoubtedly have taken him to other repositories, too.

Tayte pulled one of the records closer and set it between them as he and Jean sat down. It was a book called the *Newgate Calendar*—Volume II. It bore the subtitle *The Malefactors' Bloody Register*. He'd come across the *Newgate Calendar* before. It began as a monthly publication of the Ordinary of Newgate's account of executions, the Ordinary being the prison chaplain, who made money selling his accounts to the publishing press. These accounts were later compiled into six volumes that were once among the top three books to be found in the family home along with a bible and *The Pilgrim's Progress*. They encouraged moral correctness through fear by showing illustrations of people like Thomas Hunter, the knife-wielding child murderer, with one boy lying lifeless at his feet while another, caught by his hair, is struggling to free himself. The publications were against Catholicism, the Commonwealth, and anything outside of the Common Law or Bloody Code as it was later known, instead favouring the Church of England and the monarchy.

Tayte put on a pair of the white gloves that had been provided for them and turned to the index, feeling the old book's uneven edges as his fingertips passed over them. There were several pages of names, and he had a good idea what he expected to find. He turned one page and then another. Then he underlined an entry with his forefinger, drawing Jean's attention to it. It read 'REV. CHARLES NAISMITH of St Mary's Whitechapel. Executed at Tyburn, 23rd of April, 1708 for High Treason.' He found the indicated page: a body of text split into two tall columns, above which was the heading 'The Ordinary of Newgate his Account of the Behaviour, Confessions, and Dying Speeches of the Malefactors that were Executed at Tyburn, on Monday the 23rd of April, 1708.'

'High treason,' Tayte whispered, glancing at Jean.

'We must be on the right track,' she whispered back.

Tayte began to read the text, noting some of the archaic spellings and how the author used capital letters seemingly at random, perhaps for emphasis—a practice that was common in the early eighteenth century.

AT the Sessions held at Justice-Hall in the Old-Bailey, on Wednesday, Thursday, and Friday, the 4th, 5th, and 6th instant, several Persons (viz. 5 Men and 3 Women) who were Try'd for, and found Guilty of several Capital Crimes, receiv'd Sentence of Death accordingly, and Two others were call'd to their former Judgment. Of all these Ten Malefactors, Five being Repriev'd, viz, the Three Women for their Pregnancy, and Two of the Men by the QUEEN'S most gracious reprieve (which I hope they will take care to improve); 5 are now order'd for Execution.

Tayte's interest in Naismith extended to the other four men who were hanged with him, and he wondered if there was a connection. He continued to read, catching the opening paragraphs and skipping ahead to find the relevant material:

While they lay under this Condemnation, I constantly visited them, and had them brought up twice every day, to the Chapel of Newgate, where I pray'd with them, and read and expounded the Word of GOD to them... On the Lord's Day the 8th instant, I preach'd to them, both in the Morning and Afternoon, upon part of the Gospel for the Day, viz. Luke 21. 27, the Words being these; And then shall they see the Son of Man coming in a Cloud with Power and great Glory...

Tayte sighed. The Ordinary of Newgate seemed nothing if not thorough in his piety. Tayte reached the bottom of the page and began again at the top of the next column. As well as providing spiritual care to the condemned, it was the Ordinary's role to solicit a confession from the accused wherever possible, such that their souls might enter heaven. As Tayte reached the end of the second column, the text still knotted in God's holy word, he thought he would have confessed to just about anything if he had to listen to this all day. He turned the page and slowed when he was half way down the first column, seeing that the subject matter had returned more directly to the accused:

I have here dwelt the longer upon these respective Heads or chief Points of my Sermons to the Condemn'd Persons, because I may have but little else to fill this Paper with; which (as I take it) should be excus'd from the Tax, being a Paper that (for the most part) contains Matter of Divinity and Devotion, and is chiefly intended for the Instruction and Reformation of Sinners. These who are the Subject of it, and are now order'd for Execution, gave me small account of their past Lives, and present Dispositions, as follows...

Tayte read five names and five brief accounts, which amounted to little more than statements of innocence against the charges of supporting the Old Pretender and the Jacobite cause. They stated their loyalty to Queen Anne and to the Church of England and upheld that no evidence to support the accusations of high treason had been proved. The Ordinary noted with disdain that these five men protested their innocence all the way to the Tyburn tree and during their pithy dying speeches.

Tayte wished they had given the Ordinary a better account of themselves. He wrote the names in his notebook below the entry that was already there for the Reverend Charles Naismith, adding Dr Bartholomew Hutton, Lloyd Needham, Sir Stephen Henley, and William Daws. Five men connected in death, hanged as Jacobite supporters. He read the last paragraph of the Ordinary's account and began to wonder what might have connected these five men in life:

I finally commended their Souls to the Mercy of God in Christ, and retir'd from them; leaving them to their private Devotions, for which they had some time allotted them: And then the Cart drew away, and they were turned off, all the while calling on God to have Mercy upon their Souls. This is all the Account here to be given of these dying Persons, by me THOMAS LAING, Ordinary. Friday, May 4, 1708.

Tayte closed the book and they took a break, returning to the ground floor where the café hubbub after the quiet of the reading room was as welcome as the caffeine. Jean sat in a chair by the window and Tayte sat opposite. Officers Hampshire and Hues kept their vigil by the main doors, where they remained standing with their drinks and were no doubt bored to distraction.

'So, what do you make of it?' Jean asked.

Tayte sucked the foam from the top of his coffee. 'Well, after your history lesson yesterday, I guess I don't really see how five men who say they were loyal to Queen Anne could qualify as Jacobites. And Naismith was Church of England clergy.'

'Jacobitism wasn't just a Catholic thing. No more than its supporters were all Scottish.'

'Movies and storybooks again?'

Jean nodded. 'Although the majority of longer-term supporters were Scottish Catholics, and that's probably what the storytellers latched onto.'

'But what about their loyalty to Queen Anne? Didn't you say that to be a Jacobite was to be loyal to the Old Pretender who called himself James III?'

'Strictly speaking they were loyal to the bloodline—to his father, James II. Support came from those who believed that his blood was the true royal blood.'

'So in a way Queen Anne's blood was also Jacobite blood?'

'Technically, I suppose it was. The word 'Jacobite' comes from the Latin for James, which is *Jacobus*. A Jacobite is literally a follower of Jacobus—in this case, James II.'

Tayte half drained his coffee cup. 'And that's what doesn't make any sense.'

'How do you mean?'

'Well, Queen Anne was still alive when these men were hanged. You said she died in 1714, six years after the hangings.'

'That's right.'

Tayte scoffed. 'Well, if someone openly supports the current monarchy, how can they be hanged for high treason? I mean, one contradicts the other, doesn't it?'

'Maybe they were lying about their allegiance,' Jean said. 'They might have said anything to escape the hangman's noose.'

'But they didn't escape it. Why keep up the lie if that's what it was? They were religious men, judging from what we've read. Surely they would have chosen to die with a clear conscience—cleansed their souls. At least one out of five would have spoken out.'

Jean seemed to be coming around to the idea. 'I suppose if they were Jacobites in the way we understand Jacobitism today then no, they wouldn't have hidden that fact if they knew they were going to die anyway. They would have died proud and loyal men.'

Tayte raised a brow. 'Things aren't quite as they seem here, are they?'

They finished their coffee and headed back upstairs to the Document Reading Room, where one record remained to be viewed.

Keep following the clues, Tayte told himself. *See where they lead.*

At his office in Central London, politician Trenton McAlister gazed out of his window towards Trafalgar Square. His eyes were fixed on Nelson's Column, taking in nothing of the morning rush hour, which was as much a part of the view as the enduring pigeons. He was deep in thought, not really looking at the effigy of the man whom after all these years he felt he knew so well, but through it. He was subconsciously tapping his foot, feeling both excited and overwhelmed by the news he had just received.

McAlister was in his fifties, clean-shaven with dyed brown hair that he had cut twice a week to keep up the impeccable image he strove to maintain. He wore a pinstripe suit, shoes polished to a high shine, and a tie that bore the red, white, and green stripes of the British republican tricolour. He was as proud of his support for a British republic as he was open about it, and having built his career from humble beginnings, he liked to think of himself as the perfect role model for a New Britain, engendering the belief that possibility was for all and not just for the lucky few. There were no skeletons in McAlister's closet. At least, none that anyone had ever found.

When a tap came at the door he turned away from the bright window with a tear in his eye. Like the foot tapping it was something he hadn't been overly aware of until he felt that tear roll down his cheek. He quickly wiped it away with the back of his hand, but little escaped the attention of his long-serving assistant, Beatrice, who had just entered the room.

'Anything wrong?' she asked as she set McAlister's morning cup of tea down on the desk.

'Thank you, Bea,' he said with a smooth Edinburgh Scots accent. He sipped his tea and turned back to the window.

'Well?' Beatrice said. '*Is* something wrong?'

'Far from it,' McAlister said. 'I've had some good news. Great news in fact.'

'Tears of joy then?'

McAlister turned and smiled, flashing whitened teeth that any Hollywood actor would have been proud of. 'If I'm feeling a little emotional this morning, it's because I believe that all my campaigning might finally be getting somewhere. And maybe sooner than I'd hoped.'

'Anything you want to share?'

'In good time, Bea, in good time.'

'Suit yourself,' Beatrice said. She turned to leave, adding, 'Your 'news man' confirmed seven-thirty this evening. I'm sure you'll tell him what you're feeling so emotional about, won't you?'

McAlister ignored the question and checked his watch. 'He called already?' he said, surprised at such an early response to a message left no more than half an hour ago. 'My, but he's a keen one, isn't he?'

As Beatrice left the room McAlister sat down and sipped his tea again, smiling to himself as his thoughts turned to his two sons. They were both in their thirties now and had taken up the republican campaign with him as soon as they were old enough to deliver pamphlets door to door. He had no doubt they were both equally proud of him, but he hoped he would soon make them prouder still.

For the first time in Trenton McAlister's political career, he believed he might actually see his efforts come to fruition in his own lifetime. The dream felt almost tangible, but there was still much work to be done. Public opinion polls showed that around 70 percent of the nation believed that Britain would be a republic in fifty years' time.

Fifty years, he thought, chuckling to himself. If his caller made good his claim, then he believed Britain could see its first president long before that.

Tayte couldn't recall having seen a copy of the centuries-old newspaper he and Jean were now looking at inside the Document Reading Room, which by now had begun to fill with visitors. It was called the *Daily Courant.* He knew of it but he'd never actually held a copy—not that he could quite do that now as this single sheet newspaper was inside a clear protective cover. Even so, he liked to see original records whenever he had the chance. Marcus was right about that. It wasn't the same as looking at a digital scan on the Internet or a copy on a microform reader.

He thought about Marcus again and about technology, adding newspapers to the list of diminishing physical documents that would be available for future generations, since people could already have their favourite newspaper delivered digitally to a PC or e-reader. He supposed that things were certainly going to be different for the genealogist of the future. *But not quite yet,* he thought as he leant in and studied what was reputedly England's first successful daily newspaper, published between 1702 and 1735. This edition was dated Thursday, April 7, 1708—a little more than two weeks before the hangings he and Jean had read about in the *Newgate Calendar.* The text was similarly divided into two heavily worded columns.

Tayte raced over it. Something had to be related, but what? There were a few paragraphs of translated foreign affairs and a large section concerning the debates of Parliament. He saw an account of a hanging and thought that was it until he reminded himself that this newspaper was published too early for such a report to be relevant. Then Jean made him jump.

'There!' she said, forgetting where she was.

Tayte felt the weight of a hundred eyes on them, although Jean was so caught up in their research that she seemed not to realise that people were suddenly staring at her. Tayte sank lower in his chair and followed the line of Jean's index finger to an advertisement section at the bottom of the righthand column. It wasn't quite what he'd expected, but he saw a name he'd recently scribbled into his notepad.

At the Sign of the Cheshire-Cheese, a Tinshop in Walbrook, near Stocks-Market, Liveth a Gentlewoman, the Daughter of eminent Physician and Royal Society Fellow, Dr Bartholomew Hutton, who has practis'd in London upwards of thirty Years. She has an Ointment call'd the Royal Ointment, for the Gout, and Rheumatick Pains, and of great Ease and Comfort to both Sexes at Home and Abroad. NB. Originally prepar'd by this Gentlewoman, and sold for her no where else.

Dr Bartholomew Hutton was one of the men who had been executed with Charles Naismith. Tayte hovered a finger over the words 'Royal Society.' That had to be what Marcus had drawn from this record. He scanned the remainder of the text and found nothing of further interest—nothing concerning any of the other hanged men and nothing more for Dr Bartholomew Hutton. He got up and Jean followed, prompting Hampshire and Hues to stir into life. They paced towards the exit with them, one in front and one behind.

Once outside the room, Tayte approached a member of staff. 'Is there somewhere I can get access to the Internet?'

The girl smiled and pointed. 'Computer facilities are provided in the Open Reading Room on this floor,' she said. 'It's the first reading room you came to on your way in.'

Tayte thanked her, and when they arrived in the Open Reading Room, he stood and turned in a slow circle while he looked for an available workstation. It was already a busy area. He thought he would have to go down to the foyer to get his laptop from his briefcase, but Hampshire and Hues were on the case. Hues leant in over the keyboard nearest them and flashed something at the man sitting there: a badge, Tayte supposed. He saw a few calm words being mouthed, and a second later the man got up and left.

'I guess that's all part of the service,' Tayte said to Jean as he sauntered over.

They sat down and Tayte brought up the website for the Royal Society. 'It has to be the connection,' he said. 'The five men were hanged together for the same alleged offence. It stands to reason they knew each other.'

'Maybe they have a list?' Jean said.

'That's what I'm hoping.'

From the website's home page Tayte navigated through Fellows to the History Pages. At the bottom of that page he saw a link inviting him to *Search our database of Fellows*. He clicked it and began the search, first with Charles Naismith. Two minutes later they were both smiling. All five men were listed in the Royal Society archives.

'Touchdown,' Tayte said. Technology had its advantages, too.

Each entry had a brief curriculum vitae appended to it: a résumé of information such as where the subject was born, their professions and fields of research, their key activities, and their published works. Tayte sent copies to the print queue, and when he returned with them, he lined them up on the desk.

'Somewhere in here we should find our next direction,' he said.

They leant in on their elbows and began to correlate the data. The five Fellows had all lived in London at the time of their enrolment into the society. They had addresses from Bayswater in the west through Clerkenwell to Whitechapel, but Tayte thought there had to be something else that connected them apart from the fact that they were all hanged on the same day. After a long and silent ten minutes Jean sat back, took her glasses off, and pinched the bridge of her nose between her eyes.

'It would help if we knew what we were looking for,' she said. 'The only useful connection I can see is the society itself.'

Tayte was coming to the same conclusion. The professions of the five Fellows all varied: one was a member of the clergy, another a physician; there was an astronomer, an ex-soldier, and a politician. They seemed an eclectic bunch. Even their fields of research seemed entirely disparate: mathematical statistics in the case of the Reverend Naismith; anatomy for Dr Hutton; geophysics and hydrography for Lloyd Needham; architecture for the ex-soldier, Sir Stephen Henley; and field physiology for William Daws. Mathematics of one discipline or another was common to three out of five, but since it was the language of science, Tayte figured that was to be expected.

'What would Marcus have drawn from all this?' he said, thinking aloud. 'What direction did it give him?'

'I don't see how he could have made any further connection,' Jean said.

Tayte thought about that.

'You're right. So Marcus would have concluded that he needed more information. The connection for now must simply be that they knew each other through the Royal Society.'

'We're overcomplicating things,' Jean said.

Tayte nodded. 'I think we've found all we're going to find here.' He grabbed the mouse and scrolled to the bottom of the screen. 'It's time to move on,' he added as he scribbled the address for the Royal Society into his notebook. 'Marcus would have wanted to find out more about these men and so must we.'

DI Jack Fable spent the morning in a briefing at New Scotland Yard. Apart from a few MI5 heads, the cinema-like room was half-filled with representatives from a cross section of Metropolitan Police units: a hundred people give or take, who were largely from Royalty Protection Branch, Counter Terrorism Command, Firearms, and the Territorial Support Group. It had been an awareness briefing. That's about all it could have been, given how little they had to go on. The attendees were simply made aware of a likely but as yet unspecified threat to national security that may or may not have a treasonable, and thus potentially royal, connection.

Fable couldn't wait to get out of there, have a smoke, and get back to the job. Two and a half hours without a cigarette made his hands shake. He lit another and headed back inside the building, adopting the slow, familiar pace he knew would see it finished by the time he reached the door. He was still thinking about the brief, and how Chief Inspector Graham Tanner had stepped in as soon as he'd heard that the Security Service were involved and the case had become high profile. Fable had to listen to Tanner as he took the questions Fable himself should have been answering, fielding them in the vague manner of a seasoned politician because the man knew even less than the rest of them.

There was a Royalty Protection supervisor Fable couldn't quite shake from his head, too. Maybe it was his severe crew cut or his towering height that made him stand out. Or perhaps it was because of the questions he'd asked. They had been all the right questions, such as did they have any idea where the threat was likely to come from? What form would it take? Did they have any suspects at this time? Fable didn't know the man, but he disliked him just for being the one to remind him so publicly that he didn't know a damn thing about whoever had killed Julian Davenport or Marcus Brown, any more than he knew why.

But Fable was resolved to change that.

It was almost two in the afternoon by the time he got back to his office. Before he'd gone into the briefing, he'd called in the details on Douglas Jones who, along with Julian Davenport, was the subject of Marcus Brown's genealogy charts. Jones had been dead twenty years, having died at an indicated age of thirty-four. He had been a young man at the time of his death, and Fable wanted to know how he died. He'd expected to find a lone coroner's report waiting for him: something simple with a straightforward cause of death, like an accident or an illness of some kind. But the pile of information on his desk made him think again. Such causes of death never generated this much paperwork. This was something else entirely.

In another part of London, a man stirred from sleep. He was a night person who liked to be active when it was dark outside and quiet. Nighttime was usually when he worked, but sometimes it was necessary to go with the flow, and for him these were exceptional times. The high-pitched beeps that had woken him sounded again and he sat to attention, throwing back the bedcovers, revealing a muscular torso that tensed and rippled as he moved. He grabbed the mobile phone from his bedside table and silenced it. This was not a phone to be switched off or ignored, even for sleep. He read the text message. That was how it worked. Strictly no voice calls.

Be ready.

That was all it said—all it needed to say. He smiled to himself as he deleted it. Another chance was coming, that was the thing. And that was all he wanted to know. He leant across to the bedside table again and reached into the drawer, retrieving a Browning semi-automatic pistol. He checked the clip. It was full. Thirteen standard NATO 9mm rounds—the Hi-Power, as used by armed forces around the world in more than fifty countries. It was a common handgun, and the serial numbers had been filed off. Origin untraceable.

He got out of bed, eyed the grey suit on the back of the door, and walked naked to the bathroom, flexing and stretching, thinking that this time he would be more than ready. He'd failed to kill the historian twice now, and that pissed him off. But he hadn't expected there to be anyone else.

The American threw you, didn't he? he thought, knowing that this time there would be no surprises.

Chapter Seven

Tayte and Jean were outside the premises of the Royal Society of London, a Grade 1 listed building located at Carlton House Terrace between Buckingham Palace and Trafalgar Square. They were standing with Security Service Officer Hampshire in the early afternoon sun beneath the pillared monument of Frederick Augustus, the grand old Duke of York, which, along with the pedestrian walkway that led down to The Mall and St James's Park, divided the terrace into two Corinthian-columned blocks. Officer Hues had insisted on 'going in first,' making their entry into the building seem a little melodramatic to Tayte, but what did he know? Hues wasn't gone long.

Once inside the building they headed across a marble floor to the information desk. The foyer was busy with tourists, and there was no one waiting to meet them this time. It would have taken too long to arrange, and Tayte figured the Security Service badges would get them access to whatever they needed to see. He wasn't wrong. After the introductions and a brief explanation of their purpose, they were following a member of staff to the society library, easing their way past the throng of sightseers who, according to the noticeboard, were waiting to take in one of the society's lectures. The eager-looking man who had been appointed to them for the duration of their visit was called Rakesh Dattani. He was a slim man in an olive green suit with a white shirt open at the neck.

'The society was formed by twelve men in 1660,' Dattani said as they walked, his voice conveying the elocution of a fine public school education. 'It was after one of Sir Christopher Wren's lectures at Gresham College. Their purpose was to promote natural philosophy or 'science,' as we call it today.'

'From the Latin, *scientia*,' Jean said. 'Knowledge.'

'A Latin scholar?'

'Once upon a time. It sort of goes with the job. I'm a historian.'

Latin was one of Tayte's weakest subjects at college, and he'd done little since then to improve his understanding. 'I saw something written in Latin on the way in.'

'*Nullius in Verba*,' Dattani said. 'The Royal Society's motto, taken from Horace. It more or less means to take no one's word for it.'

'To prove it,' Jean said.

'Precisely. After all, that is the essence of science, isn't it?'

They continued walking, passing gilt-framed portraits of former notable Fellows such as Sir Isaac Newton and John Flamsteed, the first Astronomer Royal. Dattani paused when he came to a portrait of founder member and diarist John Evelyn.

'Did you know that when the society was founded, it was called the Invisible College for the Promoting of Physico-Mathematical Experimental Learning?'

'No,' Tayte said. 'That's quite a mouthful.'

Dattani gave a small laugh. 'Quite. Which is why in 1663, when King Charles II gave the society his royal charter, it became known as the Royal Society of London for Improving Natural Knowledge. Or more commonly now, the Royal Society of London. It's the oldest society of its kind in the world.'

'How long have you been at these premises?' Jean asked.

'We've been here at Carlton House Terrace since 1967,' Dattani said. 'Before that the society made its home at Burlington House for almost a hundred years after moving from cramped accommodation at Somerset House.'

They reached the library through a carved, oak-panelled door, and Hampshire and Hues, who had dropped behind, were suddenly at their heels again. Tayte thought the room looked just how a library should look, with high ceilings and decorative stucco work on the walls and on the ceiling cornices. There were plaster busts of other past Fellows between the carved bookcases that lined the walls, and a long mahogany table dominated the centre of the room, which was surrounded by carver chairs upholstered in green to match the carpet. Tayte thought the place smelled right, too: old books and polish.

'We've over seventy thousand titles in our library,' Dattani said.

Tayte was still taking the room in. 'How far back do your records go?' He was keen to confirm that the records covered the dates he and Jean were interested in.

'Our earliest records date circa 1470,' Dattani said. 'Although locked away in temperature-controlled vaults in the basement, we have a document that dates as far back as the twelfth century.'

Tayte arched his eyebrows, thinking that the early 1700s should be no problem.

'The archives are pretty much all digitised now,' Dattani added, noting Tayte's interest in the few keyboards and computer screens at the end of the table.

Tayte opened his briefcase and pulled out his laptop. 'Okay if I use this? I'm used to the setup.'

'Of course,' Dattani said. 'Everything's online. I'll sign you in for the day. There's an Ethernet cable if you need wired access.'

Tayte wasn't surprised to hear that the Royal Society had gone digital. Pay-per-view documents were big business, and this was one time when he was happy to forgo the sights and smells of old documents in favour of a powerful search engine. He knew it would have otherwise taken far too long to find all the information the society had on the five Fellows they had come to learn about. Jean sat at one of the keyboards, and Tayte sat beside her with his laptop. It only took a few minutes to get set up and logged in.

'So, who are we looking for?' Dattani said, sitting at the keyboard opposite Jean, clearly intending to help.

Tayte had no problem with that. It would be easy to miss something given the time constraints, and three heads were definitely better than two under the circumstances. He brought Dattani up to date on their findings at Kew, telling him about the fate of the five men and the charges of high treason.

'It doesn't surprise me,' Dattani said. He tapped at his keyboard. 'I just entered 'Jacobite' into the search field of our Library and Archive Catalogues. There are twenty names listed—John Byrom, Robert Harley, Voltaire. Even Sir Christopher Wren is reputed to have held secret Jacobite meetings after lectures.'

Tayte read out the names and dates from his notebook, and Dattani confirmed they were all on the list.

'In what context?' Tayte asked.

'Let's see,' Dattani said. A moment later he added, 'The Screw Plot. 1708.'

'I know a little about that,' Jean said. 'It was at St Paul's Cathedral.'

Dattani nodded. 'They were arrested for plotting to assassinate Queen Anne, accused of loosening the screws in the support beams above the Queen's seating area.'

Jean looked incredulous. 'But it was proved to be a hoax. Something the Tories used to discredit the Whigs. The loose screws were attributed to poor construction work.'

'I really couldn't say,' Dattani said. 'But I do know that Dr Bartholomew Hutton was Physician in Ordinary to several members of the Royal Stuart family at one time or another. He attended Anne during the five years leading up to her coronation. I'm sure you're right. I can't think why he would have been caught up in an attempt on Queen Anne's life.'

Tayte and Jean exchanged glances. It seemed to Tayte that—in those times of limited investigative means—it would have been all too easy to frame these fellows of the Royal Society to make it look like they had been involved in a plot to assassinate the Queen. But why?

'He was into anagrams, if I'm not mistaken,' Dattani continued.

'Anagrams?' Tayte repeated.

Dattani nodded. 'They were very popular in his day, what with the likes of Jonathan Swift and Alexander Pope. They formed a group called the Scriblerus Club. But that was in 1712—four years too late for Dr Hutton. Although I'd be surprised if he didn't know them.'

They each began to feed the names into the archive search engine.

'Given the dates,' Dattani said, 'we need only concern ourselves with the *Philosophical Transactions*. That was the Royal Society's publication at the time. It first appeared in 1665—it's the oldest English language journal in the world.'

Tayte was already looking at a scanned image on his laptop. It bore the lavish title *PHILOSOPHICAL TRANSACTIONS. Giving Some ACCOUNT of the Undertakings, Studies and Labours of the IN-GENIOUS in many Considerable Parts of the WORLD. VOL. XXIII. For the Years 1701, 1702.*

Tayte began his search with the Reverend Naismith, whose field of research was mathematical statistics. Several results were returned, and he noted that the majority were letters. As he read the heading for the first matching entry, which was entitled 'Some New Observations Drawn from the Constant Regularity Observ'd in the Mortality of Infant Births,' he knew their research was going to take some time.

Heading east along the busy Mile End Road near Stepney Green, a man in a smart grey suit was driving a silver Ford Mondeo, killing time in the traffic.

Waiting.

If you're going to steal a car, he thought, *you do it no more than an hour before you need it. Two hours at most. That's the trick. It's a mistake to be too prepared. Steal the car the night before, and the owner has time to notice it's gone, has time to report it, and someone else has time to spot it and point the finger. That's the way of the amateur—people who think that if they leave it until the last minute they won't be able to find a car to boost in time.*

He shook his head. 'That's not the way to do it,' he said to himself.

There's always a car to be had in London. You just have to be confident. It's not like you care what colour it is. Who gives a shit if it's got leather and a decent stereo? You're not going to be together very long, are you? It's not like you've just taken out a five-year loan to pay for the thing.

And that's just it.

You never hang on to it. Not ever. When it's served its purpose, the thing to do is drive a mile out from the scene, park up anywhere you like, and calmly get out and walk to the Underground with everyone else. You take the Tube from there. That's how you do it. That's the confident way. You don't take it home to bed for the night in case you need it again the next day.

He laughed to himself and muttered, 'That's just plain stupid.'

And it will get you caught.

The mobile phone in his breast pocket began to beep. He slowed the car and checked the display. It was the text message he'd been waiting for. As he read it his face gave no hint of the pleasure he felt. Conversely, his body began to tense and tingle with such energy that he could barely control it. His hands were clenched so tightly on the wheel that his knuckles looked ready to pop through his driving gloves. He liked the gloves. He liked how a steering wheel felt through the leather in the same way he liked the sense of command and control he felt when his gloved hand was coiled around the grip of a gun.

He arrived at a junction and slammed the brakes hard, veering right and using the hand brake to help spin the car around before he floored the accelerator. He knew London like the owner of the black cab he'd stolen twenty-four hours ago to take care of Marcus Brown. He'd made a point of knowing his way around town. Being familiar with your environment was key to survival; he'd had that drummed into him enough times. As was blending in with that environment. Going unnoticed. For that, a grey suit was the perfect urban camouflage.

He glanced at the message on his phone's display again and hit the delete button. He was heading west now to an address he knew was close to The Mall—the Royal Society at Carlton House Terrace. It wouldn't take long to get there. He would have plenty of time to learn the area, to confirm his vantage point and available exits.

After countless cups of coffee and almost three hours of research at the Royal Society, Jefferson Tayte sat up and pushed his laptop away. He rubbed his dry eyes and glanced over at officers Hampshire and Hues, who could not have looked more fed up if they tried. He checked his watch. The glowing red digits told him it was almost five o'clock. Time to wrap things up for the day.

'Okay, let's see what we've got.' He looked across the table at Rakesh Dattani, who still appeared as fresh as when they had started. He was upright and perky in his chair as though he still had plenty of research time left in him. 'Rakesh, why don't you kick us off with our soldier, Stephen Henley.'

Rakesh Dattani stopped taking notes. 'Sir Stephen 'Naseby' Henley was—'

'Naseby?' Tayte interrupted. 'As in the battle of Naseby?'

'1645,' Jean said. 'The English Civil War.'

'Same spelling,' Dattani said. 'I expect his father or even his grandfather fought in the battle and they adopted the name. Anyway, Sir Stephen Henley was later wounded during the Battle of the Boyne in 1690 and withdrew from military service. After that, as an architect, he worked in collaboration on the designs of several country estates. He most likely trained under Sir Christopher Wren at some time or another. He was a wealthy man, making several sizeable donations to the society during his Fellowship.'

Jean took the astronomer, Lloyd Needham. 'Needham studied geophysics, and for a short time in the late 1600s he was hydrographer to William III, providing navigation studies for sea voyages and naval expeditions. His letters and accounts chiefly concern themselves with related experiments and findings.'

Tayte sat forward again and read over his notes. 'I was particularly interested in our mathematical statistician, the Reverend Charles Naismith. It appears that he was also something of a genealogist like me.'

'By royal appointment from 1702,' Dattani said.

'When Queen Anne came to the throne,' Jean added.

Tayte noted the connection. 'Further interests in heraldic studies. Several letters concerning statistical analysis, with a focus on infant mortality.'

'That set me wondering,' Jean said. 'The study might have come about because of Anne's problematic attempts to have children.'

'How problematic?'

'She went through eighteen terms of pregnancy. Miscarried several times, and apart from one child, William, Duke of Gloucester, who died aged eleven, all were either stillborn, died the same day they were born, or only survived for a year or two. It's interesting, too, that her sister's children shared the same fate. All three of Queen Mary's babies were stillborn.'

Tayte was putting notes together as they spoke, and he raised an eyebrow at hearing that, but he stuck to gathering the information for now. 'And what did you make of our politician, William Daws?'

'Fascinating,' Jean said. 'Politically he was Tory, in opposition to the Whig party, which was out of favour at the time, although that all changed when Queen Anne died. That's the first interesting thing.'

'The Screw Plot,' Tayte said. 'You told us the Tories blamed the Whigs in an attempt to discredit them.'

Jean nodded. 'So why would the Tory-supporting William Daws and the rest have been blamed for it? It doesn't make sense.'

'No,' Tayte agreed, confirming his thoughts that for reasons as yet unknown, someone wanted these people dead. And what more discreet and seemingly lawful way was there than to let the hangman do it for them?

'As a field physiologist,' Jean continued, 'his main concerns were with public health, and perhaps most interestingly, his letters detail a great deal of research into the study of human blood with a focus on proving parent and child relationships.'

That had caught Tayte's attention, too. 'Daws was on the right track, wasn't he?' he said, thinking that it had taken science another two hundred years to make any worthwhile breakthrough in the field of blood-type analysis.

'I found it particularly intriguing,' Jean said, 'because after the birth of James II's son, who was later known as the Old Pretender, Queen Mary claimed in a letter to her sister Anne that the child was supposititious. She publicly charged that the boy was illegitimate, smuggled in via a bed-warming pan to replace the king's stillborn baby. There was no proof, of course.'

'*Nullius in Verba*,' Dattani said.

Tayte thought about that motto again. 'So maybe Daws was looking for a way to prove it,' he said. 'Or maybe it wasn't about them at all, but it got him thinking. His research could have been driven by the need to prove someone else's bloodline.'

'Necessity being the mother of invention,' Dattani said.

'Exactly,' Tayte agreed. He moved on. 'That just leaves Dr Bartholomew Hutton—our anagram man. He was an anatomist, and as you said earlier, Rakesh, he was a royal physician. Not a bad artist either, judging from the anatomical drawings I came across.'

Jean adjusted her glasses and checked through her notes. 'Much of his focus seems to have been on the circulatory system.'

Dattani agreed. 'I picked up from one letter that he was interested in the absorption of orally digested chemicals by the bloodstream.'

'Like how long it takes to lose a headache after popping a couple of Advil?' Tayte said.

'That sort of thing, yes.'

The room fell silent. Twenty seconds later, after putting together everything he'd read and heard, Tayte summed things up as he saw them.

'So, we've got connections to Queen Anne, either direct or via her sister, Mary II, and Mary's husband, William III. We have one of the men studying infant mortality, and we can't overlook the fact that Queen Anne went through eighteen terms of pregnancy, or that both Anne and Mary died without issue, leaving the throne of England in contention. We have a physician and anatomist looking into the circulatory system. And we have a physiologist looking for a way to prove parent and child relationships. I'm not sure where that fits, and I don't think we can draw any specific conclusions about our architect or astronomer just yet, but add in the probability that these men were hanged for something I don't think any of us now believe they did, and what have we got?'

Silence again.

Tayte couldn't help but think that the motto to which these men adhered was both poignant and ironic. *Nullius in Verba*—Take no one's word for it. Given the circumstances surrounding their deaths, he wasn't about to.

When at last someone stirred from their thoughts, it was Jean and she sounded excited about something.

'What are your views on conspiracy theories?' she asked.

'No smoke without fire,' Tayte said. That was his motto, and he was open to just about anything right now.

Jean got up. 'Good,' she said. 'There are some people we should go and see.'

Chapter Eight

Having thanked Rakesh Dattani for his help, Tayte and Jean left the Royal Society and headed back to the car, which Hues had parked at nearby Waterloo Place. It was a quiet area, not a major thoroughfare. The trees in the gardens opposite Carlton House Terrace outnumbered the people Tayte could see as he followed their long shadows, his briefcase heavy from all the printouts he'd collected.

'So who are we going to see?'

Jean smiled over her shoulder. 'My best-kept secret,' she said, giving nothing away.

Twenty paces later, a sharp, *chirp-chirp* sound told Tayte that they had reached the car, and as everyone got in, Jean's phone rang. She checked the display, adopted a sour expression, and took the call.

'Hello, Daniel.'

Tayte understood why she was pulling faces when he recalled that Daniel was Jean's ex-husband.

'Elliot?' Jean continued. 'No, I haven't. He didn't show last night. I thought he must have changed his mind. You know what he's like.'

There was a long pause. The car started up.

'The interview? Yes, of course I remember. No,' she added, shaking her head. 'Okay, I'll do that.'

The car pulled out of the parking bay and Jean ended the call. Her hands were shaking as she put the phone away, and when she turned to Tayte, he noticed that her face had lost a little colour.

'Christ,' she said. 'I'd forgotten about Elliot.'

'What's happened?'

'He had an interview this afternoon. Something his dad set up.'

'And he didn't show?'

'No, and Daniel hasn't been able to reach him.' She tensed suddenly and thumped the seat. 'I should have called him last night. I should at least have found out where he was staying.' She thumped the seat again. Harder this time. 'And I should have called him this morning and told him what had happened—told him not to go to the flat. Why didn't I call him?'

'It's been a distracting twenty-four hours,' Tayte said, trying to pacify her with what he thought was a reasonable defence.

'That's no excuse.'

It fell quiet as the car reversed out of the parking bay. Tayte wanted to tell Jean not to worry, but he decided that telling a concerned mother not to worry about her child was asking for the same kind of thump she'd just given that seat. He turned to face her.

'We don't know if anything's happened,' he said. 'You told me last night that he often stayed with friends. Why don't you call them?'

Jean took a few deep breaths. She nodded to herself. 'Yes, I told Daniel I would.'

She reached for her phone again, and at that point Hampshire turned and put his face in the gap between the headrests.

'Let's have his details and a description, Ms Summer. I'll call it in anyway.'

Hampshire readied his pen, but as Jean began to give him her son's description, the windscreen exploded. Glass shattered into the car and everyone except Hues jumped in their seats. Hues just slumped forward over the wheel and the car began to swerve. A second later it slammed to a bone-jarring halt as it hit a parked car and set its alarm wailing.

'Stay in the car!' Hampshire ordered.

He got out, drawing a firearm from beneath his jacket as he went. Tayte didn't know whether an officer from what was fundamentally a civilian organisation was authorised to carry a gun, but he was glad he did. Through the gap where the windscreen had been, Tayte saw a man striding confidently towards them, coming fast in tactical zigzag lines. The man was wearing the same novelty Prince Charles face mask Tayte had seen on the gunman who had shot Marcus outside Rules Restaurant the day before, and he thought he was probably the same man who had later gone to Jean's apartment to kill her.

'Who the hell is this guy?' Tayte said.

As the gun in the approaching man's hand levelled towards them, one thing was clear: whoever this man was, he was relentless in his need to finish what he'd started.

'How did he know we were here?' Jean asked.

'We're following Marcus's research, aren't we? It's like I said last night—he knows exactly where we'll go.'

If we get it right, Tayte thought, concluding that they clearly were getting it right so far.

He heard two shots ring out, followed by the quick thump of the bullets as they hit the door Hampshire was using for cover. Then he heard return fire. *Stay in the car*, Hampshire had said. Tayte didn't know what to do, but he did know that playing sitting ducks wasn't it.

Jean nudged him. 'This side,' she said, shoving the door open, clearly thinking the same thing.

They crawled out, keeping low. Another volley of shots was exchanged, buying them time. The glass in Hampshire's door shattered, and Tayte heard him on his radio, calling for backup.

That was good—help would come and the area would be crawling with police in a matter of minutes. Tayte followed Jean to the cover of the parked cars and they began to weave between them. Behind him, the firefight seemed to intensify, the sounds of the gunshots in constant reverb between the buildings to either side of them.

Then it all stopped.

Tayte listened for the all clear from Hampshire, but it never came. He wanted to look back—wanted to call out to make sure he was okay—but the fizz of a bullet as it zipped past his ear told him everything he needed to know.

'Go!' he urged, and they ran.

'This way!' Jean called. 'The park's too open.'

They cleared the cars, heading north on the opposite side of the street. Common sense told Tayte they needed the crowds, but where were they? The few people he could see were running with them and ahead of them—clearing the area. As they reached the intersection with Pall Mall and hurried across, Tayte was disappointed to find it no busier. The gunshots had taken care of that, clearing a line of fire between them and the gunman.

He chanced a look over his shoulder, still running after Jean, already panting hard and wishing he'd left his briefcase in the car. There was no sign of the man in the novelty face mask, and while a part of Tayte was glad about that, it made him feel all the more uneasy.

They quickly arrived at another intersection, this time crossing Charles II Street where Waterloo Place met the bottom of Regent Street. Tayte didn't have a clue where Jean was leading him, but he figured she knew London better than he ever would. Further into Regent Street it began to get busier. He saw faces around him at last: people with no idea what had just happened.

'Did you hear that?' he heard someone say.

'Was that a bomb?' someone else said.

The pavement began to get busy, forcing their pace to an uncomfortable crawl. Then Jean came to a sudden stop. Someone bumped into her, but she was so tense she barely moved. She was looking through all the people to the other side of the road.

'What is it?' Tayte said. 'I think we lost him but we need to keep moving.'

Jean slowly shook her head, her stare unwavering. 'He's there.'

'Where?'

'He's looking right at me. He must have been running with us on the other side of the road.'

Tayte felt the hairs on the back of his neck stand up. He crouched and followed her gaze but he couldn't make out who she was looking at. There were too many people.

'Right there,' Jean insisted. 'Dark hair, grey suit. No mask. He's looking away now.'

Tayte counted no less than four grey-suited men. They all had dark hair. In the distance he heard the wail of sirens growing louder by the second. He turned back to Jean. 'Are you sure?'

'Shit!' Jean said. 'He's crossing over.'

She grabbed Tayte's arm and before he could look back to see for himself, they were moving again, maintaining a determined march as Jean guided them closer to the string of shop façades on their left, putting a wall of people between them and their pursuer.

'Where are we headed?' Tayte asked.

'Piccadilly Circus. It's after the next crossroads.'

Tayte had been to the Criterion Theatre before and he remembered a little about Piccadilly Circus. He tried to make out the Eros statue, where people always seemed to congregate like pigeons. There were plenty of roads leading off that busy junction. Maybe they could lose the gunman there.

'There's an Underground entrance,' Jean said, contradicting Tayte's thoughts as they arrived at Jermyn Street and crossed with the crowd that had become an unwitting human shield around them.

'The subway?' Tayte said. He didn't want to share such a confined space with a killer who had made it very clear that he wanted them dead. 'Are you serious? What if he makes it, too?'

'Trust me,' Jean said, and when they arrived at the steps that led down to the station, they took them two at a time.

Tayte didn't have a ticket. That fact was foremost in his mind by the time they reached the last step because he knew he didn't have time to stop and buy one. The turnstiles were busy—three or four people at each. Jean headed straight for the luggage gate and they ducked beneath it, still running, heading for the escalators and the sign for the Bakerloo line.

'Hey!' someone shouted.

Jean flashed her Oyster card. 'Sorry,' she called. 'We're in a hurry.'

They reached the escalator and Jean looked back as they began to descend.

'He's coming through,' she said. 'I'm sure he's seen us.'

'He's using a ticket?' Tayte said. He was incredulous. He imagined such a man would have leapt the barriers and come right at them, gun blazing.

'He doesn't want to draw attention to himself,' Jean said. 'Come on.'

She started down the left side of the escalator, which was clear of people not already walking or running down themselves. It was a long escalator, and Tayte knew the gunman had to be right behind them, closing in on them for all he knew. He wanted to look back but it took all his concentration not to trip over the steps as he tried to keep up with Jean, briefcase clutched to his chest.

When they reached the bottom, Jean grabbed Tayte and led him into a white-tiled tunnel that was bright with overhead strip lights. He saw maps and signs for train destinations. All were a blur as they ran through the people against a warm breeze that grew with the rumble of an approaching train. A second later they were on the northbound concourse just as a train arrived, clicking over the tracks, screeching as it slowed.

'We made it!' Tayte said.

He ran out to meet it but Jean grabbed him again and pulled him back, pinning him to the wall as people continued to pour onto the concourse behind them, all predictably heading for the train. Tayte saw plenty of grey suits go past, their backs to him and Jean as they went with the flow of the commuters heading home.

'There he is,' Jean whispered. 'Keep low.'

Then they ran back out, following the signs to the streets above where Tayte filled his lungs with the cool city air. He pulled out his phone to call DI Fable and smiled to himself, just happy to be alive.

DI Jack Fable was in a control room at New Scotland Yard studying live CCTV feeds from the national surveillance network. A manhunt had begun. All available police units in the area had been called in and a perimeter was fast being established, locking down a quarter-mile radius around the scene of the shooting at Waterloo Place, where two Security Service officers were confirmed dead. They had no idea where the passengers of the silver Audi were until Fable answered his phone.

'DI Fable.'

'Fable? It's Jefferson Tayte. We're at Piccadilly. We've been attacked.'

Tayte sounded out of breath. A little panicked.

'Try to remain calm, Mr Tayte. We know what happened.'

Fable had already seen footage of a silver Ford Mondeo blocking the road at Waterloo Place where the Audi had come under fire. He'd seen a masked man in a grey suit get out of the Mondeo, and he'd seen the Audi veer and crash. The entire gunfight between Hampshire and the assailant had been caught on camera from two different angles, right up to the point where Hampshire went down and the masked gunman walked up and put another bullet in him for good measure.

'Are you safe?' Fable asked.

'We're okay. We managed to give him the slip on the subway. I think he could have taken a train on the Bakerloo line, heading north.'

Fable cupped a hand over his phone and spoke to one of the surveillance team. 'Put a call out,' he said. 'SO19 to Piccadilly Station. Cover all terminals on the Pic line and Bakerloo.'

He went back to Tayte. 'Firearms officers are on their way to you,' he said. 'Can you give me a description of the man?'

The surveillance team had been busy working on the continuity of the images between the camera handoff points. They had followed the gunman north towards Piccadilly Circus, losing him somewhere along Regent Street as the rush hour hit full flow. They had little by way of a description to go on. After a pause, Tayte came back on the line.

'I didn't see him myself,' he said. 'But Jean did. He's about six feet tall. Medium build. Dark hair. She says she's sorry, but she can't single anything else out about him. Just a regular-looking guy, I guess.'

Great, Fable thought. *A regular looking guy with dark hair, wearing a grey suit in London during the Monday evening rush hour.*

Fable sighed, 'Okay, here's what I want you to do. There's a department store opposite the Eros statue—Lillywhites. Go inside and wait there. I'll have someone bring you in.'

'No,' Tayte said. 'We're not coming in. We're getting a cab.'

Fable thought he heard the familiar chatter of an idling diesel engine in the background. 'You're not safe,' he said. 'You need to come in.'

'We're no good to you if we do,' Tayte said. 'And we don't need another escort. They draw too much attention, and I don't want anyone else's death on my conscience.'

Christ, Fable thought, *I need a cigarette.*

He was about to suggest they at least meet up somewhere to share information. He had plenty to tell them about his investigation into the death of Douglas Jones twenty years ago, and he thought they must have something for him by now. But what he heard at the other end of the line cleared all thoughts from his mind.

'Tayte!'

He heard gunshots. Two, in quick succession. The sound was unmistakable.

'Tayte!'

His phone clicked and fell silent. He heard static. Then the call went dead.

The Frenchman Michel Levant was reclining on a Louis XIV chaise somewhere in southwest London, sipping chocolate from a delicate golden tulip cup. The sweetly rich drink, made in the old style with part cream, part bitter chocolate and sugar, was one of the many decadent pleasures he afforded himself. His thin lips pursed as he swallowed the warm liquid.

He was thinking about the American and Professor Jean Summer. He wondered how productive their day had been; what they had discovered on their predictable visit to The National Archives and on their telling visit to the Royal Society of London. He pondered these things at great length, but most of all he wanted to know who this American was—and Michel Levant was not the kind of man who waited long for anything.

Levant was an avid collector of French antiques from the Baroque period. He admired the delicate craftsmanship and the opulent gilding that embodied the style. He often thought that his appreciation came not from the furniture itself, but from his adulation for the man after whom the style had been named. Louis XIV, known as the Sun King, took many mistresses and had a highly favourable opinion of himself. He was a man who knew what he wanted and took it. At just five years of age, when called to his father's bedside and asked his name, he told him that it was Louis XIV—to which his father replied, 'I did not die yet, my son.' As far as Levant was concerned, the man who had reigned as king of France for seventy-two years was to be greatly admired. His portrait hung in each of Levant's many lavish rooms.

Levant sat up sharply when the expected knock came at his study door. He swung his legs around and slipped his bare feet into a pair of blue velvet slippers that, like his silk gown, were emblazoned with the crest of his family coat of arms.

'Un moment,' he called.

Despite living in London much of the time, he insisted that the language of his forebears be used exclusively within the walls and grounds of his far from humble abode. As far as his staff were concerned, to speak any other language in his presence was an offence that would earn their instant dismissal. He sauntered to the regal writing desk that dominated the room and set his chocolate cup down.

'Entrez!'

It was Françoise, of course. The beautiful Françoise, whom he had taken in several years ago and so delicately broken at the tender age of just fourteen. Françoise, his secret, whom he had named after the Sun King's young and secret wife, Françoise d'Aubigné, Marquise de Maintenon. Levant's Françoise wore a flowing cornflower blue dress with flat patent shoes and pure white ankle socks. How tantalising he thought she looked today as every day. She came to him and Levant slowly extended his hand, offering out the ring he always wore on his left index finger: a thick banded gold ring with black enamel detail. It was the size of a full sovereign and bore a likeness of Louis XIV, centred within a flaming sun.

Françoise bowed her head and kissed the ring. 'Monsieur,' she said, smiling, always smiling for him. 'Il y a quelqu'un pour vous.'

Levant knew that she had brought someone to see him as soon as she had knocked, just as he knew who it was. He flicked his limp hand towards the door, the ring seeming to weigh it down. 'Faites-le entrer,' he said, and she showed the man in.

His name was Cullen, although Levant never used his name and rarely saw him in person. He was a stocky Irishman who, to Levant's chagrin, spoke no French. Instead, he grunted words that were hardly recognisable as English in such coarse tones that Levant could not bear to listen to him for more than a few minutes at a time. But, *c'est la vie*, Levant thought. Cullen was too good at his job for Levant to be bloody-minded about house rules.

Nonetheless, as the man lumbered across the room with his oafish gait and his eternally dour expression, Levant regarded his every movement with displeasure.

'For me?' he said, indicating the brown manila folder beneath Cullen's arm.

Cullen nodded. He was about to speak when Levant rushed up to him and pinched the man's lips together. If he had been anyone other than Michel Levant, he had no doubt that such an act would have proven fatal—but he was Michel Levant, and he did not want the day tainted with Cullen's crass vulgarity.

'Uh-uh-uh,' Levant said, smiling through his thin lips as he snatched the folder away and retreated to his desk.

From one of the drawers he produced a thick roll of banknotes. He tossed it to Cullen and immediately tinkled an engraved glass bell, prompting Françoise to return.

'Au revoir,' he said, waving Cullen away. 'Françoise will show you out.'

Levant studied the girl with hungry eyes as she re-entered the room and withdrew again, following the contours of her dress, lingering and longing. Then begrudgingly he turned his attention back to the manila folder, reminding himself that business had to come before pleasure. It was the dossier he'd been expecting. He opened it, wondering how that oaf, Cullen, managed to do it. On this occasion he hadn't even been able to give him a name, saying only that the subject was an American genealogist and a close friend of the late Marcus Brown.

Ah, mais oui! Levant thought as he read Jefferson Tayte's name and saw his image, which he supposed had been grabbed from the Internet. Levant thought that Cullen must have obtained the American's name from the police after the interview statements were taken. He had contacts everywhere. Or perhaps it came from the list of attendees at the genealogy convention. It didn't matter.

He read the report and discovered that Tayte lived in a rented apartment in Washington, DC, where after his secondary education he had attended the University of the District of Columbia. He learnt that Tayte had been in foster care from infancy and was later adopted, and that his adoptive parents died in a plane crash when he was seventeen years old. He was unmarried, had no children and seemingly no other family connections, and he drove a 1955 Ford Thunderbird. Levant smiled to himself. Cullen had even provided bank and passport details, along with Tayte's U.S. social security number.

Levant gave a delicate sigh. For all that, it was an unremarkable dossier. It appeared that Jefferson Tayte was a law-abiding loner with few, if any, vices. Nevertheless, it was good to know your competition.

Tayte and Jean were in a black cab heading northwest on Shaftesbury Avenue, fast leaving Piccadilly Circus behind them. Jean was on the seat and Tayte was lying on the floor with his briefcase on his chest. On the other side of the safety partition, the driver was animated in his seat.

'I don't want any trouble,' he called back.

He had a middle European accent and he kept turning around and glancing down at the man on the floor as if to see whether he was ever going to get up again.

'Just drive and you won't get any,' Jean said.

They passed the Apollo Theatre towards Soho as two police cars went by going the other way with lights flashing and sirens wailing. Jean leant over Tayte just as his eyes peeled open again. His briefcase felt heavier than ever.

'You okay?' Jean asked.

'I think so.'

Tayte couldn't see any blood, and the only pain he felt was at the back of his head, where he'd hit the taxi roof as he fell in and slammed onto the floor. Had he not turned around before he followed Jean in, he would have missed the Prince Charles face mask and the man in the grey suit who had appeared at the Underground station exit they had left just moments before. That novelty mask was beginning to haunt him, but on this occasion it had drawn his eye and probably saved his life. His briefcase and a quick reflex had done the rest.

Tayte sat up and pushed his fingers through the holes in the leather. He popped the clasp and took out his laptop, which was cracked and falling to pieces in his hands; that and the weight of papers he was carrying had stopped the bullets, and he saw that his copy of Marcus's book had taken a direct hit. He kept a small digital camera in his briefcase, too, which he used to photograph headstones.

'At least my camera's intact,' he said. 'I must have dropped my phone.' He scanned the floor. It wasn't there.

As he crawled onto the seat next to Jean, the driver turned around again. 'Look, it's none of my business,' he said. 'Just tell me where you want to go, okay?'

At that point Jean's BlackBerry rang with a shrill warble that was impossible to miss. It was Fable.

'Yes, we're okay,' Jean said. 'Shaftesbury Avenue. We've just crossed Wardour Street.' There was a pause. 'Okay. We'll be there.'

She called through to the driver. 'Waterloo Bridge.' To Tayte she added, 'Detective Fable wants to meet. He says he's found something we should know about.'

Chapter Nine

Jean spent the remainder of the taxi ride to Waterloo Bridge on her phone, trying to find out if any of Elliot's friends had seen him. She looked downbeat and worried again by the time they started to cross the Thames, and Tayte didn't have to ask if she'd had any luck; her expression said it all. He spotted Fable through the conveyor belt of commuters heading home for the day. He was leaning on his elbows over the tubular white rail that ran the length of the bridge; his black suit caught Tayte's attention because it was the only suit that wasn't moving.

'Right here,' Tayte said to the driver.

He paid the man and told him to keep the change for his trouble. Then he and Jean stepped out into the cool September breeze that met them off the river. Tayte watched Fable flick a cigarette butt into the churning Thames below, and as they approached, the detective turned to meet them.

'Glad you're okay,' Fable said, although he didn't look particularly glad about anything. 'There was no sign of your attacker at Piccadilly,' he added. 'No one obvious. I don't know how he slipped through, but I reckon one grey suit looks the same as any other during rush hour. They're going over the CCTV recordings now.' To Jean he added, 'You think you'd recognise him if you saw him again? I expect they'll pull a few people in.'

'I think so,' Jean said over the constant rumble of traffic crossing the bridge behind them.

Fable nodded and lit another cigarette. He took a long drag on it, held the smoke in his lungs, and then blew it along the river with the breeze.

'Good,' he said. 'I'd like to get a composite, too.'

'No problem,' Jean said. Then she told Fable about her son. She reached into her jacket and took out her purse, from which she produced a photograph. She smiled at Elliot's image as she handed it over.

'It was taken about a year ago,' she said. 'He hasn't changed.'

Tayte caught a glimpse. It showed Jean standing beside her motorbike with an ice cream in her hand. A fresh-faced young man in a white t-shirt was sitting on the bike, the sea breeze tousling his fair hair, his bright smile lighting up the picture. Behind them was a pebble beach and an azure sky.

'An all too rare happy day out,' Jean said.

She gave Fable as much information as she could: Elliot's mobile phone number, the places he usually frequented, and his friends and family contact numbers. She didn't have his bank details but said she'd get back to him on that.

'We'll do what we can,' Fable said and Jean thanked him.

He turned back to the river and leant on his elbows again. 'We matched the bullet casings found at the scene of Marcus Brown's murder with the casings recovered from Julian Davenport's apartment. They came from the same gun—a 9mm Browning semi-automatic.'

Tayte nodded. He'd expected as much. The charts found at Brown's home as good as tied his friend's murder to the murder of Julian Davenport three months earlier, but it was good to confirm it, even though it brought the memory of that painful scene outside Rules Restaurant rushing back to him. He really needed to understand why his friend was dead. He reached into his jacket and pulled out the bullets that were meant to end his own life.

'Here,' he said. 'These were stopped by my briefcase earlier when we were cut off. I'm sure you'll find they came from the same gun, too.'

Fable produced a clear plastic zip bag from his pocket. 'I'm surprised he used the same gun. It's a common piece. Inexpensive. Why hang on to it?'

Tayte shrugged and dropped the bullets into Fable's bag. 'Maybe he's sentimental about it.'

'Yeah, maybe he is.'

Tayte knew that bullet match analysis wasn't the main reason the detective wanted to see them. 'You said you found something we should know about.'

Fable nodded. 'Douglas Jones—from the charts. His body was found beside a tree stump in Sherwood Forest, Nottinghamshire. Just the body.'

'Someone cut off his head?' Jean said.

'We get all sorts, believe me. The amount of blood found at the scene and the spray pattern suggested that someone beheaded him right there on the stump. The head was never recovered.'

'Like an old-style execution?' Jean said.

Fable discarded his cigarette butt, nodding. 'And he wasn't the only one. A week later another body was found in the same area, a woman this time. Sarah Groves. Same MO. Different tree stump.'

'Anything tie these people together?' Tayte asked.

Fable lit up again. 'I was coming to that. Have either of you ever heard of a society called Quo Veritas?'

Tayte and Jean looked at each other questioningly. They shook their heads.

'It's Latin,' Jean said, as though stating the obvious. '*Quo* can have several meanings such as this, that, from, or where. It can also mean to which or what place. *Veritas* is more straightforward. It means truth or truthfulness, depending on usage.'

'So one way or another it's about truth?' Tayte said.

Jean nodded. 'A simple translation could be 'from truth' or 'place of truth.''

'The truth about what?' Tayte mused.

Fable tapped another cigarette free from the packet even though his current smoke had only burnt halfway down the paper. 'I'm not surprised you've never heard of them,' he said. 'Until twenty years ago very few people had. Quo Veritas existed for three hundred years. Then after the murder of Sarah Groves, the society disbanded and the killings stopped.'

'So they broke up to protect themselves?' Tayte said.

'Seems that way.'

'And the victims were both members?'

Fable nodded. 'Not just regular followers, either. These were high-ranking members.'

'Three hundred years?' Jean said, almost to herself. To Tayte, she added, 'That fits our time frame.'

'What time frame's that?' Fable asked.

Tayte filled him in, giving him an overview of the five Fellows of the Royal Society who were hanged in 1708 for high treason as Jacobite supporters in what they had come to believe were highly dubious circumstances.

'I think they were up to something,' Tayte said. 'Something connected with Queen Anne, but not the attempt on her life they were hanged for. I'm sure of that.'

Jean agreed. 'Do you know what the members of Quo Veritas were about? I mean, what kind of society they were?'

Fable gave a half-smile, nodding slowly. 'It was a Jacobite society. Makes sense after what you've just said.'

Tayte wasn't so sure it did. On one hand they had five men who were hanged as Jacobites in the traditional sense, accused of plotting to assassinate Queen Anne as followers of the Catholic Old Pretender. Now Fable had turned up a Jacobite society in which at least one of its members was a confirmed descendant of the

Reverend Charles Naismith, suggesting that the family were Jacobites through and through. Yet there was evidence to suggest that Naismith and his co-conspirators supported Queen Anne and the Protestant faith, and that the Screw Plot charges brought against them had to be false. Tayte recalled Jean had told him that the word Jacobite was derived from the Latin *Jacobus*, meaning James, in this case referring to Anne's father, James II, so in a broader sense that meant that Anne's blood was also Jacobite blood. Tayte figured that had to be the significant difference between Quo Veritas and the more traditional Jacobite societies. He just couldn't think why such a faction should exist.

Fable started coughing. He turned away and came back red-faced. 'Excuse me.' He cleared his throat. 'Most of what came out about Quo Veritas was down to an investigative journalist working for the *Nottingham Post*. Someone called Ewan Stockwell.'

'Can we talk to him?' Jean said.

'Not a chance. He disappeared a couple of months after the Groves murder.'

'Anything turn up later on?' Tayte asked. 'A body?'

'Not a trace.'

They all gazed along the river in silence for several seconds, watching the boats and the varied skyline of buildings old and new. Jean was first to break the silence.

'So what's our connection?'

It was something Tayte had been considering. 'I believe the victims could all be related to our five Royal Society Fellows. We already know that Davenport and Jones were related to Naismith. Davenport might also have been a member of Quo Veritas.'

'Difficult to prove,' Fable offered, 'since it's now defunct.'

Tayte agreed. 'But the relationship between Julian Davenport and Douglas Jones, who *was* a confirmed member, connects them. They were both related to Naismith, according to Marcus's charts. And they're connected through the fact that they were both murdered. Twenty years ago the killer cut off his victims' heads, the society disbanded, and now he's caught up with them again to finish the job—only now he shoots them.'

'Different MO,' Fable said. 'It could be the same person, but I think it's more likely to be someone else.'

Tayte had to concede that Fable was probably right. Beheading someone on a tree stump was highly ritualistic. It carried with it some message that the killer felt very strongly about beyond the act of killing itself. Even twenty years was unlikely to have changed that.

'Either way,' Jean said. 'It looks like they're after the same thing, and whatever it is, it concerns Quo Veritas. And two—or maybe three—high-ranking members of the society are now dead.'

Tayte rifled through the papers in his briefcase. He pulled out a sheet of A4 paper and handed it to Fable. It contained the names of the Royal Society Fellows they were interested in, with a bullet hole just below the entry for Sir Stephen Henley.

'So let's say for now that the killer's victims are descendants of these men,' Tayte said. 'Two are already confirmed. If we can connect Sarah Groves to any one of them, I'd say my theory's sound. In which case we can work out who the next victims are likely to be and hopefully get to them first. And if we can do that, maybe they can tell us what this is all about.'

Fable studied the list. 'I wouldn't know where to begin.'

'I do,' Tayte said. 'But it would take too long to work through it by myself. We need a team. Maybe twenty people. The more the better.'

'The genealogy convention,' Jean said.

Tayte nodded. He checked his watch. To Fable he said, 'If you're quick you should be able to rally all the support you need.'

He told him about the convention at the O2 Arena and how some of the best genealogists on the planet were already in London.

'I'm sure they'll be only too happy to help,' he added, backing away as he scanned the traffic for another taxi.

'And what about you?'

'I'm sticking with Marcus's research,' Tayte said.

'We're going to see some friends of mine,' Jean added.

Tayte spotted a black cab and waved it down. 'Get a team together at Kew and tell them they need to identify the current descendants of the people on that list—the heirs via each generation's firstborn dependant. Tell them to start with Sarah Groves and work back to confirm things.'

'Firstborn,' Fable repeated. 'Got it.'

A taxi pulled up and Jean gave the driver an address for a university somewhere in the Bloomsbury area.

'Ms Summer,' Fable called. 'What about my identity parade? My composite?'

Tayte turned back. 'Identify the descendants,' he said. 'That's how you'll get your man.'

———

Lying in the pitch-black boot of an unmarked police car, the man in the smart grey suit had had plenty of time and solitude to consider how careless he'd been. He'd put himself at risk and he'd put the man who had pulled him out of there at risk—not that it had been difficult. The brief flash of a Specialist Operations Metropolitan Police Service badge as they cleared the quarter-mile perimeter checkpoints around Piccadilly had guaranteed their unquestioned passage. But it should not have come to that. He knew he had jeopardised everything they were working towards.

You never make it personal, he thought. *And you let the woman see your face. What the hell were you thinking? In and out—that's how you do it. You don't ponce about chasing people on foot. Once the element of surprise is gone, that's it. It's over. You go back to the car and drive calmly away.*

He calculated that he'd been in the cramped boot for thirty minutes or so. They were heading east. Not much further now. He was sick of the slow rush hour traffic. He wanted to straighten his legs, kick his feet right through the damn wing, but he couldn't. He couldn't relax either, and that only made things worse. The problem was that he couldn't stop thinking about the American and Jean Summer and the fact that they were both still alive.

They're making you look like a fucking amateur! he thought. And the problem with that was that it did make things personal. It made things very personal.

When the car finally stopped and he heard the driver's door open and close with a thump, he turned his thoughts to the bigger objective—to the string of binary numbers that was not yet complete.

Don't lose sight of that. You need to stay focused. Need to hurry now.

The boot popped open and daylight momentarily blinded him. When his eyes adjusted, he saw locked gates ahead and through them the shell of an Edwardian gasworks, now derelict with its bare steel framework, broken windows, and crumbling brickwork. It was quiet there. No one around to witness his activities. Just one pot-holed road in and out.

Tonight, he thought as he eyed the grey portacabin that was just inside the gates. He reached into his pocket for the keys. *You can get out of the suit. Lie low for a while. Watch the news reports and slip out again later.*

Chapter Ten

Jean's best-kept secret was a small group of history students she'd taught a few years ago when they were studying for their undergraduate degrees. They were all in their twenties and were now working on their doctorates at the Birkbeck University of London. Jean's phone call from the taxi on the way to the university had forced a change of address to a pub she knew well.

'It's their local,' she said to Tayte as the taxi pulled up outside.

'And they're your best-kept secret because?'

A smile washed over Jean's face and Tayte was glad to see it again. 'Let's just say that as far as their chosen subject is concerned, they share some pretty unorthodox views.'

They approached the bar's narrow, predominantly glass façade, and Tayte jumped ahead and opened the door for her. The gesture seemed to take her aback. She stopped and stared at him.

'I didn't have you pegged as the old-fashioned type.'

'Usually, I'm not,' Tayte said. 'I mean, I wouldn't really know. I've had so little practice.' He almost laughed. 'I guess seeing me do that would have surprised Marcus, too.'

'Is that why you did it?'

Tayte shrugged and followed Jean inside. 'Maybe.'

The bar ran deep into the stonework building. Soft lighting cast an amber glow over decor that was a blend of modern furnishings and old architecture, with arches and pillars, high tables with stools, and a long, polished brass-plate bar. It was busy and consequently loud, with competing voices that drowned out the background music. Tayte could smell the bitter tang of alcohol in the air and on the breath of the people consuming it.

'There they are,' Jean said, heading further in.

Tayte didn't have to look too hard to see who she meant. There was a gathering around one of the tables—some people sitting, others standing. The centre of attention was a young, overweight man with greasy-looking fair hair. He wore three-quarter-length khaki shorts and a black t-shirt that bore the words 'HISTORY: from the Greek—*historia*. Knowledge acquired by investigation. The study of the human past.'

When they saw Jean it seemed that everyone wanted to hug her at once. Tayte just stood back and waited for the excitement to fizzle out. He didn't know what he expected a bunch of history academics to look like—geeky nerds with bottle-bottom glasses and pale complexions perhaps—but this group seemed far from it. As soon as they let Jean go again, she gave the introductions.

There was Evie, a tall girl in skinny jeans with long dark hair and Morello cherry lips whom Tayte found intimidating. Next to her was Megan, a girl-next-door type in a blue print dress and boots, and beside her, close beside her like maybe they had a thing going, was a man called Dave. He wore a pinstripe suit jacket over jeans, and beneath the jacket was a retro black and acid yellow smiley face t-shirt. The centre of attention was called Ralph.

'And this is JT,' Jean said, turning to him. 'He's a genealogist. American.'

Ralph fetched more stools and Tayte was given a glass into which Dave poured a honeyed liquid called Old Speckled Hen from a half-full pitcher. Tayte didn't want to be a prude and refuse, but given that someone was trying to kill them, he didn't plan on drinking much either. Jean had the same.

'American, eh?' Ralph said. 'Not too much history there.'

Tayte gave him a guarded smile. 'Not as a nation perhaps, but that's not really what it's about, is it?'

Ralph looked around at his friends, smiling with amusement. 'Really? I thought it was?'

Tayte shook his head and pointed to the words on Ralph's t-shirt. 'It says right there that history is the study of the human past.' He took a small sip from his glass. 'Correct me if I'm wrong, Ralph, but given that the ancestors of around eighty million non-native Americans settled in the States from the UK, I'd say that in broad terms, give or take a couple hundred years, much of our history is pretty similar to yours.'

The reaction that followed was complete silence. Everyone around the table, apart from Jean, who just smiled at Tayte, looked at each other with frozen expressions. Then they all burst out laughing.

'Touché,' Ralph said. 'Actually, what's written here on my t-shirt is exactly what history's about. Particularly the 'knowledge acquired by investigation' part.'

Dave leant in. 'Don't forget that history is written by the victors.'

'That's right,' Ralph said. 'So we prefer to take history a little more literally.'

'We like to do our own investigation,' Evie said. 'Gather the facts and form our own opinions.'

Ralph underlined the word 'investigation' with his finger. 'That's the thing. Learning history shouldn't just be about reading a textbook and adopting someone else's view without questioning it. That's not investigation.'

'And when you do re-examine things,' Dave said, 'you can come up with some hard to ignore theories about how things might really have happened.'

'Our views can be a little controversial,' Evie said, looking at Jean.

'The history books can't be challenged,' Ralph said. 'That's the message coming in loud and clear over Radio Historia. If enough people read something and believe it to be true, it is true. They don't question it.'

'But you do?' Tayte said. He was beginning to see why Jean called them her best-kept secret.

'That's right,' Ralph said. He turned to Jean. 'And I'm guessing that as we've not seen you in a while, you're here now for a fresh take on something that's not on the curriculum?'

Jean arched her eyebrows. 'A possible royal conspiracy,' she said, getting everyone's attention.

'What, like Jack the Ripper?' Dave said. 'That sort of thing?'

'It concerns Queen Anne.'

'Great period,' Evie said. 'The emergence of the two-party system. The Act of Union.'

'Defining times,' Dave said.

Tayte got his notebook and pencil ready. 'And we're also interested in the Royal Society.'

Upon hearing that Ralph pinned his shoulders back, stuck out his chest, and in a serious voice that sounded like a bad Winston Churchill speech, he said, 'We are to admit no more causes of natural things than such as are both true and sufficient to explain their appearances.' It made him laugh, even if no one else did. 'Sir Isaac freakin' Newton?' he added, looking around for support.

Evie looked sympathetic. 'Occam's razor,' she said to Tayte.

'Like Sherlock Holmes?' Tayte said. 'Eliminate the improbable and whatever remains, et cetera?'

'Precisely,' Evie said. 'Although if that rule took its own advice, the only version we'd need would be to keep it simple.'

Tayte smiled and sipped his drink.

'Of course, they were all Freemasons,' Ralph said. 'Well, maybe not all of them, but most of them. It wasn't called the Invisible College for nothing.'

'Why was it?' Tayte asked.

'Because it existed beyond physical boundaries,' Ralph said. 'When the Royal Society began, science was still regarded as heresy in many parts of the world. The Spanish Inquisition was still going on. Masonic lodges were used as conduits to circulate matters of science around the world. I've got a whole heap of Masonic material about how they influenced history if you're interested.'

'Please don't get him started,' Evie said.

Jean struck the table a few times with her glass like it was a gavel. 'Queen Anne,' she stated, loudly, cutting back into the pack and refocusing the discussion. 'Shut up and listen up. I want to run a theory by you.'

Trenton McAlister lived in an unassuming townhouse in St John's Wood in the City of Westminster. His seven-thirty appointment that evening was with a journalist called John Webber, whose influence in the media world, combined with his strong anti-monarchist views, was precisely why McAlister had chosen him. McAlister's busy schedule had prevented the meeting from taking place sooner, and they were at his home because it was the only place he could guarantee complete privacy.

'Are you a whisky drinker, John?' McAlister asked.

He turned back from the drinks cabinet to the tall, mousy-haired younger man who by now was comfortably ensconced in one of a pair of antique winged chairs. He wore chinos and a tweed sports jacket that McAlister assumed from appearances went everywhere with him like a second skin.

'On occasion,' Webber said. 'With water.'

McAlister poured two fingers of twenty-year-old Talisker into a heavyweight crystal tumbler. Into another he poured an equal measure of cheap blended Scotch, thinking that it made no sense to waste a fine single malt on someone he knew would not appreciate it. He returned with the drinks and sat down at a low table facing the sitting room's darkening bay window.

'Thank you,' Webber said as he took the proffered glass from his host. 'No Mrs McAlister this evening?'

'She's indoor wall climbing,' McAlister said, settling back. 'I usually go myself on a Monday, but that wall will still be there next week. What I have to tell you on the other hand can't wait a moment longer.'

'Your message suggested the tide was about to turn?'

McAlister sipped his whisky and smiled. 'I hope so, John. I do hope so.'

He reached across the table and lifted up an archive copy of the *London Evening Standard*. It was dated Tuesday, August 17, 2010, and it was open on page twenty-five. It carried an image of the Australian prime minister and another of Queen Elizabeth II. McAlister handed the newspaper to Webber.

'The caption says it all, John, wouldn't you say?'

Webber read it aloud. 'Queen Must Be Our Last Monarch.'

'Our sentiments precisely, eh?'

Webber nodded. 'I remember the article well,' he said, handing the paper back.

'Of course you do, John. But it's never been more poignant, and I for one have no intention of waiting if I can help it.' McAlister shifted around to face Webber more fully. 'I invited you here tonight to tell you that I'm about to alter the constitutional face of Britain, irrevocably.'

Webber's eyes widened.

'We may very well be on the brink of the biggest political story this country has seen since Oliver Cromwell,' McAlister continued. 'As far as statistics are concerned, various MORI polls tell us that somewhere between twenty and forty percent of voters would choose to abolish the monarchy tomorrow. That's around ten million supporters, John.'

'And I count myself among them,' Webber said. 'I'd sooner see Buckingham Palace as a permanent tourist attraction. The French economy does very well out of the Palace of Versailles.'

'I'm sure it does,' McAlister said. 'But public support needs to be higher, and with your help I believe it soon will be.'

'How so?' Webber asked.

'Let's just say for now that I have something up my sleeve. You'll see soon enough. A new era is upon us and I want you to be a part of it—from the beginning. And I'm offering you exclusive access to the harbinger of that era. This is our time, John.' McAlister paused and leant towards the journalist. 'Can I count on you?'

'What do you want in return?' Webber asked, reaching for his notepad. 'Funding?'

McAlister laughed at the suggestion. 'No,' he said. 'Funds are not going to be a problem for us in our New Britain.' He locked eyes with Webber then, holding his attention as he said, 'What I want in return is very simple. I want you.'

'Me?'

McAlister nodded. 'Your media influence, John. An exclusive engagement, so to speak—around the clock until the job is done. You're to work on no other story or assignment. You'll be in my pocket and I'll be in yours. Can you commit to that?'

Webber scoffed. 'Are you kidding? For a chance like this I'd give you my soul if you asked for it.'

McAlister laughed. 'Good,' he said. 'Although it need not come to that.' He reached across and shook Webber's hand. 'Welcome to the campaign, John,' he added, still smiling broadly. 'Now let's get started.'

'Let me get this right,' Ralph said as he sat down for what Tayte supposed must have been the first time all evening. 'Our very own Professor Summer has a royal conspiracy theory about Queen Anne.' His smile looked playful and somewhat disbelieving. 'This I have to hear.'

Tayte wanted to hear it, too. He had several thoughts running riot in his head, but he couldn't settle anything into a sound theory just yet.

'Okay,' Jean said. 'Here it is.' She sipped her drink and licked the froth from her lips. 'My theory—unlikely as that may or may not be to some of you—is that the Hanoverian rise to power in 1714 was by no mere chance. I'm coming around to the idea that their succession to the throne of Great Britain was engineered.'

'A non-hostile takeover?' Dave said.

'Oh, I like it,' Ralph said. 'So how does it feel?'

'How does what feel?'

'Finally going against all those textbooks? Being one of the gang?'

Jean just shook her head and continued. 'When the Act of Settlement was passed, it placed the Hanovers next in the line of succession should Queen Anne fail to provide an heir, which in 1700, after the death of her eleven-year-old son, William, Duke of Gloucester, it appeared likely that she would.'

'Strong motive,' Dave said.

Evie agreed. 'So you think they made sure she died without issue?'

'That's the theory,' Jean said. 'But it's full of holes. Anne's age and health were against her, as was her track record as far as her many terms of pregnancy are concerned. I can't ignore the textbooks there.'

Ralph grabbed the now empty pitcher from the table and held it out to a passing waitress for a refill. 'But the Hanovers didn't have to do anything by the time Anne came to the throne. There was no heir. They just had to wait until she died.'

'I know,' Jean said. 'That's one of the holes. So maybe I'm wrong and the textbooks are right. It just seems a little too convenient to me.'

Tayte could see where Jean was going. He told the group about the connection to the Royal Society Fellows and about their fields of research: how one seemed to be looking into the odds of so many failed pregnancies and how another was interested in the take-up of various drugs by the bloodstream. It was easy to suppose that these Fellows were thinking along the same lines as they now were, and the only thing that appeared to ruin the theory was that Anne's pregnancies all failed before the Act of Settlement was passed.

They all had to think about that. Then the only person there who hadn't uttered a single word since the introductions, Megan, whom Tayte had supposed was just the quiet one of the group, began to speak.

'Don't forget Occam's razor,' she said. 'Eliminate the improbable. So it wasn't the Hanovers.'

Dave scratched at his temple, confusion furrowing his brow. 'But they were the only ones with anything worthwhile to gain from the fall of the House of Stuart.'

'Are you sure about that?' Megan said. 'The failed pregnancies didn't start with Anne, did they?'

'No,' Jean said. 'That's right. It started with her sister, Mary. So the conspiracy—assuming for now that there was one—might have begun several years before the Act of Settlement was passed, when the Hanovers were still around fiftieth in the line of succession. As far as they were concerned at the time, they had nothing to gain at all.'

'So who did?' Tayte asked.

Another pitcher of ale arrived and Ralph went the rounds with it. 'Yeah, come on, Megan, you little tease. Who else stood to gain from the end of the Protestant House of Stuart?'

'Okay,' Megan said. She paused and smiled as she added, 'The Whigs.'

'Politicians?' Ralph said.

'Of course,' Jean said, as though the bigger picture had just fallen into place. 'Anne favoured the royalist Tories. She sought to reduce the Whig majority because they wanted Parliament to run the country, giving less power to the monarchy.'

'It was with a Whig majority,' Evie said, 'that the Act of Settlement was passed.'

'Yes, it would have been,' Jean said. 'The textbooks would have us believe that the Act of Settlement was passed to ensure a Protestant line of succession after Mary's death when it seemed unlikely that her husband, William III of Orange, would remarry, or that Anne, because of her stillborn pregnancies, would be able to produce an heir either.'

'How did William III die?' Tayte asked.

'A riding accident that later proved fatal,' Jean said.

'One year after the Act of Settlement was passed,' Ralph added. 'Now am I the only one here who thinks that's a little too convenient?'

Megan spoke then. 'So another take on the situation is that the whole thing was a plot by the Whigs to gain control of the nation.'

'Same great motive,' Dave said.

Megan nodded. 'They passed an act of Parliament to ensure that the Catholic Stuarts could make no further claim to the throne while making sure that the Protestant Stuart monarchy died out, paving the way for the Hanovers, who favoured a Whig parliament. King George I hardly spoke a word of English. He was more than happy to leave the running of the country to the politicians—to the Whigs.'

'Anne was addicted to laudanum,' Ralph said. 'And she was called 'Brandy Nan' for obvious reasons. It would have been easy enough to get other drugs to her on a regular basis.'

'So the Hanovers were probably nothing more than political pawns,' Jean said. She turned to Tayte. 'Perhaps our five Fellows of the Royal Society were wise to what was going on.'

Given everything he and Jean had learnt about them, Tayte thought they might well have come to believe in such a plot. Perhaps the Reverend Naismith's suspicions had been aroused by what had amounted to an unlikely total of twenty failed pregnancies and infant deaths out of twenty-one attempts, first with Mary and then with Anne. And maybe Dr Hutton believed that someone was drugging the royal sisters to keep them in a state of ill health, particularly to ensure that they were unable to bear healthy children. Then there was that riding accident a year after the Act of Settlement was passed. Had it been orchestrated in an attempt to ensure that William III could not remarry and produce an eligible heir?

But what about the eleven-year-old William? Tayte thought. One child appeared to have slipped through the net.

'A lot rested on the young Duke of Gloucester, didn't it?' he said. 'He was the Protestant Stuarts' last real chance for an heir, wasn't he? Anyone know how he died?'

'Physically, he was a weak boy,' Jean said. 'Even as he grew up he had trouble climbing stairs without help.'

Dave got out his iPhone. A minute later he was summarising information from a palm-sized webpage.

'The young Duke reportedly wore himself out at his eleventh birthday party and retired early complaining of a headache, nausea, and a sore throat.' He flicked at the screen, scrolling the text. 'Next day the family doctor was sent for. He suspected smallpox so he bled him to lower the fever, but it came back with a vengeance later that evening. The leading physician of the time, a Dr Radcliffe, was then called for, and he suspected scarlet fever, adding that whoever had prescribed the boy to be bled had destroyed him. William died five days after his birthday.'

'I wonder if that family doctor supported the Whigs?' Tayte mused.

'Hang on,' Dave said, flicking at his iPhone again. 'There was an autopsy. It showed that William had an abnormal accumulation of fluid on the brain, although there was still some question as to whether the bleeding had fatally weakened him. A family doctor should have known what effect such a bleeding would have on the boy, don't you think?'

Tayte did. It seemed a rash choice of treatment for someone known to have been so weak that he had trouble climbing the stairs. He couldn't be sure about anything, but the alternative suggestion that Jean and her friends had provided seemed to fit well enough. Perhaps more importantly, it gave him some insight into what the hanged Fellows of the Royal Society were really into. If they did have cause to believe in such a conspiracy, then he wondered what they had sought to do about it.

He was considering how such a plot could have been proved or disproved back then and how it might be connected to what was going on now, some three hundred years later, when Jean's phone rang.

'It's Detective Fable,' she said to Tayte. 'He wants to speak to you.'

Tayte took the call and the group fell silent except for Ralph, who couldn't seem to help himself.

'Detectives?' he said. 'Whatever you guys are into, I want some.'

Tayte cupped a hand over the phone and shot Ralph a cold glare. 'No,' he said. 'Believe me. You don't.'

He went back to the call.

'JT,' he said, and he listened to Fable for half a minute and then checked his watch. It was almost eight o'clock. 'Okay,' he said. 'We'll head back to the hotel.' He nodded. 'That's right. The Hyatt in Marylebone.'

When the call ended, Tayte stood up, leant in close to Jean as he handed back her phone, and said, 'Time to go. There's been another murder.'

Chapter Eleven

When they arrived at the hotel it occurred to Tayte that a change of address might have been a good idea under the circumstances, but the prospect of changing hotels so late in the day was far from appealing. He was beat, and after the kind of day they had had, he supposed Jean was, too. The best compromise he could think of was to change rooms, taking adjacent doubles and trusting to the reception staff's discretion should anyone enquire after them.

They ate a light meal in the Regency Club Lounge, going over their research and considering their next direction, and they decided that the Jacobite society, Quo Veritas, needed further investigation. They talked about Jean's son, too, and Jean's growing concern for his safety given that it had now been over twenty-four hours since anyone she knew had seen him.

DI Jack Fable found them in the Churchill Bar, a panelled room with leather furnishings and a light oak floor. It was nine-thirty and the area was busy, yet quiet enough to hear the jazz piano music that was playing in the background.

'I got waylaid,' Fable said as he joined them at the bar. The acrid tang of nicotine hung heavy on his breath as he spoke.

'You ever find time to relax?' Tayte asked.

'Not much. I reckon I'll rest when I'm ninety and sleep when I'm dead.' He gave a rare smile. 'I read that on a t-shirt somewhere.'

Tayte indicated his glass. 'Can I get you something?'

Fable took a moment to answer. 'What the hell,' he said. 'Scotch. Thanks.'

Tayte turned to get the barman's attention, still talking to Fable. 'Don't you have a sidekick?' he said. 'I thought you cops always came in pairs.'

Fable shook his head. 'Not me. I prefer to work alone when I get the choice, and there isn't exactly a list of people eager to team up with me.'

The barman approached. Tayte finished his drink and slid the glass towards him. 'I'll take two more of those,' he said. 'And another cocktail for the lady.'

'A mojito,' Jean said.

'Did you see your bike outside?' Fable asked her. 'It's just along the street.'

'I did. Thanks.'

'Hear anything from your son yet?'

Jean shook her head.

'I've passed his details to the Missing Persons Bureau,' Fable said. 'I've got people checking the CCTV images in the areas you said he frequented. No banking transactions have shown up today—no cashpoint withdrawals.' He coughed into his hand, rough and throaty. 'We're running regular traces on his mobile phone, too, but so far it's been switched off.'

Jean tried to smile as if to say thank you.

'Oh, and don't worry about that identity parade,' Fable added. 'All the grey suits they pulled in checked out. Just people heading home for the day. I'd appreciate it though if you could drop by in the morning to sit with one of our sketch artists. A composite drawing of the man could be useful, however little you saw.'

'I will,' Jean said. 'First thing.'

They took their drinks to a table.

'It's a hell of a business,' Fable said as they sat down. 'Before I get to why I'm here though, you might like to know that we have some people at Kew working on those names you gave me.'

'People from the convention?' Tayte said.

Fable nodded and knocked back his drink.

'How many?'

Fable sighed. 'Three.'

'That's all?' Tayte knew they needed more help than that.

'Bad timing, I guess. Most of the people who were still there wanted to go home. The three we got all said they knew Marcus Brown.'

Tayte shook his head, thinking that it could take three people all week to get a single result, and since Fable had called with news of another murder, he supposed they didn't have that long.

'I'll freshen up when we're done here and head over,' he said. He turned to Jean. 'You might as well stay and get some rest. Identifying the descendants of long dead ancestors is just my thing, but I shouldn't think there'll be much for you to do.'

Tayte wondered who else could help, and Michel Levant sprang to mind. The Frenchman still left a bitter taste in his mouth, but he couldn't ignore the fact that an heir hunter would be useful to have on the team. Finding descendants of the recently—and not so recently—deceased was exactly what Levant professed to be so good at, and people in his profession had to know how to work fast because they invariably had to beat the competition to make their money. Even so, Tayte had thought the man was bad news since he'd first set eyes on him in Rules Restaurant, so he quickly dismissed the idea.

Fable got to the crux of his visit. 'I said on the phone that there had been another murder. It happened in Exeter three days ago. A forty-four-year-old man called Alexander Walsh. Same MO—eventually. He was shot twice in the chest just like Davenport, only this time it was aggravated.'

'Aggravated?' Tayte repeated, seeking clarification.

'He was beaten first. Tortured.'

'Any idea why?'

Fable nodded. 'His killer clearly wanted something from him.'

'And what about Davenport? Was he tortured?'

'No. Davenport must have given his killer what he wanted without a fuss. With Walsh it was different.' Fable paused and looked around. He stood up. 'Look, we can't really continue this here. I need to find somewhere quiet.'

Five minutes later they were shown into a business meeting room with a large LCD display at one end of a long table that was replete with glasses, notepads, and pens. They sat in a close group with Fable in the middle. As soon as the door clicked shut, he produced a small digital device from one of his suit pockets.

'It plays MP3 files,' he said. From another pocket he pulled out a set of miniature speakers onto which the MP3 player docked. 'I had the Devon and Cornwall Police send me a digital copy of the witness interview recording.'

'You got a witness?' Tayte said. 'That's great.'

'The deceased's wife. She had her two young children with her throughout the ordeal, and I believe they're the only reason Mrs Walsh isn't lying on a slab beside her husband now.'

'Soft spot for the kids?' Jean said. She sounded agitated. 'Are you trying to suggest that he's not quite as sick in the head as I've come to think he is?'

'No, I'm not,' Fable said. 'Far from it. But it's not uncommon. Whoever's doing this has a very specific purpose. He wants something from his victims. Killing young children takes a certain kind of sick individual. Anyway, don't get your hopes up.' He leant in and switched the machine on. 'No one saw anything we can use.

He wore that same mask I saw on the CCTV footage.' He paused. 'But they heard stuff. That's what I wanted to share with you.'

Fable hit the play button and a male voice stated his name and rank together with the date, time and place of the interview. He skipped the rest of the preliminaries and sat back as the interview began. The male officer spoke first.

'At approximately what time did the visitor arrive?'

'It was around seven o'clock. We'd just eaten. I pulled the net curtain back and saw a dark-haired man in a grey suit. He had a black leather bag—a holdall. I thought it was someone trying to sell us something.'

'Did he say anything when you answered the door?'

'No. He forced it open and I shouted to Alex.'

'And where was Mr Walsh at that time?'

'In the kitchen. He came out with a carving knife but the man had a gun. He held it to my head and told Alex that he'd kill me if he didn't do exactly what he said.'

'Did you see the man's face?'

'No. He had his back to me when I looked out. When I opened the door, he was wearing a mask—a caricature of Prince Charles.'

'What happened next?'

'He made us go upstairs. The kids were crying on the landing when we got there. He told Alex to shut them up or he was going to do it for him.'

'And then?'

'Then he asked if there was a chair in any of the bedrooms. He told Alex to get one and take it to the bathroom. I had to fetch a pair of tights while he held the gun on my children.'

'Tights to tie your husband to the chair with?'

'That's right. He made him strip to his underwear first.'

'You said earlier that he locked you and your children in the room adjacent to the bathroom, Mrs Walsh. Is that correct?'

'Yes. When we viewed the house we liked the fact that the doors still had most of the original locks and keys. You don't see that much these days, do you?'

'No, Mrs Walsh. I suppose not. Do you think he wanted to keep you close so you could hear what was going on?'

'I didn't know what he wanted at the time. Now I think he did, yes. He wanted to keep us scared or maybe he wanted my husband to be scared for us.'

'Did you believe he was going to kill you and your children?'

The recording went silent. Several seconds later a quiet, tremulous voice said, 'Yes.'

'Okay, Mrs Walsh. Take your time. When you're ready perhaps you could tell me what you heard.'

Silence again. Then the woman sniffed and continued.

'I heard my husband scream. I'd never heard anything like it before. The screaming came first. Then the questions.'

'What did the man want to know?'

'He kept asking Alex what his father left him in his will. My husband's father died just under a year ago.'

'And did your husband tell him?'

'Yes. He started going through everything, but it didn't seem to matter. Every time he gave an answer I heard him scream. Then the man asked the question again. He was shouting—always shouting.'

'And how long did this go on for?'

'About fifteen minutes.'

'And he didn't ask your husband anything else during that time?'

'No. Just the same question over and over until Alex told him what he wanted to hear.'

'And what was that?'

'A microscope. I'd seen it briefly. It was an old thing made of ivory and wood. Alex told me it was a family heirloom—one of many.'

'And that's what the man wanted?'

'I suppose so. It went very quiet after that. Then I heard the bathroom door open and I thought the man was going because I heard him on the stairs. But he came back.'

'So, he'd just gone to find the microscope?'

'Yes, I think so. It was in a box in the study with some other things that belonged to Alex's father.'

'And was anything else said when the man returned?'

'No.'

'Just the gunshots?'

There was no answer.

'Thank you, Mrs Walsh.'

The interview ended and Fable leant in and switched the machine off.

'Mr Walsh had been beaten repeatedly with a towel rail,' he said. 'His killer clearly meant to intimidate the family first to make them more compliant.'

'And he must have wanted to let Walsh know he wasn't fooling around,' Tayte said.

Fable nodded. 'I think it's also clear that he intended to kill Walsh once he'd got what he went there for. Given that he was wearing a mask it can't have been because he thought Mr Walsh could identify him. I suspect his motive for killing him was personal, as with the Sherwood Forest murders. That could help us.'

'Did any of the neighbours see or hear anything?' Jean asked.

'Not a thing. The house was too isolated. Once the killer gained access to the premises, he had the family all to himself.'

'No cameras?' Tayte said.

Fable shook his head. 'Forensics picked up a few grey clothing fibres this time, but that's about it.'

Tayte was wondering what this killer really wanted. 'A microscope?' he said, thinking aloud. 'What does he want with an old microscope?' He turned to Jean and knew she was now thinking the same thing he was.

'William Daws,' she said.

Tayte nodded. To Fable he said, 'Among other things, Daws was a field physiologist with a particular interest in the study of human blood and the circulatory system. I wouldn't mind betting that he's Alex Walsh's ancestor and that the microscope once belonged to him.'

Fable looked puzzled. 'But what could Walsh's killer possibly want his ancestor's old microscope for?'

Tayte didn't know. His head was suddenly spinning with random thoughts. There was Queen Anne and a possible Whig conspiracy to end the Royal House of Stuart; five Royal Society Fellows who were hanged for high treason—probably framed; Jacobites, past and present in the form of Quo Veritas; and now, three hundred years later, it seemed that a ruthless killer was collecting family heirlooms from the descendants of these men of science. It occurred to Tayte then why Marcus Brown might have urged him to hurry.

'Four murders,' he said. 'Two from twenty years ago and two more recently. If I'm right and the victims are the firstborn descendants of the men we've been researching, then we're running out of time. There may only be two descendants left.'

'Two?' Fable said. 'How's that?'

'The Reverend Charles Naismith had twins, so he counts for two lines of descent, which we know lead to Julian Davenport and Douglas Jones. Assuming for now that the other four men had only one heir each, that makes six in total.'

'Of which four are already dead,' Jean said.

Tayte stood up. He was suddenly in a hurry to get back to The National Archives. Wherever Marcus's research was taking them, it was clear to him now that current events had to take precedence. He needed to prove his theory and get to the remaining two descendants before it was too late.

He turned to Fable. 'Any chance I can get a lift to Kew?'

Chapter Twelve

Before Tayte and DI Fable left the hotel, Fable gave him the information he would need to make a start on proving Alexander Walsh's relationship to one of the five Royal Society Fellows. Twenty minutes later he dropped Tayte off at The National Archives' car park beneath a dark and starry sky.

Fable lowered his window. 'Call me as soon as you get anything,' he said. 'I don't care what time it is.'

'I'll do that.'

Tayte watched the detective drive off and then he walked beside the now dark pond that fronted the building, heading for the entrance. He checked his watch. The glowing digits told him it was a little after ten, and he thought Jean was probably in bed by now. Part of him wished he was, too, but sleep would have to wait. It was going to be a long night.

He was surprised to see The National Archives so busy given the hour and given how few people from the genealogy convention had offered to help with the research. As he drew closer he saw a crowd near the entrance. There were two uniformed police officers beneath a bright spotlight and a security guard at the door. Several other people were standing beyond the glass inside the foyer. He heard footsteps behind him and turned to see a man with a briefcase that was not unlike his own, minus the bullet holes, heading towards the building with him.

He wondered what was going on. There was even a mobile news team outside: a three-person crew composed of a female reporter, a cameraman with a shoulder unit, and a sound tech with a fluffy grey microphone boom and spotlight. The reporter looked cold, like she'd been standing too long in the night breeze that swept in off the pond. She had a small microphone of her own, which she shoved towards Tayte as he approached.

'Can you tell us how you hope to catch this killer?' she asked.

The question threw Tayte. He hadn't expected anything like this. He put a hand up in front of his face, partly because that spotlight was right in his eyes, and kept walking.

'Excuse me,' he said. 'I'm in kind of a hurry.'

He turned back when he reached the foyer and saw the man who had been behind him stop and smile for the camera. Turning away again his eyes were drawn to a woman he recognised from his earlier visit. She was standing by the reception desk, talking to someone and pointing as though giving directions. It was Victoria Marsh, the chief executive of The National Archives. When she saw Tayte, she came straight over.

'I was told you weren't coming,' she said. She looked pleased to see him.

'I wasn't. Not yet anyway. What's happening? I thought we only had three people helping out.'

'That was it to begin with,' Marsh said. 'For the first hour or so. Then more arrived and they've been pouring in ever since.'

Tayte started walking again, heading for the reading rooms. 'So how many do we have now?'

She looked unsure. 'Twenty-five, maybe thirty.'

'From the convention?'

'Some,' Marsh said. 'Most are employees and freelancers—people who knew Marcus or knew someone else who did.'

'The word's out then?' Tayte said. 'I saw the TV crew outside.'

Marsh nodded. 'They didn't waste any time getting here, either. We've closed the Archives to the public for as long as you need. Several people at the GRO are staying on to help out, too.'

Tayte was glad to hear that. The General Register Office was something he'd overlooked given the hour. They would need the GRO when it came to confirming the data on the many birth, marriage, and death records they would have to pull out in order to get the job done. They would also have to rely heavily on probate records and the census back to 1841. Other resources could be accessed online.

As they entered the Open Reading Room, where Tayte had previously used the building's computer facilities, he had to stop and stare. The team had grown significantly and they were all hard at work. The computer screens were all on, personal laptops were out, and fingers were tapping furiously. There were people staring into microform readers and others poring over books and other documents. Several members of the general staff had clearly volunteered to stay on, too, helping with record retrieval.

'Everyone, this is Jefferson Tayte,' Marsh announced. 'Aside from dear Marcus, he's the reason you're all here tonight.'

Tayte shot up a hand and felt his cheeks flush. 'Thanks for turning out,' he said. 'Your time and skills are very much appreciated.'

He sat in front of a vacant screen at one of the pods, and a young man whose full beard made him look older than his years introduced himself as David. He brought Tayte up to speed.

'We've just confirmed that Sarah Groves was a direct descendant of one of the men on your list,' he said. 'Dr Bartholomew Hutton.'

Tayte gave David a wide smile. He hadn't expected a result so soon, but looking around the room again it was easy to see how they'd come up with the information so quickly. And it confirmed his theory—Sarah Groves had been murdered along with Douglas Jones twenty years ago. Now, with Julian Davenport, they had three victims related to the hanged Fellows of the Royal Society.

'You said she was of direct descent?' Tayte said.

David nodded. 'Firstborn dependant from each generation, all the way back.'

'Good. So we know exactly what we're looking for.'

There was no grey area. With three victims confirmed, they had a pattern to follow. They could discard any brothers or sisters they came across and concentrate on the path of the firstborn male or female, confident that it was the right path. Before he got too settled, Tayte called the team together. He had new data to introduce and thought it could be used to simplify the process and speed things up further.

He stood and raised his arms. 'Can I please get your attention for a moment.' When the room quietened down he continued. 'We have another victim—Alexander Walsh. He was murdered three days ago.'

Tayte read out the information Fable had given him, knowing that it would be easier to have everyone work back from present to past, from Walsh to another of the Fellows. Then they could eliminate one more ancestor from the list as the team had already done with Sarah Groves. It had taken a little over four hours to get that result. Now, as there were more of them and they were in full flow, he figured it would take less time to do it again.

He sat down, took off his jacket and metaphorically rolled up his sleeves with the rest of the team, feeling confident that from the two remaining Fellows they would learn the identity of the killer's next victims.

Michel Levant was alone in his inner sanctuary, taking a bath. The capacious en suite, with its gold-plated fittings and green marble walls and pillars, was a special place to which he retreated every night before bed. It was a place of contemplation and reflection, a time and space to be shared with none other than the greatest love of his life—himself. To share a bath with anyone else was nothing less than disgusting to him. *Diabolique.*

He sank deeper into the hand-painted slipper bath and the therapeutic oils that Françoise had prepared for him and allowed himself to become weightless. He sucked in the scent of French lavender and something intoxicating that he couldn't quite place; something he would have to ask Françoise about in the morning when she came to him. With one hand he sipped Cristal champagne from a finely engraved coupé glass. With the other he pressed a button on a remote control, and an LCD panel on the wall in front of him clicked into life. The sound was muted.

Levant had no use for television other than to keep abreast of current affairs, domestic and foreign. On this particular occasion, the twenty-four-hour news channel to which the television was eternally tuned made him sit up and spill his champagne. He was looking at The National Archives building. A female reporter was interviewing someone he hadn't seen before, but standing behind her in the entrance was a big, dark-haired man in a tan suit that he most definitely had seen before.

'Mon Dieu! C'est Jefferson Tayte.'

The American was only on the screen for a second, but it was long enough. Levant grabbed the remote control and turned the sound on. The reporter was talking into her microphone.

'Can you tell us how genealogy could aid the capture of this cold-hearted killer?'

The middle-aged man beside her smiled nervously. 'I'm not really at liberty to go into the details,' he said. Then he proceeded to do just that. 'We have a list of people,' he added in a low voice, as though he didn't know the world was watching and listening. 'I've been told they're ancestors of the victims. We believe that from them we can identify the killer's next target.'

'And once you've done that the police intend to set a trap?'

The man's face turned red. 'I think I've already said too much.'

The reporter held the man's arm as he turned to walk away. 'Is it true that you've been granted full access to the census?'

The man faced the camera again. 'I believe so, yes. They're usually locked for a hundred years, other than in special circumstances.'

'Circumstances such as these?' the reporter said. 'How will you use the information?'

The man seemed to relax again. 'The census is invaluable when it comes to identifying family relationships. It's taken at ten-year intervals and gives us a snapshot of people living under the same roof at the time the census is taken. From there it becomes a simple matter to identify dependants by their relationship to the head of the household. That will be key to our research.'

'How far back will that research take you?'

'Too far for the census, I'm afraid. Beyond 1841, probate records often give up the same information with respect to naming dependants as beneficiaries, and there are other methods, of course. Once we have a name, we can confirm the association via their birth or baptism records.'

The interview continued for a further half minute, and Michel Levant listened with great interest. It all added up to the fact that Jefferson Tayte was making good progress in his quest to understand what Marcus Brown had been working on. It also told him where Tayte was, and that information was paramount to him. Having had Tayte and Jean Summer followed from Kew to the Royal Society earlier that morning, his man had lost them amidst the bustle and confusion at Piccadilly Circus. Now Tayte was back at Kew, and this time Michel Levant was resolved to handle the matter personally.

It took Tayte and the team at Kew until just after one-thirty in the morning to work through Alexander Walsh's ancestry, and by now there were close to forty experienced genealogists helping with the search. They had identified a direct line of descent via firstborn dependants all the way back to the Tory politician and field physiologist William Daws, whose studies into human blood—with a view to proving parent and child relationships—had so caught their attention at the Royal Society. It had taken around three hours to reach the result Tayte had expected to find since hearing the interview recording, although he still had no idea what the killer wanted with what seemed likely to have been William Daws's old microscope.

Tayte had lost count of how much coffee he'd consumed, and the bag of Hershey's miniatures he'd stuffed into his briefcase before leaving the hotel was almost empty. He drained another cup of bitter espresso, stood up, and addressed the room.

'Great job so far, everyone,' he said. 'We've matched Dr Bartholomew Hutton and William Daws. That just leaves two names remaining—Lloyd Needham and Sir Stephen Henley.'

A lady in a grey fleece stood up. 'A few of us had started on them before you arrived,' she said. She waved a notepad. 'We already have the names and particulars of their immediate dependants.'

'That's great,' Tayte said. 'Let's get the details up on the board.'

He went over to the window where a whiteboard had been set up. 'As we don't know from which of our two remaining ancestors the next victim is likely to come, I'd suggest we split the team into two groups.'

He turned back into the room and sliced a palm out in front of him like a knife, dividing the room in half. 'Left side, if you could take Henley. Right side gets Needham with me. I think we can safely say that the current firstborn descendants of these people are on someone's hit list. If we can identify them quickly, maybe we can save them. Accuracy is everything here, so please confirm your findings. We can't afford to cut corners.'

He asked the lady in the grey fleece to call out the details she had on her notepad, and he wrote everything down on the whiteboard. Then he returned to his seat beside David and the search recommenced. Within the teams they organised themselves into subgroups, with some tackling the direct research while others confirmed any pertinent information as they found it.

It was slow going until 1837, when civil registration for births, marriages, and deaths in England began. Prior to that they had to turn to the International Genealogical Index and the parish registers, which gave information on baptisms, marriages, and burials. Fortunately for the genealogists, writing a last will and testament in the eighteenth and nineteenth centuries was regarded as a moral duty by most people, expediting their research. Even so, it took almost twice as long to get another result.

The new day broke with no recognition from Tayte, and it was approaching eight in the morning when he thought he'd found who he was looking for. He had an entry on his screen from the 1971 census. It showed an address in Surrey, listing the head of the household as a Mr Peter David Harper, age twenty-six. Below that were the names of the other people living at the same address at the time the census was taken. There was only one name: Elizabeth May Harper, age twenty-two, whose relationship to the head of the household was wife.

Tayte checked the subsequent census entries for any dependants and noted that none were listed. When he checked the most recent census, he found that Peter Harper was still at the same address, but it now showed that he was living alone, suggesting that either through death, divorce, or some other form of separation, his wife was no longer with him. After confirming that Peter Harper had no record of death, Tayte borrowed a phone and called Fable, knowing that there was a fifty percent chance that he was looking at the killer's next victim.

When daylight broke at the windows of a grey portacabin somewhere in East London, a man in a navy blue security guard's uniform was saying goodbye to the skinny peroxide blonde who had been to visit him. Most of the girls he'd used wouldn't go back to the gasworks twice, but Lola Love, as she called herself, didn't seem to mind the place, or him. He followed her to the gate, having put enough cash in her purse to keep her going for another day on whatever Class A drug she was addicted to. He didn't care. He locked up again and watched her walk awkwardly down the derelict road, where weeds were growing tall through the cracks in the potholed tarmac. She had her arms crossed tightly in front of her, wearing fishnets and high heels and little else.

Does she feel the cold?

It was certainly a cool morning: clear and bright and dewy. He supposed she didn't, or more likely she no longer cared. Returning to the portacabin he plugged the main gate surveillance camera back into the recorder and smiled to himself. It was easier than deleting data from the hard drive like he sometimes had to do.

If anyone ever asks to see it, you blame the missing video on a fault. Simple. What else could it be?

No one ever asked. There was nothing of value at the old gasworks left to steal that hadn't been stripped out long before the construction company he was contracted to had bought the site. He thought about that surveillance camera as he plugged it back in. It had missed a lot recently. He'd slipped out at eleven the night before and had been gone almost five hours. But things hadn't gone to plan.

This one is smarter than the rest. Too smart for his own good.

The man he had visited in the night was quick to produce the heirloom he sought. This time it was an ebony and brass sextant inlaid with ivory that once belonged to Lloyd Needham, astronomer and one-time hydrographer to William III. But the digits were not there. In their place he saw only the gouge marks where they had been purposefully obscured by the man who scoffed at him as he told him how he'd read all about Julian Davenport's murder three months ago. This man was one of the older generation, and he knew all about the digits, too. He'd said that they were now his insurance, committed to memory to keep him alive.

And that had been his mistake.

He'll give up the digits. And you'll know if he's lying because you're good. Just like in Kuwait City.

He'd brought the man back to the gasworks with him, and ordinarily that wouldn't have bothered him, but the parameters had changed. The American and the team of genealogists he'd seen on his portable television last night gave him cause to hurry now that the new day had dawned. His guest had been left long enough in that draughty old boiler house. Left to his thoughts.

That's how you do it. You show them what they're in for, and you leave them to their own imagination for a while. They become more co-operative then.

He reached under the desk and slid out a black holdall from which he produced an old leather roll case that was once the property of a woman called Sarah Groves, descendant of royal physician and anatomist Dr Bartholomew Hutton. He untied the case and rolled it open. It contained several antiquated surgical instruments, the metal still gleaming, the bone and tortoiseshell handles clean and bright. His eyes fell on the lancet, and he smiled to himself as he considered that this simple physician's instrument, which had no doubt been used to bleed many of Dr Hutton's patients three centuries ago, was about to be used again—over and over again until Peter Harper told him what he wanted to know.

'Abducted?'

Tayte was talking on the phone with DI Fable. The detective was in Surrey at the address Tayte had given him an hour and a half ago. It was almost nine-thirty in the morning now, and the team of genealogists, who were all currently working on the last name from Tayte's list, had reached something of an impasse in the closing stages of their research. A decision had to be made that Tayte did not want to make lightly, and hearing that Peter Harper had been abducted from his home only served to compound the problem.

'When?' Tayte said. 'Are you sure?'

Fable coughed into the phone before he spoke. 'He was taken in the night,' he said. 'Couldn't say when for sure, but his bed was slept in. It was unmade and—'

'How do you know it wasn't some other night?' Tayte cut in. Knowing they had failed Harper by what could amount to just a few hours grated on his tired conscience.

'I was about to say that the last number redial facility on his phone showed that he made a call close to eight o'clock last evening. It's boy scout stuff.'

'I see,' Tayte said. 'Sorry. Go on.'

Fable coughed again and cleared his throat. 'His visitor didn't use the front door like before. We believe he went in through an open bathroom window on the first floor—must have gone up the drainpipe. It's a 1950s terraced house. Still has the original iron pipework.'

'Terraced?' Tayte said. 'Did any of his neighbours hear anything?'

'I've got people conducting a door-to-door now, but I wouldn't hold your breath. We won't know anything for a few hours. How's the next name coming?'

'You mean the last name,' Tayte said, reminding them both that they only had one more chance. He sighed. 'We've kind of lost the thread.'

'How's that?'

'The Great War,' Tayte said. 'During the Fourteen–Eighteen, a father and his young firstborn son—who must have lied about his age to get into the fight—were both killed. The father, Captain John Cornell, died in 1917 in Ypres. The son, Robert Cornell, didn't make it that far. He fell in 1916 during the Battle of the Somme, so the line of firstborn descendants from Sir Stephen Henley came to an abrupt end.'

'So that's it?' Fable said.

'I don't believe so. And this killer doesn't seem to believe so either, does he? I'm sure it's just a case of working out what contingency the father adopted before he died. Robert wasn't an only child. He had a younger brother called Joseph.'

'Well, that's your man.'

'Probably, but I don't like guesswork. There's too much resting on us getting this right. I want to be sure.'

'Look, Tayte. That might be a luxury you have in your world, but you're half into mine now. Don't call it guesswork if it makes you uneasy. Call it a hunch. Christ, I work with them all the time. Besides, what else have you got?'

'Not much.'

'So do what I would do and run with it. You said the son died in 1916 and the father in 1917?'

'That's right.'

'So the father had a whole year to make other plans before he was killed. If we're talking about handing down a family heirloom, then the younger brother was next in line to receive it, wasn't he?'

Tayte knew it made sense. He'd even considered that as the Cornells had lived during uncertain times, such a contingency might already have been established by the time the war began.

'I'm heading back to London,' Fable said and Tayte heard him groan as if he wasn't happy about it. 'I'm giving an update briefing at Thames House. The Security Service want to hear the case progress from the horse's mouth.'

'Tell them we're close,' Tayte said.

'How close? Give me a number.'

'Another hour. Maybe two.'

'Okay. Well, you call me as soon as you can. I won't be in that meeting a second longer than I need to be, believe me. I just hope to Christ we get there first this time.'

'We have to,' Tayte said. 'It's our last chance.'

The call ended with the words, *last chance,* spinning through Tayte's mind. He knew they could rest no hope on finding the abducted Peter Harper alive, and of the six current descendants of the Royal Society Fellows only one remained to be identified: the one person who might be able to shed some light on the killer's motive. Tayte was also painfully aware that it was probably his last chance to understand why his friend was dead. He needed that closure, and he had no doubt that this killer already knew who his last victim was and that he would waste no time paying him—or her—a visit now that he was so close to his goal.

Tayte turned to the 1911 census that was still on his screen. A name stood out that he'd seen before. It was a family name, handed down since it had been adopted after the English Civil War in 1645. The name was Naseby. It had been given to Sir Stephen Henley, and despite a change or two in surnames through marriage over the years, it had also been given to John Cornell and to his sons, Robert and Joseph. That unusual name, if its usage had been continued by the descendants of Joseph Cornell, would make the remainder of their work at Kew all the easier. He went to the whiteboard and wrote it down, hoping that it was the right name, knowing that they could ill afford the delay if it was not.

Sitting on a low wall outside The National Archives, Michel Levant snapped the collar up on his beige designer mac and recrossed his legs as he continued to watch the main entrance, waiting for Jefferson Tayte to emerge. He rarely diverted his gaze, having done so once to assess the weather as high white clouds came and went in the blue, and another time to watch a pretty teenage girl go by, unable as he was to resist what he considered to be such a simple pleasure.

The number of visitors to the Archives surprised him that morning as they arrived and were turned away again. Clearly they had neither seen the news last night nor read the morning papers, or they too would have known about the American genealogist and his team, whose work for the police had forced the Archives to close. It was of no consequence to Michel Levant. If anything, the volume of people coming and going helped to mask his presence. And he would sit there all day if he had to.

Chapter Thirteen

It was late morning by the time Jefferson Tayte left The National Archives. Despite feeling drained from having worked through the night with the rest of the team, he sprinted to the taxi that was waiting for him, hoping again that the hunch DI Fable had suggested he run with was right and that this time they wouldn't be too late.

The taxi smelled of pine forest air fresheners from all the little paper trees that were hanging on the rearview mirror. It made Tayte cough as he got in and gave the driver an address somewhere in Clapton where he hoped Fable was going to meet him. He'd called the detective but he'd picked up his voice mail, which he supposed was because of the Security Service meeting Fable had told him about. He'd given Fable another name and address from the latest census, telling him he was going there to warn the man that his life was in danger. He'd tried to get a phone number but it was ex-directory.

As the taxi joined the traffic and Tayte settled back with his thoughts, he considered how useful the census had been. Over the decades that followed the Great War, he and the team had tracked the Cornell family from Joseph Cornell through his firstborn son, who appeared on the 1951 census living in Kent with three children of his own. Then on the 1981 census, they had tracked the family to London, where the latest census showed that the target of their research still lived. Like Peter Harper, he lived alone with no dependants.

The unusual middle name of Naseby had helped. It had remained in the family to the present day, hinting at their long-standing sense of tradition. And history had repeated itself. The man he was on his way to see was called Robert Cornell, which was the same name that had been given to the firstborn ancestor who had died in the Battle of the Somme in 1916: his subject's great uncle. Robert even had a brother called Joseph, and Tayte didn't think it uncommon. He saw the recurrence of given names on the genealogy charts he compiled for his clients all the time. Maybe their father knew their ancestors' Great War stories and wanted to remember them by giving their names to his own children.

'How long will it take?' Tayte asked the driver. 'I'm in a hurry.'

The taxi sped up briefly and then slowed for the lights.

'About another half hour or so. Forty minutes at most unless the traffic's snarled up.'

Tayte screwed his face up and slumped back in his seat. He wanted to be there half an hour ago but knew that Murphy's Law dictated the traffic today would be heavier than ever. He felt trapped but there was nothing he could do about it—not that he knew quite what he was going to say to Robert Cornell when he got there. It wasn't like he had a police badge to add any weight to his visit.

'Do you have a cell phone I could borrow?' He wanted to try Fable again.

The driver seemed to ignore him.

'It's an emergency,' he added. 'I'll pay double fare.'

The driver slowed down, leant around and dropped his mobile into the change bucket in the partition. Tayte grabbed it and from his wallet he found Fable's card and dialled the number. The call went straight to voice mail again and he didn't bother to leave a message this time, hoping that Fable would pick up his earlier message soon and that he would be there in Clapton when the taxi arrived.

He was about to hand the phone back when he thought about calling Jean, remembering that she'd written her phone number on his copy of Marcus Brown's book. He quickly found it, and his call rang for what seemed like an age before she picked up. Her voice sounded small—like she was further away than he wanted her to be. He was smiling as he spoke without really knowing why.

'Jean, hi. It's JT. I hope you slept well.'

'Not really,' Jean said, reminding Tayte of the situation with her son. She sounded upbeat enough though, despite everything.

'No news about Elliot?'

'Nothing yet, no.'

Tayte didn't know what he could say that wouldn't amount to putting his foot in it, so he redirected the conversation with that most common of all mobile phone questions.

'Where are you? Still at the hotel?'

'No, I've been in Nottinghamshire since around half eight. I set off early on my bike.'

Tayte hadn't expected to hear that. 'Did you just say Nottinghamshire?'

'I couldn't just sit around,' Jean said. 'I've been looking into the Jacobite society Detective Fable told us about—Quo Veritas. Actually, I'm on my way back now. I was making a fuel stop when you rang.'

Tayte was impressed. 'Did you find anything?'

'I think I might have. I've been looking through the local newspaper archives—the *Nottingham Post*. As well as reporting on the Sherwood Forest murders twenty years ago, the journalist who covered them, Ewan Stockwell, also ran an exposé piece on the society. They were a very serious bunch.'

'You think that's why he went missing?'

'Maybe. His research ran pretty deep but it's left me confused.'

'How so?'

'Well, I've also been looking into other Jacobite societies such as Na Fir Dileas, meaning The Loyal Men, and another called A Circle of Gentlemen. They still exist, and they've survived to this day because of their beliefs and because most of their members are angry at the injustice as they see it. They all stand for the divine right of kings and the Stuart bloodline in a very traditional Jacobite sense. They support the cause through James II's son, the Old Pretender, and the Young Pretender, Bonny Prince Charlie—in other words, through the Catholic bloodline. Of those I checked—and there were plenty of them—I couldn't find a single society whose beliefs differed from that.'

'Apart from Quo Veritas?' Tayte offered.

'Apart from Quo Veritas,' Jean repeated. 'The society's members were very clearly *against* the Catholic Stuart bloodline. Instead of the white cockade as a symbol of support, their emblem depicts a self-consuming dragon called Ouroboros, forming a ring around a fleur-de-lis.'

'Why a fleur-de-lis? Isn't that French?'

'It was part of the royal coat of arms between the fifteenth and nineteenth centuries, asserting England's claim to the French throne. It's strongly associated with Queen Anne, not least because she considered herself queen of France. Quo Veritas held a strong belief that Queen Anne's bloodline represented the true line. Do you see the problem with that?'

Tayte wasn't sure he did.

'The problem is that up until twenty years ago, Quo Veritas still believed it. They supported a bloodline that's supposed to have died out three hundred years ago. How could that be?'

Only one thought crossed Tayte's mind. 'They had to believe it still existed.'

'Exactly. So what if it still does?'

Neither spoke for several seconds.

'I need to get my head around it some more,' Jean said. 'But I can't see any other explanation.'

'Are you suggesting that Queen Anne had a legitimate heir to the throne of England?'

'It was Anne of Great Britain by the end of her reign, but yes, why not? Quo Veritas had to believe she did.'

'A secret heir?' Tayte said. 'All these years?' The possibility made his head spin, but if there was any truth to it, he could see now why Michel Levant was so interested. It would be the ultimate heir hunt.

'We can discuss it more later,' Jean said. 'How did you get on at the Archives?'

Tayte was still considering the connotations of what Jean had just said. He took a moment to answer. 'It went well.' He paused again. He didn't want to tell her that one of the descendants they had traced had gone missing. He'd spare her that detail for now in light of the situation with Elliot.

'Did you manage to identify the descendants?' Jean asked.

'We did. I'm on my way to meet one of them now. Someone called Robert Cornell.' Tayte looked out the window. They were crawling along. 'Look, why don't you meet me there. We need to talk this through face to face, and maybe we can get some answers from Mr Cornell. If I'm not mistaken, either he or his father would have been a member of Quo Veritas. Do you have a pen handy?'

Tayte gave her the address.

'I'm an hour or so from Clapton,' Jean said. 'The traffic won't be a problem on the bike.'

The way his journey was going, Tayte thought she would probably get there ahead of him. The taxi was stuck in a queue at a set of lights, and all around him the traffic was either at a standstill or crawling along. A tap on the partition brought his focus back inside the taxi. The driver wanted his phone back.

'Look, I've gotta go,' Tayte said. 'Have a safe trip back. We'll talk more then.'

As the taxi pulled away from the lights, all Tayte could think about was the seemingly impossible idea that Queen Anne—a queen who had supposedly died without issue after as many as eighteen attempts—had somehow left an heir. His mind raced. He thought about the Royal Society Fellows and William Daws in particular, whose research had focused on proving parent and child relationships. As incredible as it seemed to him right now, things were beginning to make sense. If there had been a secret heir to the throne and these five Fellows were somehow involved, they would need a bona fide way to prove it. And how better than through science?

Tayte was suddenly in a greater hurry to get where he was going, and he didn't care how much it cost as long as he reached Robert Cornell in time. He called through to the driver, 'Do you know any shortcuts? I'll make it worth your while.'

Despite the taxi driver's best efforts, the journey to Clapton still took close to an hour, although to Jefferson Tayte, who was counting every second, it felt more like two. He was left standing on the pavement with his briefcase, looking up at a small, mid-terraced house that was nothing like he'd expected. He'd supposed the descendant of such a prominent man as Sir Stephen Henley would have lived somewhere more prestigious, but here was a good example of how a family's fortune could change over time.

The address was one of a hundred or so similar houses that, together with parked cars, lined the narrow Victorian street. The sash windows had almost all been replaced with double-glazing, and the tiny, low-walled gardens that fronted the houses were now paved over with grey slabs, the general appearance being further destroyed by an army of plastic wheelie bins and a regimented line of satellite dishes.

Tayte waited on the pavement longer than he meant to, partly because he still hadn't worked out what to say to Robert Cornell and partly because he hoped that if he waited long enough DI Fable would arrive. When he decided that that wasn't going to happen anytime soon, he took a deep breath, opened the small ironwork gate, and walked the path to the front door, wondering if there would be anyone home. The man was in his forties. It was Tuesday lunchtime. As he knocked and stepped back, for all his haste that morning he began to question the likelihood.

It took several seconds to find out. Then he heard the door latch, and a man with a shaved head wearing a white shirt and navy blue trousers opened the door. He was thin lipped, with a muscular jaw and a stocky build. Tayte didn't know if this was the man he'd been so anxious to see, or whether Robert Cornell was the right man at all, come to that, but he gave him a cheesy smile that must have looked like he was there to sell something.

'Hi there,' he said.

'No thanks. I'm not interested.'

Tayte stepped closer and the door slammed shut in his face. He rapped his knuckles on the glass panel. 'Mr Cornell?' he called. 'Robert *Naseby* Cornell?' He could see the man's shadow through the glass. After a lengthy pause the door opened again.

'Who are you?' the man asked. 'What do you want?'

'You *are* Robert Cornell?'

'Yes, I'm Cornell.'

Tayte extended a hand and when the man ignored it he withdrew it again. 'My name's Jefferson Tayte,' he said. 'I'm a genealogist.'

'A genie-what?'

'Family history. I'm assisting the police with a murder investigation, and I believe you're in danger. Can we go inside?'

Cornell looked up at Tayte and then he looked out into the street. 'Where are the police?'

'They're on their way,' Tayte said, hoping it was true.

'And you say I'm in danger?'

'I think so, yes.'

'From what? What kind of danger?'

'The worst kind, believe me,' Tayte said. 'Look, we might not have much time.'

'There's enough time for you to tell me what this is about.'

'Quo Veritas,' Tayte said. 'You know about Quo Veritas.' It wasn't a question.

Cornell said nothing.

'You have something that someone else wants—a family heirloom of some kind.'

Cornell seemed to measure Tayte then. 'How do I know you're not the one I'm in danger from?'

'If I was,' Tayte said, 'it would be too late already. Now can we get off the street?'

The man paused again, studying Tayte closely. Then he stepped back and invited him in.

The hallway was tight, with two doors to the left and a staircase straight ahead. Tayte followed Cornell through the first door into a lounge that was stuck in the seventies, with peeling box-patterned wallpaper and abstract brown carpet. The furniture was older still, but cheap looking rather than antique.

Tayte sat down. He was too tired to wait for an invitation. 'I'm glad I caught you home,' he said. 'I thought you might be at work.'

'I just finished,' Cornell said. 'Another half-hour and I'd have been in bed.'

'Night worker?' Tayte said. 'I can relate to that.'

'You work nights, too?'

'I did last night.'

'Well, don't get too comfortable,' Cornell said. He was across the room by the window, looking out through the faded net curtains. He turned and picked up his jacket. 'If someone wants to kill me, this is the first place they'll look. You found me easily enough.'

Tayte thought it had been anything but easy. 'I could use a coffee,' he said, standing up. 'I saw a place out on the main road.'

'No, I'll drive us to the police station,' Cornell said. 'My car's outside.'

As Cornell passed Tayte, he wondered again whether the research had led him to the right man—if the hunch had been correct. 'Was anything passed on to you from your father?' he asked. 'Something that's been in the family a long time?' He thought about Fable's interview recording and about the Royal Society. 'Was it a scientific instrument?'

Cornell paused at the door and turned back. 'I don't want to talk about it here. Not until we're at the police station and I've confirmed you are who you say you are.'

They went back out into the hall, and Cornell put his jacket on as he walked. It was a close-fitting jacket, short and boxy.

'You're a security guard?' Tayte said.

'So what?'

'Nothing. The jacket's a giveaway, that's all. I was wondering what kind of job you had.'

Cornell picked up a mobile phone and a set of keys off the shelf. 'Well, now you know.'

'Looks like you cut yourself shaving there,' Tayte said, indicating his shirt. 'You've got blood on your collar.'

Cornell gave a small laugh. 'I'm always doing that.'

He rattled his keys, and seeing the phone again made Tayte think of Jean.

'I just remembered,' he said. 'I'm expecting someone to meet me here. If we're going to the police station, she won't know where to find me. You mind if I give her a quick call?'

'Not on this,' Cornell said. 'Work gets funny about it.' He slipped the phone inside his jacket. 'You can call her from the lounge. But don't be too long.'

Tayte went back into the lounge and Cornell followed him.

'You know what,' Cornell said. 'I could use a coffee myself. Tell her to meet you at the Star Café. It's just around the corner on Lower Clapton Road. It's the place you probably saw on your way here. We'll go on to the police station from there.'

'Great,' Tayte said. He dialled Jean's number, and as expected he got her voice mail. He left a message. 'She's on the road,' he said. 'Motorbike.' He ended the call and followed Cornell outside.

Cornell was about to close the front door behind him when he stopped. 'Damn,' he said. 'I'd put the grill on just before you arrived. I won't be a minute.'

When he came out again he showed Tayte to a red VW that was parked a few spaces along the street. Tayte got in and the car pulled away.

It only took a few minutes to get to the Star Café, a greasy spoon with red vinyl seats over black and white linoleum. The place was busy with lunchtime trade and the air was thick with the smell of all-day breakfasts and old cooking fat. Tayte sat next to his briefcase with Cornell opposite, Tayte looking into the café, Cornell looking out. They each ordered a black coffee, and against his better judgement after seeing just how greasy the place really was, Tayte ordered a ham and cheese sandwich to go with it. Cornell didn't say much. It wasn't like they could talk about what was going on in such a public place. He stared out the window for several minutes before breaking what had become an uncomfortable silence.

'How long do you think she'll be?'

Tayte checked his watch. 'Not long now.' He sipped his coffee. 'So, you're not married.'

'Was that a question?'

Tayte realised it wasn't. It was just another weak attempt at small talk to fill the time. He knew from his research that Robert Cornell was a single man, and now another snippet of information caught up with him. It was something that applied to both the abducted Peter Harper and Robert Cornell, and it suddenly struck him as odd. He figured he must have been too tired to see the significance before.

'This heirloom that's been passed down through your family—'

'I told you I didn't want to talk about it until we got to the police station.'

'I know,' Tayte said. 'But I was just thinking. You're in your forties, unmarried with no children. So it ends with you, doesn't it?'

'You seem to know a lot about me,' Cornell said.

'Enough to know that you're bucking the trend. Every one of your ancestors seemed to make a point of marrying early and starting a family. I figured it was because they felt it was their duty—that they each had to ensure that whatever had been passed down to them survived to the next generation. I was just wondering why that's not the case with you.'

'It's like you said. It ends with me.'

'What does? Why now?'

'You'll get your answers soon enough,' Cornell said. He scanned the room. 'But not here.'

'Okay. I'm sorry.'

Tayte knew he'd done well to get Cornell to trust him this far, so as much as he wanted to push the matter he thought better of it. Cornell was right. This wasn't the place. He finished his coffee in silence, supposing that as whatever was set in motion by the hanged Fellows of the Royal Society had remained a secret for three centuries, it could wait a little longer.

A lanky waitress in a pink t-shirt and blue jeans arrived carrying four plates of food in her arms. 'Ham and cheese?' she said with an Eastern European accent.

Tayte put his hand up, and with an awkward delivery, the waitress set his sandwich down in front of him, rebalancing the remaining plates.

'Can I get another coffee to go with that?' Tayte asked.

'Of course.' The waitress turned to Cornell. 'Anything else for you?'

'No thanks.'

The waitress turned again and at that moment she lost one of the plates. It flipped off her arm towards Cornell and he recoiled, scraping his chair back as the contents of what looked like another full English breakfast splashed down on the table and onto the floor in front of him.

'I'm so sorry!' the girl said as she rushed away.

Cornell didn't say anything. He didn't look too happy though, as he dabbed at his trousers with a napkin. The waitress quickly returned with a cloth and an ill-advised smile, clearly trying to make light of the incident.

'Did I get you?' she said.

'It's nothing. Don't worry about it.'

She cleaned up and left, taking Tayte's lunch with her. 'I'll get you another one,' she said. 'No charge.'

Tayte didn't see the girl or the food go. All his attention was on Cornell. As he'd recoiled on his chair, Tayte saw the nickel-plated grip of a handgun and the leather sheen of a shoulder holster beneath his jacket. It had appeared like a splice of subliminal advertising: a momentary flash that left him wondering if he'd seen it at all. He realised then that he was still staring at Cornell's jacket. He looked up and their eyes met.

'I didn't think British security guards were allowed to carry firearms,' Tayte said.

'We're not. I picked this up for personal protection. I read the papers. You came here yourself to tell me my life's in danger.'

'I see,' Tayte said, not sure that he really did. 'Is that what you went back inside the house for?'

Cornell nodded.

'Better not let the police see it when we go to the station,' he said. 'I don't think they'd understand.'

'No,' Cornell said.

Their eyes remained locked, and Tayte suddenly felt like they were the only people in the café. The noise around them, of people talking and eating and clanking their cutlery, had all but faded to a low static hiss.

Cornell smiled coldly. 'You're not going to buy that, are you?'

'No, I don't think so,' Tayte said. He'd already made it obvious enough. To deny it now would be futile. 'We were never going to the police station, were we?'

'No.'

Tayte wondered then how he could have overlooked the possibility that the killer might have been one of the descendants they'd spent the night researching. But he was tired and he'd been caught up in the chase, thinking only that he had to identify the remaining descendants in order to protect them.

Cornell touched his smooth scalp, drawing Tayte's eye. 'All that's missing now is the wig and the mask,' he said, and before he'd finished speaking, his other hand had the gun trained on Tayte beneath the table. 'If you try to run, I'll kill you. If you try to warn anyone, I'll shoot you dead before a single word leaves your mouth. Are we clear?'

Tayte nodded. Having seen how confident this man was, he didn't doubt him for a second. His mouth felt so dry that he didn't think he could speak even if he wanted to.

'You've done your friend Marcus Brown proud,' Cornell said, almost smiling. 'You found his killer. But how ironic is that?' He tapped the gun beneath the table.

Tayte said nothing.

'I knew you were looking—it's all over the news. I just didn't think you'd find me so soon.' He smiled fully then. 'But you're already too late.'

'Too late for what?'

Cornell shook his head. 'Smile,' he said as the waitress came back with his coffee. 'If she senses anything's wrong, you're both dead.'

Tayte did as he was told and the girl left again. He reached for his coffee, slowly. 'I guess you would have shown your true colours soon enough anyway. I was about to ask if I could borrow your phone to call the police and give them our new location. You couldn't have let me do that, could you?'

'No.'

'That's the real reason you wanted to get away from the house, wasn't it? Because you knew they were coming. That would have been awkward for you, wouldn't it?'

'Not as awkward as things are going to be for you and your girlfriend.'

Jean.

She was heading into a trap and it was all his fault. No wonder Cornell had changed tack when he'd said she was coming to meet him.

Two birds with one stone.

A moment later, Tayte heard a motorbike outside and his heart missed a beat. He watched a slow smile crawl across Cornell's face. Then Tayte turned to look out the window, but the kick he received pulled his eyes back to the man sitting opposite him.

'Get up,' Cornell said. 'And don't forget your briefcase. We're going to meet her at the door.'

Chapter Fourteen

Detective Inspector Jack Fable arrived at Robert Cornell's address barely half an hour after picking up Tayte's voice message. He knocked on the door again and then walked back to the gate where he turned and looked up at the windows, then along the street. Clearly Robert Cornell wasn't home, but where was Tayte? He wished now that he'd thought to lend Tayte a mobile phone when he'd had the chance. At least he would have been able to call him.

He went back to his car and leant on the bonnet, not yet ready to leave. He was annoyed that his meeting with the Security Service at Thames House had overrun and that he'd had to break away from getting on with the job in the first place just to tell everyone how badly the investigation was going. The worst of it was that being incommunicado for almost an hour and a half had forced Tayte to act on his own initiative and without support. He didn't blame him for that under the circumstances, but he wished to Christ he knew where he was.

He got back into his car and slammed the door behind him. Then he made a tight three-point turn and headed back out the way he'd come, pulling out onto the busy main road where he soon came to a small parade of shops: a newsagent, a bookmaker, an off-licence, and a café. He thought the only thing missing from the lineup was a greengrocer, but they were disappearing rapidly, along with the sense of community he'd once known. He stopped at a pedestrian crossing in the middle of the parade and watched an old lady pulling a bag on wheels. She ambled across the road as if reaching the other side was a rare treat not to be rushed.

That was when he saw Jean Summer's motorbike.

There were cars parked bumper to bumper outside the shops to either side of the crossing. The bike was just beyond: a very recognisable yellow BMW. He sat up and read the number plate to be sure. H15 TRY. It was the right registration.

A horn sounded behind him. He checked his mirror and pulled over onto the kerb. The bike was illegally parked, half on and half off the no-stopping lines, and there was no disc lock on the wheel. He figured Jean couldn't have planned on leaving it there long. The café across the pavement drew his eye, and he thought Tayte must have brought Robert Cornell there to get him away from the house. Clearly Jean must have met them. He got out of the car and went to check, thinking they must still be inside.

Three minutes later he was back outside again. Yes, they had recently served a big, dark-haired man with an American accent wearing a bright tan suit. Yes, he was with another man: a bald man in a security guard's uniform. No, there was no one else with them, and the waitress who had served them hadn't seen them leave, but she'd said it couldn't have been more than five minutes ago.

So why is Jean Summer's bike still here?

Fable stood beside it and put a hand on one of the big, twin-cylinder heads. It was still warm. Five minutes or so would be about right, but he couldn't imagine Jean would just leave it there, hanging over the pedestrian-crossing zone like that. She would have known it would be towed away.

So why did she leave it? Where are they now?

Fable felt the telling knot in his stomach begin to tighten, and instinctively he knew the answer was not good.

Tayte and Jean were heading east in a black cab. Beyond the partition a football match was playing loudly on the radio, filling the driver's ears. They were side by side on the back seat and Robert Cornell was on the pull down, facing them, his gun held low so the driver couldn't see it but Tayte and Jean could. It let them know who was in control. It made them fear for their lives. That's how Tayte saw it from Cornell's point of view, and that's exactly how he felt it.

'Sorry,' he whispered to Jean, and before he'd finished the word Cornell cracked the butt of the gun into his kneecap.

'I said no talking.'

Jean had a menacing stare fixed on Cornell. It was clear to Tayte that she was over the confusion of seeing him leave the café with the gunman she probably recognised from Piccadilly Circus, and she was over the fear of seeing that gun thrust into her face for the second time. She was at the loathing stage now, deeply ensconced in the kind of hatred that would consume you if you let it.

'Where's my son?' she asked.

'Goes for you too, bitch.' Cornell put a finger to his lips. 'Shh. There's a good girl.'

'I don't care what you do to me,' Jean continued. Defiant. 'I want my son back.'

'Do you care about the cabby? He's just doing the daily grind. I bet he has a nice family. Couple of kids.' Cornell leant towards Jean. He spoke slowly, his voice low and deliberate. 'Now shut your mouth or I'll shoot him. Plenty of cabs in London.'

Tayte had no doubt he'd do it, too. He nudged Jean's leg with his and she seemed to get the message. She sat back and knotted her arms.

'Try anything—anything at all,' Cornell said, 'and I promise you, I'll pay the cabby's family a visit. All of them. You understand me?'

The journey continued in silence. Tayte stared at his sorry-looking reflection in the partition as he listened to the rise and fall of the football commentary and the shared sense of anguish and excitement from the driver. Jean continued to stare at Cornell, who occasionally stared back. Fifteen minutes passed. Then the driver spoke.

'You sure about the address? Looks like a building site.'

'Take the lane there,' Cornell said. 'Next left.'

The driver shrugged and the taxi turned onto a dusty, potholed track. There was a high barbed-wire fence on one side, trees and overgrown shrubbery to the other. The track went on, slowly rocking the taxi as it dipped into the potholes for two hundred yards or so. Then they came to a double gate.

'I get it,' the driver said as he pulled up. 'You work here, do you? I saw the uniform.'

He turned around for his fare and without hesitating Cornell put two bullets through the partition. Both found their target and the driver fell sideways. Jean was already out of her seat, arms reaching for the gun, and Tayte was about to follow but Cornell was too quick. The butt of the gun cracked into the side of Jean's head, knocking her back. Then the muzzle was suddenly pressing hard into Tayte's forehead.

'Not so brave now, are you?'

Cornell elbowed the partition where the bullets had cracked it. It fell away enough for him to reach across for the door release, not taking his eyes off Tayte and Jean as he did so.

'Get out,' Cornell said, and as though reading Tayte's mind he added, 'If you try to run for the trees, I'll cut you down before you're halfway there.'

Cornell got out of the taxi on the opposite side, removing any opportunity they might have had to jump him if he followed them out the same way. Tayte and Jean were looking in through the driver's window when he caught up with them again, and Jean had a very different expression on her face now. The fear had returned and it had stuck: fear for the man she had just watched Cornell shoot, wondering if he was dead or alive, and fear now for herself since Cornell had so effectively reminded them how deadly serious he was. He opened the driver's door, and to remove any doubt he put another bullet in him.

'Get him out!'

Tayte felt every bit of the kick Cornell gave him. It shoved him towards the taxi, and he grabbed the dead man's legs and swung them out. He lifted them and paused as Jean moved in to support the man's head. He noticed she had tears in her eyes, and he silently wished she was anywhere else but here.

'Get on with it!'

Tayte knew there was no delicate way to get the dead man out of the taxi, so as much as he didn't like to, he pulled his legs and the man's body fell off the seat. Jean tried to hold on to him, but all that dead weight was too much for her. They all fell to the ground, blood from the dead man's wounds soaking into the dirt.

'Get up!' Cornell shouted.

As quiet as the area was, Tayte had the feeling that Cornell didn't want to stay out in the open too long. He looked around. There was an old building beyond the wire fence and some kind of industrial landscape further back beyond the trees. They were somewhere in East London, two hundred metres from a road that few people seemed to use, perhaps half a mile from the nearest occupied house. As far as he could see they were in the middle of nowhere.

'Pick him up!' Cornell shouted. 'Big guy gets the bloody end.' He flicked the gun at Jean. 'You get his feet.'

Tayte linked his arms around the dead man's chest and started to drag him by his heels. 'I can manage by myself,' he said. He would have spared Jean that, but Cornell was having none of it.

'Do it,' he said to Jean, pointing the gun at her. 'I want your hands busy.'

They carried the body to the gate, which Cornell unlocked and opened ahead of them. Once inside the compound, he flicked his gun towards what was left of one of the gasworks buildings a hundred or so feet away.

'We can make it,' Tayte whispered to Jean, though by the time they got there he was panting so hard his chest hurt, hindered as he was by the taxi driver's lifeless arms as they kept slipping through his own.

They went in via an arched doorway at the side of the building. There was no door, just the opening and the draught that constantly rattled through the place. The corridor they were led down looked like a blowtorch had been taken to it: the walls were peeling, repelling the many layers of paint that had been applied over the years. It was colourful, but in an unsettling way. There were splashes of graffiti here and there, and the ceiling had fallen through in places. Around the broken windows nature had begun its reclamation, binding everything it touched with pale ivy runners and anaemic-looking leaves.

'In here,' Cornell said.

There were several doorways. The one they took led down several iron steps into a room that was lit by high glassless windows. As Tayte descended, he began to wonder if he would ever make it out again. It was clear that Cornell planned to kill them, and he thought he would do it just as soon as they reached wherever they were going with the body and were of no further use to him.

'Drop him there,' Cornell said. 'In the corner.'

That's where Tayte thought it would happen. He kept his eyes on Jean's the whole time, willing her to understand what was in his mind. He wasn't just going to stand there and let this man shoot them. Now that Marcus Brown was gone, he knew there was no one left in his life to mourn his own death, but there were still things he needed to do: important things like finding out who he was. He just kept thinking that there were two of them and one of him. That had to give them a chance.

They reached the corner in shadow and gently lowered the body to the ground. As Tayte rose again, his only thought was to charge Cornell, but at that moment Cornell said something that stopped him.

'Now pick up your girlfriend.'

That confused Tayte. 'What?'

Cornell came closer but kept his distance with the gun. 'Pick her up. I want you to carry her out.'

'Oh, I get it,' Tayte said. 'Busy hands, right?'

'You're catching on.'

Tayte wasn't sure he had enough strength left to carry a bag of groceries let alone another person, but after the taxi driver, Jean felt light in his arms. As they left the room and headed back outside, Tayte wondered why Cornell had passed up such an easy opportunity to kill them. Clearly he had something else in mind, and that worried him.

They crossed the barren yard outside, past a grey portacabin and the main gate with the black cab beyond. There was a brick outbuilding with a tall chimney ahead of them, and they made straight for it.

'What do you plan to do with us?' Tayte asked as they reached it.

Cornell gave no reply. He paced ahead and opened the door, flicked his gun, and ushered them inside.

'You can't walk away from this, Cornell,' Tayte said as he crossed the threshold and was met by a gust of warm air. Flies buzzed in his face. 'The police know who you are now. It's over.'

'I never planned to walk away,' Cornell said. 'And you're wrong. It's not over. It's only just beginning.'

At that point Jean screamed in Tayte's ear. He almost dropped her as he spun her around and lowered her to the ground. In the corner of the room, opposite the entrance, was a thin, elderly man who seemed to be crouching amongst the pipework and the rubble. He was painted red with what Tayte supposed was his own blood, and his face seemed locked in a perpetual scream. It looked like some macabre waxworks diorama, and the sight of it made Tayte retch. He turned to Cornell.

'You sick—' he began, but the butt of Cornell's gun silenced him instantly as it smashed into his temple. Then he was falling and the world was suddenly black.

Standing outside Robert Cornell's front door for the second time that day, DI Jack Fable recalled the time when he didn't have to stop to consider if what he was doing as a police officer was lawful. PACE had changed that—the Police and Criminal Evidence Act. Passed in 1984, it legislated against the arbitrary searching of property or persons without just cause. It protected a person's civil rights. Fable understood the need for legislation, but to his old-school mind, it was just more bureaucracy to wade through. It had done nothing but slow the pace of an investigation as far as he was concerned.

Fable had a gut feeling and now it was his turn to run with it. The notion that Robert Cornell was the man he was looking for made perfect sense to him. Killers are often known to their victims, if only by association, which in this case was Quo Veritas. And on this occasion, that connection, together with seeing Jean's motorcycle where no right-minded person would leave a vehicle for any length of time, gave him all the 'just cause' he felt he needed to enter and search the property. He gave the word and a firearms officer smashed the lock through with a steel battering ram. Two more officers ran in through the doorway, weapons drawn.

'Armed police!' one of the men called.

The other officer dropped the ram and followed them while Fable and two other regular uniforms waited outside for the all clear.

There was no one home. Fable hadn't really expected anyone to be there, but firearms officers were a necessary precaution. They cleared out and the regular officers moved in to begin a search of the property, looking for anything that might incriminate Robert Cornell. If they found any corroborating evidence to support the notion that he was the man they were looking for, Fable would call in SOCO for a top-to-toe search, but he needed the evidence first.

He went into the lounge looking for photographs. They told him a lot about a person: if they were married, whether they had any children, where they liked to spend their holidays, and if they were close to anyone. And he could learn a lot about a suspect from the photographs he didn't see, too.

He saw a group of three frames on a low table by the front window. They told him that Robert Cornell was a military man like his late father and his younger brother. One showed a tank of some kind beneath a blue sky, with two young boys sitting up on the barrel. They were saluting while their father stood beside it in full dress uniform. Something about it made Fable think of the Gulf War—the pale camouflage. Another photograph showed the two boys in their own uniforms, twenty-something years old, smart and proud and fresh-faced.

Fable thought the third image an odd subject for a coffee table. It showed a military funeral in mid-procession, with a Union Jack flag draped across the coffin. The two boys were at the forefront, older still and with their heads slightly bowed.

What he didn't see by way of photographs told him that Robert Cornell was single or divorced and that he had no children—or none that he cared about enough to put photographs of them alongside his father and brother.

He put the photographs back and began to pace the room, taking everything in as he wondered how much longer the background checks on Cornell would take. It had been twenty minutes so far, and he figured it wouldn't be much longer. Then he would have a better picture of the man. His military record might provide some telling information, and he would find out where he worked now. He already knew from the waitress at the café that he was wearing a security guard's uniform. There would be a useful lead somewhere in the data: something or someone to tell him where Cornell was or where he would eventually go.

One of the uniformed officers came into the room. 'Better take a look at this, sir.'

Fable followed him upstairs. In what was the only room in the house that was made up as a bedroom, they had found a box of ammunition—9mm. A common bullet, Fable knew, but he also knew that it was extremely uncommon for any law-abiding citizen to keep ammunition in a bedside drawer. And it was the same calibre bullet that had killed Julian Davenport and Marcus Brown—the same calibre bullet that had been stopped by Jefferson Tayte's briefcase.

Fable ended the search there. He'd seen enough to warrant calling forensics in before too much else was disturbed. What he really wanted was the gun to go with the bullets so they could match the casings to the murder weapon, but maybe they would find something else that tied Robert Cornell to one of the victims—a fibre perhaps, or a trace of blood on an item of clothing.

As he went to make the call, Fable was even more convinced that Cornell was the man he was looking for, and he hoped he was right. He needed progress. But if Cornell was his man, the absence of a gun in the drawer with the bullets only served to nurture his concern for the safety of the genealogist who had found him and for the historian who was now with them.

With them…

It occurred to Fable then that although Tayte no longer had a mobile phone, there was a good chance Jean Summer did. It hadn't been long since he'd seen Jean's motorcycle outside the café, but he shook his head at himself just the same for not thinking to call her sooner. He had her number. Even if she didn't answer, triangulating a mobile phone's location via the cellular network was common practice. If Jean's phone was switched on, it wouldn't take long to identify her general location. Fable made the call knowing it was the best hope he could give them for now.

Chapter Fifteen

When Jefferson Tayte opened his eyes again following the blow Robert Cornell had dealt him, he saw the man by a high recess in the wall to his right. He was standing in front of a tall open fireplace. There was ash on the ground, and bright embers were glowing in the makeshift fire basket that looked to Tayte like old iron railings that had been thrown down over the rubble to suspend the coal. He watched Cornell take a bag from a pile to his right and throw it in.

A dull and repetitive throb on the side of Tayte's head reminded him why he'd blacked out. As he regained his senses and smelled the dust and the metallic tang of blood in the air, he saw that he was sitting against a wall with his legs out in front of him. His arms were secured behind his back and his ankles were bound with something he couldn't see. His initial instinct was to get up, but a small voice stopped him.

'It's no use.' It was Jean, speaking in a whisper. 'He made me put nylon cable ties around your wrists and ankles. There's another one looped around the pipe.'

She was sitting next to him, bound in the same fashion with her hands behind her, secured to a length of four-inch steel pipe that was bolted at intervals to the concrete floor.

'You okay?' Tayte asked, immediately seeing that for the dumb question it was. Of course she wasn't okay.

Jean gave no reply.

Several feet beyond her, Tayte saw that the door was still open, pouring light onto the man crouching in the corner opposite: a man whom Tayte now realised had to be the recently abducted Peter Harper. He seemed to stare at them, but Tayte figured him for a dead man now that he could see him more clearly. His body was slumped rather than crouched, supported by the walls, and Tayte supposed he must have lost more blood than it was possible to survive.

Despite Jean having told him it was no use trying to struggle free, Tayte pulled and twisted at the cable ties anyway. His movement drew Cornell's attention, and the man turned slowly away from the fire, which had already begun to spit and flame through the column of smoke that was rising into the chimney.

'Mr Tayte,' Cornell said. 'I'm glad you're back.' He came over and squatted beside him. 'I was beginning to think you were dead already.' He leant closer. 'Can't have that, can we? Not yet.'

Tayte stared the man down and got straight to the point. He wanted answers. 'How did you find Harper and the rest? Anything to do with Quo Veritas? Did they have a members' list or something?'

Cornell laughed at the suggestion. 'You found them easily enough, didn't you? You found me.'

Yeah, Tayte thought. *And look where that got me.* He looked over at Peter Harper again, unable to stop himself out of morbid curiosity. 'You like inflicting pain on people, don't you? I guess a man like you must get a kick out of it. Is that it?'

'Oh, it's much more than that,' Cornell said. 'Although it's not really my fault.' He sat back and crossed his arms. 'I'm a product,' he added. 'You can't ask a man to do the things I've done without expecting it to change him. That's not right. It's not fair. Results were all they cared about, and I got them. The people who wanted those results made me who I am.'

Tayte doubted that. 'Let me guess. The military?'

Cornell didn't answer directly. Instead, he gritted his teeth so hard that the muscles at his temples bulged. 'Then they criticise your methods, and before you know it you're a fucking bus driver!'

He grabbed a chunk of rubble from the debris and hurled it against the wall beside Tayte's head. Fragments of brick shattered around Tayte and he flinched away. He knew the best thing to do now was to shut up, but he had the man talking. That was good. Keep him busy. Buy some time.

'So what about Harper and Walsh?' he said. 'You weren't following orders then, were you? Walsh had a young family, for Christ's sake.'

Cornell was suddenly right in Tayte's face. 'Don't expect any sympathy from me. I enjoyed their suffering. I enjoyed it almost as much as I'm going to enjoy watching you suffer.' He stood up. 'And you're wrong. I'm still following orders, only these orders were written three centuries ago.'

He got up and blew Jean a sickly kiss as he passed her and went to the door. He was almost outside when her BlackBerry rang, shrill and loud from inside her jacket. It brought Cornell back at a sprint, and he went through her pockets like a frenzied animal to find it. When he did, he read the display, dropped the phone, and crushed it beneath his boot.

'Who's Daniel?'

Jean spat at him and he slapped the back of his hand across her face, sending her glasses flying. The blow knocked her onto her side, and when she got up again Tayte saw that there was blood on her lip. Cornell raised his hand again, and Tayte figured she didn't owe her cheating husband enough to go a second round with this madman.

'He's her ex-husband,' Tayte said. He looked at Jean apologetically, but he couldn't see that it mattered. What mattered was that they did have a phone and now they didn't.

Cornell lowered his hand. 'That's all I wanted to know,' he said, speaking softly to Jean. He retrieved her glasses, straightened one of the arms where it had bent, and slid them back onto her face. 'I don't want you to miss anything.'

He searched them both then and tossed what he found across the room: Jean's motorbike keys and disc lock, a lipstick and a small hairbrush, Tayte's wallet, notebook, and a few Hershey's miniatures. When he was satisfied he went outside, closing the door behind him.

'Sorry,' Tayte said, 'but I don't think we should make this any worse than it already is. If we give him what he wants, maybe it'll give us some time.'

'Time for what?'

'For the police to get here. Fable must have worked out what's happened by now. He'll realise who Cornell is and find out where he works. And that will lead him here.'

'You really believe that?'

Tayte wasn't sure he did, and the doubt Jean had put in his mind made him struggle with his cable ties all the more now that Cornell was outside. He wrestled with them for a full minute, trying in vain to snap them from the pipework. Then he tried to force the pipe loose until his arms ached and his wrists began to sting.

Jean stopped him. 'Quiet.'

Tayte heard a diesel engine start up: the taxi that had brought them there. It grew louder, like it was getting closer. It passed around the back of the boiler house until Tayte could clearly hear it through the high windows. Then it stopped. A minute later he heard the main gate clatter shut, and he figured Cornell had brought the taxi into the compound to conceal it. Then he'd locked up again. Tayte wondered which side of the gate he was on, and it didn't take long to find out.

When Cornell came back he passed them without speaking. He crossed the room and returned with a wooden crate and a folding metal chair, which he set down a few feet in front of them. He took off his jacket and put it over the back of the chair, revealing his shoulder holster and gun against the white of his shirt.

'I have something to show you,' he said, and he walked away again, returning with a black leather holdall. From it he produced a leather roll case, which he placed on top of the crate.

'This once belonged to a physician I know you've heard of—Dr Bartholomew Hutton.' He rolled the case open and the surgical instruments gleamed in the firelight. 'More recently it belonged to a woman called Sarah Groves. I expect you've heard of her, too.'

Tayte nodded. 'She was murdered in Sherwood Forest twenty years ago. Did you steal it before or after you cut her head off?'

That seemed to amuse Cornell. He gave a wry half-smile. 'Actually, my dad left it to me.'

'Your father?' Tayte said, considering the ramifications.

'He left me this set of mathematical instruments, too.' He produced an oak box from the holdall and opened it for Tayte and Jean to see. 'I got a similar set from Julian Davenport a few months ago.' He rummaged inside the holdall again. 'Here it is. Both sets once belonged to a man of the cloth called Charles Naismith. He gave one to each of his twin sons.'

Jean scoffed. 'And I suppose your father took that other set when he murdered Douglas Jones?'

'They were weak. All of them. When it came down to it, they lacked the conviction to do what was required of them. My dad was the only one. They gave him no choice.'

'So now you're finishing what your father began?' Tayte said.

'It became mine to finish.'

'What did?'

Cornell gave no reply. He opened the holdall again, and the sight of that novelty Prince Charles face mask as he took it out and set it to one side brought the sickening tableau of Marcus Brown's murder back to vivid life. But Tayte was given little time to dwell on it as Cornell produced what was clearly another heirloom, the polished brass glowing in his hands as he lifted it up.

'This is an altazimuth theodolite,' Cornell said, offering it up. 'It's used for surveying.'

Tayte knew what a theodolite was. 'Who did you kill for that?'

Cornell stopped admiring the craftsmanship and stared at Tayte. 'No one,' he said. 'This one's all mine. It belonged to my ancestor, Sir Stephen Henley.' He paused. 'But I did kill Alexander Walsh for this microscope,' he added as he brought it out.

'What about Peter Harper?' Tayte asked. 'What did you get from him? Why did you bring him here?'

'The final piece of the puzzle,' Cornell said. He put the microscope down, and this time he lifted an ebony and brass sextant from the holdall. He brought it closer to Tayte. 'Harper thought he was being clever,' he added. 'Thought he could scratch the markings off and that would be that.' He showed Tayte the scratch marks to prove it. 'But I think the last laugh's definitely on him, don't you?'

Tayte's eyes followed the sextant as Cornell moved away again and set it down on the box with the rest. There were six heirlooms in all, and Tayte now understood that it wasn't the objects themselves that were important to Cornell but the markings on them.

Parts of a puzzle…

He was eager to study the instruments, but he didn't think there was much chance of that now. Then Cornell said something that confirmed his thoughts.

'Too bad I have to burn them.'

Tayte drew a deep breath. 'But they must be valuable.'

Cornell looked surprised. 'Sell them?' He shook his head. 'I suppose I look stupid to you, do I?' He picked up the roll case and brought it to Tayte's side. He shouted in Tayte's ear, 'Stupid Cornell! Is that it?' He took out a scalpel and showed it to Tayte: bone handle, gleaming white metal.

'Look, what do you want from us?' Tayte asked.

Cornell fixed on him with emotionless eyes—dead eyes. 'Nothing,' he said. 'And everything—for the trouble you've caused me. You forced me to take chances I shouldn't have. You got in the way, and now we're going to have to deal with that, aren't we?'

Tayte couldn't take his eyes off that scalpel. He couldn't help but say what he was thinking.

'What are you planning to do?'

Cornell showed him.

The man moved suddenly. He grabbed a bunch of Tayte's hair and yanked his head back, bringing the scalpel close to Tayte's face, hovering the shimmering steel barely half a centimetre from his right eyeball.

'Believe me,' he said. 'You wouldn't be so keen to find out if you knew.'

Trenton McAlister's office reeked of expensive cigars and fine Scotch. With him were five notable figures—distinguished gentlemen in tailored suits, both current and former MPs and members of the House of Lords. They represented an essential and powerful network of republican support that was as useful to McAlister as the considerable sums of money they had each contributed to the cause. The Scotch and cigars had been brought out merely to pacify. McAlister's associates were not happy people.

'What the hell kind of complication?' one of the men said. He was a balding, older man in charcoal pinstripes whose words were preceded by a dense puff of smoke.

'I know only what I've told you, Brian,' McAlister said. 'That the circumstances surrounding the procurement of our 'trump card' for the coming campaign have become a tad more, shall we say, involved.'

'Are you screwing with us, Trent?'

McAlister turned to a man who was perched on the corner of his desk. 'On the contrary, Michael. In fact, it could very well work to our advantage.'

'How do you mean?'

'Haste, Michael. I mean that this little complication has merely facilitated the need for speed, as it were.'

'Did he give you a timescale?'

'Perhaps sooner than I'd hoped,' McAlister said, thinking that the next call from his contact couldn't come soon enough. The people in his office had high expectations. They were paying for results out of their own pockets. He knew that to let them down now, after building them up so high, would be to his utter ruin. His career, perhaps even his life, depended on a positive outcome. He smiled as if to show that he wasn't worried in the least.

'Well, why didn't you say that in the first place?' another man said. 'That sounds like a real reason to have a drink.'

McAlister raised his glass, thinking that he'd turned the situation around rather well. 'To the campaign,' he said.

He stepped back and watched his associates drink and smoke and talk amongst themselves. His stomach was in knots, and he knew his anxiety would remain with him until his anonymous contact called again. The man held all the cards. And yet if the things he had spoken of were true—if they could be substantiated—the scandal he would unleash would surely turn the nation to their cause.

He thought about the people and tomorrow's rally, and he reminded himself that this was surely his last and best hope of seeing Britain as a democratic republic. That was all that mattered to him now, and he didn't care how it came about—whether by fair means or foul. Although, given the asking price and the covert way the deal for this information was going down, McAlister suspected the latter.

Jefferson Tayte's heart was pounding. He tried to swallow but he couldn't. The scalpel hovering millimetres from his eye locked every muscle in his body.

'Get away from him!' Jean yelled.

To Tayte's surprise and relief, Cornell obeyed.

The man seemed to study Jean as he rose, giving her his full attention. 'You'll get your turn, bitch.' He went to her. 'We've got all the time we need, and I'm really looking forward to it.' He straddled her legs and sat on them, pinning them down. From his trouser pocket he produced a rag, which he stuffed into her mouth. 'But I don't want to hear another word from you until I say so. You got that?'

He got up and put the roll case back onto the crate with the other heirlooms, setting the scalpel down beside it in clear, intimidating view. Then he went to the fire, which by now was blazing, making the room hot despite the broken windows. He threw another bag of coal onto the flames, and with a length of iron he worked it into the white heat at the base.

Tayte looked at Jean and then at the tormented figure of Peter Harper again. He thought about the recording Fable had played them—how Alexander Walsh had been beaten with a towel rail before Cornell killed him, and all while his wife and children listened in the next room. Robert Cornell was a sick man, no doubt about it. He wondered how he could spare Jean the ordeal he knew was coming if Fable couldn't figure out where they were.

Cornell came back to the chair and the collection of heirlooms. 'Soon be hot enough,' he said. 'I'll get started on you two afterwards.' He laughed to himself. 'And to think I'm getting paid for this.'

He removed something from inside his jacket. He showed it to Tayte. It was a slip of folded paper, white on one side, blue and patterned on the other. On the clear side, Tayte read an unfamiliar name and saw several numbers and the word 'Payroll.'

'That's right,' Cornell said. 'Mark Jennings. Who the hell's he?' He put the pay slip away. 'I thought it best not to give my employer my real name, so no one can trace me to this place. I thought I'd show you, because I don't want you to think the cavalry's coming. I want you to know how hopeless your situation is, and I want to feel your despair before I get to work on you.'

Tayte snorted. 'That's a little melodramatic, don't you think?'

Without warning, Cornell brought the flat of his hand hard up into Tayte's face, sending the back of his head into the wall. Tayte tasted blood. He coughed and spat onto the dusty ground. Then he smiled defiantly at Cornell, blood in his teeth.

'Tell me about the markings,' he said. 'On the heirlooms. You're going to kill me anyway. Don't I have a right to know why?'

'You don't have any rights,' Cornell said. 'Not in here. As far as you're concerned this is hell and I'm the devil.'

He went back to the fire and stirred it again.

'Tell me about Quo Veritas,' Tayte persisted. 'What did they stand for? Something to do with Queen Anne, right? Is this a royal heir hunt? Is that really it?'

Cornell stopped stirring the fire. He took the iron out and inspected it before thrusting it back into the coals. Then he rose, turning suddenly. He grabbed the microscope and brought it close to Tayte's face.

'Is this what you want to see?'

Beside Cornell's finger at the base of the microscope, Tayte saw a line of digits. Numbers without meaning.

'Binary numbers,' he said under his breath.

Cornell put the microscope back and snatched up his forefather's theodolite. 'Here's another. See?'

He held the theodolite in front of Tayte long enough for him to see that there were four binary digits engraved on the brass. This time he noticed a single decimal number tagged to the end.

'Do you want to know how the heirlooms survived?' Cornell said. 'How they remained with their respective families for three hundred years?'

Tayte nodded. That many years represented around ten generations.

'It was very simple. Each descendant had an obligation to fulfil. All they had to do was have a child who would inherit each heirloom. If one of the descendants didn't produce an heir, his life was forfeit—and there were five others whose duty it was to take it, to ensure the digits were passed on. You never leave Quo Veritas.'

'So the society was run less out of loyalty to a cause than out of fear of death?'

'It was merely a safeguard. Loyalty was enough most of the time—until *his* generation.' Cornell pointed at the bloodied figure in the corner of the room. 'Twenty years ago, when the time came to act, every inner member was tested, and all but one was found wanting.'

'Your father?' Tayte said.

Cornell nodded. 'It became my family's duty to do what had to be done—to gather the heirlooms and bring the digits together.' Cornell turned away. 'But what can any of this mean to you?'

It meant that with the heirlooms now gathered, the string of binary digits Cornell and his father had collected from their victims was complete. That left Tayte wondering, what next? What did Cornell believe had to be done? How did he mean to use the digits, and to what end? A treasonable end, Tayte supposed—one that threatened Britain's national security.

'The digits mean nothing to you!' Cornell continued, aggravation in his tone, but he was wrong.

'It's an ahnentafel number,' Tayte said.

He recalled that as well as being keen on mathematics and heraldic studies, the Reverend Charles Naismith was also a genealogist, by royal appointment for a time. In light of what else Tayte knew, he understood that this binary code could be nothing else. The decimal number at the end merely denoted the order in which that piece of the ahnentafel code fitted in with the rest. And if Jean was right about Quo Veritas and their purpose, it was an ahnentafel number that pointed to Queen Anne's heir.

But why?

If such an heir existed and could be found, Tayte wondered what Cornell expected to do with him—or her. What was his end game? Tayte didn't know, and right now he couldn't think straight, partly because in light of their current situation it seemed academic to him anyway, but mostly because Cornell had started throwing the heirlooms into the fire. He was clearly destroying them not only to obliterate the digits they had carried all these years but also because they were incriminating evidence against him—evidence he would have been foolish to keep or try to sell, as he had earlier intimated. Tayte watched the penultimate piece fall into the flames, where it burned and began to melt with the rest, thinking that Cornell must have recorded the digits elsewhere.

'I take it you wrote all those numbers down first?' he said. It was stating the obvious, but he wanted to know they had another chance to see them if they ever got out of that room alive.

Cornell turned away from the fire, his face red from the heat. He tapped the side of his head.

'You memorised them?' Tayte quickly did the maths: six heirlooms, four binary digits inscribed on each. 'You memorised all twenty-four digits?'

Cornell smiled but there was nothing pleasant about it. 'I've had a long time to remember most of it. Zeros and ones. It's not like there are many actual numbers to remember, is it?'

He picked up the last of the heirlooms. It was the roll case of surgical instruments. Leaving the scalpel behind, he squatted between Tayte and Jean and slowly introduced the other pieces to them, leaving them to imagine how he might use them. Then he drew a deep breath and stood up again.

'You know what? Sod it,' he said as he tossed the roll case into the fire. He pulled out his gun and came at Tayte like he was going to hit him with it, but he paused instead and pressed it to Tayte's forehead. 'I think I'll just shoot the pair of you instead. I've got important things to do.'

Tayte swallowed hard and clenched his jaw. His head was shaking without awareness as Cornell twisted the muzzle of the gun into his skin. Tayte's head was so far back against the wall now that he was staring at the ceiling. Beside him he heard Jean yell something indiscernible into her gag.

'At least my life has purpose,' Cornell said. 'Can you say the same thing about yours?'

Tayte thought about that; anything to take his mind off that gun. What had he done with his life? He figured then that he'd wasted most of it feeling sorry for himself because he didn't have the family he yearned for. Where was his real flesh and blood mother? His father? Did he have a brother or a sister somewhere? What about *his* family history?

That was it.

He'd spent most of his life looking for ghosts, and you can't find ghosts, right?

Wrong.

His conviction couldn't have been stronger. At times it had bordered on unhealthy obsession. They weren't ghosts. He'd only ever called them that when he wanted an excuse to stop trying. He silently cursed Cornell for giving him cause to question himself. He began to push back against the muzzle of the gun with a new sense of defiance. His life had as much purpose as any life. Who did this arrogant son of a bitch think he was to presume otherwise? He began to struggle with the cable ties again. Then he heard Jean's voice.

'Leave him alone!'

She'd managed to spit her gag out and now Cornell turned on her. He stood over her and put the gun to her head.

'If there's anything you want to say to your girlfriend, I'd suggest you do it now.'

Tayte saw the fear in Jean's eyes as they stared at one another. He was shaking his head, unable to think or say anything.

'Too late,' Cornell added.

Then he paused just long enough to take in the sense of utter helplessness that had washed over Tayte before he smiled and pulled the trigger.

⁓

Jack Fable was sitting in his office, breaking the occupational health and safety law that prohibited smoking in the workplace. Tanner could shit on him all he wanted over it; he didn't care. It was his office and he was the only person in the damn thing. Usually he stood by the window when he needed a covert puff, but he didn't have time for that now. He was breaking the law for several reasons that all seemed perfectly reasonable to him. He was disappointed that the phone trace on Jean Summer's mobile had come up empty, and he was angry with himself for not being able to procure a single lead that could tell him where she or Tayte or Robert Cornell were. He had people on the streets where Cornell lived, visiting the pubs and shops with photographs, asking questions, but he wasn't holding his breath.

Like looking for piss in a bathtub, he thought.

Several folders and loose sheets of A4 cluttered his desk. An MoD file painted a far from exemplary picture of Robert Cornell, who began service as an officer cadet, receiving training at Sandhurst before gaining his commission as second lieutenant, which Fable figured was mostly on account of his highly decorated father. Cornell junior, on the other hand, had been in trouble for fighting and bullying on several occasions before being busted back to the regular soldier ranks, ultimately being discharged for misconduct during the occupation of Iraq. No specific details about the nature of his misconduct were provided.

After that, Robert Cornell had been a London bus driver for a few years, and for the last two he'd been unemployed, claiming benefit, which to Fable's mind made the man a bum; he figured he could have continued working as a bus driver somewhere, but it seemed he had chosen not to bother. When it came to the killer Fable was looking for, Robert Cornell's profile was an ideal match.

All he had to do now was find him.

And his brother.

Joseph Cornell, like Robert, was a single man who had served in the British army, but that was where any similarity between them ended. Joseph had served his full term, and judging from his military record, Fable was sure that his father would have been very proud of him. Flying colours was an understatement as far as Joseph's career was concerned. And yet he was perhaps the main reason Fable was chain-smoking in his office. He couldn't find Joseph either. He wasn't at home and he wasn't at work. But it was where he worked—and for whom—that really bothered the detective.

It was all there in the internal profile on his desk. Joseph Cornell currently worked for the Metropolitan Police in SO14: Specialist Operations Royalty Protection Branch. Another sheet of A4 somewhere in the jumble of papers told him that he'd been present at the first briefing Fable had given in that very building less than thirty-six hours ago. He stared at Joseph's photo ID again. He recalled seeing him. He was the tall SO14 supervisor with the severe crew cut who had spouted a mouthful of questions he hadn't been able to answer.

As far as any of his records were concerned, there wasn't a single black mark against him. If anything, Joseph Cornell was too good to be true.

Fable knew he couldn't arbitrarily tar both brothers with the same brush. On paper at least, he was looking at opposites—one good, the other far from it. Maybe their lives today were just as contradictory, but he knew from the photographs he'd seen at the house in Clapton that they had been close at one time. Either way, he supposed Joseph would know where to find his brother, and right now he was the only lead Fable was interested in. And while he didn't know where he was, he knew where he was going to be. He was rostered on duty in two hours' time.

Click!

Cornell pulled the trigger but nothing happened. He stepped away from Jean, laughing. 'You should have seen your face,' he said to Tayte. 'There's no round in the chamber.' He held the gun up and purposefully racked the slide, making sure he had all Tayte's attention. Then he took aim and fired two shots at the wall above Tayte's head, making him cower as fragments of brick showered the room. This time the sound was deafening.

Cornell laughed again. 'Oops, there is now, but don't worry about the noise. No one else can hear us.' He went to Tayte and pulled his head back again. 'No more Russian roulette,' he added. 'The next one's for real, and if it's any consolation I'm going to spare your girlfriend for now. She's too pretty to waste so soon.'

Cornell was trying to force the gun into Tayte's mouth when the boiler house door swung open and a man in a beige mac walked in. It was Michel Levant, and he was seemingly unfazed by the bloodstained body in the corner of the room.

Cornell froze, his face expressionless as Levant took a step closer and fired a Taser gun at him. Two wire coils streaked across the room and fixed into Cornell's chest. His face twisted and contorted as his muscles locked and went into spasm. A second later he fell to the ground, kicking up the dust.

Tayte's jaw dropped. What was Levant doing there? He had just about given up any hope of a rescue, but Michel Levant? He was the last person Tayte expected to see.

Levant dropped the Taser and sprang at the crate where the heirlooms had been. The scalpel was still there and he grabbed it and proceeded to cut Jean's bonds.

'Amazing what you can pick up these days,' the Frenchman said, indicating the discarded Taser.

He went to free Tayte, and as Jean stood up Cornell began to groan and stir. She went for the Taser gun to give him another blast while the wires were still attached, but Levant stopped her.

'It's only good for one charge.'

Cornell was suddenly on his feet, still dazed and unsteady. He flicked the Taser darts off his chest and Jean didn't waste a second. She ran at him screaming.

'What have you done with my son?'

She crashed into him and he staggered back, but he stopped himself, recovering fast. Tayte was on his feet then. His eyes quickly found the gun on the floor where Cornell had dropped it. He saw that Cornell was looking right at it.

'Jean, be careful!' he called, and as he and Cornell went for the gun together, Jean charged Cornell a second time.

'Tell me!' she screamed.

She knocked Cornell back. Tayte reached the gun and took aim but Jean was in the way. He watched Cornell throw a loose punch like a brawling drunk, and Jean easily avoided the blow that came with such force that in his unbalanced state it spun Cornell around. Then with all her adrenaline-fuelled anger and hatred for the man who had come so close to ending their lives, Jean kicked him hard in the side and sent him tripping over the pipework and the rubble.

'Jean! Get down!' Tayte called.

She turned to him. He had the gun trained on Cornell, and given what that man had put them through, he knew he would have no hesitation pulling the trigger. But he didn't have to. Cornell was caught up in his own momentum, unable to steady himself on the debris that littered the ground. Tayte lowered the gun, staring wide-eyed as he watched Cornell trip and fall headlong into the fire. The mesh grate collapsed under his weight as he landed, and the white-hot coals fell in around him and began to consume him.

Cornell made no sound as he burned.

His back arched impossibly as he twisted and thrashed in the flames, kicking hot, smoking coals from the makeshift grate that had now ensnared him. As Tayte reached Jean, all he could think about was her son and the ahnentafel number—both of which now appeared to be lost to them. Out of humanity Tayte tried to grab the man's boot, thinking to pull him out, but the heat from the flames, augmented now by Cornell himself, was too intense. In just a few seconds it was too late.

Cornell was dead.

Jean stepped back with her hands to her mouth. 'Elliot,' she said. 'What have I done?' Her voice was tiny, almost lost in the hiss of the fire and the roar of the flames in the chimney.

Tayte put an arm around her and turned her away. 'It was an accident. You didn't mean to kill him.'

Jean kept shaking her head.

'And we'll find your son,' Tayte added, leading her away from the heat.

As they approached Levant, who had backed away towards the door, Tayte saw Jean's personal effects and his own wallet in the rubble where Cornell had thrown them. He gathered them up and returned Jean's things to her: motorbike keys and disc lock, lipstick and hairbrush. The Frenchman was still staring at the flames when they arrived beside him, an expression of disbelief hanging limp on his face.

'Thank you, Mr Levant,' Jean said, snapping him out of the daze he was in.

Tayte still couldn't understand how Levant came to be there, but he figured there was plenty of time to ask. Right now all he wanted to do was get out of there.

'Do you have a phone?'

'Oui, of course, but—'

'Are the police on their way?'

'No,' Levant said. He took his phone out and showed them why. The display was blank. 'The battery's dead. I must have forgotten to charge it last night.'

Tayte made for the door, taking Jean with him. 'The cab driver should have one,' he said. 'We'll use that.'

'What about the key,' Levant said. 'For the gate?'

Tayte stopped. 'It's locked?'

Levant nodded and Tayte eyed him with scepticism.

'Just how come you're here, Levant? And how did you get in if the gate's locked?'

Levant sighed. 'Ah, I must confess. I've been following you. Just like I followed dear Marcus. That's why I was at Rules Restaurant the day he was murdered.'

Tayte asked why. He had a good idea, but he wanted to hear it from Levant.

'Marcus was on to something. I knew it. Something big. Now you know it too, eh? I've been following you since Kew this morning. You were on the news last night.'

Jean cut in. 'Well, Mr Levant. I for one am glad you were following us.' She shot Tayte a glare.

He sighed. 'Yeah, I guess some thanks are in order. But I'd still like to know how you got in if the gate's locked.' He eyed Levant's slight and feeble frame. 'I know you didn't climb that barbed fence.'

Levant pursed his lips and smiled playfully. 'No, of course not. The taxi I followed you in stopped at the end of the cul-de-sac. By the time I walked up to the gates, you were gone and the gate was open. I went through and saw you coming from the main building, so I hid behind the portacabin. When I heard that gunshot I had to do something.'

Tayte wished he'd done it sooner. 'You always carry a Taser around with you?'

Levant shrugged. 'Personal protection,' he said. 'It's more effective than Mace, and I'm afraid I would be quite ineffective in a fistfight.'

'I'm going to get one myself,' Jean said. 'Now can you leave Mr Levant alone so we can get the keys and get out of here?'

Tayte considered himself scolded again. He went to the jacket that was still on the back of the folding chair. 'I hope they weren't in his trousers pocket,' he said as he picked the jacket up and shook it. It rattled. The keys were there.

'What about a phone?' Levant said. 'Maybe he had one?'

Tayte gave a slow nod. 'I saw him with it at the house.'

He went through all the pockets and found it. Battery good. Signal good. He checked the call history, wondering whether Cornell was the loner type he imagined him to be or whether he was working with anyone else.

'No calls,' he said. 'Not a single one, in or out.'

'Odd,' Jean said. 'What about text messages?'

Tayte checked. 'Nothing,' he said. 'It's like the phone's never been used. Unless he deleted everything as he went.'

Levant was suddenly close beside Tayte, looking at the phone's display. 'Maybe the police will find something, no?'

'Maybe,' Tayte said. He stepped away to put some space between them. Then he made for the door again. 'It's too damn hot in here. I'll call Fable outside.'

He reached the door and froze when he heard a sound from the opposite corner of the room. It seemed barely human but he knew it had to be. It came from Peter Harper. He was still alive.

Chapter Sixteen

By the time the police interviews were over, it was gone seven, and during the hours that had passed since Tayte and Jean had been liberated from their own private hell, Tayte had had plenty of time for reflection. Foremost on his mind was Marcus Brown. His death might have been avenged, but the void Robert Cornell had created inside him when he took his friend's life was still there, eating away at him, and he knew it wouldn't stop until he fully understood why his friend was dead. To achieve that he had to finish Marcus's research, but the ahnentafel number—the binary digits Cornell had memorised—was gone. Knowing that only served to make the hole inside him bigger.

Tayte caught up with Jean again outside one of the statement rooms at New Scotland Yard where he'd given his account of the events following his arrival at Robert Cornell's home. Jean had been through the same mill, both having had to relive those hours of their lives they would sooner forget, and it wasn't until the police arrived at the construction site that Jean was made aware of the full implications of her actions against their captor. She'd been told there would be an inquest into Cornell's death, but DI Fable, who had led the interviews, told her not to worry. A man was dead and there was a process to follow, but he didn't expect anything to come of it.

'We need to talk,' Fable said as soon as he joined them in the corridor. 'I can see you're tired, Mr Tayte, and you must be too, Ms

Summer, but it won't take long. Think you can give me another half hour?'

'Of course,' Jean said.

Tayte just gave a weary nod and they followed Fable to his office via a lift, grabbing coffee along the way. Through the office windows Tayte saw that the sun had all but set, slowly relinquishing the day to night and the bright city lights. Westminster Abbey, the Houses of Parliament, and Big Ben were all lit up beyond the framed glass like a nightscape painting.

'Take a seat,' Fable said. He lifted something up from beneath his desk and turned to Tayte. 'I thought you might want this back.'

'My briefcase.'

'It was found in the back of the taxi.'

Tayte smiled as he opened it and looked inside. Battered and travel-worn as it was, he figured it had fared better than he had that afternoon. Everything seemed to be as he'd left it.

'Thanks,' he said. 'Much appreciated.'

'Here, take this too,' Fable said. 'Before I forget.' He took a mobile phone from his pocket. 'It's just a loan so we can keep in touch. It's got Internet if you need it. I couldn't get you a laptop.'

Tayte took it. It was a BlackBerry, like the one Jean used to have. He eyed the tiny keyboard and the size of his fingers and figured she would have to do the typing if they wanted to look anything up.

'Business use only,' Fable added. 'I don't want to see any calls back home to the States on the bill when it comes through.'

'No problem,' Tayte said, thinking that there was no danger of that given that he didn't have anyone back home to call.

There was a pencil sharpener fixed to the end of the desk by Jean's elbow. She studied it as she spun the handle slowly around. When she stopped she looked up at Fable.

'Do you think I'm ever going to see my son again?'

The many rivulets on Fable's face deepened into chasms as he turned to her. He was an honest man and he gave her an honest answer. 'Right now, I don't know,' he said. 'I wish I had something more encouraging for you. I'm sorry.'

Jean just nodded.

'I have recovered something of yours, though,' Fable said. 'Your bike. It was illegally parked outside the Star Café in Clapton. Don't worry. I had it taken to the hotel.'

Jean thanked him. 'And what happened to Mr Levant?'

Tayte wanted to hear the answer to that, too. He thought the Frenchman was probably waiting for them outside.

'He's long gone,' Fable said. 'We had to caution him for the Taser—that's now the property of Her Majesty's government. After his interview he was released with the thanks of the Metropolitan Police Service. Last I saw, he was talking to the news people camped outside. They were all over him.' He sighed. 'I'll give the wolves a statement later this evening.'

'And Peter Harper?' Tayte said. 'Did he make it?'

'So far, but don't hold your breath. He's in bad shape.'

'What did Cornell do to him?' Tayte asked, curiosity getting the better of him in light of the kind of treatment he might otherwise have been in for.

'You don't want to know, Mr Tayte—believe me, you don't. He's lost a lot of blood, though. Would have bled to death before much longer if things hadn't turned out the way they did.'

'Will he live?' Jean said.

'I'm no doctor, Ms Summer. All I can tell you is that he's critical. The next couple of hours will decide which way it goes.'

'We need to talk to him,' Tayte said.

He didn't mean to sound so cold about it, but now that Robert Cornell was dead, Harper was the last remaining descendant of the five Royal Society Fellows. He was perhaps the only person alive who could tell them what was going on and why.

'We're just as keen to talk to him as you are,' Fable said. He paused, took out a packet of cigarettes, looked at Tayte and Jean, and put them away again. 'Look, I'd normally be celebrating at this point in an investigation. Cornell is dead. We have his firearm and it won't take long to match it to the murders, but there's a complication that's bugging the hell out of me—Joseph Cornell.'

'You think the brother's involved?' Tayte said, thinking that the last thing they needed now was another menace from the same gene pool as Robert Cornell. He'd seen Joseph's name on the census, but the possibility of a double act hadn't crossed his mind until now.

'I can't rule it out,' Fable said. 'Particularly since I discovered he works in Royalty Protection. There may be others for all I know. He didn't show for duty this evening, and no one he works with has seen him since his last shift ended early this morning.'

That information crashed through Tayte's mind like a tsunami. He stared at Fable, thinking hard.

'I've had his access suspended,' Fable continued. 'His house has been searched, and we're monitoring his banking activity. Our nation is the most surveilled in the world. Three million cameras and counting—that's around ten percent of the world's total. He's been clever enough to leave his car at home or we'd have picked that up by now, but many of these cameras also have face recognition software. Our eyes are everywhere, so to speak. When Joseph Cornell pokes his head up, we'll find him.'

Tayte was only half listening. He was busy connecting the information Fable had just imparted about Joseph Cornell and where he worked with Jean's theory about Queen Anne's heir and Marcus Brown's dying words: *Treason…Hurry*. He ran through the implications. If Joseph Cornell was involved, what was his role? He had access to the royal premises—probably to the royal family. Was this the treasonable act his friend had perceived? Was there a plot to somehow resurrect the Royal House of Stuart—a twenty-first century Jacobite uprising? It seemed too wild an idea to contemplate.

'Jean was in Nottinghamshire this morning,' Tayte said, knowing that Fable was missing a vital piece of the jigsaw. He turned to Jean and saw his own concerns about Joseph Cornell reflected back. 'She was digging deeper into Quo Veritas.'

'Did you find anything?' Fable asked.

'I found a theory,' Jean said. 'It puts a three-hundred-year-old royal heir hunt at the centre of your murder investigation. It could be the motive for the murders and the executions in Sherwood Forest twenty years ago.'

'Peter Harper may be able to confirm it,' Tayte said. 'Couple that with what you've just told us about Joseph Cornell and where he works, and I think the threat to your national security is pretty clear.'

Fable was making fists with his hands, either because he was tense or because he needed a cigarette. It was probably both. 'I hope to Christ you're wrong,' he said. Then his sour expression changed to one of incredulity. 'But supposing you're right. What could they have hoped to achieve?'

'Does it matter?' Jean offered.

Tayte agreed. 'I can tell you from personal experience that Robert Cornell believed in what he was doing, one hundred percent. He had a plan and he was going through with it, whatever the outcome.'

'But Robert Cornell's gone,' Fable said. 'And this ahnentafel number you mentioned in the interview—that's gone too, hasn't it?'

'One way or another I literally saw it burn,' Tayte said.

'So maybe the threat died with Cornell,' Jean added.

Fable laughed sourly. 'I won't believe that until I've found his brother.'

'No,' Tayte said. 'I guess I won't either.'

A rap of knuckles on the open door behind Tayte drew his attention. A man in a brown sports jacket and chinos was standing in the doorway. He had a thick caterpillar moustache under his nose and a pale blue folder under his arm. He didn't wait to be invited in.

'Phone report, sir,' he said, holding up the folder.

'This is Detective Sergeant Harris,' Fable said.

Harris gave Tayte and Jean a cursory smile as he slid the folder onto the desk.

'Anything there?' Fable asked, opening it.

'The phone was unregistered.'

'Surprise, surprise.'

'Apart from the call Mr Tayte made earlier today,' Harris said, 'no other voice calls were made or received, but the service provider did manage to recover a number of text messages from their records. They were all sent between Robert Cornell's phone and one other number.'

'I suppose that was unregistered, too,' Fable said.

'It was. Most of the texts look like garbage, as you'll see, but there's a few in there you'll find interesting. Everything's in the SMS log exactly how they sent it through. Chronological order.'

Fable was already reading the contents. 'Thank you, Harris,' he said, and when Harris didn't leave, Fable looked up at him. 'Something to add?'

'There's more to it, sir,' Harris said. 'We found a mobile phone at Joseph Cornell's house. I don't know why it wasn't picked up earlier. The memory's been wiped, but the number matches with the other number on the report.'

'Interesting,' Fable said. 'Any prints?'

'None, sir. The phone's been wiped, too. The lab found traces of a chemical residue commonly used to clean computer screens—isopropyl alcohol.'

Fable nodded to himself. 'Let me know when anything else turns up,' he said. 'Preferably Joseph Cornell.'

As Harris left, Fable turned his attention back to the log. 'There's a text here dated three months ago,' he said. 'Julian Davenport's address in Bermondsey.' He flicked through a few pages. 'Here's another more recently for the Exeter murder.' He turned another page. 'And here's Peter Harper's address in Surrey. That text was sent less than twenty-four hours ago. Not long before Harper was abducted.'

Jean leant in on her elbows. Her hands were knotted in front of her. 'So Robert Cornell was definitely working with his brother?' she said. Her voice had an urgency to it, and Tayte understood why. It meant there was still hope for Elliot.

'Looks that way,' Fable said. He paused. 'Your address is here, too,' he added, skipping another page. 'And Carlton House Terrace. That was sent to Robert Cornell yesterday morning.'

'The Royal Society,' Tayte said. 'No surprise then that he was waiting for us when we left.' He tried to peer at the log. 'What's on the pages you keep skipping?'

'The garbage, I guess,' Fable said. 'That's all the actual messages there are.'

'Mind if I take a look?'

Fable spun the log around. Between the text messages providing the names and addresses of Robert Cornell's victims were a number of texts containing a single numeric character. The majority were zeros and ones, and Tayte instantly saw them for what they were. He felt goose bumps ripple across his skin.

'It's the ahnentafel number,' he said. He counted the digits, including the decimal numbers that denoted the order. There were thirty in total. 'Is there someplace nearby where we can eat? I get the feeling this is going to be another long night and I'm no good on an empty stomach. The ahnentafel number looks complete.'

'Christ,' Fable said. 'And it's been sent to Joseph Cornell.' He lowered his head into his hands, the implied threat rekindled. 'This thing isn't over at all, is it?'

'No, it's not,' Tayte said, recalling that Robert Cornell had told him it was only just beginning.

Chapter Seventeen

The restaurant DI Fable took them to was an Italian place he sometimes frequented called Franco's. It was a three-minute walk from his office, and during that time Fable smoked four cigarettes and didn't say a word. Tayte thought the place struck a fine balance between authentic Italian and touristy: the staff looked Italian, the vinyl tablecloths looked like draped Italian flags, and there was a Dean Martin CD playing in the background. The tables, topped with Chianti bottle candle holders, were nearly all occupied, and the air was lively to the extent that you could talk without having to whisper or worry about being overheard. Jean sat opposite Fable, and Tayte sat on the end beside her with the folder containing the SMS logs occupying the only vacant place setting. They ordered their meals and Fable just asked for a cup of coffee.

'Don't you eat?' Tayte asked him, helping himself to the bread and olives. The air was heavy with the smell of basil and garlic and simmering tomato-based sauces. It made his stomach groan.

Fable smiled. 'It has been known,' he said. 'But coffee's good for now.' He indicated the folder. 'So what exactly have we got here? Some kind of map to a royal heir?'

'It could be,' Tayte said. 'If Jean's theory stacks up.' He opened the folder. 'Looking at how Cornell sent these digits, I'd say it was about as safe a way to do it as there is. These text messages wouldn't mean a thing to anyone who didn't know exactly what they were looking for—just garbage, as your colleague said.'

He flicked through the sheets. 'According to the time stamps, Robert Cornell sent the first three blocks of numbers to the phone that was found at his brother's home one digit at a time over the three-month period since Davenport was murdered.'

'Three blocks?' Fable said.

Tayte nodded. 'There were already two victims from the Sherwood Forest murders twenty years ago—Douglas Jones and Sarah Groves. Davenport was number three.'

'Right,' Fable said.

Jean stabbed an olive with a cocktail stick and hovered it near her mouth. 'There was no point letting the numbers he already had go any sooner.'

Tayte held up one of the sheets of paper. 'After Robert Cornell received Alexander Walsh's address in Exeter, we see five more texts—four binary numbers followed by the decimal number two.' He found another sheet, studied it, and offered it up. 'Then late yesterday afternoon there's a text with Peter Harper's details. And just this morning, five more digits were sent in separate text messages an hour or so apart.'

He lifted out the last sheet in the log. 'These last five digits must be Robert Cornell's, or maybe it's the other way round. It doesn't matter. We have the decimal sequence numbers. All we have to do is reassemble the digits in the right order based on the number at the end of each block.'

'So after all that, he went and put all his eggs in one basket,' Fable said.

'In a manner of speaking, yes,' Tayte said. 'He had to. While he had us tied up he intimated that he'd found the descendants the same way we did. But clearly he couldn't do the genealogy required to find his victims or to understand the ahnentafel number itself once it had been compiled. He had to trust someone who could.'

'Which is where his brother comes in,' Fable said.

Tayte had been thinking about that. The other phone found at Joseph Cornell's house was hard to ignore, but it didn't add up.

'I don't doubt that Joseph Cornell's involved, given what we know. But unless there's something you've not told us, I don't think he's a genealogist, is he?'

'No, I don't believe so,' Fable said. 'Not much call for that in the military or the police service. Maybe it was a hobby?'

'Any related material found at his home? Any books on the subject? Records or certificates?'

'Not that I'm aware of.'

'I didn't think so. Working through ten generations as we had to at Kew takes a lot of expertise, and it would be hard to do all that and not leave a trail.'

Their drinks arrived and Tayte held on to the waitress's arm as he downed his cola and ordered another.

Jean sipped her wine. 'You think Michel Levant's involved, don't you?'

Tayte gathered from her tone and from recent conversations that she thought he was on some personal crusade to discredit the man who had just saved their lives. Maybe he was, but not without good reason, to his mind.

'What if the brother was just the middleman?' Tayte said.

Fable went for the sugar. 'Something as sensitive to Robert Cornell as this? Why involve more people than he needed to? Brother or not.'

'I don't know why Joseph Cornell had the other phone at his home,' Tayte said. 'But they needed an expert genealogist—or a damn good heir hunter. I don't see how it could be anyone else.'

Fable poured two sachets of sugar into his coffee and slowly stirred it in. When he looked up again, there was a subtle flick at the corner of his mouth as though something had amused him.

'Joseph Cornell looks guilty as hell from where I'm sitting,' he said. 'There's the phone and the fact that he's doing a grand job of staying off our radar. And if you're looking for a genealogist to point the finger at, I might remind you that there are a great many in London just now. How many did you say turned up at Kew? Forty or so, wasn't it? Then there's all those experts at the convention who couldn't make it. What exactly do you think you've got on Levant anyway?'

Tayte took a deep breath and held on to it, thinking. 'He was at the restaurant when Marcus Brown was murdered. They had an uncomfortable conversation just before the shooting. I told you about that at the interview afterwards.'

'And Levant told me they were old friends, catching up. Did you actually hear the conversation?'

Tayte shook his head. 'No, I didn't. But we know Levant was interested in Marcus's work. He told us as much after the interviews. So why else *is* he so interested?'

'You told me he's a probate genealogist. Maybe he got a sniff of something that made him curious.'

'Yeah,' Tayte said. 'So curious that he's been tracking our movements from the start.' He put his hand on the SMS logs. 'Now we've got text messages feeding Robert Cornell our locations—places where Levant saw us go and where Cornell subsequently attacked us.'

'It doesn't mean Levant sent the messages,' Fable said. 'Believe me, Robert's brother Joseph is more than qualified to have kept you under very close personal surveillance if he wanted to.'

'Well, what about that gallant rescue?' Tayte offered. 'All by himself? A man like that? I mean, come on.'

'Aren't all rescues gallant by definition?'

Tayte shook his head. He was losing this and he knew it. 'And I don't buy Levant's suggestion that he carries a Taser around in his pants,' he said. 'I don't buy it any more than I believe he forgot to charge his cell phone, for Christ's sake.'

'What you believe is entirely irrelevant,' Fable said. He paused. 'Look, I don't mean to give you a hard time, but you don't have a damn thing on Michel Levant, do you?'

'What about hunches?' Tayte said. 'You told me yourself you like to run with them.'

Fable knocked his coffee back. 'Yes, I do. And they can lead to solid results. You might be right about Levant, but we can't go after him with what you've just told me. As far as the outside world is concerned, he single-handedly saved the lives of the people who identified a cold-bloodied killer and took one more scumbag off the streets. The man's a hero. That's what everyone will be reading in the papers tomorrow morning.'

He sat back heavily in his seat and pinched his eyes. 'Look, I'm sorry,' he added. 'Like I said, I don't mean to give you a hard time, but you can leave the detective work to me. If Levant's involved, he'll slip up somewhere. And when he does, I'll be right in his face.' He tapped the SMS log. 'This ahnentafel number. That's your priority, and since it's complete and we know it's out there, we need to solve it first.'

Tayte bit his lip and let it go. As frustrated as he felt, he knew Fable was right, and he could hardly mistake the message he was sending him. *Stick to what you're good at, Tayte.* He went back to the folder. His notepad was still in the rubble where Robert Cornell had thrown it for all he knew, so he borrowed Fable's pad and wrote down all thirty numbers in the order they had been sent. Then he wrote the binary numbers down again in the order dictated by the decimal sequence number that followed each binary block.

'Six descendants and six four-digit binary segments,' he said. 'That's twenty-four digits and twenty-three generations.'

'So where do you start with something like that?' Fable asked.

Tayte looked at the binary string. He offered it up. 1100 0100 0011 1000 0011 1000. 'We start with the first digit,' he said. 'In this case, that's the hard part. It's the seed. Always the number one, it represents our subject—the descendant.'

'Another descendant?' Fable said.

Tayte nodded and pointed to the last digit in the string. 'Although it's this ancestor we're interested in for now. The zero tells us it's a male, twenty-three generations back from the subject. But that's all it tells us. Right now I've no idea what century either was born in, let alone whose family tree they belong to.'

Fable sighed so hard that Tayte could smell the coffee and tobacco on his breath.

'By definition,' he continued, 'a secret heir would have to have been brought up by a family that only a handful of people knew about—like our five Fellows of the Royal Society. We're running with the theory that this ahnentafel number will identify that bloodline, and in doing so will point to Queen Anne's heir. But we need to know the bloodline in the first place.'

'The chicken and egg scenario?' Fable said.

'It looks that way, but there has to be an answer. It just needs some thought and a clear head. I've told you how things look, but I can't be seeing it right.'

The food arrived and Tayte thought the nourishment would help. He watched it land, took a little black pepper and Parmesan cheese with his spaghetti bolognese, and dove right in. There was no need to tuck his napkin in. His shirt and suit couldn't get much dirtier.

Fable gathered the SMS logs into the folder. He tore the page Tayte had been writing on from his notepad and handed it to him. 'So, you've got all you need from the logs?'

Tayte nodded, concentrating on the food that tasted as good to him as any condemned man's last meal. The ahnentafel number was laid out in binary on the scrap of paper. It wasn't going to be easy to work it out, but everything he had to go on was there.

Fable's phone rang inside his jacket. 'Good,' he said, getting up to take the call. 'Just remember that we need to get there first.'

Tayte watched Fable go and saw he had a cigarette in his mouth by the time he reached the door. As soon as he was outside, he lit it awkwardly and pressed his phone to his ear as the cigarette began to dance in time with his conversation. Tayte turned back to Jean and noticed she'd hardly touched her food although her wine was long gone.

'How are you holding up?' he asked her. 'It's gone kind of quiet over there.'

Jean tried a smile. 'I've been away with my thoughts, that's all. I'll snap out of it in a minute.'

'I hope so,' Tayte said. 'I think I'm getting to like the sound of your voice. I missed it.' He paused. 'So you're not suffering from post-traumatic stress or anything like that?'

'I don't think so.'

'No, I guess not—tough biker chick like you.'

That made her smile. 'I don't think anyone's ever called me a chick before. Even when I was young enough to be one.'

'Really? We say it all the time back home.'

'You personally?'

Tayte laughed at that idea. 'No, not me. But people do, gener- ally. Or they did back when I was in high school. I think kids have an entirely different vocabulary now.'

'I know,' Jean said in such a way that Tayte knew he'd brought her thoughts back to Elliot again.

He locked eyes with her and gently squeezed her hand. 'We'll find him,' he told her for the second time that day, having no real understanding as to how he would make that happen, knowing only that he must.

Jean's pensive smile seemed to thank him for his kindness. 'Anyway,' she said, sounding a little brighter. 'How are you holding up? You're the one who just got a grilling off the detective inspector.'

Tayte snorted. 'We've both been through a whole lot worse than that today, don't you think?' He laughed. 'He was kind of grouchy though, wasn't he?'

'I'm sure he didn't mean to be,' Jean said. 'I think we'll all feel better after a good night's sleep.'

'Don't tease me,' Tayte said. 'You don't know how much I'm looking forward to that—whenever *that* might be.'

Fable returned with his wallet in his hand. 'We need to go,' he said, waving it at one of the staff. 'The hospital called.' He looked at Tayte. 'Harper's talking. He's asking for you.'

'For me? Why? What did he say?'

'Not much. "Get Tayte." That's about it. I hope he'll have more for us when we get there.'

Tayte gazed longingly at his pasta and thought the news both good luck and bad timing. The wide bowl was still half full, his stomach considerably more than half empty. He sighed and stuffed a ball of spaghetti into his mouth as he got up, realising that Harper must have heard his name at the gasworks. He must have heard the questions he'd asked Robert Cornell, too, and Tayte hoped he was about to answer them.

When Tayte and Jean arrived at the hospital with DI Fable, Peter Harper was no longer in a position to answer anything. He was dead. They received the news in a consulting room soon after their arrival and were left with a nervous-looking uniformed police officer called Wilkins, who had been with Harper since he was admitted. Fable got straight to the point.

'Well, did he say anything else besides asking for Mr Tayte?'

'He could hardly speak at all, sir,' Wilkins said. 'He asked for Mr Tayte and then he went quiet for several minutes before he spoke again.'

'Well get to it, lad,' Fable said. 'What did he say?'

Wilkins swallowed dryly. 'Well, it didn't really make much sense as I heard it. It sounded like he said 'horror-bus.''

'Ouroboros?' Jean said. 'Was that it?'

'It could have been, Miss.'

Jean threw Tayte a knowing glance. 'It's about Quo Veritas,' she said to Fable. 'Ouroboros is a self-consuming dragon, depicted in a circle, continually eating its own tail. I saw it when I went to Nottinghamshire. The journalist included a drawing in one of his articles showing it as part of the society's emblem.'

'What does it mean?' Fable asked.

Jean looked blank.

'Mr Tayte?'

Tayte puffed his cheeks out. 'Not much at this time,' he said. 'But it was a dying man's last word. Whatever it means it must be important.'

'Something to do with the ahnentafel number?'

'I don't doubt it,' Tayte said.

Fable made for the door. 'I'll drop you back at your hotel. Sounds like you two need some quiet time to get your heads together.' In the corridor outside, he added, 'Call me as soon as you get a breakthrough. And don't talk about this to anyone else. I'm your only contact.'

Chapter Eighteen

They stopped off at Jean's flat to pick up a change of clothes, and when they arrived back at the hotel, Tayte felt like a weary traveller returning home to the familiar and the ordinary after a journey that was anything but. Time seemed to run on a different clock at the hotel, and he felt it the moment he stepped over the threshold—the frenetic pace of the last twenty-four hours having been checked at the door like a heavy coat he was glad to be rid of.

As he crossed the polished marble floor in the lobby, heading for the Churchill Bar with Jean beside him, he was already thinking about his old roommate, Jack Daniels, wondering how much of his company he could afford to indulge in before his head became too foggy to concentrate. He knew it was a fine line, but after their ordeal with Robert Cornell he intended to test it.

'According to Wikipedia,' Jean said as she browsed the Web on the BlackBerry Fable had loaned them, 'the Ouroboros often represents self-reflexivity or cyclicality, especially in the sense of something constantly recreating itself. Cycles that begin again as soon as they end.'

'Like one monarch dying to be replaced by another,' Tayte said. 'The king is dead—long live the king.'

'Or queen in this case.'

'Right,' Tayte said. 'The Ouroboros circling the fleur-de-lis. Queen Anne recreated through her heir.'

'Yes, although in a broader sense it's about the continuation of the Protestant Stuart bloodline.'

They reached the bar and the bright, neutral decor gave way to low lighting and rich mahogany panelling, lending an air of relaxation to the otherwise lively environment. The room hummed with abstract conversation from the clusters of people at the tables and at the bar, which Tayte made straight for.

'But why did Harper want to draw our attention to the Ouroboros?' he said, continuing the conversation. 'As a part of the society's emblem it makes perfect sense. It compounds the theory that this is about an heir—the royal bloodline recreated—but Harper must have heard me ask Cornell about that. He knew we'd already worked that much out, so what else was he trying to say?'

'I don't know,' Jean said. 'But whatever it was, it'll have to wait. Look over there.'

She didn't point. She just nodded towards the far end of the bar where Michel Levant was sitting and smiling at them in his tight-lipped, effeminate manner. Tayte saw him raise a half-full champagne flute to acknowledge that he'd seen them, his golden ring catching the light as if to wink at them. Tayte was about to turn around again and leave when he was distracted.

'Good evening, sir. Madam. What can I get you?'

Tayte didn't answer the barman right away. He was too caught up with the internal debate of whether or not to grab Jean's hand and run.

'Sir?'

'Sorry,' Tayte said, refocusing. 'I'll take a JD on the rocks. Make it a double.' He wanted that drink, and it was too late to run now. He turned to Jean, having forgotten his manners on account of the Frenchman who was almost upon them.

'Sounds good to me,' Jean said. 'Make that two.'

Just hearing Levant's thin, melodious voice again as he approached them made Tayte's skin crawl.

'But where have you been?' Levant said as he came between them, reeking of some sickly sweet cologne that was so strong Tayte had to step away. Levant was wearing black jeans and an embossed white shirt that had exuberant, jack-a-dandy flounces at the neck and cuffs. 'S'il vous plaît!' he exclaimed. 'Let me pay for your drinks. I insist.'

At that point Jean surprised Tayte by stealing his response before he had time to unleash it.

'I think you've done too much for us already today, Monsieur,' she said, her expression neutral.

Tayte wouldn't have been so polite, but the message was there just the same. He supposed something he'd said at the Italian restaurant must have struck a chord with Jean, and it was good to see.

The corners of Levant's mouth twitched. 'Ah, to hear my native tongue spoken by one so charming,' he said. 'You spoil me, Madame.'

A part of Tayte wanted to spoil Levant's pointy little nose for having turned up uninvited, knowing that he must have followed them there at some point, too, but it was the part of Tayte that only existed in his alter ego fantasies. In case there was some chance Levant didn't already know his room number, rather than give it to the barman and be overheard, he went for his wallet to pay for the drinks, but Levant was ahead of him. Tayte missed his lithe arm as he slipped the barman the money.

'I really do insist,' Levant said.

Tayte just frowned and put his wallet away again.

Levant indicated a vacant table further into the bar. 'Shall we?' he said, heading towards it, allowing no time for debate.

Tayte eyed Jean as they followed Levant a few paces back, his expression asking what the hell they were going to do. He didn't want to sit down and shoot the breeze with this man. He was getting cranky-tired, and they had a serious puzzle to work out.

'Just go with it,' Jean whispered. 'If he is involved, I'd sooner keep him close for now. Maybe he'll slip up somewhere.'

Tayte doubted that. 'Well, don't tell him anything.'

Levant reached the table and turned back, still wearing that honeyed smile as they arrived with their drinks and sat down. Tayte figured he'd knock his drink back, encourage Jean to do the same, and then say something about it having been a long day. He thought that's what he would do, but Jean jumped straight into conversation.

'My son's missing, Mr Levant. Do you know anything about that?'

Levant looked mortified, his expression overly exaggerated like a bad actor trying too hard to get the emotion across. 'I'm sorry to hear that,' he said. 'But why would I?'

'Maybe you wouldn't,' Jean said. 'But I had to ask.' She locked eyes with him. 'Elliot is all I have. There are things I need to make up for, and I need him back. We're not close like a mother and child should be, and I have to correct that. Do you understand?'

Levant fidgeted. The penetrating eye contact was clearly making him feel uncomfortable. 'But of course,' he said. 'And I'm sure you will. You must never give up hope.'

Jean gave a short, sardonic laugh. 'I won't, believe me. I'll dedicate my life to finding my son, and when I do, whoever took him from me will wish they hadn't. I'll hunt them to the end of my days.'

Levant smiled and squirmed in his seat. 'I believe you,' he said. 'I see it in your eyes. Redoubtable!'

Jean sat back, not quite relaxing. She was still studying the Frenchman as though trying to get the measure of him, to understand whether her obvious appeal had hit the right target. 'Were you waiting long at the bar?' she asked, changing the subject.

'An hour. No more.'

'Why?' Tayte said, joining the conversation against his better judgement.

'I will not lie to you,' Levant said, turning to Tayte. 'I am, as you say, an heir hunter. And you are on a royal heir hunt, no?'

As soon as Tayte opened his mouth to reply, Levant waved a limp hand at him and tutted. 'Please, do not try to deny it. I already know as much.'

'How?' Tayte asked. Keeping his words deliberately short, his tone curt.

Levant pursed his lips. 'I overheard you at the construction site. I was outside when you asked your questions. The windows were broken. The sound carried.'

Of course, Tayte thought, trying to recall what else he'd said. Levant had been there the whole time, and Tayte figured he must have overheard everything.

Levant's eyes lit up. 'Queen Anne's heir,' he said. 'I knew it had to be something big, but I never would have guessed that.'

'It's just a theory,' Jean said.

'Perhaps so, but a good place to start, no? We can find the truth from there.'

'Quo Veritas,' Jean said under her breath.

'Excusez-moi?'

'Nothing,' Tayte said. He put his glass down with a thud. 'Look, Levant. What you did today—whatever your motives— we're grateful to you, but it doesn't make us buddies. There is no 'we' as far as you're concerned. I told you the other day that I wasn't interested in teaming up with you, and that still stands.'

Levant dismissed Tayte's words with a pinched smile. 'But if you do not need Michel Levant's help, I can only assume you have already worked it out. Is that it?'

'Worked what out?'

'The ahnentafel number, of course. The construct that will point the way to the heir.'

Christ, Tayte thought.

'I heard you mention that, too,' Levant said. 'But I thought all was lost to the flames. How did you find it?'

It was Tayte's turn to fidget in his seat. 'As Jean said—it's all just a theory.'

'But you do have the ahnentafel number?'

'Whether we do or not,' Tayte said. 'The only people who can confirm whether there's so much as a grain of truth to any of this are dead.'

'Ah yes,' Levant said. 'Peter Harper. I gather he did not survive his ordeal?'

'He died less than an hour ago,' Jean said.

'But that is too bad. I wish I had found the courage to act sooner. Maybe then I could have saved his life, too.'

It was clear that Levant wasn't going to let them forget what he'd done for them, but it wasn't cutting any ice with Tayte, who thought it equally clear that Levant wasn't getting the message he was trying, perhaps too subtly, to send him.

The Frenchman persisted. 'Did Mr Harper say anything before he died?'

Tayte knocked his drink back and stood up, scraping his chair legs over the wood flooring. 'Yeah, Levant, he did. Know what he said? He said 'get lost.' Come on Jean, I've had about as much of this as I can take.'

They rode the lift to their rooms. Tayte hit the button and leant back against the rail while they waited for the doors to close. When they did, he turned to Jean who was plucking at her hair, frowning at her image in the dark glass. However bad she felt she looked, next to him he thought she looked great.

'Can I take it your opinion of Levant has cooled off somewhat this evening?'

Jean stopped fussing with her hair and turned to him. 'Ice cold,' she said. 'I told you he'd slip up.'

'He did? How?'

'I didn't realise when I saw him at the bar, but later on when you asked him why he was there, you hit the nail on the head.'

'I did?'

Jean nodded. 'I believe he slipped up just by being there. When Cornell died, he took the ahnentafel number with him. The heirlooms had already been destroyed, and Levant would have known as much given that he was paying such close attention to what was going on. It was over. In which case, why is Levant still following us?'

The lift doors opened to a musical ping, like the sound of the penny as it dropped.

'Because he already knew it wasn't over,' Tayte said. 'And how could he unless he already knew we had the ahnentafel number by other means?'

They stepped out of the lift and headed along the hallway.

'Right,' Jean said. 'And we got the ahnentafel number from the text messages on Cornell's phone, didn't we?'

'Levant asked me if Cornell had one.'

'Exactly,' Jean said. 'He led you right to it. It was almost as if he wanted to make sure you found it and handed it to the police.'

Tayte had to admit that it stacked up. Perhaps Levant really had played them. Now he was trying to use them just as Tayte now supposed he might have used Robert Cornell.

'But why?' he said, thinking aloud.

'I get the feeling that Mr Levant doesn't like to get his own hands dirty,' Jean said.

Tayte agreed. 'Maybe he wants us to think we found the ahnentafel number for ourselves so we'll go on and work it out for him. Then he somehow means to come along and steal the prize. I wouldn't be surprised if he'd wanted Robert Cornell dead all along. He'd become a liability, hadn't he? When the last piece of the ahnentafel number was sent this morning, Levant had no further use for him, so he took him out of the game.'

'Only, I did that for him,' Jean said as they approached their rooms.

'And Levant comes across as the hero.' The idea left a bad taste in Tayte's mouth.

'What about the other phone?' Jean said. 'If we're right, what was it doing at the brother's house?'

'I don't know. Do you think Fable would buy any of this?'

Jean cringed. 'Not tonight, he won't. We still can't prove anything, can we?'

'No, we can't,' Tayte said, wondering just how smart this Machiavellian Frenchman was, and whether he would prove too smart to leave any proof of his involvement behind at all.

Tayte fished inside his wallet for his key card. 'I could use a shower before we get started on trying to work out who this ahnentafel number points to. Might wake me up some. You wanna freshen up and meet back in my room in ten?'

'Sounds good,' Jean said. 'Just don't fall asleep waiting for me if I take a little longer.' She opened her door. 'Get the coffee on. I'll be as quick as I can.'

Coffee, Tayte thought. That was the sensible choice. 'I hear that,' he said as he went inside.

Chapter Nineteen

Tayte's hotel room looked directly out onto Portman Square: a small parkland oasis in the middle of a busy circulatory system. Because of the late hour and the trees, his window was black. There were no city lights visible, just his tired-looking reflection gazing back at him. He drew the curtains, eyeing the crisp white bed linen as he passed the bed, thinking how good it would be to crawl in there for a few days, maybe a week, watch TV and live on room service. He thought he might do that when this was over.

Jean took closer to twenty minutes to freshen up, by which time Tayte had shaved and showered and set up the coffee machine that was now dripping through nicely. They were both wearing their courtesy dressing gowns, hair still damp, faces shining, and there was something about Jean coming to his room like that that felt naughty to Tayte. It was almost midnight and there they were in his hotel room, a cord's tug from a close encounter, about to share a jug of coffee and who knows what else. He chuckled to himself as he poured their drinks. Who was he kidding?

'Mmm, coffee smells good,' Jean said. 'I was thinking if we went over what we already know, something might come from that.'

'Right,' Tayte said. 'The ahnentafel number.' His mind was suddenly back on track, wondering how they were going to identify whose family tree the ahnentafel number belonged to. Only then could they hope to work out who the subject was.

They sat at the desk in a corner of the room and Tayte began by writing the ahnentafel number out on the hotel notepad. He tore the sheet off and put it to one side. Then he popped open a fresh bag of Hershey's miniatures for the long night ahead and started with one of his favourites: Mr Goodbar. He thought the protein from the peanuts might help him think.

'So,' he said, drawing the word out. 'Where do we start?'

'Let's start with the Royal Society.'

'Okay.'

Tayte tore off five more sheets of paper, and onto each he wrote the names of the hanged Royal Society Fellows.

'We're supposing these men uncovered a royal conspiracy,' he said, thinking about Jean's history student friends. 'That for political reasons the Whigs wanted to ensure the end of the Tory-supporting House of Stuart in favour of the Hanovers. Did I get that right?'

'That's it,' Jean said. 'And it's substantiated by Dr Hutton's research into the take-up of certain chemicals or drugs by the bloodstream, and by the Reverend Naismith's statistical studies into infant mortality.'

'Right,' Tayte said. 'So they concluded that something was very wrong in the Royal House of Stuart. Potential heirs were dying left, right, and centre. On what dates were Queen Anne's first and last children born?'

'Now you're asking,' Jean said. She turned to the BlackBerry. 'The last was around 1700.' She tapped at the small keyboard and then flicked her thumb over the scroller. 'Here we are. The first was on the twelfth of May, 1684. The last was on the twenty-fifth of January, 1700, when she gave birth to a stillborn daughter.'

'And she made no further attempt to have a child after that?'

'No. None during the twelve years of her reign.'

'Okay then,' Tayte said. 'If there was an heir, it had to be a baby born between those dates. So how did they pull it off?'

'Dr Hutton,' Jean said. 'Rakesh Dattani told us he was Anne's physician for a time. He could have switched babies.'

'Of course,' Tayte said. 'A stillborn child in place of the royal heir. When did Dattani say Hutton served Anne? I'm lost without my notebook.'

'During the five years leading up to her coronation,' Jean said. 'So that would have been between 1697 and 1702.'

'Good. That narrows it down.' Tayte indicated the BlackBerry. 'That thing tell you the dates of Anne's failed pregnancies between those years?'

Jean's thumb started scrolling again. 'There were four. A stillborn daughter on the twenty-fifth of March 1697. A miscarriage in December that same year. A son called Charles, who died the day he was born—that was on the fifteenth of December 1698—and the last attempt I just mentioned, on the twenty-fifth of January 1700.'

Tayte tore off another sheet of paper and wrote the dates down. 'If it was Hutton's plan to safeguard the Protestant Stuart bloodline, I think we can safely assume that the heir was born on one of those dates. Discounting the miscarriage gives us a choice of three. The substitute child had to come from another family that Dr Hutton was attending on one of those dates.' He thought about the ahnentafel number again. 'The big question is, whose family was it?'

'Do you think the mother knew?'

Tayte shrugged. 'I don't know. It would have been safer if she didn't, and how could any mother consciously agree to such a proposal? I suspect only the five Royal Society Fellows knew the identity of the heir, so let's look at them again. Naismith, among other things, was also a genealogist. We can take it then that the ahnentafel is his work, created to identify the heir when the time was right. And for that we turn to William Daws.'

'The field physiologist,' Jean said. 'Studies into human blood with a view to proving parent and child relationships.'

'Only he couldn't,' Tayte said. 'Not in his time.'

'*Nullius in Verba*,' Jean added. 'They had to stand by their own motto. They couldn't expect anyone to take their word for it. They needed scientific proof that the child was Queen Anne's legitimate heir.'

'Exactly,' Tayte said. 'And when it seemed unlikely they would be able to prove that in their lifetime, possibly because of betrayal or discovery, they divided the ahnentafel number and engraved the digits onto the scientific instruments they would each have owned at the time. Then they set up a society to protect it, handing the ahnentafel number down through the generations piece by piece as family heirlooms.'

'It explains why they called themselves Quo Veritas,' Jean said. 'They knew the truth and when they felt the time was right they could bring the heirlooms together again to prove it.'

'But the time wasn't right for almost three hundred years. Not until the discovery of DNA. The first conclusive paternity test using DNA profiling wasn't until 1988, which was around the time of the Sherwood Forest murders.'

Tayte recalled then what Robert Cornell had said at the Star Café: *it ends with me*. The father started it and the son planned to finish it.

'What about the astronomer and the soldier turned architect?' Jean said.

Tayte shook his head. 'Maybe they were just like-minded friends. Silent partners.'

They both sat back in their chairs together and exhaled thoughtfully.

'So in terms of cracking the ahnentafel number,' Jean said, 'what does all this tell us?'

The ensuing silence spoke volumes.

DI Jack Fable didn't hold out much hope of getting any sleep that night either—not since the call came in from DCI Graham Tanner, requesting his urgent attendance at Thames House. Their progress on the case had reached all kinds of people in high places, and they wanted immediate answers. Tanner wasn't going along and that came as no surprise to Fable given the late hour.

In a high-level clearance room inside the building that was home to the British Security Service, Fable was sitting at a table looking at an intense group of people: four men and one woman whose expressions suggested they had half the world's problems resting on their shoulders. The other half, Fable supposed, was everything they didn't yet know about.

He'd been there a while. Everyone was up to date on the royal conspiracy theory Tayte and Jean had come up with, and they were aware of the idea that somewhere out there Queen Anne's heir might exist, three hundred years after she was supposed to have died without issue.

'So this thing could be real?' one of the men said. He sounded sceptical.

Fable knew him as Deputy Director General Sir Anthony Harcourt. He was ex-military and looked like he still pushed weights to keep himself in shape.

'We're unable to confirm it as yet, sir,' Fable said, wondering why his palms were suddenly sweating. 'But Robert Cornell certainly appears to have believed it, yes.'

'Why can't we confirm it?'

The question came from the only female among them. Her name was Dame Celia Grice, Director General of the British Security Service. Fable had first met her when they brought Tayte and Jean in to look at Marcus Brown's genealogy files. The dogtooth suit she was wearing then was replaced now with casual attire that Fable supposed she must have thrown on when she'd been called in. He thought her complexion seemed all the more drained for the lack of makeup, and it made her jet black hair look stark by comparison, her character all the more formidable.

'We can't confirm it, ma'am,' Fable said, 'because to our knowledge there's no one alive now who can tell us, except perhaps Joseph Cornell. I believe we'll only know for sure when Tayte and Summer find what they're looking for.'

'And there's no other way to prove this thing?' Harcourt said.

'No, sir. I don't see how there could be.'

Fable heard whispers from around the table, too low to make anything out. Then Grice spoke again.

'So, let me get this straight,' she said. 'What you're saying is that around the time of Queen Anne, politicians plotted to manipulate the line of succession to the throne—possibly in collusion with the House of Hanover—so they could gain control of the nation. To achieve that, they had to ensure that no heir survived Queen Mary or Queen Anne. Have I got that right?'

'As I understand it, ma'am, yes,' Fable said.

Grice eyed him seriously. 'We're talking about the murder of royal children,' she said. 'Mere babies in most cases. And you're suggesting that King William III's riding accident was no accident at all?'

'When you put it all together, ma'am, I'd have to say that it looks suspicious.'

'And do we have any idea what the Cornells proposed to do once they found the heir?'

'Not at this time, ma'am. But while Joseph Cornell's at large, the implied threat to the royal family has to be taken seriously. Why else would he spend years of his life setting himself up in Royalty Protection Branch? It can't be a coincidence.'

'The royal family must be relocated,' Harcourt said.

'Already in hand, sir. And as Joseph Cornell knows the protocol, we couldn't use any of the regular residences. Those locations are being checked and confirmed safe, and as I'm sure you already know, the entire SO14 branch is being vetted for any association with the Cornells, military or civilian.'

'We can't be too careful,' Grice said. She sat back and stared at the ceiling. A moment later she added, 'If this heir proves to be real, wouldn't the very existence of such a person corroborate the theory?'

'I think it would add considerable weight to it,' Fable said.

Harcourt stood up, his knuckles pressing into the table as he leant over it. 'Who knows where something like this could lead?'

Grice agreed. 'We need to contain it. Bring the information in and control it until we've had time to assess the potential damage. As I see it, if we get there first, all threats are neutralised.'

'Surely it would be better to destroy this ahnentafel number.' Harcourt said. 'Let sleeping dogs lie.'

'And worry about whether it might jump up and bite us again someday?' Grice said. 'No, thank you.' She eyed Harcourt seriously. 'We bring it in. Control it. Do I make myself clear?'

Harcourt poured himself a glass of water, drank it back and sat down again. 'Who else knows about this?' he asked Fable.

Fable thought about Michel Levant and concluded that he didn't know what the Frenchman knew. 'To my knowledge, no one. We've only just put the ahnentafel number together, and we know that someone else out there has it—probably Joseph Cornell. I've told Mr Tayte that I'm to be his only point of contact.'

'That's good, Fable,' Harcourt said. 'And we need to keep it that way. If this *is* real we won't know how big an impact it's likely to have until it's too late, and that's a risk we can't afford to take. Do you understand?'

'Explicitly, sir.'

Celia Grice stood up. 'Very well then. But as far as any point of contact is concerned, I'm assigning two more officers to our experts in the field. They'll be at their hotel at first light, and they'll stay in their shadows until this thing is over.' She walked around the table until she was standing over Fable. 'In other words, Inspector, as far as Tayte and Summer are concerned, we'll take it from here.'

Harcourt rose, gathering his things. 'Chief Inspector Tanner will no doubt brief you in the morning,' he said, indicating to Fable that everything had been prearranged and authorised before he got there.

'And Inspector...' Grice said, her tone cold and flat. 'I must remind you that your silence is mandatory in accordance with the Act of Secrecy you signed when you joined the police service.'

'Of course, ma'am.'

When Fable left Thames House for his flat in Blackfriars, driving east alongside the river, he almost punched a hole in the dashboard. The Security Service had shut him out, and DCI Graham Tanner had supported them all the way.

The sycophant.

Fable knew it was just like Tanner to leave it to someone else to break news like that to him. He couldn't do it to his face, not Tanner. But there it was. The police investigation, with the exception of Joseph Cornell, who had yet to be found, was over. Their 'heirloom killer' was dead. The press were happy. It was another tick in the box for the good guys, and it would look great on Tanner's statistics sheet.

But what next?

Whatever it was, Fable knew it would happen off stage. Any mess would be covered up. All threats to national security, to the realm and to the monarchy, would be dealt with quietly.

All threats...

Fable had a badge and a signature on a piece of paper to ensure his silence—to protect him, he hoped—but what did Tayte and Summer have?

'Not a damn thing,' he mused.

If they found what they were looking for—what he had asked them to look for—his cynical side couldn't discount the idea that

Jean would go missing like her son, and Jefferson Tayte would be repatriated in a metal casket.

In Tayte's hotel room, he and Jean sat and drank coffee and threw ideas around for the best part of an hour, getting nowhere. Tayte eventually stood up and began to pace the room, scrunching his toes into the carpet, talking as he walked.

'It doesn't really help that we know the possible dates on which the subject of the ahnentafel number was born unless we know whose family tree it belongs to. What about the Ouroboros? Let's look at that again.'

Jean took off her glasses and pinched her eyes. 'We keep looking at it,' she said. 'I'm becoming an authority, but it's not helping.'

'It has to be the key,' Tayte said. 'Peter Harper would have known we'd need one—something to help us solve the puzzle. We just need to work out how to apply the key he gave us to the ahnentafel number.'

Jean sighed and went back to the BlackBerry. She started reading out much of what she'd already said, constantly flicking her thumb over the scroller. When she went quiet, Tayte returned to his chair and began to think aloud.

'Look at it logically,' he told himself. 'It's part of an ahnentafel—an ancestry chart. A genealogist put it together soon after 1700. You're a genealogist, JT. Think like one. It's family history. The past. It had to exist in his lifetime.'

The room fell quiet again—just the sound of Jean working the BlackBerry.

'It goes back twenty-three generations from the subject,' Tayte said, not to himself this time but to Jean. He sounded brighter.

'Do you have something?'

'I think I do. You see, even with today's technology and all the improvements in record keeping over the years, I'd find it next to impossible to trace just any old family history through twenty-three generations. We're talking several hundred years. Back then, unless the family history had been meticulously recorded through the centuries, Naismith couldn't have compiled such an ahnentafel.'

'So it has to be a famous family history?'

Tayte's face split into a cheesy grin. 'How about the royal family itself? That's where I was going wrong before. The chicken and egg scenario. I was thinking that to find the heir, we first had to work out their family tree. But that's precisely what we needed in order to find the heir. Like the Ouroboros, it comes back to itself, and that's the thing.' Tayte rocked back on his chair, the satisfaction of discovery flushing his cheeks. 'This puzzle starts where it ends.'

'It self-references?' Jean said.

'Exactly. To find Queen Anne's heir we have to start with the heir as though the child had lived. Which is exactly what your royal conspiracy theory proposes. The ahnentafel number is only part of the puzzle. If we follow it, it should lead us to the real heir and the family they became a part of when the babies were switched. We can confirm it easily enough.'

Tayte found the sheet of paper onto which he'd written the ahnentafel number. 'So the first digit represents Queen Anne's supposed stillborn child, or her heir if we're right. The second digit, also a number one in this case, represents Queen Anne. A zero takes the male line.'

Jean pointed to the next digit along. It was a zero. 'So that's Queen Anne's father, James II, and the next is a zero, so that's *his* father, Charles I.'

'You've got it,' Tayte said. 'Think you can keep going? It's the last person on the ahnentafel we're interested in. Something about them should give us our next direction.'

Jean took a deep breath. 'I'll try.'

She grabbed a pen and pulled the ahnentafel number towards her so she could write the names in. Then she rattled through nine of the twenty-three generations—the ahnentafel following the kings and queens that were so familiar to her—before arriving at James I of Scotland, where the ahnentafel steered away from the well-known monarchs through James's wife, whom she knew to be Joan Beaufort.

'Thank God for the Internet,' she said, turning to the Black-Berry again to follow the less familiar line.

It took her through three more generations before arriving back on familiar ground with Edward I and the House of Plantagenet, then to Henry III and to John Lackland, brother of Richard the Lionheart. She continued in this way, using her knowledge and the Web for reference until all the names were written against their respective digits on the ahnentafel. When she'd finished she set the pen down and sat back.

'So who does it point to?' Tayte asked, eager to hear the answer.

Jean turned the ahnentafel around so Tayte could read it.

'Ethelred II?' Tayte said. 'The Unready?'

'The very same. Although etymologists would tell you that the word 'unready' has taken on a different meaning over the years. In Ethelred's day it was 'unraed,' which meant 'without counsel' or 'having poor counsel.''

'Oh,' Tayte said, not really paying attention. He was wondering where this discovery had left them, and he thought that Naismith's ahnentafel number could have pointed to anyone in the British royal family tree, so why Ethelred II? 'What else do we know about him?'

'I can tell you the basics. He reigned between 978 and 1016. Became king at the age of about ten, when his stepmother supposedly murdered his half-brother, who was later known as King Edward the Martyr. Ethelred was an unpopular ruler. Had a lot of trouble with Vikings and ordered the St Brice's Day massacre to kill all the Danes in England. He was defeated by the Danish leader Canute at the Battle of Ashingdon in 1016 and was buried at St Paul's.'

'Need to look anything up?' Tayte asked, smiling.

'I don't think so,' Jean said. 'It's hard to be specific when you don't know what you're looking for.'

Tayte was still smiling. 'I think we've found it. You're referring to St Paul's Cathedral, right?'

'Not as it stands today, but yes. There's been a cathedral dedicated to St Paul on the same site since the beginning of the seventh century. The present cathedral is the fifth generation, built after the previous building was destroyed by the Great Fire.'

'1666,' Tayte said.

'Designed by Royal Society Fellow, Sir Christopher Wren,' Jean added.

'I knew that. Now you've spoiled it.'

'Spoiled what?'

'I wanted to say it—thought it might impress you.'

Jean threw the pen at him. 'I don't want to get you too excited before bedtime,' she said, 'but there's a large statue of Queen Anne outside the west portico of St Paul's. The same St Paul's that was being built during the time of our five Royal Society Fellows.'

Tayte arched his brow. 'What was it that Rakesh Dattani said of Sir Stephen Henley? He told us he'd probably trained under Christopher Wren at some point, didn't he?'

'Words to that effect,' Jean said.

'St Paul's it is then. First thing in the morning.'

Chapter Twenty

The banging on his hotel room door woke him. Jefferson Tayte got out of bed in his stars-and-stripes boxers, rubbed his gritty eyes as he slipped on his dressing gown, and checked the time. It was just after seven in the morning, and the banging was getting louder.

'Just a minute!'

He checked the peephole and saw that it was Jean, also in her gown. When he opened the door, he could see that she'd been crying.

'What is it? What's wrong?'

Jean stomped into the room and sat on the bed. She had a folded slip of paper in her hand.

'I came straight round,' she said. She sniffed, removed her glasses and wiped her eyes. 'I just found this under my door.'

She handed Tayte the slip of paper and he unfolded it as he sat beside her. He read it aloud:

'Find the heir—find your son.'

'Someone must have put it there during the night,' Jean added.

The note reaffirmed Tayte's belief that they had been set up for this all along. He read the words again, knowing that the police would have no hope of tracing the source. It wasn't handwritten. It was printed on a sheet of white A4 paper in a Times New Roman font—as common to any word processor today as Courier had been in the days of the typewriter.

Jean took a deep breath, trying to control her emotions. 'Elliot hasn't just gone off somewhere, has he? Somewhere inside me I was hoping that was all it was. But it's not, is it? They've got him.'

Tayte wondered who 'they' were, and as usual he thought about Michel Levant. Levant had been at the hotel last night. He had every opportunity to slip the note under Jean's door. Maybe he'd tried to work out the ahnentafel for himself but couldn't. Now he wanted them to do it for him. Tayte knew he couldn't rule out Joseph Cornell either, given what they knew about him, and he certainly didn't believe Cornell was equipped to solve the puzzle by himself. He heaved a sigh, thinking that it didn't matter who had Elliot just now. What did matter was that they now had another very personal reason to find whoever or whatever the ahnentafel number ultimately pointed to.

'At least now we know,' Tayte said. 'And this note must mean he's okay. They're clearly offering a trade.'

Jean nodded and Tayte realised he'd been holding her hand the whole time. He smiled and let it go again. 'Look, why don't you finish getting ready,' he said. 'I'll hit the shower. We'll skip breakfast. First one out of their room can knock for the other.'

<hr />

Within twenty minutes they were washed and dressed and pacing across the hotel lobby, heading outside to Jean's motorbike.

'Can't we take the subway?' Tayte said.

Jean slipped her leather jacket on as they walked. 'You're not wimping out on me, are you?'

Tayte feigned a smile. 'Not at all. It's just—' He held up his briefcase. 'I thought it would be easier, that's all.'

'You can hold on to it like before.'

Tayte was more worried about how he was going to hold on to the bike. 'What about helmets?'

'They're in the panniers.'

'Good,' Tayte said without conviction. 'Helmets are good.'

They reached the reception desk, and out of the corner of his eye Tayte was aware of two men sitting in the lobby reading newspapers. They were dressed in jeans and polo shirts: one had on a green fleece jacket; the other was in black leather. They folded their papers, their eyes blatantly on Tayte and Jean as they passed.

'Mr Tayte? Ms Summer?'

Tayte and Jean stopped walking. As the men approached, the one wearing the fleece produced a wallet, which he opened to show his ID.

'We're with the Security Service. I'm Officer Jackson and this is Officer Stubbs.'

The other man gave an impassive nod.

'What's this about?' Tayte asked.

'I think you know what this is about,' Jackson said. 'We've been assigned to stick with you until you find what you're looking for. There's a car waiting outside.'

'I see,' Tayte said. 'You mind if I make a quick call first?'

'Not at all.'

Tayte called Fable on their borrowed BlackBerry, checking his watch while he waited for him to pick up. It was eight-fifteen, and he figured the inspector would be on the job again by now—if he'd slept at all. When he picked up, the conversation was surprisingly short, Fable's tone drained of emotion.

'That's right,' Fable said. 'The Security Service are running things from here. Until we get a lead on Joseph Cornell, I'm going to be sitting in my office filling out paperwork.'

Tayte was sorry to hear that, but given the government's concerns, he wasn't surprised. When the call ended, he turned back to Jackson and Stubbs.

'Okay,' he said. 'Let's go.'

As they followed the officers outside, Tayte whispered to Jean, 'Don't say anything about the note.'

Jean nodded back, indicating that she understood why. The Security Service wanted them to solve this genealogical puzzle and discover the heir's identity. Yet when they did, if Jean wanted to see her son again, they had to hand the prize over to the very person they were trying to stop. Tayte felt like he was in a one-horse race he couldn't win, and the appearance of the two officers only served to complicate things. Stepping out into the cool morning, he knew they had to lose their escort. They needed to be free agents if they were going to find a way to satisfy everyone and reunite Jean with her son.

But how?

The question dominated Tayte's thoughts all the way to St Paul's.

⌣

Trenton McAlister was sitting in the back of a silver Mercedes near Buckingham Palace when the call he'd been waiting for came through. His driver had pulled over beneath the trees along Constitution Hill, hazard lights flashing while he set up the folding bicycle from the boot of the car. McAlister didn't want to arrive at the rally out of breath or heaven forbid, sweating.

His caller's tone immediately told him he was not about to receive the news he was hoping for.

'Further complications have arisen.'

McAlister felt his skin prickle. 'What kind of complications? No. Don't tell me. I don't want to hear any of the details.'

'Then let's just say that it's a matter of risk versus reward.'

'Get to the point,' McAlister said. 'What do you want?'

'I want more money.'

McAlister smiled to himself. 'Of course you do. How much?'

'Double.'

McAlister nearly choked on his dry tongue. 'As much as that? My, my.'

As a contingency McAlister had factored in half as much of the asking price again. It was human nature to be greedy, and he wasn't going to play the hypocrite now. But he hadn't figured on double. He would have to make up the deficit from his own private funds, which amounted to just about everything he had, if not a little more.

'And I want half up front,' the caller said. 'Transferred to my account within the next hour. The details will follow after this call.'

McAlister had to take a deep breath at hearing that. He hadn't parted with any of his or his associates' money yet, and he had no guarantee that he would ever hear from this man again once he had.

'Why should I trust you?'

'Trust me, don't trust me. I could tell you that I'm a man of my word but what would that mean to you?'

McAlister felt trapped. It was a gamble, but all his dreams came down to this, and he'd made promises that powerful people expected him to deliver on.

He gave a long sigh. 'Very well. But the payment fixes the price. Don't try to screw me over a second time.'

'The price is fixed,' the caller agreed.

'Good. So when am I going to get what I'm paying for?'

'It may only be a matter of hours.'

Hearing that put the smile back on McAlister's face. 'That's very good indeed.'

As the call ended and he got out of the car, McAlister wanted to call his journalist, Webber, to instruct him to begin the campaign that he believed would discredit the monarchy beyond redemption. But something told him to wait. If Queen Anne's heir proved to be real, he could show how the plot that put the Hanoverian bloodline on the throne in the first place was perhaps more than just a theory. It might cause the people to question the royal family's right to be there at all, and if a bona fide heir to Queen Anne could be produced...

McAlister snapped his bicycle clips around his ankles and took the bicycle from his driver. He felt goose bumps ripple through him as he imagined the royal scandal that would ensue: the manipulation of the royal bloodline, the heinous way in which it had been manipulated, and the cries for a royal referendum. He put on a cycling helmet and proudly took up a campaign board on which was written 'Republic Britain Now!' Then he cycled along Constitution Hill towards Buckingham Palace like Don Quixote, with the board as his lance and the small bicycle as his mighty charger, galloping to victory.

Chapter Twenty-One

St Paul's Cathedral sat on Ludgate Hill at the highest point in the City of London. Tayte and Jean were standing across the street amidst the morning rush hour commuters, facing the Great West Gate with officers Jackson and Stubbs close beside them. The air was pungent with acrid engine fumes, not that it bothered Tayte. His attention was focused elsewhere.

The Portland stone from which the cathedral was built appeared bright against the clear morning sky as Tayte continued to gaze upon it. They were all looking up at the neoclassical structure, with its symmetrical portico supported by Corinthian columns. The columns led the eye skyward to the relief on the central tympanum depicting the conversion of St Paul, whose statue stood directly above it between the cathedral's two towers.

In the background Tayte could just see the top of the great dome, and he had to smile at the hypocrisy. Judging by what he'd learnt from Jean over the past few days, the last Catholic king of England, James II, had been forced to abdicate. And later, in 1701, the Act of Settlement had been passed, formally turning the nation's back on Catholicism for good. And yet here was Sir Christopher Wren's masterpiece, consecrated barely ten years later, whose crowning glory was modelled on the dome of St Peter's Basilica in Rome—the centre of the Catholic Church.

As the traffic lights changed and Tayte turned his attention to Queen Anne and the statue that was the subject of their first line of investigation, he wondered if Anne had known this. He'd heard about Wren's secret after-hours meetings at the Royal Society in support of Catholic Jacobitism. Was this a backlash? The great architect's last laugh? The additional irony of seeing the Church of England monarch standing in the foreground certainly put a smile on Tayte's face.

He crossed the street at a pace, making directly for the statue. Anne seemed pivotal to everything that had happened, then and now. The ahnentafel, through Ethelred II, had led them here. It seemed fitting then that the statue of Queen Anne herself, standing before the west gate beneath St Paul's unceasing gaze, might have some part to play in the puzzle. He studied the figures in the sculpture under the scrutiny of Jackson and Stubbs, who hadn't spoken a word since leaving the hotel.

Tayte saw a proud monarch with a golden orb and sceptre atop a high pedestal. Below the central figure at each corner sat four ladies—allegorical representations of Great Britain, Ireland, France, and the North American colonies. To the front of the statue between Britannia and France, Tayte could see the Royal Arms, depicting the British lions, the French fleur-de-lis, and the Irish harp: those dominions over which Anne considered herself sovereign. Tayte approached the plaque on the north side and read it aloud.

'This replica of the statue of Queen Anne was erected at the expense of the Corporation of London in the year 1886.' He turned to Jean, disappointed and a little perplexed. 'It's a copy.'

'Yes, but it's supposed to be an exact copy,' Jean said. 'Francis Bird's original was sculpted from white marble. This is in stone but that should be the only difference.'

'Hmm, 1886,' Tayte mused. 'Do you know when the original was erected?' To hold any significance, he figured the statue had to have been there before the Royal Society Fellows were hanged.

Jean turned to the BlackBerry. A moment later she sighed and said, 'Not until 1712. Two years after the cathedral was completed.'

'And four years after the hangings at Tyburn,' Tayte said. He turned away and headed for the entrance. 'Come on. Ethelred led us here. Let's see what he's got to say.'

Having not long opened for the day, the cathedral was quiet. They were not the first visitors to enter, however, and within the hour Tayte supposed the place would be filled with the murmurs of hundreds of tourists. For now, though, as he peered into the Baroque interior, he could count the visitors he could see on one hand.

He looked back towards the street, wondering if anyone beyond the pediment they had just passed beneath was watching them. Given how quiet it was inside the cathedral, he figured anyone following them would be easy to see—especially if that someone was the flamboyant Michel Levant. He saw the bustle of commuters in the street, which seemed to have intensified since they arrived. No one stood out. He paid Jean's entrance fee along with his own and suggested to Jackson and Stubbs that they wait outside.

'No sense all of us paying to go in,' he said, thinking that he'd find another way out when the time came. 'I doubt we'll be more than five minutes.'

Tayte got no comment or expression from either of the Security Service officers—just their steady eyes boring into him. Jackson stepped up first. He handed the admission fee to the attendant and the pair followed Tayte and Jean in. Their rigid countenances were beginning to unnerve Tayte. He wanted to crack a joke just to make one of them smile, but instead he just tried to forget they were there, which was difficult given their insistence on maintaining such close proximity. Tayte imagined they were being overly protective because of what happened the last time two Security Service officers had been assigned to them. Whatever their motives, they were far too officious in their duties for Tayte's liking.

'I guess this isn't your first visit?' Tayte said to Jean as they walked along the nave beneath the high ceiling.

'I've lost count,' Jean said.

'So we don't need to ask for directions to the crypt?'

'No. Access is through the north and south transepts. It wasn't open last time I was here.'

'Well, let's hope it is today.'

They continued across a black and white chequerboard floor towards the quire and high altar at the east end of the cathedral. Tayte's neck was already stiff from looking up all the time, trying to take everything in.

'Queen Victoria commissioned the mosaics,' Jean said. 'She thought the place lacked colour, particularly in the quire.'

They reached the Great Circle beneath the main dome, which formed the centre of the transept crossing.

'The frescos in the cupola above us were painted by Sir James Thornhill,' Jean said. 'He was the pre-eminent painter of his day.' She guided Tayte to their left, into the north transept, passing a monument to Lord Leighton. 'Another great painter,' she said. 'Victorian era.'

'Ever thought of becoming a tour guide?' Tayte said with a grin.

Jean just rolled her eyes at him.

The crypt was open. They took a stone staircase down beneath the north transept, and Tayte was surprised by what he saw. It was unlike most of the crypts he usually encountered in his line of work. It was not the dark, eerie place he'd imagined it to be. There were no cobwebs, no creeping flora starved of daylight, and for a tourist attraction he was surprised to find no dark mood lighting to set the expected tone. This crypt looked more like a contemporary art gallery. Monuments and inscriptions adorned the walls like paintings. The pillars, walls, and ceiling vaults were coloured to match the bright Portland stone, and from every pillar the ceiling was lit with uplighters.

'The layout exactly matches the footprint of the upper cathedral,' Jean said as they walked. 'It's the largest crypt in Western Europe.'

'Really?' Tayte said, raising his eyebrows without awareness as he continued to take everything in.

'Apparently, the mosaic floor we're walking on was laid by convicts from Woking Prison.'

Instinctively, everyone looked down. Even Jackson and Stubbs.

'Tell me if you've had enough of the commentary,' Jean added.

Tayte turned to her and smiled. 'No, it's fascinating, really. You must soak up information like a sponge.'

They came to a black sarcophagus that was set on a plinth in the centre of the crypt beneath the dome.

'This is Lord Nelson's tomb,' Jean said. 'The Duke of Wellington's here, too.'

'Any idea where Ethelred's buried?' Tayte asked.

'I don't think we're going to see much,' Jean said as she led them on. 'It's not really a matter of where he's buried. There's a memorial as I recall, but that's about all. It's on the 1666 plaque.'

'The Great Fire,' Tayte said, figuring the date alone told him plenty.

Jean confirmed it. 'His tomb was destroyed along with just about everything else.'

When they came to the memorial, Tayte just stared at it and sighed. It was an unadorned grey tablet, inscribed with the names and dates of those interred at the cathedral before the fire.

'That's it?' Tayte said. 'Ethelred. 1016. King of the Angles?'

'I told you there wasn't much to see.'

Tayte thought it amounted to nothing at all. He read a few names off the plaque, none of which offered any connection.

'What are we really looking for here? I mean, I know we're looking for Queen Anne's heir, but what form is that likely to take?'

Jean's downturned expression gave him no encouragement. He thought it through, wondering how these Royal Society Fellows intended to pass the heir's identity on when the time came. Had something been hidden in the cathedral? Were they looking for a mason's mark engraved on a stone? He figured St Paul's must be riddled with such markings, but it seemed too fanciful to contemplate—the stuff of Hollywood film scripts. He kept thinking, and it wasn't until he thought about the man whom he supposed had created the ahnentafel puzzle—the Reverend Naismith—that he knew he had the answer.

'He was a genealogist,' he reminded himself, thinking aloud. 'We're trying to discover the identity of an heir. That, and something to confirm we're looking in the right place. It's all we can really hope to find, isn't it? All we need to find?'

Jean indicated the plaque. 'Like a name on a memorial?'

'Exactly,' Tayte said. 'Or on a headstone. In my room last night we established that the heir had to have been switched with a newborn baby from another family on one of three possible dates.' He went for the piece of paper he'd written the dates on, but Jean beat him to the answer.

'The first was in March 1697,' she said. 'There was a miscarriage in December the same year, which we've ruled out. The next was a year later in December 1698, and the last was in January 1700.'

'Right,' Tayte said, checking his piece of paper and taking note of the exact dates. He started walking. 'Come on. We need to check the burial registers.'

Jean went after him. 'Wait,' she said. 'That can't be right.'

Tayte stopped and Jackson and Stubbs stopped with him. 'I don't see how it can be anything else. What better way was there for a genealogist to send a message, or a name in this case, forward through time than on a headstone? The ahnentafel led us here to St Paul's Cathedral. It stands to reason that this is where we're going to find the name we're looking for.' He flicked the piece of paper he was holding. 'All we have to do is check for burials that match these dates. If we find a matching birth, or perhaps an infant burial—'

Jean stopped him. 'It can't be right,' she insisted.

'Why not?'

She grabbed Tayte's arm. 'Come with me,' she said, and she led him to the southeast corner of the crypt. 'Look. See for yourself.'

They were standing before Sir Christopher Wren's tomb. Tayte read the epitaph on the wall behind the sarcophagus. It was a Latin inscription that he didn't understand, but beneath it was a translation.

'If you seek his memorial, look around you,' he said, and instinctively he did.

Jean sighed. 'Not that. Wren was the first person buried here at new St Paul's after the old cathedral burned down.' She pointed to the inscription on the sarcophagus. 'Look here.'

Tayte read the inscription and the penny dropped. 'Died 1723,' he said. 'I guess that rules St Paul's Cathedral out altogether, doesn't it?'

'It does if we're looking for a headstone dated between 1697 and 1700.'

'I'm sure of it,' Tayte said. 'The Fellows had to pass the heir's identity on somehow. And it had to be in such a way that would stand the test of time. A headstone or some other memorial has to be the answer.'

Jean gave a humourless laugh. 'Then we're in the wrong place.'

Tayte couldn't argue with that. He started walking again, heading for the exit. 'Let's get some air. We need to think this over.'

Back outside, standing beside the Queen Anne statue again, Tayte tried to block out the cacophony of human and mechanical traffic that was raging behind him as he stared up at the cathedral.

He was thinking about the ahnentafel and about Ethelred II, wondering where else, or what else, their discovery might point to, and whether it had anything to do with St Paul's Cathedral at all.

'They were men of science,' Tayte said to himself.

His thoughts wandered with his eyes as they strafed the tall pillars all the way up to the relief of the conversion of St Paul. His instincts told him that this was not a complicated puzzle. He recalled the conversation at the pub Jean had taken him to, where he'd met her history student friends. He thought about Ralph's 'Isaac Newton' speech. *Occam's razor. Keep it simple.* It was another rule by which the Fellows of the Royal Society lived. It made sense that they would have tried to follow that rule in everything they did. The idea suggested something to Tayte that now seemed obvious.

'The ahnentafel number was the puzzle,' he said. 'The rest should be easy.'

'How do you mean?' Jean said.

'I mean once the ahnentafel number had been put together and the ancestor identified, our five Fellows must have wanted whoever was in possession of it to find what they were looking for quickly, and with relative ease. Getting the pieces of the puzzle together and understanding what it meant was the main thing.'

'So if the rest should be easy, why can't we see it?'

Tayte turned back to the cathedral and returned his gaze to the central relief. He cleared his mind, keeping his thoughts simple.

'The ahnentafel number points to Ethelred,' he said. 'That's a fact we can bank. Ethelred was buried at St Paul's Cathedral, but not at *this* St Paul's.' His gaze wandered up to the statue of St Paul himself, standing above the tympanum.

Not at this St Paul's...

'Of course,' he said, his eyes still fixed on the saint high above them. 'So what we're looking for isn't at this St Paul's, either. This isn't about Queen Anne's statue or Ethelred's tomb. And it's not about the cathedral. It can't be about any of those things.'

'So Ethelred doesn't point to St Paul's Cathedral?' Jean said.

Tayte spun around, his face beaming. 'No,' he said. 'He points to St Paul himself. What we're looking for is another St Paul's—a church.'

Jean returned his smile. Then her shoulders slumped. 'But which St Paul's? How are we supposed to know?'

'There must be a clue to that answer somewhere,' Tayte said. 'Maybe we've already seen it. When we read about the executions at The National Archives, didn't it say where the Reverend Naismith was rector?'

'Whitechapel,' Jean said. She shook her head. 'But it was St Mary's, not St Paul's.'

Tayte kept thinking but nothing came to him. 'There can't be many St Paul's churches in London that fit our criteria,' he said. 'Maybe we'll only know it's the right one when we see it.'

'It would have to be a church of Anglican denomination,' Jean said.

'And there would have to be burial plots dating far enough back,' Tayte added. 'Is there someplace nearby where we can get a coffee? We've got some research to do.'

Chapter Twenty-Two

They found a Starbucks on Ludgate Hill, not far from the cathedral. As they headed towards it, Tayte's thoughts resettled on the problem of how they were going to lose their escort. It seemed that Jackson and Stubbs would give them no easy opportunity, and he didn't think that he and Jean would get very far if they tried to make a run for it. Just the same, he concluded that he would have to devise something soon. If only he knew what.

He followed Jean inside the coffee shop, and the place instantly struck a familiar and welcome chord. The merchandise branding was the same as it was back home, and the sweet aroma of coffee and pastries was just as good. He drew a deep breath and was reluctant to let it go again. It reminded him of home, which, with everything that had happened during the past few days, was somewhere that now seemed further away than it ever had before.

They took a table by the window, where a red bus or black cab was rarely absent from the view, and Tayte noticed that the previously dominant office apparel on the people passing by began to shift with the hour to more casual attire. Jean sat down and got straight to work on the BlackBerry, and Tayte couldn't see how she was going to manage on such a small keyboard and screen.

'We could try to find an Internet café if it'd be easier,' he said.

Jean carried on tapping the keys and flicking her thumb over the scroller. 'It's okay. I'm used to it. I'll have a latte,' she added without lifting her head.

Starbucks it is, then, Tayte thought, deciding that Jean was definitely growing on him. He turned to their silent partners, who decidedly were not. 'I insist on buying you fine folks a coffee,' he said, forcing a smile.

Stubbs removed his leather jacket. 'Thanks,' he said as he sat down. 'Double espresso.'

Jackson kept his fleece on and didn't ask for anything. 'I'll give you a hand.'

Tayte placed his own hand on the man's shoulder, exerting just enough force to get his meaning across without seeming offensive. 'Take a seat,' he said, still smiling. 'They have trays.'

Jackson didn't look happy about it, but he sat down just the same. 'Cappuccino,' he said, sourly.

At least they're talking again, Tayte thought as he backed away. He stood in the queue under Jackson's watchful gaze, and he wanted to give him a wave but thought better of it. Instead, he turned his back to him and eyed the clock on the wall. They hadn't been at the cathedral long. It was still early, just before ten.

There were three people ahead of him in the queue and there were two girls serving behind the counter. It didn't take long to reach the front of the line, and when he did, another girl appeared through the staff doorway. She came straight to the till, almost shoved the girl who was already there aside, and smiled broadly at Tayte.

'Yes, please. Can I take your order?'

She was a slender dark-haired Eastern European girl in black jeans and a t-shirt that left her tattooed midriff exposed. Tayte gave his order with a twenty-pound note and waited, and as he waited he was aware that the girl kept studying him, smiling at him every time he caught her eye.

She fumbled with his change and dropped half of it back into the till. Then as she handed it to him, he could see that she was nervous about something. Her smile had gone and her heavily made-up eyes bored into his with an urgency Tayte couldn't fathom. As he took his change, she held on to his hand and leaned in closer.

'You need to use the men's room,' she said in a voice so low Tayte wasn't sure he'd heard her right.

His confused expression said enough. He felt her squeeze the change into his palm, her eyes growing larger still. She nodded discreetly towards the toilet facilities and repeated the line with greater urgency. Then she pulled away, renewed her smile, and went on to the next customer.

Tayte collected his tray and walked slowly back to the table, buying himself time to allow what had just happened to sink in.

She wants me to go to the men's room? He snorted. *What the hell for?*

Whatever the reason, it didn't matter. He had to go if only to find out. He drew a smile on his face to hide his confusion as he arrived beside Jean and set the tray down.

'I got us all a pastry,' he said as he offloaded the tray. Then to Jean, he added, 'How's the research going?'

'Good,' she said. 'I've found a church in Covent Garden that seems to fit. I've ruled several out already—Edgware and Knightsbridge and a few others that haven't been around long enough. I think I've got another possible match in Hammersmith.'

'That's great,' Tayte said. He paused. 'Look, I'll be right back. I need to use the men's room.'

Jean threw him a smile and continued the research. He turned to go but stopped when Jackson got up to go with him.

'What now?' Tayte said. 'Do you think I need a hand in there, too?' He was talking loudly, his accent cutting through every conversation, turning heads. 'Don't you think I'm big enough to go by myself?'

Jackson froze, looking around at all the people who were now looking right at him. He gave Tayte a mean stare as he sat down again and Tayte turned away. He let out a nervous sigh and made a beeline for the men's room, thinking that he definitely had to find a way to lose their escort, and sooner rather than later.

Tayte was gone a full three minutes. Too long, it seemed, for Officer Jackson, who met him on his way back.

'Everything okay?' Jackson said. He eyed Tayte sceptically. Then he leant in and sniffed him like a bloodhound. 'You went in there for a smoke?'

Tayte just smiled at him. 'I don't smoke.' He squeezed past, went back to the table and sidled up beside Jean. 'So what do we have?' he asked, letting nothing of what had just happened in the men's room affect his demeanour.

'St Paul's Hammersmith checks out,' Jean said. 'Although it was rebuilt in 1882. Every church I hit seems to have a website. Makes it much easier.'

Tayte grabbed a pastry. 'God really is everywhere,' he said. 'You can't get more omnipresent than the Internet.'

Jean laughed at him and turned back to the research. 'I've ruled out three more churches,' she said. 'One in Bow, another in Clapham, and one not far from our hotel in Marylebone. I don't think there are many more to check.' She pushed the napkin she'd been writing on across to Tayte. 'That's every St Paul's church of Anglican denomination Google could find. Just Deptford, Shadwell, and Mill Hill to go.'

Tayte hadn't heard of any of those places. He looked over Jean's shoulder, not at the BlackBerry but out the window, peering nonchalantly left and right along the street without drawing attention. He sipped his coffee and turned to the research. Jean had the website for the church in Deptford on the screen.

'No good,' she said a moment later. 'It wasn't consecrated until 1730.'

Tayte crossed it off the napkin.

'Shadwell,' Jean said. 'Built in 1657.' She paused, shoulders slumped. 'Rebuilt in 1820.'

'Oops,' Tayte said. 'The churchyard might still be intact, though. And there's the burial registers.' He drew a circle around Shadwell on the napkin. 'We'll check it out. What about the last one?'

Jean brought up the website for the church at Mill Hill. She navigated to the website's About Us page and a moment later, shook her head. 'It wasn't consecrated until the 1830s.'

Tayte crossed Mill Hill off the list, and as he looked up he glanced out the window again. He took a piece of paper from his jacket pocket. 'So we've got three churches that fit,' he said, writing them down. 'Covent Garden, Hammersmith, and Shadwell. What are their addresses?'

'We've got the BlackBerry,' Jean said. 'Might as well look them up as we go.'

'I'd sooner write them down. What if the battery dies?'

Jean pulled up the details for each of the three churches again and read out the addresses. When Tayte had finished writing them down, he asked Jean for the phone.

'There's something I want to check,' he said, and when she passed it to him he pretended to tap the keys. He nodded thoughtfully at the screen as though he'd found what he was looking for. Then he put the phone in his pocket.

'What were you looking up?' Jean asked.

'Oh, it's nothing.' Tayte sent a smile across the table to Jackson and Stubbs, who had long since finished their coffees and now looked stone-faced and bored. 'I just wanted to see how last night's Redskins game went.'

He put his hand in his pocket and felt over the phone for the battery release. When he found it he flicked it open with his thumb and held out his coffee to misdirect attention as he popped the

BlackBerry's battery out to make sure it was off. Outside the window the arrival of a flashing blue light caught his eye. He saw three cars pull up, blocking the road. One was a police car with a bold orange stripe down the side. The other two were unmarked.

'What do you suppose that's all about?' Jean said.

Tayte shrugged his shoulders, but he knew well enough.

Across the table, Jackson pulled out his phone. 'Are we done here?'

'I'm good,' Jean said, draining her latte.

Jackson pressed his phone to his ear and Tayte heard him tell whoever was on the other end that there was something going on outside—that the street looked like it was about to be closed off.

'Bring the car to the bottom of Ludgate Hill,' Jackson said. 'On Farringdon Street. We'll meet you there.'

When they got outside, several men wearing plain clothes and ballistics vests rushed them, handguns drawn.

'Armed police!' at least three of them shouted.

Tayte and Jean were clear of the doorway. Jackson and Stubbs were just behind them. The Security Service officers were clearly the focus of attention—just as Tayte knew they would be. He saw Stubbs reach a hand towards his jacket but he thought better of it.

'Hands behind your heads!' another police officer shouted.

They got no protest from either Jackson or Stubbs. Tayte watched both men raise their hands behind them and Jackson had his eyes fixed on Tayte the whole time. He thought the man looked ready to rip his head off. A split second later, the two men were on the ground with police all over them.

'Do you want to tell me what's going on?' Jean said.

Tayte grabbed her arm and they started running. 'Come on. I'll explain later.'

They ran back towards St Paul's Cathedral and didn't stop running until they found an available taxi to get them out of there. They took a left turn before the cathedral into Ave Maria Lane and picked up a black cab further down towards Amen Corner.

'Marylebone,' Tayte said. He was panting hard as he followed Jean in. He slammed the door behind him and flopped back onto the seat.

'Explain,' Jean said, wide-eyed and naturally confused.

Tayte had to wait to catch his breath. When he did, all he said was, 'Fable.'

'What? What about him?'

'He was in the men's room.'

Jean didn't look any less confused. 'Why? What happened?'

'He said he was concerned for our safety. He told me there were things going on that we should know about.'

'Like what?'

'Like the government's getting jumpy. That they'll do just about anything to stop this from getting out if it proves to be real.'

'But only if it fell into the wrong hands, surely?'

'Not exactly,' Tayte said with a humourless laugh. 'Fable didn't come right out and say it, but I got the impression that if we found what we were looking for, agents Jackson and Stubbs had another agenda to follow. They weren't there to protect *us*, if you know what I mean.'

Jean looked numb. 'Oh my God,' she said. 'They were there to protect the identity of the heir?'

'Eliminate all threats,' Tayte said. 'That was my take on the situation. Whoever's pulling our strings with that note has done well to stay off their radar. They must have understood the risks far better than we have.'

'Christ,' Jean said. She sat back, momentarily dumbstruck. A few seconds later she added, 'So Fable set all that up back there? The armed police?'

Tayte thought about the two Security Service officers lying face down on the pavement outside Starbucks and smiled to himself. 'Yes, he did. I had no idea what he had in mind. He just told me he'd handle it. I guess he must have called in their location and descriptions with a reasonable cause for an armed response unit.'

'Coffee shop drugs deal?' Jean said.

'Who knows?'

'How did he know where to find us? We didn't tell him we were going to St Paul's.'

'The BlackBerry,' Tayte said. He took it out of his pocket and showed her the pieces. 'I took the battery out so the Security Service wouldn't be able to find us again the same way. I'm sure they'll be trying, so we don't dare use it for now.'

'I don't think it's going to take them long to find us again anyway.'

'How's that?'

'Well, unless by some unlikely chance they weren't listening to a word we said back there, they know exactly where we intend to go.'

Tayte sank his head into his hands. 'Of course,' he said. 'The St Paul's churches.' He sat up again. 'So, we'll have to be careful, that's all.'

Jean eyed him doubtfully. 'Are you kidding me? Look at you. You're an outsize American with a standout foreign accent, wearing a bright—if a little smudged—tan suit. What chance have we got?'

'So we'll have to be *extra* careful,' Tayte said. 'Look, we don't exactly have time to work on our disguises, do we? This is all we've got. Besides, they don't know what order we plan to visit the churches in.'

'They'll cover all of them.'

'Probably,' Tayte conceded, 'but we've got a head start. They won't be out of that fix in any kind of a hurry.'

'Why are we going to Marylebone? The church in Covent Garden's nearest.'

'I know, but it's too predictable. Better if we start further afield. They might not expect that, and I want to avoid public transportation if we can. Didn't Fable say this was the most surveilled nation in the world?'

'My bike?' Jean said.

Tayte nodded. 'It's not foolproof. They'll be looking for the registration when they check the hotel and realise it's gone, but we'll get around quicker. Maybe we can stay ahead of them. Where are Hammersmith and Shadwell located?'

'Hammersmith's in the west—four or five miles from Marylebone. Shadwell's east. It's a little further out, but there's not much in it.'

'I wish my laptop still worked,' Tayte said, eyeing the bullet holes in his briefcase. 'I could have accessed the parish register indexes. We might have been able to pinpoint the right church from that.'

'What about The National Archives? Couldn't we access the registers from there?'

'We could,' Tayte said, thinking about it. 'But it's out of our way, and we'd need to visit the church to confirm things anyway. More often than not the registers only give names and dates.' He paused. 'There are only three churches. Let's start with Hammersmith. We'll work our way west to east across London.'

The taxi continued northwest to Marylebone. Jean stared out the window most of the way, leaving Tayte with his thoughts as she seemed to wrap herself in her own. They hadn't been able to talk about her son since leaving the hotel earlier, and Tayte imagined she was thinking about him now. When she spoke again, she confirmed it.

'Did you tell Fable about Elliot? About the note?'

'No, I didn't.'

Jean fidgeted with her hands. 'If we don't make it,' she said, pausing. She looked tearful just thinking about what might happen to her son if they didn't.

'I know,' Tayte said. He placed a hand over hers to steady them.

'Did Fable say anything about Joseph Cornell? I don't suppose they've found him yet?'

Tayte shook his head. 'He never came up.'

'He must know where Elliot is.'

Tayte didn't reply straightaway. A moment later he said, 'Look, all the while the police are searching, there's hope, right? They won't stop looking—not for Joseph Cornell or your son. I know it's hard, but let's stay focused. When we find what we're looking for, at least we'll have something to bargain with.' He squeezed her hands. 'Elliot's going to be fine.'

Jean forced a smile. She gave a resolute nod. 'Okay,' she said. 'But I hope to God you're right.'

Tayte hoped he was, too. He turned away and stared out the window, taking nothing in. All of London could have sped past him for all he knew or cared. He was oblivious to it. The real challenge had now begun. How to save Elliot was foremost in his mind, but in doing so, how could he hope to prevail against whoever had kidnapped him? He wanted no part in any implied threat to Britain's national security either, and he supposed whoever was offering the exchange for Elliot might also have been behind Marcus Brown's murder. How then could he simply hand everything over? The answer was simple: he couldn't. But where did that leave Elliot?

Tayte's head began to spin, like the Ouroboros was inside him, chasing the questions round and round, each one coming back to itself in an endless, unanswerable loop. When he factored in the latest information Fable had imparted—that the government were bent on preventing anything from getting out—he couldn't see how any of them would be allowed to just walk away from this.

He had to find a way to change that.

Chapter Twenty-Three

St Paul's Church in Hammersmith was located in the centre of town, north of the River Thames. It was besieged by fast dual carriageways and the busy Hammersmith flyover, and the swarming traffic filled the air with a constant drone. Tayte and Jean arrived little more than forty minutes after parting company with Security Service officers Jackson and Stubbs, and Tayte supposed there had been plenty of time for them to confirm to the police who they were. They would be free men again by now, and Tayte had no doubt that they were working hard to catch up with them. As Jean revved the bike up onto the pavement by the low trees that lined the church grounds, Tayte felt his heart race just knowing that they were being hunted again.

'Let's get this done with as soon as we can,' he said. 'We could have company any minute.'

They followed the path towards the early English Gothic–style church, and Tayte wondered if they already had the kind of company he was talking about, perhaps waiting for them around the corner or inside the building. He had to remind himself that neither he nor Jean knew what to look out for. These people were just like everyone else: regular clothes, ordinary cars. He'd recognise Jackson and Stubbs, but he didn't expect to see them so soon.

He scanned the area. It wasn't busy, which came as a welcome change to Central London, although he thought the whine of the traffic up on the flyover spoiled an otherwise pleasant environment. Beyond a mighty oak tree that stood adjacent to the church's impressive tower, Tayte saw a young couple holding hands as they walked the path beside the lawn. There was an elderly woman by the oak, talking to a mother who had a child in a pushchair. *No cause for concern*. Tayte wanted to see the churchyard first, so they kept to the path.

'It doesn't look promising,' he said, noting that the grounds were small and unremarkable: a strip of mown grass around the church and a barely larger triangle of grass further down. 'It all looks pretty new.'

'Even the trees,' Jean said. 'Apart from that oak.'

Given how long there had been a church on the site, Tayte had hoped to find a graveyard of considerable age, replete with crooked, lichen-stained headstones. But this was a memorial garden bereft of any planted shrub or flower. They continued around the path, and Tayte saw that several of the paving slabs were actually headstones laid horizontal. The dates he saw were mid to late nineteenth century and of no interest.

'This whole area's recently been redeveloped,' he said. He pointed to the church wall ahead. 'Look there. The headstones have been moved.'

The wall was lined with grey headstones, secured to the wall in close proximity to one another. Further inspection revealed similar dates that were too late to be of any value to their investigation. All were clearly inscribed and easy to read. They reached the end of the wall and stopped.

'I suspect the less legible stones were destroyed,' Tayte said, gazing around and seeing nothing of relevance. He headed back to the church. 'Let's see what we can find inside.'

The church appeared considerably larger on the inside than Tayte had expected, and that lifted his hopes. The walls were festooned with memorial plaques, and he concluded that the grounds had indeed diminished over the years because of the extensive infrastructure of public roads in the vicinity. The details from the headstones that had not survived were now either consigned to the parish records or had found their way into the church as plaques on the walls.

There was no service today. As they moved further in beneath a high vaulted ceiling, Tayte's eyes became alert for trouble again. He saw the backs of several heads seated in the pews, facing the altar. They were exclusively elderly people. Retired people, he supposed. Towards the altar, someone who clearly worked there was polishing brass.

So far so good.

Tayte stopped when his eyes fell on a memorial at his feet. 'This is more like it,' he said. 'Timothy Walker, 1788.'

They moved on, scanning the walkway until they found another. 'Thomas Bowden. 1761,' Jean said. 'Apothecary.'

The date was still over sixty years too late, but Tayte felt they were getting closer. When they came to a monument for Sir Nicholas Crisp, who died in 1665, he knew there was a good chance that a memorial covering one of the dates they were looking for might be there. They moved into the south aisle, where they saw several plaques dating from the eighteenth century, but all were decades too late.

'We should split up,' Jean said.

Tayte looked around. There were so many memorials. He knew that even if they did, it would take too long to check every inscription, and he didn't want to risk missing anything.

'I don't think we have the time.'

He glanced at the entrance, checking for trouble. As he looked away again, his eyes were drawn to a man in black wearing a clergyman's dog collar. He was a young man with dark hair and a six o'clock shadow that might have been designer stubble. As he came towards them along the nave, Tayte stepped out to meet him.

'Excuse me.'

The clergyman paused and smiled, and Tayte introduced himself and told him how he made his living, saying nothing of the real reason they were there. They quickly found out that the clergyman was called the Reverend Johnson, and he was interested to hear that Tayte was a genealogist.

'I'm a bit of an amateur myself,' the reverend said.

Tayte didn't want to deviate from their objective just now. 'That's great,' he said. 'Look, I was wondering if you keep any parish records here? I'm interested in the late seventeenth century.'

'Copies,' the reverend said, hesitating. 'But they're only for church use. The originals are held at the Archives and Local History Centre on Talgarth Road. You can view them there, but they're closed on Wednesdays and Fridays. You could try tomorrow.'

Jean stepped forward. 'We don't have until tomorrow.' Her tone was curt—all sense of tact undermined by the need to find what they were looking for.

The reverend frowned. 'Well, I'm sorry,' he said, 'but—'

Tayte put a hand on the reverend's shoulder. 'What my friend means is that we're flying home this afternoon,' he said, leading the reverend away from Jean towards the pulpit. 'We're trying to find someone, and she's a little upset that we're running out of time.' They stopped walking. 'From one family historian to another,' Tayte added, smiling his cheesiest smile. 'I'm sure you'll understand how important this is to her.'

'Well, I don't—'

'Perhaps I could make a donation to the church?'

Tayte reached into his jacket pocket and produced the dates they were interested in. He showed the slip of paper to the reverend, hoping to get him interested.

'I just need to know if there were any births or burials recorded at this church on or very close to these three dates. If I'm not permitted to look myself, perhaps you could check for me. How does twenty-pounds per date sound for your donation box?'

The reverend almost snatched the list from Tayte's hand. 'Wait here,' he said. 'It might take a few minutes.'

Tayte gave Jean a thumbs-up as he went back to her.

'Sorry,' she said. 'I nearly screwed that up, didn't I?'

'Don't sweat it,' Tayte said. 'I wanted to say the same thing.' He took out his wallet and removed three twenty-pound notes. He looked at the money and scoffed, adding, 'A little church bribery never fails.'

When the Reverend Johnson returned, he shook his head as he gave Tayte the slip of paper back. 'I'm sorry,' he said. 'There was nothing recorded within weeks of those dates. Maybe the person you're looking for was buried elsewhere?'

'I'm sure that must be the case,' Tayte said. He handed the donation over. 'Thanks for looking.'

As they turned to leave, two men entered the church, and Tayte and Jean froze like rabbits in their gaze. Their casual attire might not have given them away, but the instant recognition on their faces as they stopped inside the doorway left Tayte in no doubt as to who they were. A second later, he squeezed Jean's arm and pulled her close as he made straight for them.

'Come on,' he said. 'I'm not playing chase with these guys.'

He knew he couldn't outrun them anyway. He thought Jean probably could, but he also imagined they were carrying firearms, and he didn't want to find out.

'What can they do to us anyway?' he added, thinking aloud as they drew closer.

Tayte hadn't seen either man before, and he supposed they had just been sent there to cover the bases, or the churches in this case, as he and Jean had thought they would. He knew that even if they managed to evade them here, others just like them would be waiting at Covent Garden and at Shadwell. He had to deal with this now. As he approached the men, he tightened his jaw and went in bolder than he would have thought possible three days ago.

'You need us,' he said, punctuating the words. 'Call it in. I want you off our backs or this ends now.' He stopped a few feet short of the door. 'And if that happens, you lose—plain and simple. Whoever else is looking for this thing will get there first.'

One of the men stepped towards him. 'We have instructions to take you in, Mr Tayte.'

'We're not going in,' Tayte said, defiant. The adrenaline pumping through his veins was beginning to make him feel ill. All the same, he stepped closer to meet the man, briefcase ready to swing if it came to it. 'So what are you going to do about it?'

The man looked at his colleague, and his colleague reached beneath his jacket and kept his hand there, leaving Tayte with little doubt as to what he had in mind.

'Are you authorised to kill us *before* we've found what we're looking for?' Tayte saw the man's gun arm relax a little. He swallowed hard. 'I didn't think so.'

The man in front of Tayte gave a cheerless smile. 'Come on,' he said. 'Don't make this hard on yourself.'

Tayte laughed, eyeing the pair up and down. 'Do you really think you could get me to your car without shooting me first? I probably weigh more than both of you put together.'

He was exaggerating, or hoped he was, but they seemed to get the idea. He could see they were thinking about it.

'Don't try to make the decision for yourselves,' he said. 'I'm sure it's above your pay grade. Just call it in. Either we continue this by ourselves or it's over. When we find what we're looking for...' He paused, reached into his pocket and showed them the battery-less BlackBerry. 'We'll let you know.'

Tayte's eyes followed one of the men as he stepped outside. The other just kept staring at Tayte, so Tayte stared back. He could feel his legs begin to shake. A second later the remaining man went to the doorway, and he too stepped outside. After a full minute passed and neither man returned, Tayte went and peered after them.

He turned back to Jean. 'They're gone.'

Jean checked for herself. 'Wow, I'm impressed.'

Tayte gave her a sheepish grin. He wasn't trying to impress anyone. Not this time. Now it was over, all he wanted to do was sit down with a hot, sugary beverage and wait for his pulse to climb down. But there wasn't time for that.

He grabbed Jean's hand. 'Come on. They won't be far away. Next stop, Covent Garden.'

⌣

Tayte and Jean headed back to Central London via Knightsbridge, following road signs that told Tayte they were heading towards Piccadilly Circus. It was just after midday, and the sun felt hot on his shoulders as he hugged his briefcase to his chest, moving with the roll of the bike as Jean continued to manoeuvre the big BMW through the traffic with all the proficiency of a seasoned London courier.

They passed Green Park on their right, and further down Tayte saw the Academy of Arts. He craned his neck to admire the architecture and saw that they had a car close behind them. Too close. He heard its engine rev hard and observed the aggravated behaviour of the driver who seemed keen to overtake them. Then as soon as a gap appeared in the oncoming traffic, the car swerved out and swerved back in again, cutting in front of the bike. Jean hit the horn but the driver of the car—a blue Ford—seemed ignorant to the fact that he'd just narrowly squeezed into a space that was barely there.

A side road was coming up on their left. Tayte saw the Ford's indicator blink as it slowed and began to turn. Jean, who was clearly aggravated, twisted the throttle and began to overtake, giving the horn another blast for good measure.

Take it easy, professor, Tayte thought. *It's just some jerk. He'll be out of our lives in a second.*

But he wasn't.

As they drew level with the Ford, instead of turning left, it swerved right, cutting across them. Jean was quick to respond, avoiding contact, but the car forced the bike onto the other side of the road into the oncoming lanes. Horns screamed from just about every direction as Jean weaved in and out of the traffic on the edge of control. The bike's engine was suddenly screaming, and the last thing Tayte heard from Jean was, 'I'm losing it!'

Tayte hit the tarmac first. He landed with a thump that sent a jolt of pain ripping through his shoulder as Jean laid the bike down. Cars swerved around him as he rolled to the far kerb and came to a stop. In his periphery he saw the bike continue to slide into the traffic with Jean still attached. He sat up, saw Jean kick herself free and part slide, part roll across the oncoming traffic. She made it, but her motorbike did not. Tayte watched it slam into an oncoming lorry and disappear partway beneath it.

'Jean!'

Tayte was on his feet, running to her. She was moving—slowly getting up. The traffic had stopped in both directions and people had begun to gather.

'Are you okay?'

Jean didn't reply. She was looking at her bike, or what used to be her bike. 'I can't deal with this now,' she said. Then she walked away, limping slightly. She took off her helmet and threw it to the ground.

'Where are you going?'

'Covent Garden. You coming?'

Tayte didn't know what to do. He looked back at the lorry and at the driver who was inspecting the damage. He saw his briefcase in the gutter and went after it, wincing at the pain in his shoulder as he stooped to pick it up. He looked up at Jean, who was already growing distant.

'Wait!' he called after her. 'Hold on, I'm coming!'

She disappeared down a side street, and Tayte ran to catch up. Somewhere behind him he heard someone shouting, but he didn't turn around.

'Jean! Wait up!'

When Tayte caught up with her, they walked at a fast pace along several side streets until Tayte was lost. He didn't have to ask if her leg was okay. If it hurt at all it didn't show. He could barely keep up.

'We need to talk about what happened back there.'

Jean stopped. She turned to face him. 'So what do you think just happened?'

'First, you need to calm down.'

Jean took a deep breath and forced it out again. 'There,' she said. 'I'm calm.'

Tayte thought she still looked like she wanted to break something. 'So why don't I believe you?'

Jean huffed, fists still clenched. 'It pisses me off, that's all. One reckless driver—that's all it takes. We could have been killed. Then what would have happened?'

Tayte realised she was really wondering what would happen to Elliot. 'You think that was an accident?'

'I see it all the time. A thousand motorcyclists die every year in London, and the vast majority of those accidents are because of idiots like that. I hope I see his ugly face again some day.'

'Come on, Jean, it's a hell of a coincidence, don't you think?'

Jean turned away and started walking again, turning onto a busy main road. Tayte supposed it could have been an accident. The Security Service didn't want them dead. Not yet, anyway. And if they did, they would be dead already. He thought about Michel Levant and dismissed him, although he still had the Frenchman pegged for the writer of the note Jean found under her door. As he saw it, everyone involved in this for one reason or another wanted them to find what they were looking for. He thought about Joseph Cornell then and knew he couldn't rule him out. But why try to make it look like an accident? All Tayte knew was that he hated co-incidences. To his mind, someone clearly wanted to stop them from finding what they were looking for altogether, but who?

'Come on,' Jean said.

She stuck her arm out and started to run. Over his shoulder Tayte saw a double-decker bus indicate and pull over. The sign on the front read, 'Holborn via Covent Garden.' As they boarded, Jean offered him a weak smile.

'At least my glasses didn't break,' she said. Then she tugged Tayte's sleeve, drawing attention to it. 'You ripped your jacket.'

Tayte looked. It was torn at the shoulder where he'd made first contact with the tarmac. He snorted. 'Don't worry,' he said. 'I've given up all hope of taking any of my suits home with me.'

Chapter Twenty-Four

They got off the bus at the Strand and made their way along Bedford Street towards Covent Garden, entering the grounds of St Paul's Church via Inigo Place, which, Jean informed Tayte, was named after Inigo Jones, the architect who designed the building and the Covent Garden Piazza. Tayte scanned the area for headstones, but all he saw was a colourful courtyard rose garden with grey wooden benches lining the walkway. It was busier than he'd expected, but this peaceful setting amidst Victorian townhouses, coupled with the warm sunshine and the fact that it was lunchtime, made the reason entirely evident. Almost everyone he could see was eating, which did nothing to stay his own appetite.

'This doesn't look promising either,' Tayte said as they walked. He couldn't see a single memorial, upright or vertical. 'We'll go straight in this time,' he added. 'Keep your fingers crossed.'

As they drew closer, Tayte heard a familiar sound that made him think of Marcus. It was a street performer talking and laughing into a PA system in the piazza on the other side of the church. It reminded him how close they were to the restaurant where his friend had been murdered. He tried to put those thoughts aside for now as they took the few steps up to the main entrance, passing a billboard advertising a play called *Dido and Aeneas*.

'It's a theatre, too?' Tayte said.

Jean nodded. 'I read on the BlackBerry that it's called the Actors' Church. Apparently it's a long-standing tradition.'

They went inside.

'It's dark,' Jean said.

Tayte peered in, letting his eyes adjust after the bright sunlight. The interior was small and nothing like the church at Hammersmith. 'Busy, too,' he said. 'Looks like they're getting ready for a service.' He didn't know whether to pass through the inner doors or not.

'Can I help you?'

Tayte spun around to see a bright-faced woman in navy blue, whom he put somewhere in her fifties. She was carrying an armful of pamphlets.

Jean didn't say anything. She just returned the woman's smile, leaving the talking to Tayte this time.

'Hi,' he said. 'Is this a bad time for a visit?'

'Not if you want to celebrate the Eucharist with us. Holy Communion begins in fifteen minutes.' She offered them both a pamphlet. 'Would you like a service sheet?'

'No thanks,' Tayte said. 'We don't really have the time. I'm just a genealogist looking for a record. Do you keep any information at the church apart from these plaques on the walls?'

'Most of them commemorate the achievements of the various actors who've passed through here at one time or another,' the woman said. 'W.S. Gilbert of the Gilbert and Sullivan duo was baptised here.' She paused. 'But I don't suppose you're interested in any of that.'

On any other day Tayte would have been very interested. Gilbert and Sullivan had composed the music for many of his favourite musicals.

'Not today,' he said. 'Just parish registers.'

'I'm afraid we don't keep them here anymore.'

Tayte half expected as much.

'But we do have a series of books published by the Harleian Society that might be of interest to you.'

Tayte flashed his eyes at Jean. Long before the world went digital, the Harleian Society had been transcribing collections of information that were of particular value to genealogists and heraldists.

'Do you have their Parish Register series?' Tayte asked.

'I'm sure we do. I think one of the previous rectors made a hobby of collecting them. The books were here long before me, and I've been a churchwarden at St Paul's for twelve years now.'

'We're only interested in 1697 to 1700,' Tayte said. 'Do you think we could take a look?'

The woman wrinkled her nose. 'If you're quick,' she said. 'Follow me.'

She led Tayte and Jean around the congregation into a windowless room that looked like it was used for church administration. There was a desk with a computer screen and keyboard. Papers and books were everywhere.

'They're in here,' the woman said, going to a cabinet on the far side of the room. She pulled out a drawer and began to sift through the contents.

'Here we are,' she said. 'The Registers of St Paul's Church Covent Garden Vol. IV—1653–1752.' She turned to face them again. 'How does that sound?'

Tayte was smiling. 'That sounds perfect.'

The woman put the book on the desk, and Tayte eagerly flicked through the pages while Jean looked over his shoulder. When he found the end of the seventeenth century, he fished in his jacket pocket for the slip of paper containing the dates they were interested in.

'March 25, 1697,' he said, still turning pages. A moment later he stopped, looked at Jean and shook his head. 'There's just one burial recorded. It's nearly three weeks out.' He checked the next date, which was for 1698. 'December 15,' he said. There were two registered burials and one birth that month: two burials in the first week and one birth on the twenty-eighth. He flicked ahead to 1700. 'One to go,' he said. 'January 25.'

A moment later he looked up again.

'No good?' the churchwarden said.

Tayte shook his head and noted from Jean's expression that she shared his disappointment. 'One birth and one death,' he said. 'Both on the same day and three weeks too late.'

'The same day?' the warden said. She found the entry. 'Oh, yes, the Booth family,' she added, shaking her head. 'Tragic. The mother died giving birth. Then eight years later the daughter drowned in the Thames. Her poor father could never forgive himself for her death, or so the story goes.'

'That's very interesting,' Tayte said, keen to move on.

'They have an inscription in the churchyard,' the warden continued. 'There are several others there, and copies of registers are prone to error, aren't they? It might be worth a look.'

'Very much so,' Tayte said. 'But I didn't see any memorial inscriptions on the way through.'

'They're around the corner to your right as you leave. We have a row of headstones against the wall and some inscriptions on the ground.'

'Then we'll leave you to your communion,' Tayte said. 'I'm sure we've already taken up too much of your time.'

On the way out, Tayte began to question his logic. He gazed absently at the myriad plaques on the walls as they walked, reading abstract words here and there, taking little in.

'What else could it be?' he said, urging himself to think.

'Something to do with the Ouroboros?' Jean said.

Tayte shook his head. 'Too vague. Having to find any kind of mark is leaving too much to chance. The ahnentafel's like a treasure map, and those things are never vague. Its creator couldn't risk any kind of misinterpretation.'

'I suppose not,' Jean said. 'A memorial carrying a date that matches one of Queen Anne's failed pregnancies on the other hand is very specific.'

'Yes, it is.'

'So let's stick with it,' Jean said. 'We still have the church at Shadwell to try when we've finished here.' She scoffed. 'We should have started our search there. East to west. You know things are always in the last place you look.'

'Ain't that the truth,' Tayte said as they approached the light beyond the main doors and behind them the Eucharist began.

———

Tayte fell behind and caught up with Jean at the bottom of the steps outside the church.

'What kept you?'

He dropped to his knees and opened his briefcase. He took out the genealogy charts Marcus Brown had compiled for Julian Davenport and Douglas Jones and spread them out on the flagstones.

'What is it?' Jean said. 'Have you found something?'

Tayte didn't answer right away. He traced a finger over the names on Jones's chart and then did the same with Davenport's. He paused over them for several seconds, then he shook his head and folded them away again.

'It's nothing,' he said, slipping the charts back into his briefcase. 'I was just wondering whether any of those other dates in the burial register appeared anywhere else here. They don't.' He stood up. 'Let's take a look at those headstones.'

They kept to their right and walked around the church as directed. The area was bleak and colourless by comparison to the gardens they had just left. The ground was covered with grey paving slabs and there was a narrow, flowerless shrub border to one side. Everything was overshadowed by the trees that grew out of the paving, blocking the sunlight. The headstones the churchwarden had mentioned were lined up against the church wall to their right, like a row of knockdown targets at a fair.

They walked over several horizontal memorials to get there. Those that were legible bore dates from the late eighteenth century, and he saw one that was barely discernible, the inscription all but gone. He wondered whether it had been missed from the Harleian Society's publication because of its condition when the register was compiled. What if it was the very grave they hoped to find—the heir's identity now lost for all time? He wondered how that would sit with the British Security Service and whoever had offered the exchange for Jean's son.

They approached the headstones and walked the line from one to the next as though inspecting a parade, becoming increasingly disheartened with every inscription they read. The dates were mostly from the early to mid-1700s. They were old but offered no connection. Heading back to the gardens, something caught Jean's eye, and she went to the wall in shadow.

'Look,' she said, pointing to an inscription set into the corner by her feet. 'It's for the Booth family the churchwarden told us about. The drowned girl.'

Tayte knelt beside it. It bore three dates. One was for a loving husband on June 4, 1739. Another was for his beloved wife on February 14, 1700, and the third was for their daughter, who was born on the same day and died eight years later in 1708 as the churchwarden had said.

'She drowned the same year our Royal Society Fellows were hanged,' Tayte said.

'Pity she was born three weeks too late,' Jean countered.

Central to the inscription was a sentence that made it clear how the churchwarden knew that the father could never forgive himself for his daughter's death.

'I let her die,' Tayte said as he read it.

Jean knelt down and ran her fingers over the stone. 'That's very sad.'

Tayte turned away. 'I've read a thousand inscriptions just like it. Come on. Nothing here matches what we're looking for.'

Jean eyed him askance.

'What did I say?'

She shook her head at him. 'I suppose I'd come to think of you as someone with a little more sensitivity, that's all.'

They headed back around the church.

'I didn't mean anything by it,' Tayte said. 'You just see so much of a thing that it stops registering.'

'Like pathologists and autopsies?'

Tayte smiled. 'Kind of, I guess.'

They were in the garden again and Tayte noticed that there was more than one exit. 'How do we get to the last of our St Paul's churches?'

'This way to Shadwell,' Jean said, indicating an arch to their right that led out through the townhouses. 'We can take the Tube from Covent Garden station, change at Holborn, and pick up the DLR at Bank. It's on the Thames.'

'DLR?'

'The Docklands Light Railway.'

They emerged onto King Street amidst a bustle of people, whom Tayte supposed were a blend of tourists, shoppers, and office workers taking their lunch break, all heading to and from the piazza. They joined the throng and made their way towards the market square as the crowd thickened and their pace slowed to a shuffle.

'It's not usually this busy here on Wednesdays,' Jean said, almost having to shout.

'I guess it is lunchtime,' Tayte said. He wanted to hold her hand so they didn't get separated but he shied away from the idea.

Jean was trying to look ahead through the crowd, lifting her chin, walking on tiptoes. 'There must be something going on.'

They reached the edge of the piazza and the din from the street performers grew. It was a happy sound, if a little harsh to Tayte's ears, and he couldn't stop himself from trying to get a look at what all the fuss was about. There was a distinctly carnival atmosphere to the place. Beneath the pillared portico of St Paul's Church where it abutted the piazza, red, white and green flags hung like bunting between the pillars, matching the t-shirts he could now see on many of the people there.

He saw several posters bearing the words 'Republic Britain Now!' and quickly realised that the event was part of a political campaign. A small stage had been set up behind a street performer who was riding a high unicycle whilst juggling batons, warming up the crowd. It was easy to get caught up in it all and Tayte did. So much so that when he turned back to Jean to make sure he was still shuffling in the right direction, she was gone.

Chapter Twenty-Five

Tayte jumped in the air to get a clear view above the crowd.

'Jean!'

She didn't answer and he couldn't see her. He jumped again and began to turn in a slow circle.

Where is she?

Movement in the otherwise calm crowd suddenly drew his attention. Someone was pushing through the people towards him. All he could see of the man was his thick neck and his short blonde hair—and the urgency in his eyes as he came right at him. The man touched a hand to his ear, lips moving like he was talking to someone via a Bluetooth headset or a two-way radio. Then he saw someone else moving fast to his right, knocking people aside as he came in from the market.

Tayte knew there was no way he could brave this out with a few well-chosen words like he had in Hammersmith. He looked around for Jean again. Where was she? Did they have her already?

Who the hell are they?

His first two questions were answered when he felt someone tugging at his jacket. Then, as he began to sink beneath the crowd, he heard a familiar voice.

'Are you crazy? Didn't you see them?' It was Jean. She looked intense. 'The man coming from the market,' she added. 'He was driving that blue Ford.'

Tayte was too pleased to see her again to say *I told you so*. 'Why didn't you say something?'

'There wasn't time.' She pulled at his jacket again. 'We need to get out of here. Stay low.'

They filtered through the crowd like two people trying to find their way out of a cornfield, obscured by everything around them. The going was too slow for Tayte's liking, but the ever-thickening crowd made it impossible to move any faster. He was crouched low over his briefcase, eyes down at Jean's boots with no idea which way they were going. The man on the PA sounded louder, so he figured they must be heading for the portico where the street performers were.

Twenty seconds later Tayte emerged from the crowd behind Jean like a drowning man coming up for air. He saw a contortionist on all fours, staring up at him with her face upside down. Behind her he saw a man with a microphone, dressed like a circus ringmaster.

'We have a volunteer, ladies and gentlemen!'

At the edge of the crowd to his left, Tayte saw the man who had come from the market. He was a gaunt, sinewy man with hollow cheeks and a shaved head. Put a straw hat on him and Tayte thought he would have made a good scarecrow.

'That's him,' Jean said. 'Run!'

They headed for the stage where there were fewer people. One of the performers tried to grab Tayte's arm as he passed, smiling playfully, but Tayte dodged him. He glanced back. The scarecrow was coming for them across the arena. Tayte saw one of the performers reach for him, and the man made no attempt to dodge. Instead, the scarecrow slammed the base of his palm into the performer's face, knocking him down like a bowling pin.

Tayte refocused on getting out of there. They cleared the stage area beneath the portico and the gathering seemed to part for them, only Tayte soon realised it wasn't for them. The key speaker had arrived to a cheering crowd. He had a foldaway bicycle with him, trousers still clipped around his ankles.

'Ladies and gentlemen,' the man on the PA said, seeming to ignore the fracas that had just stirred the crowd on the other side of the arena. 'The Right Honourable Mr Trenton McAlister MP!'

Tayte almost ran into him. He tripped over the front wheel of his bicycle instead. 'Sorry,' he called back, getting to his feet.

At that moment Tayte saw the scarecrow again. He was at the end of the parting, not twenty feet away. A thin smile slowly split his face, prompting Tayte to grab his briefcase, turn on his heel, and run after Jean as the crowd began to close in.

The timing conjured biblical connotations in Tayte's mind. It was like Moses and the Israelites—the parting of the Red Sea now returned to devour the enemy. Tayte wished it would, but as he emerged on the other side, he knew the crowd would only buy them a few seconds. From then on they would be in the open.

Jean was waiting for him across the street, waving frantically. 'Come on! We can cut across the Strand. It's not far to the Embankment.'

Tayte didn't know what was at the Embankment and he didn't ask. As they ran down the first street they came to, all he was interested in was a taxi, but he couldn't see any. When they were halfway to the main road, he glanced back and saw their pursuers turn into the street after them. He ran harder and somehow he managed to overtake Jean. It was downhill all the way, and his weight gave him momentum. He was panting fiercely by the time they reached the main road.

'I don't know how long I can keep this up,' he said.

'Just remember they want to kill us,' Jean said. 'It works for me.'

That thought kept Tayte going. They crossed the Strand, taking their chances with the traffic. His jacket suddenly felt two sizes too small, like it was crushing the air from his chest, making it

hard to breathe. Behind him, he heard a car horn and figured whoever was chasing them had just crossed the road after them. He
thought about grabbing Jean and ducking into one of the shops,
but he didn't think that would offer any kind of sanctuary, and Jean
seemed to have a plan. He only wished he knew what it was. He
looked for a taxi again. The few he could see were either going the
other way or were already occupied. Jean turned left into a narrow
side street that ran out to a steep bank of steps, which they took two
at a time.

'You think you can make the park?' she said, indicating the
trees further down beyond the high buildings that now crowded in
on either side of them.

The street was quiet—no one else around. Fire escapes and com-
mercial bins lined their way and the air reeked of rotting kitchen
waste. At the bottom of the steps another narrow street began to
slope away. The park was two hundred metres at most.

'I'll make it,' Tayte said, hoping that he could.

They crossed a narrow intersection with another quiet road,
and the trees and mature shrubs that marked the boundary of Victoria Embankment Gardens seemed real to Tayte for the first time.
Nothing, however, seemed as real as the muted gunshots he heard
behind him as chunks of paving suddenly blistered at his feet.

'They're shooting at us, for Christ's sake!'

As he continued to run for his life, curiosity got the better
of him and he looked over his shoulder again. The scarecrow had
cleared the steps and his partner was close behind him. When Tayte
turned back to Jean, he knew he was slowing down. She'd gained
twenty paces on him and was almost at the park gate. It was a single,
wrought iron gate—a minor access point. Tayte's legs felt like lead
pendulums swinging beneath him as he focused on it. But what
then? The park was no safe haven either. What was Jean thinking?
It didn't seem to matter. Over the sound of his own wheezing lungs
he heard the scarecrow's voice for the first time.

'You're mine now!'

Tayte didn't have enough energy left to doubt it. He knew he should have ditched his briefcase when they left Covent Garden, but he couldn't bring himself to part with it any more than he wanted to lose all the paperwork that was inside. He thought about making a stand. At least maybe Jean could get away. He was the bigger man after all. But he knew he didn't have the skills. The men chasing him in all probability did, and there were two of them. They would be on him in seconds, and if that happened he thought Jean would try to help him.

That thought alone decided him. He got mad at the idea and kicked his legs harder, running flat out down the slope, barely able to control himself. He saw that Jean was now on the other side of the gate.

Why is she waiting? Why doesn't she run?

'Come on!' she yelled, spurring him on. 'Don't look back.'

Tayte shot through the opening like a sprinter crossing the finish line. Then he caught an exposed tree root and fell headlong into a flower border. He heard the gate clank shut behind him and turned to see that Jean had locked it with the disc lock from her bike. The scarecrow crashed into it, clawing at Jean through the bars as she backed away.

She yelled at Tayte. 'Get up!'

Tayte needed to catch his breath but the pop of another silenced gunshot and the puff of dirt in the border between his legs quickly got him to his feet.

'They'll be over that gate in seconds,' Jean said, grabbing Tayte's arm. 'We've got to keep moving.'

Somewhere along the way, Tayte thought Professor Jean Summer had turned into the personal trainer from hell. He was on his feet again, trying to run, but the lactic acid in his muscles was shutting him down. They crossed the colourful gardens in thirty seconds, unhindered. Jean's disc lock seemed to have delayed their pursuers, but when they emerged from the main gates, close to Embankment Underground Station, it was clear that at least one of them had thought around the problem.

The blonde-haired man had skirted the park fence. He announced himself by grabbing Jean's hair as she ran out ahead of Tayte, and without thinking Tayte charged at him, ramming him with the hard end of his briefcase. It knocked him back and they were running again, in through the Tube station entrance and out the other side, heading for the river. Tayte had no idea where the other man was and he hoped he never saw him again.

'What about the subway?' he called.

'There's no time. I saw the other one in the park. He's coming.'

They crossed the road, playing chicken with the traffic. Cars swerved and horns blared.

'The pier!' Jean said and they made for it.

There was a river boat there—a river bus according to the signs. It was red and white with blue seats and clear panelled roof sections fore and aft. Jean must have seen that it was about to leave. As they ran along the walkway, a member of staff was putting up the safety chain.

'Wait!' Tayte yelled.

The man paused long enough to allow them onto the covered platform, and within seconds the boat was moving. Looking back, with only a few metres between the boat and the pier, their pursuers came out onto the walkway after them, but they were too late. Tayte watched them reach the pier and stop. He saw the man whose gaunt face he would never forget slap the rail in bitter defeat, staring after them as Tayte turned away and collapsed into a breathless heap on the deck.

Chapter Twenty-Six

The River Tours service operated on a hop-on, hop-off basis, which Tayte thought was just as well under the circumstances. He and Jean remained outside in the sunshine, and Tayte was glad of the breeze off the river to cool him down.

'Do you stop at Shadwell?' he asked the ticket man, still catching his breath.

The man shook his head.

'How about Canary Wharf?' Jean asked.

'Service terminates at St Katherine's, after Tower Bridge.'

'Terminates?' Tayte said. 'Don't you stop anywhere else?'

'Weekdays, we run a loop from Westminster, stopping at Embankment and St Katherine's. That's it.'

'How long does it take?'

'To St Katherine's? Twenty-five minutes.'

Tayte checked his watch to get a reference: it was almost two o'clock. He paid the fares one way to St Katherine's Pier and sank forward on his elbows.

'We're screwed,' he said. 'They'll know where we're getting off.'

Jean agreed.

'How long will it take them by road?'

'Ten minutes—maybe fifteen. Depends on the traffic, but they'll need a car first.'

Tayte scoffed. 'They'll have one nearby. Those guys were organised.'

'Then they'll be waiting for us.'

'Yes, they will.'

The boat was quiet. Tayte could only see a handful of people aboard: some outside and a few more inside beneath the canopy. There were no children. As the boat headed east along the Thames at a gentle pace, Tayte wondered again who wanted to stop them from solving the ahnentafel, but he quickly concluded that it didn't matter. All that mattered was that they didn't succeed.

'I figure we've got about twenty minutes to come up with a way off this boat,' he said.

'I've been thinking about it,' Jean said. 'We need to call the police.'

Tayte knew it was the sensible thing to do. Their lives were at stake—they could have the police meet them at the pier. It wouldn't matter who else was there waiting for them. They wouldn't do anything with the police around.

'But what then?' he said. 'We'd be detained. We'd have to answer all kinds of difficult questions. Things we don't want to get into right now.'

'I meant Detective Fable,' Jean said. 'He helped us out before. He could do it again.'

Tayte thought about it. The only thing that stopped him reaching for the BlackBerry was the fact that he knew as soon as he turned it on he'd be broadcasting their location to any interested party. He figured anyone with Internet access had a good chance of locating them.

'Can you swim?' Jean asked.

Tayte peered over the side of the boat. It was a short drop into the murky river. 'I tried it once or twice in a pool,' he said. 'When I was a kid. I vowed not to make a habit of it.'

'You don't fancy it then?'

Tayte looked out, wide-eyed. 'Swim to shore?'

The boat had crossed towards the south bank and was now right of centre in the direction of travel, having just passed beneath Waterloo Bridge. The water looked choppy from the wash off the other boats, and Tayte figured that if he went in from here, his body would have to be winched out again when it eventually washed up further down.

'No,' he said. 'I don't *fancy* it at all. I guess I've spent too much of my life sitting in archive rooms when I should have been at the beach.'

'So call Fable.'

Tayte didn't waste a second getting the pieces of the BlackBerry out of his pocket. He figured whoever was trying to kill them already knew where they were anyway, so he reassembled the phone, switched it on, and was greeted with a message asking him to enter the PIN code. He hadn't thought about that. He showed it to Jean, still thinking about the river and the banquet he might yet make for the crabs and the crayfish.

'Try all ones,' Jean said. 'It's a factory default.'

Tayte did. It worked. He found Fable's number and hit the dial button. After several rings the call went to voice mail and Tayte ended the call.

'That's just great,' he said. He tried again, wondering where Fable was and more importantly, why he wasn't picking up. The call went to voice mail again.

'No good?' Jean said.

Tayte shook his head. He thought about leaving a message, but there seemed little point. By the time Fable picked it up, it would be too late. He switched the phone off and popped the battery out again—paranoia getting the better of him.

'Fifteen minutes left to come up with a plan,' he said.

DI Jack Fable was in Kew at The National Archives. Something Tayte had said at the Italian restaurant the night before had stuck in his mind—about how difficult it would be to find the descendants of the hanged Fellows of the Royal Society without leaving a trail. He'd been in a quiet corner of the Document Reading Room for the last hour, studying record request logs.

The idea was simple enough. Every record requested at The National Archives was logged in the system. All he had to do was take a line of research that the team of genealogists had already worked through and correlate the records they needed to see with any recent requests for the same information. If anyone showed a particular interest in the descendants of these long dead Fellows of the Royal Society, it would single that person out.

Fable wasn't naive enough to think that whoever that was had used their own name; he knew that a clever man would never do that, especially if he knew his research might lead to murder. But what if, when he'd first started out, he hadn't known he was identifying a killer's next victim? He might not have foreseen the need for caution then. That's what Fable was hoping.

It would take time, and Fable knew the process would have to be repeated at the General Register Office for all the other pertinent records, but he knew he was on to something. Even if the killer's researcher had used a different alias every visit, he would find the dates and times of the record requests that correlated with the genealogists' research trail. The CCTV images from the lobby could be vetted to see who had entered the building before each request, and a recurring face would soon stand out. Maybe it would be a face he or someone else recognised.

The River Tours boat that was taking Tayte and Jean to St Katherine's Pier was five minutes from its destination. The best plan they had come up with to avoid the inevitable encounter when they docked was to wait until the boat was close to the pier and then slip into the river while everyone else was getting off, staying low, using the other passengers as a curtain against anyone looking from shore. Given Tayte's lack of proficiency in the water, he was nervous about the idea and he doubted there were enough people aboard to give them the kind of cover they needed for long, but there were now very few options left open to them.

They had just come in sight of a museum warship on the south bank to their right, which Jean had said was a Royal Navy light cruiser called HMS *Belfast*. It had been in permanent dock on the Thames for forty years, she'd said, and she was still talking about it now, only Tayte was no longer listening. He was having a heart attack. He grabbed his left arm suddenly, like a wasp had stung it. He drew a sharp breath and clenched his fist to his sternum. Then he fell off his chair.

'JT!'

The few other passengers turned to see what was going on. Jean was down on her knees in an instant, trying to unlock Tayte from the foetal position he'd tightened into.

'JT, what is it?'

His words were strained. 'My heart.'

One of the staff ran over. 'What's happened?'

'He's having a heart attack.'

'Are you sure?'

'He just told me,' Jean said. 'Look at him. We had to run for the boat. It must have been too much for him. He needs a hospital.'

'Help me sit him up,' the man said. To Tayte, he added, 'Try to stay calm, sir. That's it.'

They helped Tayte into a seated position on the deck, propping him up against the side of the boat.

'Keep him still while I call ahead for an ambulance,' the man said. Then as he went to make the call, Tayte began to groan.

'Get me off this boat.'

He winked at Jean and watched her jaw drop as she caught on. The man turned back and Tayte drew another sharp breath before scrunching his eyes shut.

'What if he doesn't make it to St Katherine's?' Jean said. 'You need to stop the boat at the next pier.'

'That's Tower Millennium Pier.'

'I don't care what it's called. Just get us there.'

As the man rushed away, Jean moved in and pulled one of Tayte's eyelids open. 'I could thump you,' she whispered.

'I only just thought of it,' Tayte said. 'Besides, a genuine reaction is always more effective, don't you think?'

'You just didn't want to go in that river, did you?'

'There is that,' Tayte admitted.

Within a couple of minutes the boat was alongside Tower Millennium Pier on the north bank, and Tayte was suddenly feeling much better.

'I guess it could have been indigestion,' he said to a worried looking member of staff as they disembarked. He had an arm resting on Jean's shoulder for support, keeping up the act until they were clear.

As the boat pulled out again, heading towards Tower Bridge and St Katherine's Pier, Tayte surveyed their new surroundings. They were on a platform outside the Tower of London.

'Come on,' he said. 'Let's get a cab to Shadwell before our friends waiting downstream realise we got off.'

Chapter Twenty-Seven

Tayte and Jean arrived at St Paul's Church in Shadwell ahead of a school field trip that consisted of two female teachers and thirty or so ten-year-olds from the local primary school. Tayte watched the procession of pupils file past in pairs like a blue centipede that quickly disappeared beneath the shade of mature trees in the churchyard. He couldn't feel much of the breeze, but he could hear it rustling the treetops above as it tried to shake free the early autumn leaves.

He stood there a moment, briefcase in hand, like an estate agent assessing a new property listing. He was looking at the north-facing side of the church, which was constructed of brown brick with plain stucco dressings. He would have thought it unremarkable were it not for the impressive spire that sat above the pediment, rising in ornate pillared tiers like a tall wedding cake whose crowning glory was a high stone obelisk.

'I don't know how much time we have,' he said to Jean as they made their way through black ironwork gates towards the church.

'How do you mean?'

'I mean, I don't think it's going to be long before they catch up with us again. They knew we were at St Paul's, Covent Garden. They probably knew we were in Hammersmith given that they tried to kill us on the way back. I wouldn't be surprised if they knew we were at the cathedral, too.'

Jean agreed. 'You don't need to be a Fellow of the Royal Society to work out the pattern, do you?'

'No, you don't,' Tayte said. 'And given they know we were on a boat heading east—a boat that terminated at St Katherine's, not far from *this* St Paul's...'

He left his words hanging as the headstones and sarcophagi he could see to either side of the path distracted him. These were old memorials, judging from their worn and crooked appearance. The walled churchyard, though relatively small, clearly predated the present building, which Tayte knew from Jean's research on the BlackBerry was built around 1820.

The path led them to the entrance where a few stone steps led up to a bright red door that was set between tall white niches and iron railings. The Greek revival facade was topped with a plain stone tympanum that ran the full width of the pediment. Tayte stopped and looked back towards the road, thinking that they were probably okay for now. He figured they had maybe thirty minutes to check the place out. Any longer than that was pushing their luck. He stepped ahead of Jean and opened the door.

'Shall we?' he said.

Inside, they caught up with the school trip. The children were already neatly ordered in the pews, and Tayte could see that they had been equipped with tracing paper and crayons. He thought they all looked impatient to get outside again to begin their rubbings, but it appeared they had to take in a little church history first.

The lesson today was being given by someone who looked too young to be anyone other than a very junior member of the church. He wore a dog collar with a black shirt and jeans, and Tayte thought his fair, windswept hairstyle suited a guitar and microphone better than a pulpit and bible, but what did he know?

'St Paul's Church Shadwell is known as the Church of the Sea Captains,' the young clergyman said.

Tayte wasn't there for the lesson. He turned away, taking the place in. It was a predominantly white interior with gilded detail and galleried wooden balconies. His eyes strayed to the stained glass windows and then back to the walls, looking for pertinent inscriptions. In the background the clergyman continued his lesson.

'More than seventy sea captains have been buried in our churchyard over the years,' he said. 'And although not buried here, one important parishioner I'm sure you've all heard of is Captain Cook.'

Jean sidled up next to Tayte and studied the wall with him. 'Maybe we can talk to one of the churchwardens.'

Tayte looked around. 'If we can find one.'

The clergyman giving the history lesson was the only member of the church he'd seen, and he seemed settled for the time being.

'Does anyone know where our church got its name?' the clergyman said.

Tayte saw a hand shoot up from the pews.

'Because of St Paul,' one of the children said.

'That's right. But more specifically, it was named after a very famous St Paul's in Central London. Can anyone tell me which?'

St Paul's Cathedral, Tayte thought, not really registering his answer as he moved around the church and continued to study the inscriptions with Jean. There were relatively few, and nothing he saw came close to the dates they were looking for.

'It was dedicated to St Paul in honour of the Dean of St Paul's Cathedral,' the clergyman said, confirming Tayte's answer when none of the children did.

The words caught up with Tayte then. He suddenly found himself very interested. He turned to listen more attentively and saw that Jean was already ahead of him. He sat beside her in the pews.

'In 1669,' the clergyman continued, 'Dean William Sancroft—who later became Archbishop of Canterbury—owned the land this church was built on. It was because of his granting of the lease to build our community church that we are here today.'

Jean turned to Tayte. 'Are you thinking what I'm thinking?'

Tayte was thinking a number of things and chief among them was the self-consuming dragon, Ouroboros. 'It goes full circle,' he said. 'Ethelred to St Paul's Cathedral. St Paul to this St Paul's church, which connects us back to the cathedral and Ethelred.'

'Ad infinitum,' Jean said.

It was a good connection but Tayte needed more. He stood up, not wanting to waste another second. 'Excuse me,' he called, raising his hand as he spoke as if that made the interruption okay. 'Do you keep your own parish registers here?'

The sudden intrusion seemed to take the clergyman aback. 'No,' he said, his brow firmly scrunched. 'None.'

'Do you know where the burial registers *are* kept? Maybe the local record office?'

The clergyman nodded. 'Since the war years, yes.'

'And prior to that?'

'Everything was destroyed during the Blitz. Now, would you mind waiting until we've finished? I can answer your questions then.'

'Everything?' Tayte said, more to himself than to the clergyman. He knew the centralisation of England's parish registers hadn't begun in earnest until after the war, and he supposed such losses had prompted it. 'There were no copies?' he added, unconvinced. He thought about the Harleian Society publication he'd looked through at the church in Covent Garden. 'Weren't the registers published anywhere?'

'No,' the clergyman said. 'Everything was lost. Now I must—'

Tayte put his hand up again, this time in surrender. 'There's no need,' he said. It was clear that he was testing the young man's patience. A quick glance at the teachers sitting in the pews confirmed that he was testing theirs, too. He gave an apologetic smile. 'I'm sorry for the interruption,' he added and sat down again.

He turned to Jean, who looked mildly embarrassed for him or perhaps because of him. 'No records,' he said. 'No copies, either.'

'So where does that leave us?'

'Headstones and memorials. That's about it.'

Jean stood up. 'Let's go outside and take a look at the graveyard. Before we're thrown out.'

They took a clockwise route around the church from the gate they had entered by, checking every memorial they came to for a date that matched one of Queen Anne's failed attempts to provide an heir—a grave that should not be there. They walked side by side, like crime scene officers looking for the smallest piece of evidence. Typically, they found that many of the inscriptions were worn and difficult to read.

'This is going to take a while,' Tayte said. They had cleared ten or twelve graves and he was anxiously aware that the clock was ticking.

'We can't afford to cut corners,' Jean said.

Tayte knew she was right, but he had a feeling it was going to take more time than they had. He began to wonder when their expected company would arrive, thinking that if he had to run anywhere else today, the heart attack he'd feigned on the boat would hit him for real—if running was even an option. The churchyard was all but empty. He'd only seen one other person: a groundskeeper tending the border by the far wall they were heading towards. They would be easy targets.

They continued in silence, focusing on the dates, quickly ruling out every memorial they came to. Then as Murphy's Law would have it, the silence was shattered by thirty school children as they ran out into the churchyard armed with their tracing paper. Tayte just wanted to get this done and get out of there. Now an army of ten-year-olds was running riot, covering the headstones they needed to see with tracing paper.

Tayte pushed a frustrated hand through his hair. 'That's just great.'

'Maybe you could recruit them,' Jean said, smiling to herself.

Tayte thought about it. 'That's not a bad idea. Better to have the horde with you than against you, right?'

'I was joking,' Jean said. 'Anyway, you'd never get past the teachers.'

Tayte was going to try anyway, but just as he was about to find a teacher to ask, a white-haired man in a green shirt and tan corduroy trousers came over and spoke to them. He was the groundskeeper Tayte had seen, although he looked several years past retirement age.

'Sightseeing, are you?'

Tayte thought it a reasonable assumption given that the man had probably seen them musing over every inscription they came to. 'No, not really.'

'Looking for family, then?'

Tayte shook his head. 'I'm a genealogist looking for a date.'

The man laughed to himself. 'Then you're looking in the wrong place. Everyone's dating online these days.'

Jean laughed with him. Tayte just smirked.

'I'm sorry,' the man said. 'I couldn't resist. What name are you looking for?'

'We don't have a name,' Jean said.

'No name?' the man repeated. 'Pity. I might have been able to help.'

'We're looking for a headstone dated somewhere between 1697 and 1700,' Tayte said.

The groundskeeper drew a long breath. 'Then you're still looking in the wrong place. You won't find anything that old out here.'

'Why's that?' Jean asked. She didn't seem ready to believe him. 'This graveyard's been here since the mid-1600s, hasn't it?'

'That might be so,' the man said. 'But there's not so much of it now as there used to be. Back in the 1840s it was twice the size, but the London Dock Company compulsory purchased the land for development. All the older graves went. Then in the 1920s much of what was left was cleared for a nature study area.'

Jean chewed her lip. 'What about a crypt?'

The man scratched behind his ear, shaking his head. 'Times change,' he said. 'Space is a precious commodity in London, as in any big city. The church crypt was turned into a community centre in the 1980s. I'd not long started working here then.'

Tayte and Jean exchanged glances, saying nothing. Then Jean turned away and Tayte thanked the man. He caught up with her and they walked a few paces in silence, passing puddles of children who had settled onto the grass in pairs: one holding the tracing paper, the other rubbing the crayon.

'I guess that saved us some time,' Tayte said, trying to focus on the positives.

Jean stopped abruptly and turned to him. She gave a cheer-less laugh. 'Time for what?' she said. 'Don't you see? It's over.' She crossed her arms and locked eyes with him. 'This is the last church on our list,' she added, drumming the reality home. 'We've got a connection back to St Paul's Cathedral, which leaves me thinking that this is probably the right church, but where does it leave us? All the old graves are gone, and the only records were destroyed during the Blitz.'

Tayte knew she was really worrying about where that left her son and it was easy to understand why. How would things turn out for Elliot if they had nothing to exchange for him? He'd already considered the ramifications, but now was not the time to stand around discussing it. He grabbed Jean's hand.

'You may think it's over but it's not,' he said as they walked. 'There are people who still want us dead. They don't know it's over, so we need to leave this place.'

They reached the street and Tayte looked for a taxi. It was late afternoon and the traffic was building. He was about to start walking again, if only to get away from the church, when he heard something that sent a shiver through him. He turned towards the sound, back to the churchyard. One of the schoolgirls was turning in slow circles between the headstones, singing his name.

'Jefferson Tayte…Jefferson Tayte…'

Tayte sprinted back through the gate and stopped several feet from her. In her hand she had a letter and a toy rabbit.

'Are you Jefferson Tayte?' she asked.

Tayte stepped closer. 'Yes, I am.' He indicated the letter. 'Is that for me?'

The girl gave a quick nod and held the letter out.

'Thank you,' Tayte said as he took it. Then he turned away and ripped it open as Jean caught up.

'What is it?' she said.

Tayte showed her. 'Further instructions. There's a number to call when we've identified the heir.'

Jean knelt in front of the girl. 'Who gave you this?'

The girl pointed towards the road—to the iron railings and the path that ran alongside them. 'The lady.'

There was a woman dressed in black, heading off to their right. Tayte dropped his briefcase and ran across the graveyard.

'Hey!'

The woman turned and Tayte saw that it was a girl who looked like she was in her late teens. She had gum in her mouth, a silver stud through her lip, and she wore dark makeup, goth style.

Tayte showed her the letter through the railings, sidestepping to keep up with her. She eyed it briefly and turned away again, unfazed by the fact that he knew she'd delivered it. Clearly, this was not her note.

'Who gave this to you?' Tayte asked.

The girl turned back to him. 'Man in a van,' she said. 'Gave me twenty quid and a cuddly toy for the girl.'

Tayte looked along the street. There was no van there now. 'Did you see this man? What did he look like?'

'Fat,' the girl said, snapping her gum in Tayte's face.

'What kind of van was it?'

'A white one, stupid.'

The railings ran out. The girl kept walking. Tayte gave a frustrated sigh and turned back. He figured it was no use pursuing the matter. The girl clearly wasn't interested, and the man in the van was probably a couple of miles away by now. Tayte supposed he'd probably been paid for his services, too, but by whom? And how did they know where to find him? He was sure no one could have followed them from Covent Garden. He returned to Jean who was waiting by the gate with his briefcase. He didn't have to say anything. His expression said it all.

'Let's get out of here,' he said, and they started walking with the flow of the traffic.

They hadn't long cleared the church when Tayte saw a taxi and stuck his arm out. Then as it pulled over, he froze. A blue Ford he recognised was heading towards them.

'They're here.'

Chapter Twenty-Eight

As soon as Tayte saw the blue Ford approaching St Paul's, he crouched beside the taxi he'd just hailed and pulled Jean down with him. As she got in, Tayte watched the Ford arrive in a hurry and pull up onto the pavement outside the church. Two men he recognised got out, and he didn't wait around to find out whether they had seen them. He threw his briefcase into the taxi and jumped in after it.

'Thames House,' he said to the driver.

Jean was looking out the rear window and Tayte looked with her. One of the men, the gaunt-looking scarecrow of a man, was heading into the churchyard. His blonde associate remained by the car, watching the street.

'They can't have seen us,' Tayte said as the taxi pulled away. He faced the front and slid lower. 'Better keep down until we're clear, though.'

Jean turned back into the taxi and sank down beside him. She eyed him questioningly. 'Thames House?'

Tayte nodded. 'We're going in. It's the only way to stop this. The people at the top of the chain need to know it's over. Maybe then they'll leave us alone.'

'You think?' Jean said. She sounded doubtful.

Tayte settled back for the ride. 'I don't know what to think,' he admitted. 'The way I see it, though, is that if the heir can't be found—if this thing can't be proved one way or the other—why kill us? And that goes for Elliot, too. Why harm him if there's nothing to gain from it? I don't see why anyone would.'

'I wish I shared your faith in humanity.'

Tayte reached into his pocket, pulled out the pieces of the BlackBerry, and reassembled it. He read the note again, the last part aloud.

'Once the heir is confirmed, Elliot will be released.'

'Only, the heir can't be found,' Jean said. 'War and redevelopment have seen to that over the years.'

Tayte stared at the phone, hesitating.

Am I doing the right thing?

When it came to it he couldn't see any other way through this. He began punching numbers into the phone. 'And that's the message I'm going to deliver,' he said. 'The heir is lost. It's over.'

Jean began to protest but Tayte stopped her.

'You need to trust me.'

He pressed the phone to his ear, and the call picked up on the second ring without greeting. He'd expected an answering machine but he got a real voice; it was a young and clearly perturbed male voice.

'Speak your information clearly,' he said, like he was reading from a cue card. 'Once it has been confirmed, I will be released.'

'Elliot?'

The colour drained from Jean's face. She grabbed the phone. 'Baby? Is that you?' She had tears in her eyes.

'Mum!'

Tayte heard the plea. He took the phone back and put the call on speaker. 'Whoever's listening to this,' he said. 'The trail ends at St Paul's, Shadwell.' He paused. Silence. 'It's over,' he said. Then he explained why, laying out the trail they had followed from the ahnentafel to St Paul's Cathedral, then to the St Paul's churches, and ending at Shadwell. 'You can confirm it easily enough,' he added. 'The heir is lost, you hear me?'

When Tayte paused again, waiting for a response, all he heard was a click from the speaker.

'Elliot!' Jean called. Tears streaked her face.

Tayte put an arm around her. 'It's no use. They've hung up.'

'They're going to kill him!'

'No,' Tayte said. 'They're not.'

He believed it, too. He still thought 'they' meant Michel Levant, and he figured he was too smart a man to kill someone without good reason, so since the trail had ended at Shadwell, Tayte couldn't see what the Frenchman would have to gain from doing so. He knew it was a gamble, but he'd witnessed Levant's reaction to Jean's plea back at the hotel the night he'd shown up uninvited. Something she'd said had reached the man, he was sure of it.

As the taxi passed the Tower of London on their left, heading east along Lower Thames Street, Tayte picked up the phone again.

'Who are you calling now?' Jean asked.

'Fable.'

Tayte selected his number from the address book. This time the detective picked up.

'Tayte,' he said. 'Sorry I missed your call earlier. Everything okay? I tried to call back.'

'The phone was off,' Tayte said. 'And no, everything's not okay. We're coming in. The heir hunt's over.'

'Where are you going? Scotland Yard?'

'Thames House,' Tayte said. 'The heir can no longer be identified and your Security Service needs to know that. Can you meet us?'

'I'm twenty minutes away.'

'Good. We'll meet you there.'

Tayte ended the call and noticed that the taxi had slowed down. Looking out the window he could see that the traffic had built since reaching Central London. There were traffic lights every few hundred yards—queues of ten or twenty cars at each. Tayte loosened his seat belt and leant towards the driver.

'How long will it take?'

'In this traffic, maybe half an hour.'

Tayte sat back again and closed his eyes as Lower Thames Street slowly drained into Upper Thames Street. When he opened them again they were on tree-lined Victoria Embankment, tracking the river on their left, where he caught glimpses of the London Eye and Waterloo Bridge, passing boats in permanent mooring that at night became restaurants and nightclubs.

Jean had gone very quiet and Tayte couldn't think of anything to say that would make her feel any better, so they shared an uncomfortable silence for a time. Further down, when they came to Westminster Bridge, the taxi turned right, making a left turn at Parliament Square towards Millbank, where the traffic cleared a little and they picked up speed.

'Not far now,' the driver called back.

Tayte recognised the view from their first visit to Thames House: the heavy shade from the mature trees to either side of the road, the tall, stone buildings to their right, and the gardens that had momentarily replaced the river to their left. That was just two days ago but it felt more like two weeks.

He turned to Jean, but when he saw that her eyes were shut tight he turned away again. He felt he had to say something. He didn't know what. Anything. It didn't matter. Just something to get her talking again and maybe take her mind off Elliot for a few minutes. He was about to say how nice the river had looked in the late afternoon sun—just useless small talk—but as he turned to her again the words stuck in his throat. Through the window he saw a blue Ford careering towards them.

'Look out!'

He pulled Jean towards him as the Ford rammed the side of the taxi. It swerved and began to snake in the road.

'The phone,' Jean said. 'They must have tracked it.'

'Who the hell are these people?'

Whoever they were they were coming at them again. This time they slammed hard into the driver's door and the taxi veered left, skidding with the blow. Up front, the driver was shouting obscenities as he fought to control the vehicle, but Tayte knew he was losing it. They mounted the kerb with a jolt that lifted Tayte out of his seat. He caught glimpses of people scurrying out of the way. Then ahead through the windscreen he saw the tree.

The bonnet of the taxi seemed to explode on impact, rising in a gush of steam from the burst radiator before slamming down again. Tayte and Jean lurched forward, seat belts engaging, stopping them both from being body-slammed into the driver's partition. When Tayte recovered, through the cracked windscreen he saw the Ford pull up ahead. It was the only car that did. The rest of the traffic kept moving.

'Go!'

Jean was already pulling at the door handle. 'I can't. It won't open.'

It didn't take long for Tayte to realise why. The red light was on. The doors were locked and the release switch was up front with the driver. He slapped the palm of his hand repeatedly on the partition. 'Hey!' he called. 'The door release. We need to get out!'

The driver didn't move. He could have been dead for all Tayte knew. Looking out through the windscreen again he saw the hollow-cheeked face of the man who had previously tried to kill them as he came now to finish the job.

Tayte banged on the partition some more. 'Hey!'

The driver groaned. He stirred briefly then faded again. Beyond the windscreen, trouble was fast approaching. The scarecrow was in the road. The other man was on the pavement. They were coming at them on both sides of the taxi.

Tayte sat back and repeatedly kicked the partition. It was slowly giving out but it was taking too long. 'Come on!' he yelled at the driver. 'Let us out of here!'

Nothing.

Jean joined in. 'Hey!' She thumped the screen but it was no use. The driver was either dead or out cold.

Outside his window Tayte saw that the few people who had scattered when the taxi mounted the pavement were returning—coming to their aid at last. Behind him he thought he heard a car pull up. Then as if to counter all hope, a gunshot scattered the people again—this time for good.

Tayte looked ahead and saw that the scarecrow had removed the silencer from his gun. He'd let off a warning shot to deliberately clear the area and it had worked. He was coming for Jean, and through his window Tayte could see that his partner was coming for him. He thought his and Jean's murders would be on the front page of the newspapers in the morning: man and woman shot dead in London taxi. Read all about it.

The blonde-haired man approached Tayte's window, lifted the hem of his sweatshirt, and drew a handgun from the top of his jeans. He levelled it at Tayte through the glass, and Tayte faced him, steel jawed. There was nowhere to go. No way to fight back. He wasn't about to cower. All around him seemed suddenly calm, despite Jean's now frantic attempts to break through the partition.

When the gunshot came, Tayte shut his eyes tight. It took him a while to realise that the man outside his window hadn't fired it. And it took the sight of that man falling at the glass, his face sliding slowly down it, for him to understand that the shooter himself had been shot. The ambient noise returned to Tayte then, as suddenly as if someone had just released a mute button.

Gunfire erupted behind him.

He looked at Jean who was now crouched into a ball on the floor. He checked for the scarecrow again and saw him duck behind the bonnet. They locked eyes briefly as the man rose again to take a shot, but a close bullet pinged the coachwork and made him think again. It forced him to backtrack for better cover, returning fire as he went.

Chancing a look out the rear window, Tayte saw two people he wouldn't have thought he'd be so happy to see again.

'It's MI5,' he said to Jean. 'Jackson and Stubbs.'

Jean looked up, staying low. 'They must have been watching at Shadwell.'

'And they've followed us in,' Tayte said.

He heard a tap on the door and Stubbs poked his head up at the window.

'Get back!'

The next thing Tayte saw was the butt of a gun as it smashed through the glass. He heard covering fire from Jackson, and then like an echo two shots were returned.

Tayte gave Jean a nervous smile. 'You'd better go first,' he said. 'In case I get stuck.'

Stubbs knocked out what remained of the glass and Jean didn't waste a second getting out. Tayte watched her slip through the opening like it was something she did every day. He thought it would be easier for him if he sat in the frame first, but that would mean putting his head in harm's way.

'Come on,' Stubbs said. 'Crawl out. Stay low.'

Tayte put his hands through the frame and paused. He thought about his briefcase lying on the floor and figured this was where they parted company. He refocused on the gap where the window had been. It seemed wide enough. He wasn't that overweight, was he? He made it halfway before Stubbs had to start pulling. Below him he could see his assailant's dead body, and not wanting to wind up beside him, Tayte kicked his legs, trying to work his midsection through a little at a time like a caterpillar. He was almost out when a gunshot reported to his right and in that same instant Stubbs jerked back. He clutched his shoulder and staggered, letting go of Tayte, who fell the rest of the way out. Another volley of shots was exchanged as Jackson returned fire from the other side of the taxi.

'Help him up,' Jean said.

She took off her jacket and as Tayte sat Stubbs up against the side of the taxi, she pressed it to his wound. Two more shots cracked out, and Jackson came around from the back of the taxi. He squatted beside Stubbs and checked his wound.

'Is he going to be okay?' Tayte asked. He felt more than a little responsible.

'He should make it,' Jackson said, stone-faced as ever. 'Services are on their way.'

Another bullet clipped the taxi with a dull thump, letting them know this wasn't over.

'This guy's persistent,' Tayte said.

Jackson snorted. 'Yeah, well, he's going to have more heat than he can handle in a minute. All we've got to do is stay put.'

'Is that a good idea?' Jean said. 'He knows where we are.'

'We stay put,' Jackson said again. 'The cab's good for cover as long as we stay down.'

Jean turned to Tayte and quietly said, 'I don't like not being able to see him.'

'I don't like it any better when we can,' Tayte said. 'But I know what you mean.'

Jackson was doing his best to find out where the other gunman was. He kept peering over the bonnet and around the trees along the pavement. It went eerily quiet. No cars. No other people. Even the birds had fled from the trees, and there wasn't a soul to be seen in the gardens beyond the railing. Tayte figured someone must have stopped the traffic when the firefight kicked off. There was a bus lane and chevrons down the middle of the road—plenty of room for the emergency services to get through, but where were they?

The seconds that followed that thought came and went in a confused blur. Tayte saw the man who was trying to kill them appear suddenly at the rear of the taxi. He thought he must have worked his way around them on the other side of the street. He heard a shout from Jean and saw Jackson turn and squeeze off a wild shot that missed by a mile, or might as well have. Then he saw Jackson buckle over as Stubbs tried to get a shot off, but the gun was kicked out of his hand.

And suddenly Tayte was running again.

Jean had his arm, leading him past the blue Ford towards Lambeth Bridge. Sirens began to wail, the sound coming from all direction, but they did nothing to deter the man who just would not stop. He didn't seem to care if he was killed, just as long as he succeeded in killing them first. The next bullet splintered a tree as they reached it and ducked behind it, still running.

'It's not far,' Jean said.

Tayte had heard that before. He'd lost hold of her now and was already falling back.

'It's just past the bridge,' Jean added. 'We'll make it if we can keep the trees between us. I can see police lights ahead.'

Tayte thought the bridge and the police lights looked too far away. He felt like he hadn't stopped running since Covent Garden and vowed to join a gym if he ever saw his homeland again. But that seemed like a hollow promise to him now. He watched Jean make it to the next tree and knew he wasn't going to reach it. When he thought the man behind him was about to take another shot, he stopped and turned to face him. He wasn't going to take a bullet in the back. He wanted to see his killer as he pulled the trigger.

And there he was.

Up close Tayte liked the look of him even less. When the man saw that Tayte had stopped, he slowed to a fast walk and smiled a thin crack of a smile that accentuated the dark hollows beneath his cheekbones. When he was no more than ten feet away, he raised the gun and for some reason Tayte smiled at him. He didn't know why at first, but he soon realised it was because of the car.

It seemed to come out of nowhere, and before another shot was fired, a ton and a half of automotive machinery had bucked up onto the pavement and swiped the scarecrow's legs out from under him.

Tayte jumped back and watched the man bounce off the bonnet, then roll like a discarded cigarette towards the garden railings.

The passenger door shot open.

'Get in!'

It was DI Fable, on his way to Thames House to meet them.

Chapter Twenty-Nine

Jefferson Tayte was lying on the bed in his hotel room, staring at the ceiling. He'd not long checked his watch, keeping an eye on the time. It was almost eight-thirty in the evening, and the hours that had passed since DI Fable had saved his life at Millbank had for the most part been consumed by the questions that had been fired at him by the people he'd met at Thames House soon afterwards: people who needed answers and who eventually seemed satisfied with what he'd told them. All that was over now, he hoped.

The general sense of disquiet he still felt as he lay there was entirely because of Jean's son. He kept telling himself that he'd done all he could—that no harm would come to Elliot if it turned out that the hunt for Queen Anne's heir was a lost cause and that there was nothing now for his captor to gain. But every minute that had passed since he'd made that phone call in the taxi tied the knot inside him tighter.

When DI Fable had dropped them back at the hotel, Jean had told Tayte that she had no appetite for a meal, which he understood, although he was surprised she didn't want a stiff drink at the bar with him after everything they had been through. But as anxious as Tayte now felt, he knew he could multiply those feelings a thousand times as far as Jean was concerned—if that even came close.

'I need some time to myself,' she'd said. 'Call for me later. Nine o'clock.'

That was all she'd said. Then she'd disappeared behind the lift door as it closed, and Tayte had gone to the bar and started drinking for both of them. He wasn't drunk—not even close. His appetite had kicked in before the alcohol took hold, and he'd gone into the restaurant and eaten for both of them, too. He could still feel her parting kiss on his cheek, or liked to think he could.

Tayte checked his watch again: eight-forty.

He'd already shaved and showered, and he figured he looked about as good as he was going to, given what little he had to work with. At least his hair was clean again, and tidy for a change, and he thought the aftershave he was wearing smelled nice, which was something. He wanted to see Jean again. He wanted to see her smile again, too: the kind of smile he'd seen the day they first met in Rules Restaurant when Marcus introduced them.

Marcus...

Tayte thought about his old friend and he felt bad for not thinking of him more often, but the events of the past few days simply hadn't allowed him to do so. He supposed he would have plenty of time to mourn his friend's passing once his life found its rhythm again, but he still hadn't resolved everything. Not yet. Marcus's murder had been avenged, but he still had to complete the research that had led to his death. He knew how much Marcus hated to leave his research unfinished once he'd started, and he thought he would do that for him in the morning, knowing as he did that there was more to this royal heir hunt than he had let on.

He started drifting with his thoughts, tripping down memory lane with Marcus Brown, the greatest genealogist he'd ever known or was ever likely to know. He thought about his college years, as he often did. He was fond of that time. It was somewhere he went back to when he needed a happy thought. He supposed everyone had a place like that in their lives. He thought of his first introduction to Marcus, recalling his passion and his wisdom, and the hope it had given him when he first started out in genealogy. Tayte felt he owed it to both of them now to resolve his own unfinished business, and he was just beginning to feel the familiar weight of all those failed attempts begin to smother him again when he was saved by the telephone. He sat up and swung his legs off the bed to answer it.

'Hello.'

'Mr Tayte? It's Jack Fable. I'm down at reception.'

Tayte hadn't expected to hear from the detective again so soon. 'What is it?'

'We found Joseph Cornell. More by chance than good police work.'

Tayte thought that was good news, but he had the feeling Joseph Cornell wasn't the reason the detective had come to the hotel so late. His next words confirmed it.

'There's something else,' Fable added. 'Something that can't wait until morning. I tried calling Ms Summer's room, but she's not answering.'

That said it all. 'You found her son?'

'I'd rather talk to Ms Summer in person,' Fable said. 'You think you can call on her and bring her down to the bar?'

'Sure,' Tayte said, and every bad scenario he could think of began to tumble through his mind. 'We were going for a drink at nine,' he added, putting his loafers on. 'Jean was probably getting ready when you called her.'

'Yeah, that must have been it,' Fable said. 'I'll see you both shortly. Oh, and tell her to bring her jacket.'

When he saw Jean again, Tayte didn't go into the details of Fable's call—not that he really had much information to share. What he did have was enough to worry him though, and he thought he'd spare her that for now. After all, Fable hadn't really said anything about Elliot. It was just his concerns over the probability that it now appeared Cornell had kidnapped her son, not Michel Levant. He knew the kind of man Robert Cornell had been, and at this point he didn't suppose his brother was much different.

'Why does he want me to bring my jacket?' Jean asked as they walked to the lift.

'I guess you're going somewhere,' Tayte said, praying it wasn't to the city morgue. 'Let's just wait and see what he has to say.'

Fable was sitting at a table in the Churchill Bar when they entered. It was quiet. A young couple were sitting on stools at the bar. A few other tables were taken. Background conversation was barely audible. Fable stood up as they approached, and they all sat down together as a waiter came to take their drinks order. Tayte ordered a Jack Daniels to continue where he'd left off an hour ago, and Jean had the same. Fable declined.

'This is becoming a habit,' Fable said to Tayte. He reached down beside his chair and lifted Tayte's briefcase up. 'What is it with you and London taxis?'

Tayte smiled as he reacquainted himself with it for the second time in as many days. 'Thanks,' he said. 'I'll try not to let it happen again, believe me.'

Fable held something else out. It was a black plastic box the size of a slim matchbox. 'They found this taped inside.'

'What is it?'

'It's a GPS transmitter.'

'A tracking device?' Tayte said. He scoffed. 'Good place to put it. My case goes everywhere with me.'

Jean sat forward and took a closer look. 'So that's how they knew we were at St Paul's Church in Shadwell.'

'I guess it is,' Tayte said, wondering who had access to his briefcase recently. A second later, he said, 'Michel Levant. He could have put it there when I left it in the taxi the first time around. He followed us to the construction site where Robert Cornell worked.'

'And whoever put it there wrote the notes,' Jean said. 'And they kidnapped my son.'

'What notes?'

Tayte felt his cheeks flush. 'I wanted to tell you, Detective. I just needed room to think.'

Jean explained everything and Fable looked disappointed. 'You damn well should have told me,' he said. He paused, letting it go. 'Look, before you go jumping to conclusions about who put this in your briefcase, there are things you need to know.' He cut right to it. 'Joseph Cornell is dead. His body was discovered at a flat in Islington earlier this evening.'

'Dead?' Tayte said, considering the ramifications. 'How? When?'

'Someone reported hearing a gunshot earlier this evening, or what sounded like a gunshot. Turned out they were right.'

'Who was it,' Tayte asked. 'A neighbour?'

'Anonymous call from a payphone. Local. People don't always like to get involved.'

'What happened?' Jean asked.

'Joseph Cornell was found sitting in an armchair with a hole in his head. A handgun was found on the carpet beside him. Time of death coincides with the call we received. Suicide seems the probable cause but it's yet to be confirmed.'

Their drinks arrived, suspending the conversation. When the waiter left again, Jean knocked half her drink back, eyes on Fable the whole time. 'Why did you want me to bring my jacket?'

Fable leant towards her and gave a reassuring smile. 'It's good news, Ms Summer. Your son was at the flat.'

Tayte waited for Jean to say something but she didn't. Instead, she continued to look at Fable until her eyes welled with tears. Then she stood up, sniffed, and put her jacket on.

Fable rose with her but he beckoned her to sit down again. 'Finish your drink,' he said. 'He's in safe hands.'

'Where is he?'

'Guy's Hospital, but he's okay. He's being checked over, that's all. Just routine.'

'They didn't hurt him?'

'He has a few bruises. A possible cracked rib. Nothing more. He probably struggled at first.'

Tayte thought about the phone message he'd left for Elliot's kidnapper. It was over. That's what he'd said. The heir could not be found. He thought Cornell must have seen no other way out.

But what about Levant?

Tayte couldn't get past the fact that the Cornells needed a genealogist. And he couldn't see how Joseph Cornell could have planted that tracking device in his briefcase. Apart from when he'd left it in the back of the taxi at the gasworks, it had been by his side every step of the way. If Joseph Cornell had been there, surely he would have intervened when Levant showed up.

Jean stood up again. Her cheeks glistened beneath the ceiling lights, and her hands were shaking as she downed the rest of her drink. 'I want to see my son,' she said. 'I want to see him now.'

'Okay,' Fable said as he rose. 'Let's go see him.'

As they walked, Tayte asked how officers Jackson and Stubbs were.

'They're going to make it,' Fable said without elaborating.

'What about the man who shot them? Did they pick him up?'

Fable shook his head. 'The manhunt continues. He probably made it to the river, and my guess is that he's one highly resourceful son of a bitch. I doubt we'll see him again.'

They reached the lobby. In her haste, Jean had pushed ahead.

'Any idea who he was working for?' Tayte said.

Fable sighed. 'Does it matter?' He sounded beat. 'It's over, Tayte. The people at Thames House bought your story, even if I didn't.'

Tayte said nothing. He just looked at his shoes as they headed across the lobby.

Fable stopped halfway to the door. 'Someone didn't want you to find what you were looking for,' he added. 'I'm sure Joseph Cornell was a marked man, too. Maybe he killed himself. Maybe he didn't. There are powerful people out there who'd rather let sleeping dogs lie, if you know what I mean. My advice to you is to do the same and move on.'

'And what about you?' Tayte said. 'Are you moving on?'

'There seem to be a few loose ends still, don't there?'

Tayte nodded, thinking about Michel Levant again as they caught up with Jean. He gave her a smile and changed the subject.

'Well, I'll let you take it from here,' he said. 'I'm sure you'd like some time alone with your son.'

'Thank you,' Jean said. 'And don't wait up. I don't think I'll be coming back to the hotel tonight. Elliot's dad will want to spend some time with him, too, so I guess we'll go there.'

'Oh, okay,' Tayte said. 'Well, I'm glad things turned out.'

Jean nodded. She turned away, then she quickly turned back again. 'How about lunch tomorrow?'

Tayte's face lit up. 'That'd be great. Where?'

'The National Portrait Gallery. I'll meet you there around midday?'

Jean leant in and kissed Tayte's cheek for the second time that evening, and Tayte suddenly felt light on his toes. She glanced back as she followed Fable to the car, and Tayte thought that was a good sign, too. He was still smiling to himself when he reached the lift, thinking that all he needed now was an early night. If he was going to continue this royal heir hunt and finish Marcus Brown's research in time for lunch with Jean, he needed a good start on the day.

Chapter Thirty

Tayte left the hotel the following morning with purpose in his stride. He stepped out onto the pavement between a row of stone pillars that tried in vain to lend a sense of grandeur to the hotel's otherwise uninspiring facade. He looked at the park across the street in Portland Square, then up into the changeable sky before turning right, making his way alongside the taxi rank further down.

It was thirty-seven minutes past eight precisely, according to Michel Levant's bejewelled Cartier watch. He'd been studying the hotel entrance from a bench in the park for the last hour, having chosen his location carefully so as to avoid being picked up by any of the street surveillance cameras in the area. He was watching intently through a pair of antique, mother-of-pearl opera glasses, which he now slipped into the pocket of his coat. He got up to follow Tayte, but he was pressed into his seat again by a firm hand, the arrival of which was accompanied by a dense plume of cigarette smoke.

'Inspector Fable,' Levant said, smiling thinly to disguise the consternation he felt at seeing the black-suited detective standing like some contemporary Grim Reaper beside him.

Fable sat down and nodded towards the hotel where Tayte had now passed the taxi rank, still walking. 'He must be taking the Tube from Marble Arch this morning,' he said. He took another drag on his cigarette and blew the smoke across Levant's line of sight. When the air cleared, Tayte was gone.

Levant's lips remained tight, his smile wavering.

'I thought I'd find you around here,' Fable said. He held out his hand. In his palm was a small black box. 'Know what this is?'

Levant shook his head. 'Should I?'

'It's a GPS transmitter.'

'Really?' Levant said. 'But I'm afraid technology and Michel Levant do not mix well.'

Fable looked sceptical. 'I doubt that,' he said, putting the device back in his pocket. 'It's not active anymore,' he added. 'But I'm sure you already know that. That's why you're here, isn't it? So you can follow Tayte the old-school way.'

Levant crossed his legs and turned to face Fable more fully. 'Is it a crime, Inspector?'

'That all depends,' Fable said. 'But it's not why I'm here.'

Levant fidgeted. 'Then why *are* you here?'

'I'm here because I knew this is where I'd find you, and because murder most definitely is a crime.'

Levant laughed—a small laugh that belonged to a child.

'As is being an accomplice to murder,' Fable added. 'Like finding a man and passing his name and address to someone you know intends to kill him.'

Levant was suddenly wide-eyed at the suggestion. 'Inspector, I hope you're not suggesting that—'

'What I'm suggesting,' Fable cut in, 'is that you were hired by the Cornells to find the descendants of certain long dead Fellows of the Royal Society. I'm suggesting that you started with Julian Davenport and ended with Peter Harper.'

'But that is absurd!'

Levant tried to stand up for a second time, but Fable forced the Frenchman down again.

'Is it?' Fable said. 'So there's no point in checking the records Marcus Brown requested at The National Archives and at the General Register Office when he researched Davenport's family history?

There's no point checking to see who else requested those documents recently?'

Levant gave no reply. He pulled a gold enamel cigarette case from his inside coat pocket and offered one of the thin cigarettes to Fable.

'French?' Fable said.

'Mais oui. Of course.'

'No thanks.' Fable lit another of his own. 'I've got news for you, Levant,' he added, getting back to the conversation. 'I already checked those records.'

'And what did you find, Inspector?'

'I found what was possibly your only mistake in all this. I found you.' Fable smiled to himself. 'You must have really kicked yourself for using your own name when you realised what was going on with the Cornell brothers. If you'd stopped at Davenport, you might have been okay. How were you to know what they intended to do with the information you gave them?' He paused and took another long drag on his cigarette. 'But you didn't stop, did you? You became someone called Alan Smith. Not a very imaginative nom de plume, as you might call it, was it?'

Levant laughed the suggestion off. 'But I am not this Alan Smith,' he protested. 'What if I told you I did stop when I heard of Monsieur Davenport's murder?'

'Then I'd say you're a liar.'

Levant gave a sickly grin. 'But surely, it is not a matter of what you believe, Inspector, but what you can prove.'

'You're absolutely right,' Fable said. 'And The National Archives CCTV footage will prove that you were there prior to each and every one of Alan Smith's record requests.'

'It's a little weak, Inspector. Don't you think?'

'I think it's a good place to start,' Fable said. 'Whoever requested those records was an accomplice to murder. And I can put you at the scene, so to speak. By the time all the footage has been checked and all the records correlated, I'll have enough to get you in front of a jury.'

Levant laughed again, but only to hide his growing discomfort. Win or lose, such a trial would do nothing for his reputation. He had found Julian Davenport, after all. That record trail alone would incriminate him.

'And you worked all this out by yourself?' Levant said with more than a hint of sarcasm.

Fable eyed him sourly. 'It only takes one good copper to nail a scumbag like you.'

After a pause, Levant sighed and said, 'You always get your man, eh, Inspector? However smart he may be?'

'Don't flatter yourself, Levant. As soon as Mr Tayte got me thinking about that record trail, it was easy.'

'Ah, Monsieur Tayte,' Levant said. 'He has been quite an adversary, I think.' He stubbed his cigarette out on the arm of the bench and let it fall to the ground. Then he sat up and slapped Fable's thigh. 'Bravo, Inspector!'

Fable shifted uneasily. He brushed his leg where Levant had touched him as though his hand had left a dirty mark. 'Do that again and I'll break your nose.'

'Tut-tut, Inspector. But you should thank me.'

'What the hell for?'

Levant settled back again. 'The Cornells were fanatics like their father. They came to me with the idea that together we could resurrect the Royal House of Stuart. They told me the fantastic tale of Queen Anne's heir and promised me great wealth and reputation—both of which I adore, of course. But their plan was quite ridiculous.'

'Don't tell me,' Fable said. 'Once you'd found Queen Anne's living descendant, Joseph Cornell would use his position in Royalty Protection to assassinate the royal top table? We already had that figured out.'

'I'm sure you did. They believed it would pave the way for a new heir to come forward, and in the confusion, who knows? Maybe the Stuart bloodline would reign again, or perhaps the monarchy of Great Britain would end altogether. Either way, they didn't mind.'

'Better no monarch than the wrong monarch?'

'Oui, Inspector. That is exactly how they felt.'

'And if it had all worked out, you would have received a huge finder's fee for your trouble.'

Levant gave a small clap with the tips of his fingers. 'Bravo again, Inspector. But as I've said, their plan was quite ridiculous. I tried to talk them around to a more realistic proposal, but they would hear none of it. Alas for them I had already seen another, more realistic way to make the game worthwhile.'

Fable coughed into his hand. 'How's that?'

'I simply went from two desperate men to another—a politician of no consequence. I offered him ammunition for his republican campaign, and it was easy to convince such a vulnerable man that he needed the information I wished to sell him.'

Fable scoffed. 'And when Jefferson Tayte identified Robert Cornell, the man became too high a risk, is that it?'

'He had to go, Inspector. In many ways, Monsieur Tayte did me a great service. I wanted to stop him at first, but I saw a way to use them both. Such was Professor Summer's rage that she saved me the trouble of killing Robert Cornell myself as I effected my rescue.' Levant's face suddenly lit up. 'Imagine my delight.'

'What about his brother?'

Levant pursed his lips. 'Let's just say for now that I'm not surprised you couldn't find him.' He took out his cigarette case again and offered one to Fable as he had before.

Fable ignored him.

'Of course,' Levant said. 'Silly me. You don't like French cigarettes.' He lit one for himself and drew slowly on it, savouring it as if it were his last. 'I thought I framed poor Joseph very well. The mobile phone I planted at his home must have excited you, no? Then when you found him dead and Elliot Summer alive...'

He paused, reflecting on how Elliot Summer had served his purpose in the end.

'Michel Levant is no barbarian, Inspector. I thought that if Jefferson Tayte wanted to play games, I would play also. I love a good game, don't you? With Monsieur Tayte believing he had duped us all into thinking that Queen Anne's heir could no longer be identified, he is off his guard, no? The rest would have been easy, but alas...'

Levant toyed with the Sun King ring on his left index finger, admiring it briefly before checking the time. He watched several seconds tick slowly by.

'Do you know, Inspector, it took three strong men to hold Joseph Cornell so that he couldn't struggle. It had to look as though he took his own life, but it was Michel Levant who pulled the trigger.'

That last confession seemed to strike Fable dumb.

'Of course, you were right,' Levant added. 'I had no knowledge of the Cornells' plans until it was too late. I suppose they tested me at first—as if they needed to test Michel Levant!' He took on an indignant air. 'They came to me with a name—the Reverend Charles Naismith. They hired me to find his living descendant—his heir—and that is what I did when I gave them Julian Davenport. It was only after I read of his murder that I was truly aware of what I had done.'

Levant let out a long sigh. 'Do not get me wrong, Inspector. If I had known my research would lead to murder, I would still have done it given the prize. Only I would have been more careful, of course.'

Levant stood suddenly and Fable did nothing to stop him this time. 'But enough of this chitter-chatter,' the Frenchman said, discarding his cigarette. He turned and faced Fable, studying him.

Then he leant in and kissed his forehead, noting that the detective's skin had turned a pallid shade of blue.

'I am disappointed, Inspector Fable. You underestimated Michel Levant, I think.' He shook his head. 'C'est la vie. You were not the first to make such a mistake.'

With that, Levant walked away, heading for the taxi rank outside the hotel. As he opened the door to an available taxi, he heard a scream and looked back to the park. Fable was now lying on the bench. A woman was beside him, looking around for help. But Levant knew it was too late. Just as he knew that he had given his confession to a dead man.

He got into the taxi and gave the driver a random street name, thinking as he sat back and the taxi pulled away that he would take a sojourn to Paris. A visit was long overdue, and London was already beginning to leave a bad taste in his mouth. It always did, given time.

He knew there would be an autopsy. It was a matter of procedure in all cases of unexpected or unexplained death—especially the death of a policeman. Until then it would appear to the layman that DI Fable had perhaps had a heart attack, and who would be surprised. The autopsy, however, would reveal that Fable had died from asphyxiation.

As the taxi turned the corner, Levant studied his Sun King ring again, and this time he made sure the needle in the band was fully recessed. It would never do to prick himself with it as he had pricked Fable's thigh when he slapped him to hide the sting.

The lethal substance was called succinylcholine chloride, a synthetic equivalent of the naturally occurring curare, found in the jungles of South America and used by natives to tip their darts and arrows. In hospitals, tiny amounts were used in a muscle relaxant to keep patients still during delicate operations. Once it had taken effect, the neat alkaloid had quickly paralysed Fable's entire body, preventing his lungs from functioning, rendering him unable to breathe and yet unable to draw anyone's attention to the fact that he was slowly dying.

By the time Fable reached the pathologist's table, Levant knew that the poison would have broken down, leaving it all but impossible to detect. Puncture marks were unavoidable, though, and even if they went undetected, questions would be raised as to how the detective seemingly died from asphyxiation on a park bench in broad daylight. Suffocation and foul play would no doubt be the verdict, and Levant did not intend to stay and read about it.

He smiled to himself as he considered that the inspector had had some small triumph in his last moments. Levant's unresolved business with Jefferson Tayte would have to wait. After all, how could he risk further involvement now? No hunt was worth the hunter, however great the prize, and with the Cornell brothers dead, there was no one left in the game to blame for the demise of Detective Inspector Jack Fable.

Chapter Thirty-One

It was raining by the time Jefferson Tayte arrived at his destination, battered briefcase once again in hand. He had no umbrella but that didn't bother him; it had only been a short walk from the Underground station and the rain wasn't heavy. The streets were all the quieter for it, and he liked the way they smelled when the rain first arrived and mixed with the dust. It reminded him of old things, like antique books and boxes of old photographs that hadn't been opened in a while.

He passed through a pair of tall iron gates that led onto Inigo Place, and he recalled the conversation around the table at Rules Restaurant four days ago about technology and its effect on genealogical research. He considered that as records were changing—e-mail instead of letters, photographs on a hard drive instead of the pages of an album—so too were churchyards diminishing: headstones being swallowed whole by urbanisation and cultural progress. The thought saddened him, not least because it made him think of his friend again.

He thought that, like the Ouroboros, the assignment he had taken upon himself when Marcus was murdered had ended where it began, in Covent Garden. He walked towards St Paul's Church between the grey benches that were now empty and wet, through a memorial garden that without the sunshine and the people had lost much of its former vibrancy. Or maybe that was just his melancholy tainting the view.

There seemed to be twice as many steps leading up to the church than he remembered. They felt taller, too, because of his aching leg muscles. He climbed them laboriously, passed the advertisement board for *Dido and Aeneas,* and went inside. Not far inside. Just far enough to see the black and gold board on the wall that he'd seen when he last left the church after Jean and had fallen behind to read it.

The board commemorated past churchwardens, whose contributions to the Actors' Church had earned them their place on the list. The dates ranged from 1638, when the church was consecrated, to 1820. Tayte figured there must be another board somewhere covering more recent additions, but this was the only list he was interested in.

He found the name that had previously caught his eye, and to reaffirm what he already knew, he took Marcus Brown's charts out from his briefcase as he had on the steps outside with Jean the day before. He soon found the match. It was next to the entry for the Reverend Charles Naismith: Oliver Naismith, who according to the list on the wall had been a churchwarden at St Paul's Church between 1698 and 1709. The charts told him that Oliver was one of Charles Naismith's twin sons, who had carried his part of the ahnentafel number through to the next generation and had been a founder member of the society created to protect it: Quo Veritas.

Tayte slipped the charts back into his briefcase, thinking about Occam's razor and the idea that once the ahnentafel number was complete, the rest should be easy. Having already seen the connection, he knew that to those Fellows of the Royal Society who had created the puzzle, it *was* easy. The ahnentafel number pointed to Ethelred II, who pointed to St Paul. The fact that Oliver Naismith was churchwarden at St Paul's Church in Covent Garden would have been apparent to every one of them at the time.

Keep it simple...

Tayte smiled to himself as he went back out into the morning drizzle. It stood to reason that the Fellows needed someone on the inside if they were going to fake a burial, which was what they had to do. He made his way around the church to his right—to the few headstones and memorials that the current churchwarden had told them about. The answer to the puzzle had been right under their noses.

He supposed it was something you either saw right away or you didn't see at all. And Jean hadn't seen it. That was why he had seemed so insensitive to the tragedy of the mother who had died giving birth to a daughter who drowned eight years later, and whose father felt so responsible as to believe that he had let her die. Tayte had wanted to get Jean away from that memorial before she saw the truth.

He turned the corner making for the memorial now, sheltering from the rain beneath the trees that seemed to crowd the limited space between the church and the townhouses, darkening what was already a dull and forgotten space. He turned another corner, around the north transept, considering as he came to the memorial that the Fellows had chosen its placement well—of course they had, given what was at stake. As he was now sheltered from the elements by the canopy of trees and by the church itself, so was the memorial, giving the inscription the best chance of survival.

Tayte reached into his briefcase and took out his digital camera. Using software to enhance the shadows and highlights, he could make difficult-to-read inscriptions legible, although he didn't need any help on this occasion. He took several shots of the memorial from different angles and then took out a pad and transcribed the inscription, underlining the subject of the search: Maria Jane Booth. Born February 14th, 1700. Died March 21st, 1708.

It was a lie. Tayte could clearly see that now. He supposed the date of birth had been fabricated to remove any association with Anne Stuart, who was not then Queen of England. It would have been easy enough to falsify the date of the mother's death and the birth of their daughter by a mere three weeks, and it had worked. He and Jean had been looking for a date that matched one of Anne's failed pregnancies and had found none recorded in any of the Anglican parishes connected to St Paul.

But the date was not the marker.

It was the father's apparent display of guilt that left Tayte in no doubt that he had found Queen Anne's heir. He knelt before the inscription and read it again, murmuring the words beneath his breath.

'I let her die.'

He thought about Dr Bartholomew Hutton, who had been Anne's physician until his execution in 1708 and who, according to Rakesh Dattani at the Royal Society, had a penchant for anagrams. 'I let her die' was just that—an anagram of the name the ahnentafel number had pointed to: Ethelred II.

Tayte's eyes drifted to the mother's name on the memorial, knowing from it that she had died when the child was born. He thought about the timing. To make something like this work, the substitute baby had to be born on the same day as the heir. Dr Hutton would have known when Anne went into labour, but it puzzled him as to how the Booth family—who must have been in on the deceit—could have engineered the birth of their own child to coincide so precisely.

The only answer he could think of was that the mother's labour had been forced as soon as Dr Hutton gave word. And it had killed her. Tayte considered that the poor child was already forfeit, and he supposed the baby would either have died during what must have been an extremely traumatic birth, or had been suffocated immediately afterwards. That was the real tragedy to his mind. He wondered at the lengths this family must have gone to in order to fulfil their part in protecting the Royal Stuart bloodline. Perhaps 'I let her die' had a much deeper, truer meaning.

His thoughts wandered. He questioned why there had been any need to feign the child's death and hide her away, and the answer came quickly to him: it had happened in 1708. He recalled that the five Fellows of the Royal Society were hanged on April 25, 1708. Maria Booth had apparently died a month earlier.

Were they betrayed? Did they know that they had been discovered?

He thought they must have. The child's apparent death would deter anyone from looking further if they suspected who she was. And the Fellows' elaborate ahnentafel puzzle would find her again when the time was right: when science could irrefutably prove her Royal Stuart bloodline.

Tayte stood up, stiff and aching, like his joints were rusty hinges exacerbated by the damp. His eyes remained fixed on the inscription. For all it now seemed to be, it was still nothing more than so many words on a memorial. No genealogist of any repute would take such findings at face value, however good the connections. A good genealogist would go on to confirm his findings.

He supposed that if he looked he would find another burial record for Maria Jane Booth, perhaps in some faraway parish, many miles from the faces that might otherwise have recognised her. It would prove that she had not drowned in the Thames in 1708 but had lived on. He supposed he would find a record of her marriage, too, and baptism records for her own children. And from there he could trace her descendants to the present-day heir.

If he chose to.

He considered that his friend's research was now all but complete, and he questioned whether Marcus would have wanted to take it any further. Tayte couldn't know for sure. What he did know was that it had proven a deadly game, then and now, and he supposed no good could come from digging deeper. What if he did go on to identify an heir? What if through DNA testing they proved the conspiracy was no theory at all? He had little doubt that he would just be putting more people in danger. 'Move on,' Fable had said, and Tayte fully intended to.

He collected his briefcase and headed back out the way he'd come, considering that everyone involved had to believe the heir hunt ended in Shadwell and that Queen Anne's heir was a lost treasure that could never be found.

And it had worked, hadn't it?

He looked over his shoulder at the church and wondered if it really had. He scanned the area as he made his way back along Inigo Place to the gates and the main road beyond, and by the time he reached them he was laughing at himself for being so jumpy. As he stepped across the threshold, he popped a Hershey's chocolate into his mouth and left all thoughts of heirs and ahnentafels behind him. He was thinking about buying a new shirt and suit before lunch—thinking about Professor Jean Summer and how much he was looking forward to seeing her again.

Chapter Thirty-Two

She was waiting for him at the bar, gazing absently into the restaurant at nothing in particular, much as she had been at Rules Restaurant the first time he'd seen her. The black dress, patent leather heels, and overly bright makeup Jean had been wearing when Marcus introduced them had gone in favour of a simple dress, low heels, and a cardigan. She had her glasses on, hair tied up, and if she was wearing any makeup at all, it was subtle. Tayte thought the look suited her perfectly.

Something else about her had changed, too. It was something intangible that Tayte couldn't put his finger on. Perhaps it was because of everything they had been through in the past few days, or maybe it wasn't her at all. Maybe it was him. He'd never felt protective of anyone in his life—never had to. But he did right now, just looking at her. He was already smiling when she saw him in his new tan suit.

Then she was smiling, too.

'I just got here a few minutes ago,' she said. 'Shall we have a drink first?'

'Sure,' Tayte said, wondering why he suddenly felt so nervous.

He put his briefcase down and sat on a stool beside her. They ordered champagne cocktails, and as Tayte settled, he turned and took the place in. It was an airy, modern interior with polished wood flooring and wire-frame chairs and tables. His eyes were instantly drawn to the windows and the cityscape panorama beyond.

'Great view,' he said, picking out Nelson's Column, Big Ben, and the apex of the London Eye.

'Shame about the rain,' Jean said, frowning. 'It's much better on a clear day.'

Despite the grey backdrop and reduced visibility, Tayte thought it looked just fine. They watched the barman make their cocktails, and when he set them in front of them they looked at each other as they clinked glasses.

'Here's to the end of a very eventful week,' Tayte said.

'And good riddance,' Jean added.

Tayte snorted. 'Amen to that. So how's Elliot?'

'Better than I'd expected. He's back with his father—a little sore, but he'll mend. We're spending a few days together next week.'

'That's great,' Tayte said.

Jean nodded. 'It's too early to hope for much long term, but we'll see.' She paused. 'And what about you? What did you get up to this morning?' She laughed as she added, 'I wouldn't be surprised if you stayed in bed.'

Tayte laughed with her, considering his reply carefully. Jean had every right to know the truth, and he wanted to tell her everything he'd done, in what he considered to be everyone's best interest. He wanted to explain how he'd seen what was possibly the only way out of their predicament while they were at St Paul's in Shadwell, even though it had meant taking a risk as far as Elliot was concerned. He didn't think she would ever forgive him for that, and he wouldn't blame her. It was something he would face up to someday, but he knew that to tell her everything now could put her life in danger again, and that he would not do. As for the current British monarchy, Tayte knew Marcus would have wanted no part in bringing something to light that might ultimately threaten such an institution, however great or small the impact might be, and neither did he. He wasn't usually one to leave the past unresolved if he could help it, but on this occasion he felt it was the right thing to do.

'I went to see Marcus's wife Emmy before I came here,' he said. 'The funeral's tomorrow at ten. I thought I'd stay the rest of the week and fly home Sunday.'

He thought he saw Jean's eyes open a little wider at hearing that, or maybe he just imagined it. He wanted to see her again. They hadn't even sat down to lunch yet, and he already knew it would not be enough. Sure, he'd see her tomorrow at the funeral, but then what?

'I was just wondering,' he began.

He faltered. *What's wrong with me? Why can't I just say it?*

He knew why. It was the perennial fear of rejection that had stalked him and taunted him since learning that his own mother hadn't wanted him.

Why should Jean? What if she says no?

He couldn't ever recall feeling like this before. Somehow he'd made it to forty, and there he was stumbling over feelings that were entirely new to him. He wasn't sure he liked it, either. It was so much easier to crawl back into his hole, wasn't it? But he felt light-headed to the point of being giddy, and it wasn't because of the champagne cocktail.

Even my palms are clammy.

'What is it?' Jean asked through her smile.

Tayte sat on his hands and cleared his throat. He was going to do this. He had to.

'I was just wondering,' he said. He was blushing. He could feel the heat in his cheeks. 'When will I see you again?' He rushed the words out and immediately thought that he'd had all his life to think of a good line for when it really mattered, and all he could come up with was some damn song title.

'Do you want to see me again?'

Tayte smiled and nodded like a puppy in a pound waiting for someone to want him in return. 'We never got to see that show Marcus wanted to take us to, did we?'

'*Les Mis?*'

Tayte nodded again. His mouth was dry. He swallowed hard. 'I was wondering if you'd care to see it on Saturday. With me,' he added, like such a caveat might adversely affect her decision.

'Well, I don't know.'

Tayte buried his face in his cocktail. 'Oh,' he said. He took a sip that was more like a gulp. 'Sure, that's okay,' he added. 'I just—'

Jean cut in. 'What I mean is, are you only asking me because Marcus would have liked it?'

'No,' Tayte said, quickly. 'Of course not. I'm asking because *I'd* like it.' He looked right into her eyes then and said, 'I'd like it very much.'

Jean toyed with her glass, delaying her answer. Then she smiled and said, 'In that case I'd love to.'

Tayte knew he had a cheesy grin all over his face, and he didn't care. 'Great. That's really great.'

'But I'm afraid three's a crowd,' Jean added, suddenly serious again.

'How do you mean?'

She looked at the floor and couldn't keep a straight face as she said, 'I mean, don't even think about bringing that bloody briefcase.'

Epilogue

Two weeks later.

Jefferson Tayte had been out for a morning jog in DC's Lincoln Park wearing brand-new running shoes, the likes of which he hadn't owned since college. Ordinarily, he would have hit the shower as soon as he got back to his apartment, but today the morning mail delayed him. On top of the usual pile of junk mail was an airmail letter from England, and it had piqued his curiosity. The postmark told him it was from London, and as he took it into the kitchen with him and poured himself a coffee, it made him think about Jean again.

She was coming to visit him next month, and he was looking forward to seeing her again more than he'd looked forward to anything in his life. He kept telling himself that he'd bought his new running shoes because he'd made that promise to himself and because that was what people did when they turned forty, but he knew the real reason was because he'd met Jean. He thought about her every time he put them on.

As well as exchanging e-mails every day, they telephoned one another regularly, and through those conversations Tayte learnt of Fable's death. It had saddened him more than he would have thought the death of such a casual acquaintance could. A suspected heart attack is what Jean told him it said in the newspapers, but when Tayte had called New Scotland Yard he was told that the verdict was open and that no further information was available—at least not to him.

Fable's death had made him think about Michel Levant. His instincts still told him the Frenchman was somehow involved, and he hadn't ruled out the possibility that he was also partly responsible for his friend's murder. He knew there was unfinished business between them, and he was in little doubt that their paths would cross again someday. He had denied the heir hunter what was arguably the ultimate heir, and he figured you couldn't get the better of someone like Michel Levant without repercussions. That suited Tayte just fine, but he knew he'd have to watch his back.

He sipped his coffee and sat down with his letter. The name at the top of the headed notepaper read Goldman, Goldman & Rose, Solicitors. He scrunched his brow.

A law firm?

The letter was brief. It was from the executors of the late Marcus Brown's will, and by the time Tayte had read it the colour had drained from his cheeks. He went over the salient points again to be sure he'd read it right.

There's a key to a safety deposit box waiting for me in London. They're only at liberty to discuss the matter further in person, but have been instructed to inform me that it concerns my family.

My family?

Acknowledgements

My continued thanks to all the online forum members who have supported me since I published my debut book in 2011, and to those readers who have written to me and/or written reviews for my work. Your encouragement and support will always be very much appreciated.

Special thanks to Inspector Pat Rawle for continuing to help with my enquiries, to Kath Middleton, Sherie Sprague, Sue James, Karen Watkins, Susanne Meyers, and Judith Allison for their help with editing and proofreading this book, to Emilie Marneur for inviting me to join Amazon Publishing, to my copyeditor Julie Hotchkiss, and everyone else at Amazon Publishing who has contributed in any way to this work, and as always to my wife Karen, for so many reasons.

About the Author

Credit: Karen Robinson

Steve Robinson drew upon his own family history for inspiration when he imagined the life and quest of his genealogist-hero, Jefferson Tayte. The talented London-based crime writer, who was first published at age 16, always wondered about his own maternal grandfather—'He was an American GI billeted in England during the Second World War,' Robinson says. 'A few years after the war ended he went back to America, leaving a young family behind and, to my knowledge, no further contact was made. I traced him to Los Angeles through his 1943 enlistment record and discovered that he was born in Arkansas ...'

Robinson cites crime writing and genealogy as ardent hobbies—a passion that is readily apparent in his work.

He can be contacted via his website www.steve-robinson.me or his blog at www.ancestryauthor.blogspot.com.